Patricia Duncker is the author of *Miss Webster and Chérif* (shortlisted for the Commonwealth Writers' Prize in 2007). She is Professor of Contemporary Literature at the University of Manchester.

THE STRANGE CASE OF THE COMPOSER AND HIS JUDGE

New Year's Day, 2000. Hunters, in a forest in the Jura, stumble upon a half-circle of dead bodies lying in the snow. A nearby holiday chalet containing children's presents and decorations indicates a seemingly ordinary Christmas. Searching for clues, the judge, Dominique Carpentier and Commissaire André Schweigen find a strange leather-bound book, written in mysterious code, containing maps of the stars. The book leads them to the Composer, Friedrich Grosz, who is connected to every one of the dead. And so the pursuit begins. Carpentier and Schweigen are drawn into a world of complex family ties, ancient beliefs and seductive, disturbing music. Carpentier, proud of her ability to expose frauds and charlatans, likes to win — has she met her match in the Composer?

Books by Patricia Duncker
Published by The House of Ulverscroft:

MISS WEBSTER AND CHÉRIF

PATRICIA DUNCKER

◆

THE STRANGE
CASE OF THE
COMPOSER
AND HIS JUDGE

Complete and Unabridged

CHARNWOOD
Leicester

First published in Great Britain in 2010 by
Bloomsbury Publishing
London

First Charnwood Edition
published 2010
by arrangement with
Bloomsbury Publishing
London

British Library CIP Data

Duncker, Patricia, *1951* –
  The strange case of the composer and his judge.
  1. Suicide pacts- -Fiction. 2. Composers- -Fiction.
  3. Police- -France- -Fiction. 4. Women judges- -
  France- -Fiction. 5. Detective and mystery stories.
  6. Large type books.
  I. Title
  823.9′14–dc22

  ISBN 978-1-44480-427-0

Published by
F. A. Thorpe (Publishing)
Anstey, Leicestershire

Set by Words & Graphics Ltd.
Anstey, Leicestershire
Printed and bound in Great Britain by
T. J. International Ltd., Padstow, Cornwall

For S.J.D.

I saw Eternity the other night,
Like a great ring of pure and endless light,
All calm, as it was bright;
And round beneath it, Time in hours, days, years,
Driv'n by the spheres
Like a vast shadow moved; in which the world
And all her train were hurled.

Henry Vaughan

Gelobt sei uns die ew'ge Nacht . . .
Let us praise eternal night . . .

Novalis

1

Hunters in the Snow

The bodies were found early in the afternoon of New Year's Day. Hunters in the forest were rounding up their dogs, pulling their hats close over their ears against the frost, and heading for home. Several centimetres of snow had fallen in the night, and by dawn, when they had set out, the air sliced their lungs and faces, clean and hard. The trails on the lower slopes remained clear, but slush and ice rendered the tracks on high ground above the rocks impassable. They bagged two hares, and watched the deer rushing through the mangled green, leaping the fallen trunks left by the storms, but let them go. The hunters waded through the snow, discouraged by the devastated landscape and blocked paths. Every endeavour to negotiate clear space was thwarted and baffled. New Year's Day. Someone proposed a tot of eau-de-vie, hot coffee and his wife's chocolate-cream gâteau. A small fête for the New Year. Let's go home. They called out to one of their number who was pissing against a pile of frozen logs. But he didn't move or turn. He had seen something strange in the clearing below him.

This man, who lived just eight kilometres away from the white space where the bodies were discovered, had already seen the cars, five of

1

them, massed at odd angles around the holiday chalet where, it was assumed, the gathering had passed their last night. He had noted the registrations — not one from the local department — and the wealth to which the vehicles bore witness: two Land Cruisers, 4 × 4s, a Renault Espace, a plush black Mercedes. Big slick vehicles from Paris, Nancy, Lyon. One of the cars was registered in Switzerland. He had noticed the CH sticker on the boot. But at that moment, when he raised his eyes from the steaming arc of his own piss, he did not associate the pattern in the snow beneath him with the visitors to the mountains. He peered forwards, uncertain. Were they tree trunks, already severed and arranged, awaiting transport? Surely he imagined the bare patches in the bark, which looked like faces, and the branches splintered open, like palms facing upwards. Two of his friends trudged over to his side and followed his stare down the rock face to the clearing.

All at once they knew that these were people, real people, tranquil, beautiful, arranged in a symmetrical half-circle, lying in the snow beneath them, and that every single one was dead.

There is no need for urgency if death has gone before us. Yet still they hurried, clambered in rapid silence down the icy fissure in the rock face, shouldering their guns, scuffing their gloves on the boulders. Quick! We must get to them. We must call for help. The dogs whined, yelped, then set off round the longer sloping route through the trees, their noses snuffling the hardening snow. They blundered downward, frightened, eager. But when they stood, puffing and confused, their breath condensing in clouds, before the silent, frozen forms, lapped in fresh snow, they lost all inclination to speak or act. They held back their dogs and spoke in whispers.

'Appelle les pompiers. Et les flics. Call the emergency services. And the cops. Qu'est-ce que tu attends? What are you waiting for? Go on, do it.'

The hunter's hands, which had killed many times and were always steady on his gun, now slithered and twitched over the buttons on his mobile phone. His dog circled the bodies, wary, uncertain.

But the signal fluctuated. How many? Where? You're breaking up. Give me your exact position. The hunter gestured helplessly to his friends, and now they all had an opinion. This is the easiest way to find us. This is the road to take. Mais non, passe-moi le portable! Each one of them knew the body of the forest like a lover, all her secrets fingered and touched. They had walked every trail in all seasons; they knew the thickets, the buried cleft with the soft falling water, the deep pools. They nosed out the scents of the forest with an instinct as uncanny and subtle as their dogs. They knew every sound, every spoor, could smell the earth as keenly as the creatures they hunted: moss, water, fear. They would stand silent for hours, watching over their prey, tenderly plotting their kill, with the impassioned concentration of a bridegroom, waiting for the beloved to stir. Now they huddled together at the edge of the clearing, giving one another advice, puzzled, insecure, their voices lowered, not out of respect for the frozen dead, but in case they could hear.

Eventually it was decided that one of them should descend to the lower trails, where the mobile phone could locate a clear signal and the emergency services, taking the dogs with him, to wait at the crossroads where the tarmac ended and their abandoned vans nuzzled the forest. He could guide the police, pompiers, premiers secours, all the necessary procession which promised the help no longer needed. As he tramped away into the misty, declining light the others gathered together, fearful guardians of whatever had been accomplished in the clearing on the brink of the ravine. They did not study the bodies but looked out over the snowy hills and shattered tunnels of broken trees. Mist boiled in the distant valleys; the white light, deepening to blue, veiled the horizon. The best of the day had already gone.

They began counting the dead.

The bodies lay close together, woven into a pattern. Nine adults, partially exposed in the soft wash of snow, stretched out upon their backs, settled into a sedate, reclining curve. Their elbows were bent back, their hands raised, palms facing upwards, as if they had all completed a complex movement in the dance, and died in the very act. The hunters did not pry too closely, but stood back enthralled, for they were used to death. The dead and the moment of dying

4

accompanied them through the forest, their daily companions, who held no secrets from them. But this was an event of a different order.

The black fixed eyes gaped open, gazing at the winter sky, their lashes and eyebrows white with frost. The hunters kept their distance, not because they were afraid, but because they were disturbed by the bodies of the children.

The children formed a smaller group, nestled at the feet of the adults, like loyal greyhounds carved on the tombs of heroes. The curled figures were wearing pyjamas beneath their outdoor coats and heavily swaddled in blankets; their arms and fingers tucked away, invisible in gloves and mittens. Two of them embraced half-chewed fluffy animals, a panda, a small grey koala bear. The youngest child looked tiny, perhaps just over a year old. Who would murder little children and then lay them with such careful tenderness at their parents' feet? The woods cracked and whispered with the coming frost. As the light shrank into the pines the hunters heard the murmur of diesel engines, then voices approaching from the left, at last, the crunch of heavy boots breaking the snow's crust. Dark figures, laden with bulky equipment, arc lights, cameras, grey plastic coffins roped to sledges, rose towards them, moving slowly through the trees.

★ ★ ★

The officer in charge of the police investigation rummaged in the pockets of his hooded coat.

There was still enough light to make out the tracks around the half-circle of bodies. He began to draw upon a pad.

'Vous n'avez rien touché? Are you sure you didn't touch the bodies?' He accused the hunters, without even looking at them.

'We haven't gone near the bodies.'

'So whose tracks are these?'

Three sets of indentations in the snow marked the outer circle. The most recent belonged to the dogs.

'Deer. Those tracks were left by deer.'

The deer had come very close. They must have stood over the dead, then gently stepped away, back into the shadowed green. The oldest marks were half filled with fresh snow. A flurry of tracks hovered near one of the bodies. This corpse occupied a central place at the circle's core, and they could now see that it was a woman's face, pale and shocked by the suddenness of her death, her mouth gaped slightly open, her white tongue visible. She was not young, but her face was drawn in strong lines and bold gestures, her dark hair flooded back, escaping from the furred hood of her coat. The Commissaire stared at her face for a long time, then blew on his fingers and continued drawing the scene, while his white-suited myrmidons, all looking puzzled rather than shocked, staked out the circle to include the tracks. No one looked closely at the children.

'Any sign of the Judge yet?' snapped the Commissaire. 'I rang her over an hour ago.'

The hunters felt excluded from their discovery. No one asked their opinion. Why weren't

6

they suspects? They had seen enough crime scenes on TV to know that whoever admitted to the discovery of the body had usually committed the murder, except in the case of dead wives, where the husband, absent or present, was always the only one with the motive. And here they were, armed to the teeth, with enough ammunition to massacre the forest, yet no one had even asked for an alibi. The hunters were not ignorant men. They were trained to read signs, even small signs, a broken branch, a snapped twig, a disturbance in the waters. They watched the white ghosts of the police scientifique moving quickly, staking out the bodies, photographing each face in turn, the flash slapping the snow in a sudden white flare. And then they realised what was missing from each man's face. No one balked on the brink of the circle as the hunters had done. They strode forth like conquerors, buckled beneath the weight of their equipment. They carried the right things. They had expected to see this strange gathering of the dead, arranged in precisely this pattern, hidden from the world on a remote outcrop in the forest. They had all known what awaited them. They had seen this before.

'Voilà. Vous pouvez disposer. Come into the main station tomorrow morning at 9 a.m. to sign your statements. This officer will take down your names, addresses and telephone numbers. We will interview you again before the end of the week. Cartes d'identité? Thank you. And please don't talk to the press. Do you understand that? Not a word to the journalists.'

They were dismissed.

Yet these men were the first witnesses to the events in the forest, the first to ask questions about the unfinished circle and the bodies of the children. These three men were the first to debate whether the members of the gathering had been murdered or chosen their own deaths, the first to wonder why the circle remained incomplete, the first to marvel at the children, tucked carefully into the space created beneath the feet of the men and women who had given them their lives and then, for the hunters assumed that this was so, had watched them die. The hunters strode down the ice trails, their boots leaving complete treads in the mud beneath the cracking sheets of ice, past the wooden chalet now surrounded with yellow tape, overrun with gendarmes and dark men without uniforms probing furniture, digging in suitcases. The cars were all opened, and painstakingly examined under the sizzling glare of artificial lights by men with supple white gloves, as if the machines themselves were also cadavers concealing their secrets. All the doors and windows of the chalet stood open to the leering cold.

The hunters retreated, clutching their guns, and their breath gleamed white in the twilight as they descended the mountain, climbing the fallen trunks, avoiding the police armed with chainsaws, who were clearing the trails. They could hear the muffled howls of their dogs, locked in the vans, long before the half-hidden vehicles loomed through the pines. A large dark car, wheels churning the slush, rose past them.

They stepped back, nodding to the woman within. She returned their gaze with a flat blank stare. They feared that she was one of the relatives, one who had been summoned, one who already knew. Now the forest rustled with voices and the chortle of machines. The hunters slipped away.

★　★　★

The winter sky surrendered cold blue into engulfing dark beneath the pines as the Judge's car, a borrowed Kangoo, one of the more recent models, fitted with four-wheel drive, lurched up the track. She surged past the startled men standing in shadow, all armed with rifles, apparently captured in the process of vanishing. The car slithered to a standstill on the rim of the scene around the chalet, which now resembled a film set, trailing wires, arc lights and cameras, the actors busy in rehearsal. The Judge wore mud-spattered boots, an old brown overcoat and red leather gloves. Everyone stood back respect-fully as she hovered outside the circle, gazing inwards. Her glasses had black frames and the thick lenses glittered under the lights. No one spoke. Everybody waited to take the next cue from her. She was now the principal element to be reckoned with in this eerie drama. One of the men stepped forward.

'Madame le Juge? Monsieur le Commissaire is waiting for you. I'll take you up.' He carried a large torch, which was not yet necessary as they retraced the hunters' tracks through the pines in

9

the half-light. The earth hardened beneath them. The Judge could smell the ice forming, a rigid, fresh smell of damp, oozing resin and wet earth.

'There's a sheer rock face just behind them,' said the officer, 'so I'll take you round. It's a bit longer, but enough of us have already been over the ground.'

The Judge nodded.

'We'll have to carry them down on stretchers. The track is blocked at too many points by fallen trees for the pompiers to get up there. And the snow's too deep,' he added as an afterthought.

The Judge slipped a little in the murky slush. He put out his arm to help her. She waved him away. They could hear the faint hum of activity somewhere above them. He clicked on the torch. A yellow circle of light appeared in the churned snow before their advancing boots. The faint crunch as they broke the first crust of ice steadied their passage.

'Monsieur Schweigen told us not to touch any of them until you got here. He said that you'd want to see the pattern that they make in the snow.'

The Judge nodded again, but did not reply. The white path juddered and shook in the torchlight, then slithered into a firebreak, sliced up the vertical slope. The going was slower in deep snow. The officer waited for her as she rummaged in the powder with the toes of her boots, trying to find solid ground. She stretched out her arms like a tightrope walker, hesitated, then found her uneasy balance once again. The light renewed itself in the open, a distinct,

10

luminous and deepening blue; but the mountain's flank seemed to warp the space and sounds above, which sometimes ballooned outwards into the valley, so clear that she could hear individual voices, then shrank away into whispers and echoes that thumped dull against the heavy, laden green.

'La voilà!'

Schweigen peered down the dark cliff where the rocks dripped icicles from the overhang and saw her coming, a tiny dark figure following one of his officers. He watched her bowed head and cautious steps, jubilant and relieved. She had been in Strasbourg with her brother's family, just over an hour away, and listened without comment to his agitated, rushing talk — the hunters have found the bodies in the snow. Then she simply said that she would leave at once. And now here she was. He watched her clutching the rock to steady herself in thick fallen snow at the foot of the cliff. Red gloves. He remembered those red gloves from that long winter investigation in Switzerland. She was wearing the same red gloves and she was directly below him. As if aware of his beady stare, she looked up, raising her face to his. He stretched out his hand in greeting as if to draw her up towards him. She smiled slightly, but did not hurry. The light was almost gone. I want her to see them before the light goes, before we ignite the generator and the whole place looks like a frontier outpost under siege. He slithered towards her, engulfed in a spray of wet earth, cracking branches and hardening slush.

11

'Bonne Année, Madame le Juge!' A small wry smile appeared in her eyes. He was so close to her that his breath steamed up her lenses. She took off her glasses and wiped them on her scarf.

'Bonne Année, André. Although best wishes do seem a little out of place here.'

He stood before her, excited as a schoolboy, full of his own prowess; he had summoned her up and she had come to him.

The Judge stepped into the blue circle of the last light on the mountains and surveyed the fan of bodies in the snow before them. The freezing gendarmes, many of them still bleary from their millennium celebrations, rustled in the slush, tense and shifty, discomfited by the tiny wrapped bodies of the children that Schweigen had forbidden them to touch. The Commissaire babbled in the Judge's ear.

'They celebrated their departure. We've found the remains of their final meal, champagne, bûche de Noël, extra presents for the children. They'd actually decorated the entire chalet.'

The Judge said nothing. She hunched her shoulders and shrank inside the hood of her winter coat, tense and bristling against the cold. For a long while she stood silent, absorbing the scene, her boots gently sinking as the melted crust of fresh snow crumbled beneath her heels. Then she set out around the periphery defined by the tape, with André Schweigen clamped to her side, gabbling quietly.

'The hunters left prints everywhere. So did their dogs. The dogs also made those marks — that scratching in the snow. There were trails left by deer too, but those were nearly gone. More snow must have fallen in the small hours. The hunters say they didn't touch the bodies. I don't think they did. It's hard to tell what the poison was. Cyanide, I should think. Like the Swiss departure. But listen, there's one — one of them — '

Schweigen's excitement became uncontainable. He stepped in front of her.

'Dominique, écoute-moi bien.' His voice dropped to a hiss. 'One of them's been shot. The woman at the core. Just as it happened in Switzerland. And the gun's not there. It's gone. We'll comb every inch. I'll sift snow through sieves if I have to, but I think the gun's gone. Obviously we'll have to wait for ballistics to confirm the facts, but I'm willing to put money on the bet that it's the same gun. Even after six years. Someone walked away from the mountain last night. And that's not suicide, it's murder.'

'Calme-toi,' replied the Judge softly. They stopped, facing the half-circle of the enraptured dead. 'Of course it's murder. How could those tiny children consent to their own deaths? We're looking at a crime scene, André, whatever the results from your ballistics lab.'

He stopped talking and took her arm. No matter what happened this was now their investigation. They were no longer trailing in the slipstream of the Swiss, who had buried the last departure, along with the dead, in a sarcophagus of platitudes: a tragic waste, incomprehensible and heartbreaking. But for Madame le Juge nothing remained incomprehensible or beyond

13

the reach of pure reason. The mysteries of this world stained the bright radiance of eternity. Her method, tested and consistent, was to analyse the stains. They trudged onwards, the snow sucking at their boots. The Judge gazed impassive at the white faces of the dead, absorbing each one in turn, as if every detail should be remembered for ever. The smallest children were wrapped in furred cocoons, their puckered features scarcely visible. She lingered for many minutes over the fading face of the older woman at the centre of the half-circle.

Schweigen leaned into her cheek.

'That's her, isn't it? The sister?'

'Yes. That's Marie-Cécile Laval.'

Finally the Judge stopped, stood perfectly still, and raised her eyes to the devastated forests on the surrounding slopes; the great trees, like liquidated giants, piled one upon another, their roots, naked and undignified, sprawled in their wake, the shallow holes already filled with snow. At once beautiful and desolate, the bare curves of the mountain stretched away towards the Rhine Valley and the shadows of the Black Forest in Southern Germany. The bodies all faced towards the east, to greet the rising sun. They had died in the night, certain that one short breath, wasted in this temporary world, riddled by time, was the prelude to their eternal awakening, promised in the stars.

She looked again at the huddled soundless children, tenderly enveloped in hoods, scarves, mittens. What train of reason led a woman to protect her child against the night cold then fill

14

his mouth with poison? She slouched down into her coat, and shivered against the quiet, thickening night. Reason had nothing to do with it. Before her on the forest floor, lay an extraordinary witness to the passion, that instinctive act of love. I will never leave you; I will never abandon you in the kingdom of this world, smothered by time, age, pain, heartbreak. I shall take you with me. Lord, remember me when thou comest into thy kingdom. This day shalt thou be with me in paradise. The Judge stared at the still, frozen face of Marie-Cécile Laval. Her unimaginable act represented one last gesture of boundless love, the love that had gathered up these children and borne them forth in triumph.

★ ★ ★

The sound of a heavy vehicle thumping against the branches in the distance disturbed the motionless, iced air. The Judge raised her head like a deer at bay. Schweigen was watching her carefully.

'Have the press got hold of it yet?'

'We've had one call. The hunters found them. No matter how often you tell them not to blab, people talk.'

'Then let's get to work. But keep it quiet as long as you can. I'll need to interview the men who found them. I'll do that tomorrow morning early. Before they start seeing things in their heads and imagining details that weren't there. Have you got all the photographs?'

'Yes. And something even better than that.' Schweigen presented her with the drawings, the measurements between each body carefully noted. His record of the scene looked slightly sinister, for alongside a careful diagram showing the positions of each corpse was a sketch of the older woman's face, the open eyes and the expression of startled amazement, exactly caught.

'That's excellent,' said the Judge, thrown off guard by Schweigen's unexpected talent and the grotesque, disturbing subject.

'I was all set for the Beaux-Arts,' he said, with a small shrug of regret. 'It's harder to draw faces you've never seen before. She's the only one I knew.'

The first shift of actors surrounding the spectacle began to pack up, ready to bear the bodies away from the darkening apse of the mountain; the lorries from the morgue were stuck further down the slope. The second shift of forensic experts hovered on the brink of the circle, ready to sift through the snow, their searchlights tilted at odd angles, picking out the whitened, laden branches of the pines. Schweigen was relieved that none of his team knew any of the dead and said so. The Judge stood over the men as they lifted the children, ostensibly daring them to be anything other than gentle with the stiff, small forms, but in fact giving them something else to think about, in case anyone shuddered or cracked. She eyed them carefully. Some seemed too young, far too young, to touch the dead. As each corpse was packed up and gently zipped into a yellow folded sack its outline became momentarily visible upon the forest floor, then appeared to fade. The dead left barely a shadowed trace behind them. The gathering at the foot of the rock cliffs had already melted into the past.

'Le Parquet rang me right after you did,' said the Judge, 'and just as well he did. I had to listen to it all again and pretend I didn't know. You don't give me instructions, André, he does. If he knew that you had already been in touch with me he'd think that you were running your own private war against these people.' She gestured towards the empty clearing, now ablaze with lights as each morsel of snow was stabbed and turned.

Schweigen, unabashed, put his drawings away inside his coat and took her arm again.

'But aren't you glad I did?'

The Judge smiled slightly and they set off together, concentrating on their boots, heads bowed as if they were the chief mourners, following the slow procession into the darkness and the freezing trees.

★ ★ ★

No heating was turned on in the chalet and there was no question of turning it on until the boiler and all the electrical devices in the house had been examined and cleared. The investigating team worked into the night, swathed in mufflers, their gloved hands searching, recording, collecting. Boxes of odd personal material, diaries, notebooks, wallets, car-registration documents, meal plans, the rubbish rota, dry-cleaning stubs, were all inspected, listed and removed. There was a moment of horror and excitement when the mobile phone in one of the Land Cruisers sprang into luminous life and began to sing. The relatives had still not been contacted or informed.

'Leave it,' snapped the Judge, noting down the incoming number. The echoes of the Christmas theme tune, 'Jingle Bells', died into silence. The Judge turned to Schweigen.

'We have all their identities now. I think you can begin contacting whatever's left of their families. Let's look at that list.'

The chalet was privately owned and littered with the personal clutter that every household generates year after year. A cork poster board, overrun with holiday photographs, showed some of the dramatis personae from the clearing on the mountainside, ebullient on skis, or with raised glasses, sitting around candle-covered cakes. The local free newspaper lay abandoned behind the sofa. Schweigen checked the date. A wilted heap of flowers slumped on the table, withered with cold. The air, glacial and still, shifted like a curtain as the Judge passed softly over the threshold into the kitchen. The possessions of the dead lay scattered in the convivial disorder of a Christmas family holiday. Here were presents still resting in their wrapping paper, washing-up neatly stacked on the draining board, but not stowed away. A light still glimmered, eerie and blurred, on the telephone's screen. The words were in English: *You were called at 12.31* . . . and the red eye glared with the threat that *the caller has left you a message.*

'Écoutez la bande, Madame le Juge,' Schweigen suggested in respectful, formal tones. Two of his men were working in the kitchen.

'I want that board of photographs recorded,' said the Judge. 'We have to track down everyone in those pictures who isn't already on the slab in the Institut médico-légal.' She looked at Schweigen. 'All right. Play it.'

She noted down the number. It was the same one that she had recorded from the car's mobile phone. A shiver of sadness washed over her shoulders. Someone was out there, trying to get through, ringing again and again, someone who didn't know. The tape hissed and clicked. Then a man's voice spoke in English, leaving the briefest possible message.

'Cécile? Happy New Year. Please ring me today.'

And the line went dead. Schweigen checked his list.

'He's after Madame Laval. The only one who wasn't apparently poisoned. One bullet to the left temple. Very little blood loss. And the only woman whose children weren't with her.'

'Impound the tape. And I want a list of all calls to and from the chalet as far back as you can. When did they get here? December the 23rd?' She steadied her glasses and looked closely at the numbers. '0049? Isn't that Germany?'

Schweigen nodded. He plucked out the tape and labelled the bag, then looked over her

19

shoulder at the number.

'It's a mobile. A German mobile.'

'Identify it.'

'Could be one of her family trying to get through. We should contact her children.'

'That was the voice of a man her age. Or older. Find out who he is.'

Three entire families, nine adults and seven children, had perished in the forest clearing: Marie-Cécile Laval, another older woman, possibly a grandmother, a teenage boy of seventeen, three married couples and all their children, some of them barely toddlers. They had taken their children with them. Here were all their papers, cartes d'identité, driving licences, car insurance documents, credit cards, abandoned either in the chalet or in their cars. The money left in handbags, drawers and coats amounted to over five thousand francs. The Judge sat at the dining table in the main room of the chalet, wearing a pair of gloves borrowed from the police scientifique. Her red leather gloves, the ones that Schweigen had recognised, stuck out of her pocket. She checked all the jettisoned labels on the Christmas presents and decoded the Christmas wishes, scratched in biro on the decorated wrapping she had fished out of the waste-paper basket. Had anyone else taken part in the celebration and then returned from the mountain? The presents themselves still littered the rooms: an amber bottle of Coco from Chanel, a CD rack shaped like a giraffe, a motorised truck for one of the children that could be controlled with a télécommande, a new

20

DVD player and a handful of war films. What on earth had possessed them to spend so much money just before they died? She began noting down the names, terms of endearment, generic names, pet names — who was 'ma petite chouchoute'? My beloved wife? That could have been any one of the three women. Before her lay a little solid pile of mobile phones. She activated each one in turn and went through the calls dialled and received and the entire mass of text messages. Hours later, she fixed André Schweigen with a steady glare, her mind elsewhere.

'They died last night. They went up the mountain long after midnight.'

'They did?'

'Yes. All the text messages on the mobiles saying Bonne Année have been read.'

'Join my team.' He grinned at her. 'Do you want to look at these photographs now or shall I bag them up?'

'Pass them over.'

He gave her a small halogen torch to amplify the light above the dining table that was still draped with swags of green pine and ivy from the forest. Jaunty strings of fairy lights flickered on the Christmas tree, changing the colours of the swaying crystal baubles. Schweigen turned off the flashing trails that chased each other round the picture rails and across the perked ears of a wild boar's head, stuffed and mounted above the sofa. The Judge settled down to study the photographs. Two men shouldering a canoe. Sports Day. A child dwarfed by his safety helmet, winning the cycle race. A woman on a driveway

21

lifting a tiny toy dog towards the camera. No family pets had been left locked in the chalet. Where were the animals? The Judge got up, still carrying the photographs, and went through to look over the kitchen floor: no bowls, no rugs, no basket, no cat flap. She shrugged and continued peering into these lost lives. Tropics. Very possibly Martinique, all the signs are in French. Here is a black man on a beach carrying a calabash. The images were of family, anniversaries, holidays, moments of success. But who takes pictures of their loved ones at nine-thirty on a November night, sunk into the sofa in front of the television? Here were life's landmarks: the weddings, birthdays, sports day, the new baby in her grandmother's arms. And surely this was Madame Laval, swinging on a ski lift, beside one of the women who died in the forest, with another young girl clinging to her arm, smiling — the same smile. This is her daughter.

'What's Laval's daughter called? Laval's a widow, isn't she?' Schweigen consulted a printout, the Judge recited the names.

'Un fils, Paul, né le 15 octobre 1971, et une fille, Marie-Thérèse, née le 2 novembre 1983. We never interrogated either of them after the Swiss departure. They weren't there. The boy was still at university in Paris and the girl was too young.'

She reached down into the mass of salvaged Christmas paper and handed him a small crushed heap of green-and-white stripes, holding out the matching card beneath the light. He studied the curling script. *To my darling*

Marie-T, Je t'aime, ma petite chérie, Bisous, Maman.

'Find that girl for me, André. No one else in last night's departure is called Marie-T. And this present, whatever it was, has been opened.'

She measured the size of the wrapping paper and noted the pattern of the first folds. Schweigen turned the card round in his hand.

'Yes, but do the two go together? This paper and this card? The card's not attached to anything and the DVDs were wrapped in the same paper.'

'We must check.'

Schweigen strode outside to use the radio car. The Judge laid out a newspaper flat upon the table and emptied the contents of every single waste-paper basket that could be found, downstairs and upstairs, on to the table. She began to examine the scrabbled pile of objects in turn, raising each strange scrap into the air, tissues, used biros, the last cylinder from a lavatory roll, discarded plastic bags, an empty can of Coca-Cola Light, a broken stapler and an exploded balloon. She gazed at each pointless, redundant item with an intense and tender concentration. The forensic team tiptoed around her; a small cloud of her warm breath billowed into the cold.

★ ★ ★

The forensic pathologist from the university hospital lab rang Schweigen at 1 a.m. Everyone looked up expectantly. He stood in front of the charred logs left in the massive fireplace, black volcanic stone, with a huge slab of dark slate beneath the irons, and simply listened. The team lost interest and continued their travail de fourmi, the ant-like crawl, turning over all the daily objects, touched by the dead. Schweigen's team was known for its thoroughness; one of them dusted off the plastic fridge magnets, in case they revealed a different set of prints, and photographed the cheery plastic alphabet, arranged into insane, compelling poetry.

'Well?' The Judge glowered at him. Schweigen consulted his notes.

'Exactly the same pattern as the Swiss departure. He won't say anything definite. You know what he's like. And he's being very cagy about the exact time of death. Apparently he's got to measure the potassium content of the fluid in the eye. All the bodies were as cold as the ground beneath them. But here's the basics: apart from Laval, who was shot, and we don't yet have the ballistics report, they all died of potassium cyanide poisoning, except for the children, who seem to have been dosed with a mild form of chloroform, then injected with sodium thiopentone. But he's only examined two of them so far. We've sent down the syringes we found in the bathroom. The old lady was diabetic and he thinks they're hers. It looks as if they murdered their children while they slept and then carried them up the mountain.'

'No.' The Judge contradicted him. 'They wouldn't have done that. They would have knocked them out down here and then killed

24

them on the spot. How many of your people are still up there?'

'About five. I can't get a signal from their mobiles.'

A young woman in a white plastic overall and red scarf stepped up to the Judge.

'I'll go up. We're now looking for one or more disposable syringes in the clearing. Right?'

The Judge inspected the unlined face before her. Surely this girl was too young to be staring at these monstrous deaths?

'Yes. That's right. Off you go. Take this torch.' The Judge got up, stretched her arms over her head and then accompanied the girl to the door. The frost had now hardened the earth into a sparkling crust that glinted in evil buckled sheets across the muddied tracks and spattered snow.

'Will you be OK?'

The girl smiled. 'I'm not afraid of dead people and I don't believe in ghosts.'

The Judge grinned back, a warm merry smile, which the young forensic technician had never seen before; the Judge never looked young, or mischievous, and they were all terrified of her famous Medusa glare.

'Quite right,' said the Judge, 'neither am I. Hot coffee when you come back down. André!' She called back into the arctic chalet. 'If you've finished in the boiler room and this place is not wired to blow up, let's turn the central heating back on.'

2

The First Departure

André Schweigen had a wife and son. His boy had been born six years earlier, shortly after the Swiss departure on Midsummer's Night 1994. On that night sixty-nine men and women, some of them barely teenagers, had either killed themselves, or been assisted on their passage into eternity, in a mass suicide, the finale to a huge gathering at a remote mountain resort in Switzerland. They had swallowed the poison as a toast at the end of their festivities, and even the Judge, looking carefully at the macabre photographs depicting a Roman feast of death, commented on the radiance inscribed on every countenance, a luminous, transfixed, untrammelled joy. They had died in ecstasy. The rigid glory of their faces reflected that of men and women long at sea, perceiving at last the distant blue outline of their native land. Their clenched, joined hands bore witness to the tenacious ferocity of their Faith. And that single designation was all that the Judge could glean about the nature of their beliefs, even after years of research, numerous dead-end interrogations, secret trails followed and abandoned. She knew whom they were, what they did, how much they earned, but precious little else. Nothing could prise open the mysterious credo by which they lived. They were members of the Faith.

The young dead faces, for there had been many in that first departure, or so it seemed to Schweigen, then in flower with proud paternity, were those of a primary school, an école primaire let loose on a treasure hunt, anxious to pounce upon the first clue. Curiosity, expectation and excitement blossomed in their dead eyes. They had stepped, jubilant, hopeful, accompanied, across the threshold. This struck Schweigen, whose baby son demanded love and food every four hours with fervent regularity, as particularly obscene. He tramped in a diminishing circle around the Judge's office, explaining his position. That office, a huge high-ceilinged room bulging with dossiers, store cupboards and filing cabinets, and invaded by monstrous plants, crouched in the backside of the Palais de Justice. Mid-May in the Midi, almost a year after that first collective departure, and already explosively hot outside; the shadows sliced the pavements in half as the light crested the tiles, three floors above. Schweigen warmed to his theme: their deliberate exclusion from every aspect of the case.

'The Swiss never let us in. We weren't ever part of the investigation. Thirty-eight of the dead were French citizens. Most of the children were French. Some of them came from Strasbourg. They involved me because I speak German too. And the local dialect. I can just about understand Schweizer Deutsch. But we weren't given access to all the necessary evidence. The Swiss were anxious to wrap the whole thing up

27

as quickly as they could. All that bilge in the newspapers — a tragic destiny, unforeseeable, unstoppable, a suicide sect, which, thank God, has eliminated itself for good and all. But it was murder, Madame le Juge. And the Swiss investigators wouldn't pursue the fact of the missing gun. It was their guru, the Grand Master, whatever he called himself, who got shot. Or shot himself. An ordinary revolver, .22, double-action weapon, all the traces present on his right hand. Where's the bloody gun gone? If a man's shot himself and the gun's gone, then someone walked out of that room alive. Who? Nobody wants to know except me. Can they find the gun? No. Do they worry when they can't find it? Do they just! All they can think about is calming the press and informing the relatives. Stifle all the nasty questions. Ignore the evidence which doesn't fit.'

'And the money? What about the money?' Schweigen found himself in full roar, several decibels higher than was necessary, and discovered that the office possessed an operatic echo. 'I had the Brigade Financière investigating the accounts of every French citizen who died. They were all as rich as Croesus, and the month before they take off on their summer holidays and top themselves they'd all made vast donations to the association that fronted the whole thing — Les Amis des Étoiles — meditation, bloody yoga, lectures to rapt audiences of middle-aged women, that kind of nonsense. And when we seize the accounts where has all the money gone? Anton Laval withdrew ten million

28

francs from the bank before the departure. A bank draft made out to him personally. But what for? And where has he put it? All that cash has vanished. It's a crucial part of their empire. And he must have passed it on to someone. He can't spend it where he is.'

'Who took the money?' André bellowed at the grotesque fronds of a phoenix palm bursting out from a blue pot shaped like a Greek amphora.

The Judge's Greffière, a very young woman in her first proper job, dressed as a goth in ripped black with a green jewelled nose ring and a death's head hollowed out by a glowing prism eye on her right forefinger, ceased tapping her machine and glared at Schweigen.

'Should I go on recording all this? It's lunchtime.'

Dominique Carpentier shook her head and lifted her chin. Schweigen stood still, mid-stride, in his decreasing spiral, confronted with her dark eyes enlarged by the thick, black frames.

'No, Gaëlle, I think Monsieur le Commissaire needs to let off a good deal of best unrecorded steam.'

Schweigen immediately began to apologise. He had raved, uninterrupted, for nearly an hour, hardly noticing the silent women seated before him. The Judge suggested a private lunch, over which they could continue to share information.

'Can I go?' Gaëlle adored the Judge, which was not uncommon, but remained completely unafraid of her, which was. They exchanged the briefest of glances as Gaëlle bolted for the door, revealing an extraordinarily unsuitable black leather miniskirt, just covering her arse, long bare thighs and lace-up black suede boots. Schweigen blinked, incredulous.

'That's your Greffière?'

The Judge smiled. 'She's very efficient. Never creates muddles or misses anything. And she speaks fluent English, which is very necessary in my line of work. They all have to do a language test. She got 20/20.'

'How did she get to be so good?' Schweigen's English had never advanced much beyond 'My tailor is rich', and a healthy spattering of gangsta rap.

The Judge selected a small blue notebook for her briefcase and a yellow dossier with the tapes tied tight.

'She studied comparative European law at the LSE in London and paid for herself by becoming a dog-walker. You know, you must have seen them if you are ever in London. They patrol the parks, matin et soir, with a pack of other people's dogs.'

'But the point of having a dog, if it isn't a chihuahua or a Rottweiler, is to get the exercise.'

'Ah, Monsieur Schweigen, there you touch upon one of the deeply irrational aspects of modern life. Anyway, some people have dogs to go with their coats and handbags.'

The Judge stood up and Schweigen realised that he towered far above her. He suddenly felt misshapen and bizarre, Polyphemus facing Odysseus. How old was she? Her smart white blouse and beige trousers made her look like a convent girl. Schweigen struggled to open doors, to stand back, to become small. The irony in her tone brought him to heel. She drew forth a huge set of old keys.

'I'd better lead the way, Monsieur Schweigen. Vous ne connaissez pas le chemin.'

Schweigen gave up playing the gentleman, ceased shrinking into his jacket and trailed along behind her crisp, clinking wake.

★ ★ ★

Dominique Carpentier was a famous woman long before that day in midst of the Midi spring, 1995, the year following the massacre in Switzerland, when she first encountered André Schweigen. She was known as 'la chasseuse de sectes' — the sect hunter. That title headed up the late-night documentary about her life and work on Antenne 2, where, when interviewed by Christine Ockrent, she offended almost everyone involved in alternative therapies and bogus paths to salvation, both in this world and the next. That name and her strange, elegant face gleamed on the cover of *Le Nouvel Observateur*, which ran a two-part series on the madder categories of pseudo-religious sects. Dominique Carpentier came from a large, wealthy family of vignerons in the Languedoc; studied philosophy and psycho-analysis at the Centre Michel Foucault in Paris, before completing her degree in law, and then returning to work in the Midi where she was born. At first, when she was still living in her father's house, her mother never missed an opportunity to plead the cause of marriage,

31

children, and the pressing necessity of a proper home. The matriarch sometimes spent whole mealtimes in full persuasive flow, even when the dear local curé, our adored Father, always placed at the head of the feast, sat stuffing charcuterie into his cheeks. Dominique's method of dealing with her mother, a mixture of humour and ruthlessness, demonstrated, to her colleagues at least, an impressive and pitiless efficiency. Her career as an advocate had proved to be solid, but not spectacular, until she encountered her first sect. The case was assigned to her because a distraught mother had initiated the proceedings. Carpentier's good at dealing with mothers. Push that one her way. But this apparently insignificant affair signalled the beginning.

Madame Cordelier, Isabelle, née Varrière, à Florensac, 43 ans, was the mother of three children, but the youngest, her only daughter, had fallen into the claws of a pernicious older companion during her last year at school. At first the friendship seemed harmless enough — weekends away at the beach, meetings mid-week at which they sat quietly, listening to charismatic visiting lecturers telling them how to achieve a perfect work/life balance by bringing the mind and body into eternal harmony. The first alarm signal exploded over breakfast one morning with sudden demands from the daughter for a substantial loan — eight thousand francs — to attend a weekend course. Madame Cordelier read the publicity carefully and then threw the mother-of-all enraged fits.

Le Corps Harmonieux presented itself like a

32

church. Everything necessary was on offer: a gospel, a prophet and a promise. *Our moment in history has brought us to a point where we can no longer see the way ahead. Our bodies are alienated from our souls; we are in a dangerous, unbalanced state. But this was not always the case, for we are not really born from this earth. We originally descended from a distant planet where we once achieved an evolutionary level far above human. We stood taller, we were more beautiful, our brains fully enlarged, working at maximum capacity; we possessed the power of foreseeing the future. And in that long-forgotten time, that golden age buried in oblivion, but still dimly perceived and remembered by the chosen, we walked with gods. We enjoyed perfect health and never aged. Through the apparently miraculous process of cloning, a gift we were once able to perform by the simple laying on of hands, a procedure that the laboratories of our holy movement are* even now bringing back to perfection (and for which we need to gather in large sums), *we shall live for ever, advancing and improving the body and mind, locked in an ever more perfect balance, as the physical structure is re-created flawless, to greet the newly housed soul. And we may yet return to this extraordinary state, which is in fact our natural plane of existence, when we reclaim our power to heal ourselves. Our divine duty shines before us: to achieve our full potential by bringing our minds and bodies back into that harmonious and peaceful balance which unleashes and reveals our supernatural powers. Jesus himself is one of* our great guardian leaders, who showed us the Way, the Truth and the Life before returning in his spaceship to that far-distant planet where he continues to evolve towards perfection.

Le Corps Harmonieux promised eternal health, eternal happiness and the chance to become one of the chosen few for a mere eight thousand francs. The guru of this sect proved to be a fascinating character. Now in his forties, he had already made some impact on the world as a failed rock star, advertising agent and Florida time-share holiday-home salesman. He spoke well, in an intense, persuasive manner, looming down upon his clients with a hawklike nose and terrible blue eyes. More seriously, he revealed a deep need to have his cock sucked by adoring adolescent girls. Madame Cordelier's daughter became one of his small chosen circle, destined, with the aid of his laboratories, to remain perfect gorgeous nymphs, for ever lovely and for ever young.

Madame Cordelier cut off the funds and ordered an end to all association with the guru and his disciples. Her daughter promptly moved out, after stealing her mother's credit card and emptying her account. She moved in with the guru, whose constant supply of sixteen-year-old girls, but preferably even younger ones, proved a daily necessity to reassure himself that his own body and soul were in perfect balance and good working order. The daughter willingly complied. Madame Cordelier stormed off to the police.

It is in the nature of the law to chew over desperate situations very slowly indeed. By the time the case reached the courts it was three years on from the day of Madame Cordelier's daughter's departure, intent on embracing the bliss of balanced body and soul, united in love and faith upon that higher plane. The guru had discarded her in favour of a thirteen-year-old and she had returned home, weeping and broken, persuaded that she had failed him in some awful way and therefore been deselected.

Dominique Carpentier took up the case. She eventually discovered, while meticulously dissecting his accounts, that the fiery preacher's eyes owed their commanding authority to tinted-blue contact lenses; even in court, however, she never gave away that little secret. The guru claimed that he was in fact an extraterrestrial, and therefore exempt from French income tax laws. Dominique Carpentier never suggested that he had not actually seen the inside of a spaceship. Instead she attacked on three fronts: corrupting the morals of minors, fiscal irregularities of immense proportions and publicité mensongère — fraudulent advertising. If he conducted his business on earth he was subject to local laws controlling that particular corner of the planet.

When Gaëlle came to read this dossier, years later, as she set about acquainting herself with the Judge's methods of working and the nature of her chosen enemy, she emerged from the dusty paperwork astounded by the dozens of dépositions, official statements from loyal members of Le Corps Harmonieux, all persuaded to a woman and man that an evil injustice had been perpetrated upon their noble saviour and upon themselves. They were certain that he was inspired by voices from another world and that he had been sent to warn them of this evil society that offered only alienation, repression and death. His words brought them direction and comfort. He pointed out the Way. He would lead them onwards into a libertarian utopia of freedom, beauty and light. The dissenters who turned against their master could be counted on one hand.

'How could they believe all this shit?' she demanded, waving one of the little brochures which the Judge had proved to be a raft of undeliverable claims. The presence of the soul, its precise nature and the practicalities of its transference from one human body into another, could not be verified. The soul, in any case, has no legal existence. The laboratories did not exist and human cloning, although manifestly possible, was still illegal and of uncertain efficacy. The Judge studied her assistant's spiked hair, held in place by a gel whose consistency resembled transparent cement, and then made one of her speeches. Gaëlle always treasured these moments when the Judge addressed her as if she were Madame la Présidente, with the whole court in closed session before her.

'We shouldn't judge them too hastily, Gaëlle. We must understand these people, their motives and their faiths. They are not all deluded fools, frauds and charlatans. Their leaders often sincerely believe that they are preaching a precious truth or imparting a crucial revelation.

36

But we must stop them exploiting the fears of the more vulnerable members of society — whether they do so unwittingly or otherwise. We have created a world where many men and women live alone; they no longer feel that they belong to a tribe or a community. They see this world as a desolate place. They long to live supported and secure within a discipline or creed, anything that offers the illusion of certainty, a way to comprehend this world and hope for the future. Their faith is often unconditional. We need to understand rather than condemn their beliefs. We must grasp the urgency of this spiritual need. For into that empty space, left without form and void when the great religions roll back, the sects sweep in. Read on, Gaëlle. You'll see how they resemble and differ from each other. My only weapon is the law. And I will use the law to defend our citizens.'

Gaëlle rose to her feet and clapped. The Judge grinned.

'Don't be too cheeky, ma belle. Look at the dates on those dossiers. Le Corps Harmonieux is a classic 1970s sect, because it relies on extra-terrestrials and flying saucers. The logical finale is Spielberg's *E. T.* There are some far more sinister ones in the cabinet on the right, with militaristic Fascist connections. One group was responsible for desecrating a Jewish cemetery. You won't jeer at them so easily.'

'But what happened to the guru and Le Corps Harmonieux?'

'He paid the massive fine, got three years'

suspended sentence and went back to Florida. Most of the faithful went with him. They're all there still, on a sort of ashram in beach huts. The laboratory now exists and their cloning claims are on the rise. They get a lot of media attention in the States. They make a lot of money. I keep in touch.'

Gaëlle imagined the Judge's eyes, travelling like searchlights, picking out the sects across the globe, and surveying their very thoughts from her office in Montpellier. But the Judge was not omniscient; and until that day in May 1995, when she kept her first appointment with André Schweigen, sent to her by a frustrated Procureur de la République, who had got as little joy out of Switzerland as the bilingual Commissaire, she had never encountered the Faith.

★　★　★

Almost a year after the massacre in Switzerland Schweigen's initial meeting with the Judge took the form of a continuous monologue. He thundered unchecked over lunch, which happened outside in a shady inner courtyard. He blossomed like a desperate client confronting his psychoanalyst for the very first time. The Judge changed her glasses to an identical pair with blacked-out lenses, which, given their dimensions, were clearly adjusted to her sight. The courtyard around them smelt damp with watered pots, wet green leaves and hot stone. The paving was flooded every morning in summer and pockets of water remained, shimmering in the natural dips and crevices worn into the flagstones.

Schweigen presented her with folders of papers, then took them all back to check they were the right ones. He radiated heat and discomfort. Yet he babbled courageously on; the Judge took notes. There had been no one left to interview and no living witnesses. The members of the Faith had hired a remote mountain hostel, just for themselves, and brought in all they needed: food, sheets, bedding, towels, soap.

'The place looked like a stage. Very theatrical, all the props arranged. And what were they doing during their last days? What do you think? Walking, swimming, yoga and meditation. Pony rides for the children. A long weekend of bracing exercise, specially organised for people committed to the outdoor life.'

They had been seen marching through the sunlit fields in groups, their arms around one another, singing. They left no suicide notes, and no explanations.

'But the odd thing is,' Schweigen argued away at an imaginary audience, 'they weren't the sort of people who go in for mad cures and diets. They weren't lacking anything. They were all rich, educated professionals. Two were in medical research, an endocrinologist and a skin-cancer specialist. They had positions, money, prospects. They were people who'd made it. They had everything to live for.'

The Judge laid down her pen and looked straight at Schweigen. He had taken off his jacket and there were damp sweat patches under his arms. He began waving his hands in an attempt to present his views in a manner that was more rhetorically persuasive.

'They weren't dropouts or hysterics. I don't know — but the sects you deal with — don't they just gather up the dross and the lost? People with no money and no future? Who want to be told what to believe?'

The Judge nodded slightly. 'But what makes you think these people were not among the lost?'

'They had all the things of this world. Worldly goods, I suppose you'd say. Yet they wanted something more. Somewhere else.' He glanced down at the fixed rictus of joy clamped across the dead faces spread out upon the tablecloth. His voice rose, incredulous, baffled. 'And they believed they were going there.'

'Apocalypse sects, or suicide sects if you like, always have a powerful vision of paradise,' said the Judge. She scanned the list of names, counting entire families. 'Or their ideal place, Utopia, Eden, the Golden Kingdom, whatever. The Faith probably conforms to this pattern. I assume you interviewed any surviving relatives? Employers? Friends?'

'We did. Everyone we could dredge up.' Schweigen sat fidgeting in the heat; he wiped his razored head, now damp with sweat; the black hair on his forearm stuck to his watch. The Judge observed him carefully.

'Shall we go inside? They have air conditioning.'

'No, no, it's fine. It's just that — I'm not really dressed for holiday weather.'

40

The Judge lowered her glasses and looked at him over the top so that he could see her eyes. The pupils were huge and dark, the deep brown rings surrounding them appeared to widen. He shrank away, taken aback by the sudden intimacy of the gesture.

'Monsieur Schweigen,' she leaned towards him and lowered her voice, 'why don't you nip inside and take off your woollen vest? Here, put it in this.'

She handed him a blue plastic carrier bag and shunted him off to the Gents as if he were a little boy. The lavatory turned out to be unisex and tiny, smelling of face powder with an undertow of bleach, and as he stood there, wrestling with his unsuitable layers, he shuddered with embarrassment, as if he were undressing in front of the Judge. She had a reputation for being disconcerting and direct, but he had not quite imagined the mixture of arctic formality and the almost physical familiarity of her manners. How did she know that the thing was made of wool? He suffered from the uncomfortable sensation that an unwritten line had been crossed. She was surveying his body, assessing his garments, giving him the once-over. He turned on the cold tap and splashed his naked chest, face and neck with cold water. Then he took off his watch and placed his wrists under the chilled stream, as his mother had taught him to do. He cooled down at once and peered into the mirror. He still looked disconcertingly pale and hot. He noticed the odd grey hair among the black at the centre of his chest and pulled on one of them. They proved to be much longer than the black ones and sprang back into a damp coil. Schweigen shook out his slightly crumpled shirt, then put it back on, turning up the sleeves and smoothing down his ruffled sense of dignity.

When he got back to their table he found that the Judge had ordered a pitcher of iced water for him and was sticking Post-its on all the documents she needed immediately.

'Vous allez mieux?' She pulled back his chair and made him welcome at the table. Now, for the first time, he looked hard at the Judge, discounting her reputation and her intransigent opinions; he studied the woman herself. She had been observing him like a laboratory specimen, sweating under the lights, now he returned the compliment. The quality that struck him most forcefully was her stillness. She was reading fast, absorbing both the details and the larger shapes revealed in the documents before her; she gutted his careful paperwork, as if peeling the flesh off a fish. He could not see her eyes and wasn't sure that he wanted to see them so nakedly again. She was lizard-smooth, her bare arms hairless, olive-skinned, no rings at all, just two gold studs gleaming in her ears, and a thin gold chain with a tiny disc and a small wrought charm barely visible beneath the folded collar of her blouse. What did the charm represent? Unless he buried his face in the small dip below her collarbone, he would never know. As the thought crossed his mind he shivered slightly and at that moment the Judge looked up. There was a strange pause. He still could not make out the expression in her

42

eyes; Schweigen stared at her, transfixed. Slowly, slowly, as if her entire body was unfolding from its coils, the Judge began to smile. She handed him a broad, generous smile, like a luminous gift.

In all the years to come, when André Schweigen tried to recall every moment he had spent with Dominique Carpentier, every reverie eventually condensed into that extraordinary slow smile.

'You look much better already. Here, drink this.' Cold drops ran down the perspiring glass. As he began to drink the virgin glass of pure, cold water she lowered her dark glasses, as if to encourage him, and meeting her gaze, he drank the lot, an unflinching Tristan to her Isolde.

'Santé,' said Schweigen, setting down the empty glass. And the languid, erotic smile metamorphosed into a merry, childish grin.

'Santé, Monsieur le Commissaire,' she laughed, raising her glass to him. Had he already fallen in love with her? Or was this just the moment when he noticed that he had? That smile, full of humour and affection, doomed to be Schweigen's undoing, ensured that from then onwards his every third thought was dedicated to the black-haired, dark-eyed Judge, whose ruthless efficiency, terrifying discipline and legendary self-control drove her colleagues to drink.

'You mustn't get so worked up, Monsieur Schweigen. I know it's frustrating. But it wasn't your investigation. You would have done things differently. But consider — what we have here are the threads. If we follow them carefully we'll soon have the whole tapestry before us. Be patient. Listen. Wait.'

But that was her method, not his. Schweigen needed to calculate the advantage and the risk, then to act.

'Tell me all you know about the founders of the Faith,' she said, and the invitation was as gentle and reassuring as if she had proposed an afternoon in bed.

*   *   *

What did they actually know? Not much, in fact. A central figure, which they had identified from the sparse existing literature, was known simply as the Professor and another as the Guide. The Faith appeared to conform to a classic pattern common to many religions: a complex mysticism of eternal transcendence whose followers nevertheless believe that it is meet and right to intervene in the kingdom of this world. The reactions of the surviving relatives, and the statements given by colleagues and employees to Schweigen and the Swiss police, made it clear that no one who knew the dead had any idea whatsoever that their friends were involved in a religion at all, let alone a suicide sect. The same phrases came up again and again: she never talked about this — we had no hints, no indications — but he appeared to be quite normal, happy, full of plans — they were doing well, he had just been promoted to a better post — but they loved their home and family — she was devoted to her children, I can't believe she would have let them come to harm — it's simply not possible, we would have known, she would have told me, this cannot have happened to us. So they were looking at a secret sect, a hidden fellowship. There were no public lectures, no proselytising, no published gospels. But what became clear immediately was the fact that these members of the Faith were hand-picked: they were the chosen.

'Look at this pattern. They nearly all have higher degrees or advanced qualifications. Some of them went to the same universities — all well-known prestigious institutions. They've all achieved an exceptional level of education. Most of them are not just experts in their fields — they are the sole expert. That's why you have such a cautious lot of obituaries. And why the Swiss hushed the whole thing up. They were famous people. It's embarrassing, peculiar. Hmm, predominantly scientists. Only a few come from the arts, and when they do they are always linked to music. Gerhart Liebmann. He was Swiss, an opera producer and director of the Berliner Staatsoper. I've seen his work discussed in the papers.' The Judge was already pulling at the threads. 'So that explains the patterns of recruitment. They draw in the people they already know, and recruit from the circles in which they move.'

'And this mass suicide took place on the summer solstice. So they operate on a system that is linked to the moving cosmos.'

'All religions do,' said Schweigen, sugaring his coffee well beyond the normal dose.

'Exactly. Well, nearly all. Noël is simply the winter solstice festival left over from the pagans. The Muslims generate their holy days through the lunar calendar, as do the Jews. But this Faith seems to have a closer union with the stars than either the Muslims or the Catholics. What's this?'

The Judge drew forth a grubby photocopy of a smeared graph, traversed by two undulating lines and covered in random dots. She could see no writing on the chart at all. It looked like a musical score for some complex form of Gregorian chant. She turned it several ways up, trying to read the paper from different angles. Suddenly her face cleared.

'I know what this is. Look. It's a chart of the middle heavens. This curved belt contains the stars of the zodiac — it's that part of the sky where you can always see the sun, the moon and the bright planets. And these marked dots are star clusters. Look — these are the stars in Taurus, here is Orion, and this group here are the Pleiades. Where was this found?'

'It was pinned to the noticeboard in the kitchen. It's not the original. That was clearer and some of the stars were highlighted.'

'Do the Swiss still have this chart?'

'God knows.'

'Find out. I want a colour photograph. As clear and detailed as possible. The original would be better. And it's only going to rot in a box if the Swiss have wound up their investigation.'

'There was a full moon on the night they died,' ventured Schweigen, alarmed by this astrological development. 'How will this chart help?'

'We can't assume that they were all killed off in Switzerland. More of them may be out there. And this chart may tell us if and when the next departure is due to take place. And it may also tell us where they think they're going.'

She peered again at the faces of the dead, framed as portraits, with their names, ages, professions, next of kin listed below, but now she was looking for something unambiguous, a face she expected to find.

'One of them must spend all his time peering down a telescope or looking at charts on his computer. Which one is the astronomer? Or the astrophysicist?'

Schweigen flicked over the pages in the file, unhesitating.

'This one. And he's the man who didn't take the poison. He was shot.'

Anton Laval, aged 56, born Lyon, senior researcher with the CNRS at Grenoble, often featured as one of the consulting scientists in the popular late summer television programme, La Nuit des Étoiles. The Judge studied the calm handsome face for some time. If she recognised him, she gave no sign.

'Maybe that's our Professor,' said Schweigen. 'On the other hand at least twelve of them were Professors.'

'It says here he wasn't married. Who was registered as his next of kin?'

'One sister. I saw her yesterday.' The Judge raised her darkened eyes to his face, her mouth remained inscrutable. 'She lives about eighty kilometres to the north-east of here, a huge

47

domaine, beyond Nîmes. She was still distraught with grief when I asked about her brother. I had to stop and wait while she pulled herself together. She couldn't tell me much. No more than she gave to my colleagues last year, just after the event. They were asking very silly questions though. Did he have any enemies? Who might want to shoot him? There were nearly seventy other people lying dead all around him. It looked like he was just following the fashion.'

'And as far as the secret sect is concerned she seemed to think it quite extraordinary that he could believe in anything to the point of sacrificial martyrdom. She's the devout Catholic and he's the sceptic. Or that's more or less what I gathered. She's in the local curé's pocket. She kept saying how much she missed her brother, but she's absolutely convinced that she will see him again and that they will be reunited. I thought she was a bit mad.'

'She's a widow, but she always kept her nom de jeune fille because she runs the estate. She's on that list. Marie-Cécile Laval.'

★　★　★

But five years earlier neither Schweigen nor the Judge had suspected Madame Marie-Cécile Laval of being a member of the Faith. She cooperated willingly with the investigation, talked frankly about her brother, unfailingly loving in everything she said. Her unflinching tenderness seemed odd. When someone commits suicide the reaction of disbelief is usually followed by rage against the person who has so brutally slammed the door and gone. Madame Laval's gentle, emotional forgiveness disarmed her interrogators. She opened her house to them, handed over her brother's papers, presented a countenance of such cultivated intelligence that all suspicion faded.

Schweigen always remembered Madame Laval as he had first seen her, surrounded by beautiful eighteenth-century furniture, gilded mirrors with dusty Cupids, a cabinet inlaid with rosewood and mother-of-pearl, family portraits by once famous artists, stiff sofas covered with replicated material, exactly matching the original patterns but too bright to be genuine. The Domaine teetered over the edge of fading splendour; the baroque fountain was beginning to lose its shells, moths had nestled in the drapes. Lay not up for yourselves treasure upon earth, where moth and rust doth corrupt, and where thieves break through and steal. Madame Laval sat quietly in a corner of her depleted elegance, weeping over the corruption of all earthly things. Her sole desire was to bring her brother's body home. Where your treasure is there will your heart be also.

Schweigen had indeed called upon Madame Laval the very day before he first met the Judge in the flesh, and those days, which he now thought of as the first days, seemed private, secret. Madame Laval lurked in the middle distance, an unknowing, silent witness to what had taken place between André Schweigen and

49

the Judge. Two weeks after that first meeting in May 1995 the Judge called him at work.

'Monsieur Schweigen? Dominique Carpentier à l'appareil. Thank you for the map of the stars. Very clever of you to get hold of the original.'

'Well, that wasn't hard. The Swiss didn't want it.'

There was a pause. Schweigen clenched his left fist. He had sounded ungracious. How could he keep her on the line? But she had already moved on to the next step of the dance.

'I've discovered that Madame Laval has at last managed to secure the release of her brother's body and she is bringing him back to the Domaine for burial. I thought we might attend the funeral together and pay our respects.'

'The funeral?'

'Ah yes. She is holding a full-blown Catholic requiem Mass at the church in the village, then the cortège will retreat to the family mausoleum for a private burial in the vaults. The curé is up for the full Mass with choir and speeches, because she hasn't asked for burial in the graveyard. I'm not sure he could have accepted a suicide.'

'How do you know all this?'

'The curé is my uncle.'

'You actually know the Laval family?'

'Not so well any more. But I did once. My family are also vignerons — in the same commune. Everyone will be there at the funeral, including my parents. It would look very odd if I wasn't.'

'Why didn't you say so before?' Schweigen snapped. He felt cheated. He suspected that his

50

temper might not be reasonable, but he couldn't stop himself. The Judge sounded faintly amused.

'It wasn't relevant before. Now it is. So I've told you.'

Schweigen became even more incensed. His investigation had been hijacked. 'But you knew who Marie-Cécile Laval was and you didn't say anything.'

He was stamping his feet like a child. Regarde-moi. Occupe-toi de moi. I'm the person who's important here, moi, moi. The Judge ignored his enraged squeal.

'Can you come?' An immense patience flooded the line. Schweigen caved in.

'Mais bien sûr. Where shall I meet you?'

'At the church. The funeral is at 15.00 heures. Can you get there by 14.30 at the latest? I will already be there and I want to be inside the church.'

★ ★ ★

Unexpected, aggressive and ferocious, the heat assaulted his black suit and bound him fast as he teetered off the plane at Nîmes. None of the hired cars within his budget had air conditioning. He roared sweating through the vineyards with all the windows open, the hot air rushing past. Already the land seemed parched and gasping. Cicadas rattled in the trees; a glassy haze coated the green. He never took his family south in the summer, no matter how hard his wife pleaded with him; the heat was simply unendurable.

51

The little square in front of the church glimmered in a leopard skin of light and shade, shadowed with great plane trees. A café colonised the paving. The village smouldered quietly behind closed shutters. He heard the chink of plates being collected in the half-dark. Only the tourists ate outside; and the season had barely begun. The café had piled away some of the tables to make room for the arriving cars. Strangers in fine clothes and dark glasses already patrolled the square. The great west doors of the church, siege barriers covered in nails, stood open. The hinges had been renewed; crows perched on the corbel table. Only brides and coffins entered through the great west doors. The undertaker's men, eerie, comfortable and sinister in black, skulked just inside, waiting.

Schweigen imagined the hearse like a large refrigerated meat van. Anton Laval had been dead for nearly a year. What was the point of prising him out of the vaults in Switzerland and hauling him home — a poison bag of blackened skin and rotting bones? He was nearly an hour early and yet so many people were already there. Schweigen parked under the trees. The heat billowed around him. He sat for a moment with his eyes closed, wondering if he could put his jacket back on at the very last moment. The cicadas were deafening.

Then the car door opened on the driver's side and there stood the Judge, within his grasp, her black hair, slick and tight, wrenched into a thick plaited coil. She leaned over him; he smelt the crisp folds of her sleeveless black linen shift, absorbed her dark glasses with fine golden rims and black high-heeled shoes.

'Bonjour, Monsieur Schweigen.'

He stood up, stiff, sweating and off guard, wondering if he would ever, in all his life to come, desire a woman again as powerfully as he wanted this calm, untouchable Judge. She stepped back and stretched out her hand towards him. He could not read her eyes, and so he hesitated; then he took possession of her cool fingers in his clammy grasp.

'I think you need something to drink,' said the Judge.

★   ★   ★

He watched the people with whom she shook hands, tried to calculate which ones were family and which ones were probably more distant friends and acquaintances. One woman with opulent olive breasts clasped the Judge firmly in her arms and demanded her 'nouvelles'. Schweigen retreated into the church, occupied a pew with a clear view of the altar and lectern and chastised himself for unreasonable jealousy. He regained control of his emotions and his face in the shadow of a pillar, and became altogether calmer in the musty dark. He had not set foot inside a church since his son's baptism. The Judge slithered in beside him and produced a handwritten list of names, some of which were marked with an asterisk. She moved her briefcase to the other side so that her thigh rested against his and whispered against his cheek; even her breath cooled his simmering flesh.

'All these people are relatives of members of the Faith who left in the last departure. Some others are colleagues and friends. I may not have all the names. This is my uncle's list for the enterrement, which I compared with the one in the dossier. But it won't be complete. People just turn up at funerals, others don't even at the last moment. But if any members of the Faith still exist, then they may well be here in this church. Don't worry about photographs. I've had the entrance wired with CCTV. We'll have a video for cross-reference with the information we already have. This seemed such an excellent opportunity.'

Schweigen noticed a prowling journalist carrying a tape-recorder and microphone. The television cameras set up in the square were excluded from the church, but the journalist slipped inside.

'The press are here,' he hissed.

'No wonder. A government minister will be too. My uncle told me. These aren't ordinary people, André, they have not only position, but power. Why do you think I'm so interested?'

All he could think of was the fact that she had used his first name. In the midst of their conspiracy she had drawn him closer, closer. He looked down at her bare knees and then round at the packed and rustling church and the gathering of hushed and waiting mourners who loitered in shadow, just out of reach of the afternoon glare.

'Won't your CCTV camera be noticed?'

'Goodness, no. It's part of the church's ordinary security system. Plenty of tourists are thieves. That Virgin dates from the twelfth century. The altar is wired up to all kinds of alarms.'

'Then you know this church well.'

'I should do. I was baptised here.'

And suddenly he found himself staring into her intimate hidden past — her catechism classes, her first communion. He tried to imagine her as a young girl and failed. Her strange calm face, the eyes masked by the dark glasses, swivelled round towards him. He confronted her ironic smile.

'Is your uncle going to say Mass?'

'Oh yes. But not the address. I am especially interested in the tributes. One of Laval's closest friends is due to speak. He's a German Composer apparently. Uncle has only met him briefly, but I noticed the musical connection. Quite a few people here are members of his orchestra. Ah, here they come.'

Members of the congregation, rummaging in their laps for the order of service and alerted by the deep whistle of the organ, lurched to their feet. A murmur of smart clothes and hushed, cultivated voices rose and died away. The minister appeared with his wife and bodyguard, who suppressed the journalist. There was a dreadful hush. They could hear the hearse and the family arriving outside. A small choir entered, following the cross. *Dona nobis pacem.* Schweigen recognised Madame Laval. The entire

Mass was being sung in Latin. He shuddered slightly; the whole thing gave him the creeps. He had attended a boarding school, lodged in the mountains of the Haute-Savoie and run by Dominicans, passionate advocates of corporal punishment, which they believed essential to the formation of a solid, honest character. Schweigen continued to associate the Church with hot tears and incipient violence. He edged closer to the Judge. *Requiem aeternam dona eis.*

The coffin swung slowly up three steps into the nave and at its head marched a man taller than the others, which caused a disturbing disequilibrium in the distribution of its weight. His white hair gleamed against the oak, his lined face and clenched jaw shone hard in the bright light for a moment then vanished into shadow. Despite clearly being older than the other bearers he was broader across the shoulders and chest; his stride was longer and he was forced to curb his steps to an uneasy shuffle so that the coffin, draped with an eerie velvet pall and crested with a crown of white lilies, ceased to list, like a rolling ship. He measured his slow stride, but it was still a relief when the massive coffin descended safe upon the catafalque and the unsteady progress down the aisle passed off without disaster. The congregation exhaled a gentle puff of gratitude and the funeral began.

Afterwards, Schweigen couldn't remember much about the funeral; he was too hot and still uneasy in the Judge's presence. But he did remember the address. The white-haired man who had carried the coffin rose to speak. He

56

stood still for a long time before addressing the congregation in hesitant, careful French. He did not speak to the deceased, but the survivors. And he was the only person who gave any indication that Anton Laval had not died peacefully in bed, full of years and surrounded by his grandchildren.

The substance of the Composer's opening words proved conventional enough; the traditional professional tribute to a distinguished scientist, enumerating his honours, describing the importance of his research and highlighting the fact that he had pinpointed three of Saturn's many moons. Then his tone changed. He laid down his text, fixed the assembled shifting crowd with a terrible glare, and spoke from the heart.

'Anton was my friend. I cannot and will not judge the actions of my friend. But if anyone here were to feel angry and bereft because they do not understand the reasons why he has left us I would say this. You will never comprehend him or consent to his departure without understanding his belief that all things are eternal, that our very mortality is the sign that we shall be transformed. In the midst of life we are in death, but that life is ours for ever; it is that eternal life which awaits us beyond death, the glory of an eternal union with all that we have ever loved. We are not only earth and water; we are fire and air. And we are surrounded by signs, the pathways to a higher, greater nature, the Great Mind that extends beyond us, goes before us, leads the way. That Great Mind is Love itself, the place towards which all desire leads, the home for which we yearn. I loved Anton. And I know he loved, and still loves, every one of you.'

The effect on the Judge was electric. She shifted against the wood and lifted her head like a cheetah that has just seen the wildebeest, ambling towards the river. The funeral felt like a cover-up, a fraudulent paint job, disguising a fissure that would bring the house down. So the speaker's last words rattled the pews and the plaster statues; as he turned to caress the coffin, his head bowed, his giant hands seemed to cradle the dead head and lost bones; even the four vast candles encircling the catafalque guttered in the swift rush of air.

The strange, gaunt figure returned to the lectern and gazed into space as if listening to something that only he could hear, then sat down suddenly next to Madame Laval, who leaned against him, dislodging her black veil. Then they heard another voice, another foreign accent of a rather different nature, booming out next to the coffin. The curé, standing a little to the left of the altar, bowed down in prayer, and the congregation followed. The Judge consulted her order of service, but nothing special was marked after the address. The small figure was masked by the Composer's giant shoulders and remained invisible. He was nothing but a voice, a foreign voice shaking in the air. Schweigen realised that he was speaking English and grasped the incantatory rhythm, but missed the words. So did the Judge.

Pray, pray for my soul — that the Dark

Host may embrace me and restore me. Let no evil approach my dwelling. Anoint my servants with the holy oil of sanctuary that we may pass safely across these dread waters and that at our rising the Dark Presence shall grant us joy perpetual.

The Judge craned her neck to see who was speaking, failed, then fished a small black notebook out of her bag and wrote three words: *The Dark Host*. Then she wrote: *Prayer for the dead? Where is it from and who was speaking? Ask Uncle.*

When the moment came for each member of the congregation to circle the coffin, spattering the arum lilies with holy drops of water, the Judge reached out and drew Schweigen back into the gloom next to the font.

'We don't show ourselves,' she hissed, 'we're not the only ones watching.'

Schweigen's flesh prickled where she had touched his arm. Every part of his body felt vulnerable, as if cut open; he was caught in the giant tide that swept all things towards her. He swallowed back the unprofessional hysteria which threatened to engulf him and clutched at the choir's disturbing roar: *Libera me.*

Libera me, Domine, de morte aeterna
In die illa tremenda
Quando coeli movendi sunt et terra
Dum veneris judicare saeculum ignem

Deliver me, O Lord, from eternal death

On that awful day
When heaven and earth shall be shaken
And you shall come to judge the earth by
fire.

Schweigen felt slightly deranged. The only
Judge he could now imagine stood next to him.
And he was already undergoing a trial by
fire. Everyone rose and faced the coffin as the
unsteady procession left the church, and in the
scrum that followed they lost each other in
the crowd. Schweigen scuttled after her, trying to
fix her glistening coil of black hair that was
definitely pushing against the stream. He caught
up with her beside the vestry door. She produced
a giant key from the briefcase; then opened the
back door into the square.

'We'll take your car. I'll drive.' She bundled
him into the front seat.

It was now well past five in the afternoon. The
heat was still there, but its savagery had ebbed.
They sped down a tiny walled road with vines on
either side, then up into a rocky outcrop covered
in shimmering Mediterranean pines. The country stretched away into layered hills, shaggy with
stunted oaks and white rocks. The soil glowed
red and stony. Humped between the vines, a
series of small stone caverns, with domed roofs
like prehistoric houses, punctuated the geometri-
cal vineyards.

'I won't ask where we're going. You obviously
know.'

Schweigen sat back, delighted to be no longer
responsible for whatever was going to happen

next. The sensation of recklessness was both erotic and exhausting. The Judge stopped the rented Clio behind one of the stone buildings and then led the way, clambering up the rocks. Her black high heels were swiftly coated with red dust. The small bulge in her bag, which he had decided must be a ladies' gun, turned out to be a pair of birdwatcher's binoculars.

'Here you are. I thought we'd check if anything untoward happened at the interment.'

'Do you mean we can see it all from here?'

'Stay within the pinède; then they won't see us. All the main buildings face the other way. I know the geography of the Domaine. I used to go to the dances in the Great Hall at New Year.'

The buildings of the old mas had slit windows and great bulging walls like a fortress; and the glimmering heat painted the adjacent family crypt in odd shades of white and grey. The mausoleum looked like a tasteless nineteenth-century church and was surrounded by rusting railings. For a long time nothing happened. Schweigen was being munched by passing insects; he fidgeted and scratched. The Judge crouched silent and simply watched. They shared the binoculars.

Then she said, 'There's my uncle!'

And behold the priest tottering down the uneven path towards the doorway of the mausoleum. As he opened the great metal gates they saw the gaping dark of the opened tomb beyond him. The undertakers had taken over completely and were shunting the unstable coffin down the track on what looked like a hospital gurney. Madame Laval followed slowly, carrying the wreath of lilies. All the bearers and all other relatives had vanished.

'Here they come.'

They took turns to watch. The action unfolded like an unedited film from which the soundtrack had been lost. The white-haired Composer who had spoken so forcefully at the funeral was not there, nor was the immediate family. The last group accompanying Anton Laval to the ancestral vault consisted only of his sister and the priest, four undertakers and two builders with a bucket of cement and a discarded pump, ready to seal the stone. They whipped off their hats as the coffin wobbled past. Then everything froze as the priest opened his book to read the final prayers. The coffin tilted on the brink ready to descend the steps. At the last moment Madame Laval stepped forwards, removed the velvet pall, handed it to the builders and unfolded a small cloth, which she draped across the plaque like a fallen soldier's flag. The undertakers straightened the cloth and began to lower the coffin into the gulf. The Judge had the binoculars.

'Very interesting. Look.' She passed the glasses to him, but all he saw was Madame Laval, supported by the curé, and the descending coffin covered by a flash of deep, glittering blue.

'What was it? The fleur-de-lys?'

'No,' said the Judge, her face inscrutable, but every tendon in her shoulders stretched and tense. 'It was covered in stars.'

★ ★ ★

Neither of them spoke on their way back to the village. Schweigen had lost all interest in the case, the funeral, the sect known only as the Faith, any possible political connections; all he cared about now was how to contrive some method of remaining beside the Judge for as long as he could. He had no idea what to do. Ask her out to dinner to discuss the funeral? Tear up his return plane ticket and invite himself to stay? Sabotage the car? What if she had a husband and children waiting for her at home? He knew nothing about her. She was simply 'la chasseuse de sectes', and he was sitting next to her; noticing the tiny freckles on her bare arms, her strong small hands and short, unpainted nails, the fact that she drove in one gear too low so that the car roared, and possessed an apparent immunity to heat — this was all he knew, and it made him feel slightly sick, reeling with desire, which loomed before him like a ghastly tunnel with no exit.

'What is it?' asked the Judge, as the village reared up out of the vineyards in the distance.

Schweigen risked all.

'Stop the car.'

She pulled up on a small track by the edge of the vineyards. A little row of olives and two dark pillars of cypress trees, brushing one another, marked the rim. They could be seen, clearly, from all directions. The Judge switched off the engine and turned her dark gaze upon him. He reached up to her dark glasses and took them off. Her nose twitched and she blinked. Schweigen realised that she could no longer see him clearly and that she was swallowing a huge gust of laughter.

'What's so funny?'

'You are.'

She leaned towards him; he could smell her hair and the perfume on her dress. Her lunge across the gear stick was so sudden and unexpected that Schweigen cringed back against the passenger's door. One hand shot out and caught his head, her fingers sticking into his short damp hair, and with the other she hauled his shoulders round to face her so that her savage kiss, hard against his lips, almost dislocated his collarbone. Schweigen shook with fright like an assaulted virgin. She covered his face and neck with light, dry kisses. Then just as suddenly as she had come she drew away, like a serpent recoiling, choosing the next bare patch of skin to bite.

'There,' she said, 'wasn't that what you wanted?'

Schweigen recovered himself completely. His confidence galloped back through every vein, like a horse flying riderless across open fields, charged with pure joy.

'Yes,' he said, looking her straight in the eye, and allowing all his sexual intent to glimmer and shine with expectation and demand. 'That was exactly what I wanted.'

'You taste of salt,' smiled the Judge and flicked her tongue swiftly across her lower lip.

3

The Book of the Faith

Now, five years on from that day at the funeral, Schweigen's emotions rolled back and forth as he rummaged through the chalet where Madame Laval had spent her last days. He stomped about the bedrooms overseeing his forensic research party; he felt tricked and betrayed by this stately woman, who had followed her brother to the grave, staging an exact replica of the earlier events. But through the manner of her death Madame Laval had brought the Judge back to him. There was the woman he loved, sitting downstairs, bending over the evidence, in charge of his investigation. The trail glowed warm again. He had an incontestable excuse to speak to her every day. He found himself smiling into the linen cupboard.

André Schweigen could never quite remember the Judge with sufficient clarity between their rare encounters ever to be reassured that she was not, in fact, a mirage created by desire, which he had ingeniously conjured up. He wrote her name upon his telephone pad, over and over again, simply for the pleasure of watching the letters take shape, just as the younger son of Sir Rowland de Boys had plastered *ROSALIND* all over the woods, defacing stiles and gateposts, oaks and silver birch trees. If he tried to remember her smooth, cool shape he could see nothing but her eyes and hands. He couldn't remember her clothes. Did she always wear black as she had done five years before at Anton Laval's grotesque requiem Mass? She is half my size. I can hold both her hands in one of mine. All her movements are sly and deft. She makes me feel huge, ungainly, clumsy and stupid. Her hair. Now I can see her, I can see every flick and shimmer of her black hair as she bends forward with her head upside down and brushes her hair downward, then up she comes, acrobatic and precise as a circus act, and it settles round her shoulders and across her face like an affectionate animal. Then she raises her left arm, comb braced and ready, rakes it all upwards, then sculpts the mass into a coil, no stray threads, and fixes the creature at the nape of her neck, with that tortoiseshell clamp that her mother brought back from the Maldives. And the last thing she does as she smoothes her shirt into her trousers is reach for her glasses.

I have watched her do this every time I have made love to her. She moves like a dancer. Now I can see her eyes and hands. But I cannot imagine her face. A cold swell of panic rushed through him and lifted the hair on his forearms. I cannot see her face. And so the Judge vanished.

Schweigen found himself perpetually on the brink of announcing to his oblivious wife that he was in love with a Judge. This rendered his family life precarious and intolerable. Had he been able to confess that the Judge was merely another woman, the matter would have been simpler, less strenuous, more easily explicable. He would then have fallen into that banal category of men, who, after an erotic debut with a woman they have known for some time, settle down into about eight years of emotional and economic debris; in which they purchase the villa, plant the trees, make do with one car when the wife works part-time, eat dinner with friends who are doing the same thing, have one child, decide they cannot afford another, and thank God it's a boy, buy surfboards for Brittany, skis for les vacances d'hiver, mountain bikes and walking boots, eat sensibly, despite the chips, decorate the house for Christmas and decide that they are happy. On the edges of this seeping bliss the husband — or the wife — will have the odd adventure. A few doors will be slammed when all is revealed, discovered or confessed. But the steadiness that has been established by routine and that daily engagement which is required of long-married people, who, after all, rub along like comrades in the trenches, will restore the balance; and a provisional equilibrium, that long swell in the Atlantic, which means you have reached the middle passage, steadies the ship. The possibility of catastrophe had already been avoided by intimate friends, once, twice, and Sabine Schweigen prepared herself, not only to take these side steps in her stride, but to ignore them steadily, as wise wives often do.

She therefore did not notice, or refused to do so, when Schweigen lay beside her, prostrate, unsleeping, like someone electrocuted, nor did she comment when he sat sagging and crumpled at the table in the mornings, black rings beneath his eyes, like an elderly rag doll. The first investigation proved traumatic. Small wonder. Who would not be shaken by the sight of dozens of poisoned people, some no more than children, murdered while they slept, and by their parents' own hands? Madame Schweigen was a nurse who specialised in intensive care. She frequently worked night shifts, so that her mother was recalled to babysitting duties when her husband's journeys dragged him away from home. She remained unperturbed when his life heaved into disturbance and uproar; with an inquiry of this nature anything else would have been extraordinary. Besides, he still ate a substantial breakfast.

But Schweigen's inner life had been laid waste by an emotional electric storm, which had fused the synapses in his brain. The Judge dominated the investigation and therefore his working life, but worse, far worse than this, she occupied his imagination, like a conquering army, whose troops and tanks, camped out at every street corner, now controlled all access to his soul. He gazed at his wife, desperate. For every action was now performed before the cool, appraising eyes of the all-seeing Judge, about whom he still knew next to nothing.

In the beginning, five years before, the Judge created all the circumstances that could reasonably lead to another meeting. Almost a month after Anton Laval's funeral, when all attempts on Schweigen's part to contact her had been greeted with a shattering clatter of the portcullis, he had begun to plan reckless measures. He could not accept that this affair was a matter easily settled in one afternoon. Then her voice, steady and precise, appeared in his ear, as if they had just finished speaking some moments before.

'Monsieur le Commissaire? C'est Dominique Carpentier à l'appareil. I have arranged to meet the judge who dealt with the Swiss departure. Just to talk things over. Given that so many of the families are agitating about the lack of an enquiry. Have you seen *Le Nouvel Observateur*? Non? Marie-Cécile Laval has written an article about her brother that has provoked a good deal of correspondence. It reads more like a self-justifying obituary than an explanation. But you should read it. I've brought you a copy, just in case.'

'Where are you?' snapped Schweigen, incensed by her cool and aroused simply by the sound of her voice.

'At Strasbourg airport. On my way to Bern. Would you be free, by any chance, and able to join me?'

The hotel in Bern overlooked the Parliament buildings and a famous café, which the government patronised, strolling across the square, bent on consuming mid-morning coffee and cakes during the breaks between sessions. The scale of the buildings, both the Parliament and the political coffee house, allowed them to settle comfortably alongside one another, domestic and charming. As they sat in the restaurant the evening sun illuminated the crisp yellow linen tablecloth and the Judge's olive arms. Schweigen counted the ribbed stitches on the front of her white shirt, and noticed that the veins in the semi-precious stones in her ears were not symmetrical. He looked everywhere rather than into her face, the large glasses and the fabulous, magnified eyes. He heard the amusement in her voice, like a melody played on the oboe, every time she ceased to speak about the investigation and addressed him directly as a man to whom she had once made love.

'I've booked a suite with two rooms. Just in case you wanted to endorse our respectable cover story.' She grinned at him.

'How could you be so sure I'd come with you?' Schweigen had actually told the truth at home, or at least the geographical truth — that he was called away to Bern, activated his mother-in-law, and hurtled off to Switzerland, trailing in the Judge's first-class wake on the midday train.

'Ah well,' said the Judge, 'here you are.' And he was granted a smile more beautiful, more generous and affectionate than he had ever dared to long for during all the manic hours he had spent gazing at her handwriting, whispering her name. André Schweigen felt quite unhinged. This awkwardness, which accompanied his passion like a drinking chorus in the middle of Mass, then proved his undoing.

Upon the table, beside their scraped dessert plates, was a Sträußchen, a little bouquet of wild flowers in a decorated pot. The hotel, now owned by a chain, had succumbed to the desolate economics of capitalism and replaced the fresh scented flowers, which had once enchanted visitors to the former family-run establishment, by an authentic plastic-textile cluster of edelweiss. Schweigen tipped the candle too close to the green-and-white bouquet, which caught fire at once and began to smoulder. For a moment he did not notice what he had done. A dramatic shift in the Judge's attention triggered the alarm and a cloud of black smoke rose up from the table. The worst of it was that no one else, not even the waiters, or the two businessmen sitting next to them, who actually had a computer open on the table, took the slightest bit of notice. Schweigen tried to quell the flames with his bare hands, burning his thumb in the process. The Judge snatched up her yellow linen napkin, folded it rapidly in two and smothered the blaze in one swift gesture. The plastic flowers sizzled faintly beneath her ruthless grasp and then went out. She tipped her water glass over the napkin as a precaution, so that a small damp heap of charred remains defaced the table.

'Have you burned your hand?' The Judge was genuinely concerned. 'There's a sinister smell of roasting flesh.' Then she laughed softly. 'Come upstairs, André. I've got some antiseptic cream in my suitcase.'

And that was the second time she had called him by his first name. For ever afterwards he always remembered this combination of emotions, chagrin, embarrassment, pain and joy

71

— the pure joy of acknowledgement and recognition. She loves me, she loves me not, she loves me. He no longer cared about anything else; the woman he loved without let or hindrance had gazed upon him with undisguised tenderness and addressed him by his name. She loves me.

★ ★ ★

The heating in the chalet had not yet risen to the first floor. Schweigen prowled through the children's rooms, full of video games, bright activity centres, plastic picture books and half-built constructions in Lego. The toys were beginning to get to him. He saw building kits, battleships and play-stations that he had bought for his own boy, the same baseball cap with the bright logo, similar boots. He bristled at these abandoned rooms and young lives sliced in two; his anger now rising in exact proportion to his approaching exhaustion. He wished them all back here, now, so that he could prosecute the lot. As he retreated from the main children's room he turned out the light, and it was then that he became aware of the stars. André Schweigen looked up.

Above him, all across the ceiling, glowing with soft phosphorescence, glittered a pattern of lights, carefully designed to mirror the night sky at the winter solstice. The children had gazed at that sky night after night and then died, their faces raised to the same pattern of stars, churning across the void, following the earth where they lay, staring wide-eyed into eternity. Schweigen completely forgot his self-imposed formal manner towards the Judge, which he reserved for professional occasions, and yelled down the stairs, 'Dominique! Viens ici. Viens vite!'

The Judge pattered up towards him, steadying her glasses and buttoning her coat. They stood, side by side, gazing at the gleaming stars. There was the sign, the same one that the Swiss police had pulled ruthlessly from the kitchen notice-board, tearing at the edges, as they rushed to eliminate all the unintelligible symbols that only augmented their fears and the apparent complexity of the case. Schweigen had the creeps; it was like entering a pharaoh's tomb.

'Well, what's the matter, André?'

She lowered her voice. He was reassured by her steadiness and her immediate perception of his unease. He no longer felt the jubilant flush of adrenalin; the horror of the massacre on the forest floor pressed against his back, with the stealthy weight of an animal, hunting him down.

'It's the children. The toys. I don't know — ' He petered out. She peeled off her right red glove, reached up towards him, and gently touched his face.

'They'll never come home. All their things are here. My boy's got the same things. And they'll never come home.'

The Judge put her arms around him, and rocked him close to her warmth. He looked into her magnified eyes, illuminated by the fraudulent night sky above them, and flung away the strange unease, which padded back into the children's room and coiled around the bunk beds.

'Shhhh, André, don't take on so. Their parents believed they were going home for ever. To their real home.'

'But the sky was overcast last night,' Schweigen declared bitterly, 'for most of the night. The temperature rose. It snowed after midnight. They never saw those stars.'

'But they knew they were there,' whispered the Judge.

★ ★ ★

One of the forensic team emerged from a bedroom across the corridor.

'Madame le Juge? We've just found this.' She held out a book bound in leather covers, like an accounts book or a family Bible. The thing was massive, and resembled a Grimoire, a gigantic book of spells. A curious clasp sealed the pages and a gold inlaid pattern, worn away in places, circled the rim. No title marked the spine, just three worn gold crests.

'Where did you find it?' Dominique Carpentier replaced her white surgical gloves and reached for the evidence.

'In Madame Laval's bedroom. Under her pillow. I thought it might be a diary, but it isn't. It's too big. We did look. It is printed, but we can't understand the languages.'

They retreated downstairs. The Judge set aside her Christmas wrapping paper and holiday snaps and began to study the book.

'André, is there anyone in this departure who has the initials R.B. or F.G.?'

There was a pause as Schweigen scanned the list.

'No. Neither.'

'Or anyone in the Swiss departure?'

'God knows. All those papers are back in my office. And yours.'

'No. The details are all in my computer now. Gaëlle has scanned everything. And that's in the car. Can you fetch it for me? We can check.'

* * *

At first, as she turned the pages, she sat startled by the enigma before her. The book was indeed written in no immediately recognisable language. A blocked-out code, which resembled unaccented Hebrew, filled the entire page. She tried to decipher a pattern, but could see none. Then she began to notice a sequence of recurring signs in Greek, which did not form part of the code. And she recognised these: *Ursa Minoris, Ursa Majoris, Centauri, Tauri, Cygni,* the unknown language addressed the stars. The Judge sat very still, frowning. Strange diagrams, carefully drawn, finely marked, printed on plates and protected by soft interleaved sheets, fine as muslin, were interspersed throughout the blocked-out sheets of opaque printed code. She ruffled the pages, and suddenly saw a language that she knew. *Wir sind auf einer Mission: zur Bildung der Erde sind wir berufen.* She turned to the man who was working through the bookshelves, borrowed a pencil and set to work. *We are here on a mission; we are called to educate the earth.* The German sentences lay scattered, like fallen columns amidst the code. Beside both languages, crouched in the margins, were two sets of handwritten annotations, the initials added carefully after each comment or interpretation: R.B. and F.G. The manuscript interpretations by one of the scribes also appeared to be written in German, but the minute, flattened Gothic script defeated the Judge. The observations signed by F.G. were all handwritten in the obscure code. Nevertheless, she noted each page where the marks occurred for the university philologist who helped them in their investigations, and then translated each printed German phrase carefully, pausing over the sentence structures, brooding on the verbs. The unintelligible language appeared to be a commentary upon the German or vice versa, but the German sections, taken together, suggested something of great constancy.

Leben ist der Anfang des Todes. Das Leben ist um des Todes willen. Der Tod ist Endigung und Anfang zugleich, Scheidung und nähere Selbstverbindung zugleich. Durch den Tod wird die Reduktion vollendet.

Life is the beginning of death. Death is the purpose of life. Death is at once an ending and a beginning, a separation from the self and at the same time a closer bonding with the self. That gap is made perfect in death.

*Wir träumen von Reisen durch das Weltall:
ist denn das Weltall nicht in uns? Die Tiefen
unsers Geistes kennen wir nicht. Nach innen
geht der geheimnisvolle Weg. In uns oder
nirgends ist die Ewigkeit mit ihren Welten,
die Vergangenheit und Zukunft.*

We dream of travelling through the universe:
but does the universe not lie within us? We
know nothing about the depths of our souls.
The secret path leads inwards. Eternity with
all her worlds, past and to come, lies within
us or nowhere.

Suddenly she stumbled over a sentence in
English. *If you have no faith in yourself or your
own judgement, find your faith in the Guide,
who reaches for your hand, ready to lead you
into the Kingdom.* They had never located the
Guide, whoever he might be. Or was this book
itself the Guide? The Judge began a separate
column of references to the Guide, as if he were
a burglar, still at large. She began to underline
passages in her own pencil translation. Schweigen came back into the chalet clutching her
computer. He stood beside her and peered at the
text.
'But some of it's in German! We can read
that.'
She was defeated by an entire verse of poetry.

Getrost, das Leben schreitet

Zum ewgen Leben hin,
Von innrer Glut geweitet
Verklärt sich unser Sinn.
Die Sternwelt wird zerfließen
Zum goldnen Lebenswein,
Wir werden sie genießen
Und lichte Sterne sein.

Schweigen stood over her and pointed to the words, translating on sight.

'Comforted, life strides towards eternal life — clothed, or consecrated, I'm not sure which, by an inner fire, our senses are transfigured. The world of stars will melt into the golden wine of life, which we will savour and become illuminated stars. There you are, Dominique, it's madness. That's a hymn. It's supposed to be sung. They all spent too much time with their eyes fixed on heaven.'

'You have no grasp of mysticism, André. Stars are metaphors. And I think they did sing this. Listen. *Die Außenwelt ist die Schattenwelt: sie wirft ihren Schatten in das Lichtreich.* The external world is a world of shadows, which casts its shadows in the Kingdom of Light. Reality is like the veil of Maya, which hides the truth. This world is an illusion.'

Schweigen shrugged. 'I sometimes wish it was.'

So this was the core, a cult of death as the gateway and the threshold. Their eyes were turned inwards, towards darkness. Death signalled the ultimate union with the soul, the end of all yearning and separation. It was that anticipation of blessedness, which had filled their hearts. For now she saw them, swinging up the mountain into darkness, carrying their children in their arms, the promise of the Faith pouring from their lips in exultation, ringing in their ears through the silence of the snowy forest. They were stepping through the wall of shadows into the brilliance of their Kingdom.

'That's where they've gone, André — they've departed, to their Kingdom of Light, and their Guide is somewhere among the stars.'

'They're all on the slab in the Institut médico-légal in Strasbourg,' snapped Schweigen gloomily, looking up from the computer. 'But I think I've found our F.G.'

The Judge slapped down her pencil.

'Well? Who is he?'

Schweigen scrolled down.

'Guess. No surprises here. But he isn't one of the dead. Do you remember Gerhart Liebmann, the opera director? A great friend of his. And of Anton Laval. I'm willing to bet F.G. is the famous Composer with his own orchestra who spoke at the funeral. His name is Friedrich Grosz — F.G.'

And into the doomed chalet with its polished wooden walls and floors, its Christmas-candle arrangements and untouched boxes of choco-lates, fruits confits and marrons glacés, rolled a name from the past, the man who had refused to be interviewed, refused to cooperate either with the Swiss or with Schweigen. This was the Composer with the irreproachable alibi, the man who had been conducting a concert in Berlin on

79

the night of the Swiss departure, the man who had been seen by three thousand people, who had denied all prior knowledge of the mass suicide and yet had known every single one of the dead. How dare you question me, he snapped at Schweigen. I accepted their decision to depart. Leave me alone with my grief. His high-handed arrogant face, all lines and shadows, the dramatic white hair, which stood on end when he conducted or rehearsed his orchestra, materialised before her; there he stood like a figure conjured up in ectoplasm at a séance. There he was, a man in his mid-sixties, powerful, unpleasant, enraged. And now she could hear his voice, vivid on the video of the funeral, speaking with absolute conviction: *In the midst of life we are in death, but that life is ours for ever; it is that eternal life which awaits us beyond death, the glory of an eternal union with all that we have ever loved.* He cannot have been speaking on behalf of his dead friend. He was speaking for himself.

The Judge looked at André over the top of her glasses. All the scratching and sifting around them suddenly ceased. Everyone stared at the Judge.

'But wait, listen,' said Schweigen, 'it gets better. The voice on the tape — that's his voice. I've traced the mobile. He was ringing this chalet repeatedly last night. After they'd all trooped off up the mountain.'

The forensic team began to murmur, pleased. The Judge weighed her words carefully. She tapped the great book on the table before her.

'Large chunks of whatever this is are written in German. If he is F.G. and this is his handwriting, then at last we have some hard evidence of his involvement.'

Her thoughts were less careful. Someone walked away from both of these massacres, carrying a gun. I don't believe in his innocence or any of his protestations. He knew about the Faith, and he knew about the first mass suicide. He probably knew about this one. She looked down. At the bottom of the open page was a simple handwritten sentence in ordinary German, followed by a small set of initials: *Gelobt sei uns die ew'ge Nacht. Let us praise eternal night. F.G.* This book belongs to him.

4

Not Death, but Judgement

Gaëlle stood waiting beside the Air France check-in desk at Montpellier airport, banging the tickets and her carte d'identité against the handle of her suitcase. The giant metallic hangar with marble floors gleamed in the early light, substantially cooler than the outside world, where the phoenix palms, now free of winter plastic, erupted into fresh green. Midweek, and the first flight fully booked; everybody else had already clambered up the escalator, passed through security, grappling with their computers, and sailed onwards towards the gates, bound for Paris. No sign of the Judge.

The Judge never showed up late in the normal course of things. Therefore something must have happened. If she didn't appear in the next ten minutes they would miss the connection at Roissy, which would carry them on into Germany. Gaëlle's mobile suddenly illuminated and thumped out Motorhead's heavy metal retro-beat. Technically, this was the office phone, but Gaëlle had customised the theme tunes and somehow appropriated the number.

'Hello. What the hell's happened to you?'

Gaëlle did not look at the tiny screen. She expected the Judge; it was Schweigen.

'Gaëlle? She's switched off her phone. She

82

won't answer. Can you give her a message from me?' Gaëlle abandoned her suitcase and began to pace in a widening circle.

'Have you had a row? I'm not a dating agency.'

She heard a huge sigh from Schweigen, she could almost feel his breath hot against her ear.

'I'm just anxious that she should have all the information she needs at her fingertips before she does the interviews.'

'You mean you want to be there and do it all yourself. Just like you did last time,' sneered Gaëlle, 'with the same success you had in February.' The investigation had suffered a dramatic setback when Schweigen's aggressive technique had resulted in the withdrawal of all cooperation by the Famille Laval. A reminder about the fiasco at the Domaine, the exact details of which Schweigen had concealed from the Judge, rubbed a sufficiently raw wound to draw blood; the sigh turned into a snap of rage.

'There's no need to be so bloody rude.'

Pause.

'OK. I'll tell her to turn her phone back on so that you can have a fight with her yourself.' Gaëlle cut him off, then stood fidgeting with the mobile; Schweigen was capable of ringing straight back. This proved to be one of his strengths. No one ever escaped his persistence.

★ ★ ★

Ever since New Year's Day, three months earlier, when Schweigen and the Judge had stood side by side, contemplating the bodies in the snow,

83

Gaëlle's working life had developed an unexpected dimension of emotional upheaval. Schweigen was uncontrollably in love with the Judge; concerning his feelings there could be no doubt. His passion crashed ahead like a battering ram, an obsession that he would not, or could not, abandon or disguise. I want, I need, I desire. Gaëlle expected him to rave on through all the verbs of love every time she heard his voice on the line. But what was Dominique Carpentier's position on the matter? And as for the history of the affair, very little information could be gathered. The Montpellier office endured a state of documentary siege, battered by e-mails, faxes and registered deliveries, avec avis de réception. Sign here, please. The Judge flicked the telephone system over to Gaëlle's desk and so it was her Greffière who usually fielded Schweigen's demands. Gaëlle knew that the Judge had never married and lived alone. Schweigen, however, had a wife and child, tucked away somewhere in a Strasbourg suburb. And yet he was the Lover, the ardent suitor, desperate in pursuit. The Lady hardly raised her eyes to acknowledge his fanatical insistence. Was he or had he ever been successful in claiming her attention, let alone eliciting an amenable response? Gaëlle had her suspicions, but no proof. She worked her sexual way through queues of men and occasionally women too, without making any hard and fast commitments. There was time enough for households, school runs, family holidays, and sleeping with more or less the same person later on. Time enough. But the Judge had at least fifteen years start on her

84

Greffière in the great enterprise of life. And to Gaëlle's fairly certain knowledge the Judge had never been swept off to the theatre in evening dress or wheedled into consuming long, exotic dinners by any man at all, during the five years since Schweigen's first arrival in the office, and her tenure at the desk.

Was there a childhood sweetheart? When Gaëlle stalked off home or out to the bar, the Judge plunged onwards through the giant paper valleys created by her dossiers. She was last seen at six-thirty on the previous night, calmly reading a book in English about the Apocalypse sect at Waco. Gaëlle peered over her shoulder: she discovered the Judge in the midst of a three-cornered negotiation between the FBI, the Branch Davidians and God. Did she pick up the telephone, come dinnertime, and summon her lovers? No personal photographs decorated the office. If there was anyone important to her she kept him well hidden. Gaëlle suspected that the Judge was absorbed by exactly what she appeared to be doing — researching the sects. An eclectic collection of books dappled the tall cream shelves and a lavish series of technical volumes on astronomy and primitive myths of the universe and its origins, in several languages, had recently appeared.

'Most ancient peoples chose their own names for the stars,' explained the Judge, when questioned about the textbooks in Arabic. 'I may as well acquire them all. Look, here is the night sky in January, with Orion's belt very visible, follow the line here and you come to Canis

Major and this is the brightest star, the greatest in this constellation.' Her fingers spread gently across the map of glimmering dots. 'This is Sirius, here in the south. And far over there within Taurus are the sister stars, the Pleiades.'

Gaëlle gazed at the astronomical maps in baffled wonder. Here was the universe — labelled, gendered, painted, named. Wherein lay the significance of this charted mass of stars? Why did the Judge take them so seriously? Surely the Faith was no more than another batch of suicidal lunatics with someone, somewhere, creaming off the cash? Had the Judge scented something rich and strange in this fabulous emptiness? She puzzled for hours over the books and patterns. The stars glittered with their own immortality, a gift from the loving gods. Mortal lives were inscribed in the heavens, transformed into fragments of eternity by the immortals, who had been forced, through extraordinary circumstances, to turn their eyes earthwards and remember how to love.

'The love between a mortal and an immortal being is always doomed,' explained the Judge. 'This accounts for the terrible disappointment of the saints. Sacrifice your life to God and take up meditation in a desert with only lizards and scorpions for company, and your reward will be grief and unending loneliness.'

The importuned gods never listen when they are besieged with petitions and laments. They withdraw to great distances. Wait, wait in faithfulness and patience or pick your way through the meadows of Illyria and their

86

all-seeing eyes will rest upon you. Here comes the god, in a rush of foul breath and black wings. His fatal embrace will be the last thing you know in your mortal flesh; and then the stone doors of your predetermined fate will roll shut behind you, and the tomb will be for ever sealed. What remains for infatuated mortals in passion's wake, when the weeping deity retreats to Olympus, the charred ashes of his lover still warm upon the altars built to worship him? A frigid immortality stretched out between the stars.

That's Schweigen's fate, grinned Gaëlle to herself. Cold stars, cold distant stars. She looked down at the mobile. One missed call. Schweigen's at the office. Numéro masqué. Number withheld.

Will all passengers for Air France Flight 306 please proceed to Gate 22 where boarding has begun. And here she comes, scudding through the shifting groups of business suits, smart deep-green jacket and black trousers, her glasses slightly dark against the dull electric glare. Here she comes, the Judge and her whirling suitcase, smouldering flashes of aluminium light glinting from her polished chariot wheels. She slammed the case down on the conveyer belt.

'Excusez-moi, Gaëlle. I had André Schweigen on the phone.'

'So did I.'

'Hmmm.' The Judge wrinkled her nose. 'It's more or less your private number now, isn't it? He shouldn't ring that number.'

'But he does. Frequently.'

They assailed the escalator at a gallop. The

security men at the top wore white like the angels of the Apocalypse: white shirts, white coats, white gloves. They beckoned to the racing women. Hurry, hurry, hurry.

'Well?' said the Judge, as they stood breathless before the voracious machine, which guzzled down their boarding passes. 'What did he want? I expect there will be a message from him waiting for us at the hotel in Lübeck.'

The Judge paused to read Gaëlle's black T-shirt, which, across her breasts, declared *PEACE AND LOVE*, but announced a rather different politics across the back: *FUCK THE SYSTEM* in fluorescent yellow. Gaëlle handed the return plane tickets over to the Judge and grinned, rueful and defiant.

'I only wear it when I'm travelling.'

The Judge merely smiled.

★　★　★

Gaëlle and the Judge touched down amidst the long shadows of a late-afternoon sun just before four o'clock, and they had other things to think about. Their alarming descent seemed like stepping back into winter. The trees were dusted with a fragile spring green and the migrating birds, in ragged mass convoys, cried above them in the gusty sky. Barely ten degrees outside and an evil wind, straight from the Baltic, crackled across the runway. They scuttled over the damp tarmac and into the dim cream buildings, which looked like an abandoned wartime installation. The Judge paused to watch her bags being unloaded on to the trailer wondering if her russet cashmere shawl was at the top or the bottom. Gaëlle's bum-freezer jacket and black elastic miniskirt shrivelled against the gruelling wind.

'I've got to buy new clothes. Can we take a taxi? And can I put a new coat on our expenses?'

'Yes and no,' said the Judge.

Gaëlle moaned all the way to the baggage reclaim. 'But I'm here on behalf of the Republic, and the state ought to save me from freezing.'

'You knew where you were going, ma petite chérie,' said the Judge peacefully. 'North.'

The Judge balanced her open briefcase on one knee and settled two files side by side. One was labelled *GROSZ* and the other, thicker file was marked *LAVAL*. She tapped her shivering Greffière on the nose with her fountain pen. 'It's up to you to dress suitably when you're sent on a mission.'

Gaëlle stamped up and down beside the baggage conveyor belt, pulling faces and shuddering with cold. The Judge grinned at her. At least no one could now read *FUCK THE SYSTEM* scrawled across her back.

The cobblestones before their hotel glistened in the damp. The Judge decided that the first, urgent thing to do would be to get dressed all over again in a warm pullover and flat shoes, for her tiny heels skidded and stuck in the gaps between the rounded shining stones.

'Sous les pavés, la plage!' murmured the Judge. Gaëlle stared. 'Beneath the pavement, the beach! They obviously don't have riots here, or they'd asphalt over the lot,' explained the Judge, hauling her suitcase up the steps.

Gaëlle shivered, gloomy, incredulous, blank-faced, as the Judge paid off the taxi and pocketed the receipt. They stood side by side at the top of the steps, gazing down the Trave at the white boats, the ducks squawking, disconsolate, along the edge; the gabled brick buildings on the opposite shore had sunk, lopsided, into the bank. Everything before them seemed alien, northern; a little city of faded wealth and past medieval glory, nevertheless game and ready to make the effort to be modern, delighted to confront the spring, by planting dozens of indestructible pansies in window boxes.

'Quick! Inside!' Gaëlle bounced through the swing doors.

The Lübeck Music Festival was plastered all over the lobby and the wind section of the visiting Berlin Orchestra had already appropriated the third floor. The hotel proclaimed itself full, smug with artistic talent. Reception assumed they had come for the Festival and plied the Judge with brochures and programmes. Safe in her room, she flattened out the duvet, which towered up in the shape of a crown, ate the chocolate left in the middle of her pillow, and sat down to assess her collected information. For here on the cover of the Opera *Spielplan* was the face of the man she was hunting down, the gaunt, lined cheeks, a mass of white hair, rimless glasses and that glare of passionate intensity she had seen in the Romanesque church of her childhood, five years before. Was he much changed?

Perhaps the publicity photographs had been taken years ago? No, the face was remarkable for its stillness, concentration and timelessness. He would look the same when he was eighty. She noted down the times and dates of his appearances. *Friedrich Grosz will conduct a concert of his own music in the cathedral. Tickets from the Festival box office.* She compared the programme with the information Gaëlle had down-loaded from the Internet. Then she laid out all the silent evidence on her puckered duvet. Here was the coded book they had found in the chalet, their only guide, unfolding the dark philosophy of the Faith, safely stowed in plastic covers. And here was the letter he had sent, agreeing to grant her a rare interview.

We have to ask, we cannot demand. He's not a French citizen; and he's a famous, busy man. We have no evidence linking him to the New Year's Day departure beyond a coded book, with its sinister annotations and a mobile phone message to the sister of his dead friend. But he is part of this. I can smell it; I can feel it on my skin. All the people he loves, or those he says he loves, end up dead with bullets in their brains before the gun vanishes. Who is this man with his brilliant career and his strange, ageless face? How does he come to own a copy of this coded missal, privately printed, and — I am assuming this — distributed only to members of the Faith? I know that he can read and speak that coded language — if it is ever spoken. How many other copies were printed? Or, for the thought struck her then, is this the only copy that exists? He is irrevocably implicated in this dark puzzle whose meaning remains obscure.

Yet he is not obliged to see me, or to answer any of my questions. He can withdraw at any time. Be tactful. Bait the hook with respect for his position and authority. Let him take all the time he needs. Ask, ask; but don't give him any clues to your paths and your directions.

> Lübeck
> 1 March 2000
>
> Chère Madame,
>
> *I am, of course, willing to cooperate with your enquiry although I fear that I can be of little use to you. If my assistance will ensure that the children of my dearest friend, Marie-Cécile Laval, will no longer be harassed by your over-zealous police force I shall be glad to answer all your questions. They must be allowed to grieve in peace without these remorseless intrusions.*
>
> *As you know, I am a busy man with many engagements abroad. I shall however be at home in Lübeck during the month of March for the annual Music Festival of which I am the Artistic Director and will be able to see you on one of the following Wednesday mornings indicated below. Please contact my secretary by e-mail or at one of the office numbers in Berlin.*
>
> *Yours sincerely,*
> *Friedrich Grosz*

The letter was written in English, dictated,

typed, the signature an added scrawl. But this is his voice. I am hearing his voice. And he is standing between me and the Laval children. André Schweigen has already botched that avenue in this investigation. She wrinkled her nose in irritation, stood up and looked out upon the cold crimson glow, which illuminated the tiny, shutterless windows of the Salzspeicher. She heard the traffic hissing on the wet streets outside. Then she dressed in warm clothes, flat shoes and her red gloves, prepared to cast her own chill remorseless light into the dark places before her.

The early spring braced itself for frost. As she set off in the gathering cold her breath surrounded her face like a nebula. She tucked the red leather gloves inside the black sleeves of her coat, pulled the hood over her head against the drizzle and marched down the Obertrave in the direction of the Dom. The cafés gathered in their chairs and tables, which had appeared on the pavements, optimistic in the midday sunshine. All the windows were double-glazed with a small shelf between the layers of glass. Here was the Music School, ablaze with light and bustle, voices, discordant instruments, the charmed sadness of a saxophone speaking to a piano. The Judge slid softly past, aware of how much smaller she was in comparison to this powerful mass of excited musicians in evening dress, disgorged into the streets, wielding large black cases shaped like weapons. She caught the odd word, but could make no real sense of their urgent shouts. The lower reaches of An der

Obertrave appeared to contain only houses, silent, domestic. On her left the gabled buildings stood uncurtained, lit up, like the backdrop of an Advent calendar. She peered into their bright interiors, the gold pine tables decorated with candles and yellow flowers, vivid cushions and low lamps, half expecting to see hosts of angels and bewildered shepherds, receiving the good news. Planted vats of flowers and bulbs lurked by the festive doorways, many already filled with tiny green spears, rising to meet the inexorable spring. On her right, beyond the fragile early green of the trees, swam the river, shimmering dark, a faint mist hovering above the ripples and the lost floating leaves. She paused, examining the washing lines. These strange structures, the wires almost invisible, stood by the river, and the white sheets, hanging in still folds, now hardened, kissed by the plunging frost.

The interior of the cathedral sizzled with humming floodlights and the orchestra, clamped in a semicircle, their heads bent over their illuminated scores, resembled a Vatican conclave of dark cardinals, buried in prayer, before casting lots. Then the second violin raised her head, and began. The terrifying sadness of these high, yearning notes sliced through Dominique Carpentier's concentration, but only for a moment. The underlying cold beneath the heaters, the muggy damp and halogen brilliance sent her scurrying down the side aisle, keeping close to the darkness beside a parched white row of baroque tombs. The massive structure of red brick was painted white inside; huge white

94

Gothic vaults, dusty and darkened with candle smoke, loomed above her, harbouring the cold. Everywhere else was filled with sound technicians and cables. The concert was being recorded and broadcast live later that night on Nord Deutsche Rundfunk. The Judge sought out a secure perch from which she could observe, without being seen.

The nave was divided into distinct sections with raised seating beneath the west windows, and across a dozen of these fixed rows sprawled a mass of bored young people in white shirts and dark jackets, clutching floppy green scores of music. The choir, waiting. Around the altar spun the orchestra, in an ever-widening arc, and before them, white head bowed, listening intently, stood the giant, skeletal form of the Composer. The Judge faded into a pillar for a moment, to be quite sure, and to assess the difference made by five years. He wore a black jacket over a white T-shirt with a faded symbol across his chest; his white hair hung over his eyes and forehead as he bent down, studying the score, gently marking time as the solitary violin steadied and soared. Then suddenly he looked up and the floodlights coupled with the rimless glare of his eyes; the orchestra flexed, like a great beast awoken. The strings raised their bows, expectant, tense.

The Judge took hold of her shawl, drew its mask more closely round her face and tiptoed up the steps beneath the Gothic clock beyond the apse. The font, a brass treasure with a giant candelabrum poised just above it, dripping real wax, lay in a sunken circular pit surrounded by chairs. She had just vanished into a large straw seat with oaken arms and a high back when the low murmur from the strings arose, blocked out the woodwind and settled into a peculiar, haunting monolithic sound, subtle and vast, at once near and distant, as if the notes originated in some far corner of the world, but came back, bearing an echo of silence and darkness, by a special grace. The Judge caught her breath, arranged her shawl and settled her nerves. She found herself corralled by painted Gothic saints, somewhat larger than life, brandishing symbolic animals, doves, parrots and a chubby leopard, their dusty eyes all fixed upon the Virgin. She watched the Composer, and him alone; the rest was nothing but the backcloth. She had not expected to see him, conducting a rehearsal, but now she intended to put the moment to good use.

Dominique Carpentier had all the subtlety and patience of a good psychoanalyst. She listened like a stoat, ears alert for any change in the bushes and the grass. Now she calculated, space, shadow, distance. Could she remain here, unobserved at the Composer's back, watching him at work, beneath the savage lights? The music bit into her consciousness, strange, monumental, solid as the painted brick pillars, a dense intricate texture of embroidered sound. She listened carefully, finding herself unable to follow any single section of the orchestra, aware only of the layered change when the brass entered the dance, steady and mannered as a pavane. The Judge disliked music for the simple reason that it muddied her emotions. And she never went to concerts. The occasion was therefore unusual, provocative as well as interesting, for here was her subject, unwitting, unguarded, performing on this Gothic stage before her. The music shuddered and broke off. A shocking silence followed in which an unfortunate trombonist attempted to slink in unnoticed and was called to account. The exchange took place in English. The Judge heard every bellowed word, magnified by the booming acoustic.

'I'm sorry sir, I just — '

'Take your place. I do not accept excuses as you well know. Speak to me afterwards. SILENCE! Again, from the entrance of the oboes.'

The choir sat taut, upright, like naughty children whose knuckles smarted from the cane. The Judge concentrated on the Composer's hunched back and shoulders. She watched his anger dissolving as the music returned. She could learn a lot about someone from studying how he worked. How did he treat his colleagues? What mattered most to him? Suddenly, he stopped them all again.

'No, no, no. Dah, dah, dah, dah. Don't change the pace. More volume, more breath, but keep the pace steady, steady.'

Pause.

'Again.'

He raised his baton. She watched them rise like a wave into the eerie toll of the music and descend, rise, sway, fall, again and again. Outside, the last red light glowed and died in the clear glass windows. Darkness.

'Better, better. Alison, you are a fraction late coming in.' He bent down to the second violin. 'I need to hear you just a moment before I do.' Suddenly he threatened her. 'If you can't get it right I'll hand the part back to Johann.'

The first violin, who sat waiting, patient, mute, looked up, outraged.

'Now from the beginning again right through to the episode with the brass. Tu n'as pas la partition? Pourquoi? Pourquoi? Réponds-moi!'

The Judge was sitting behind the rood screen, or the Lettner, so that she was looking at the underbelly of the cathedral, the blank boards, crossbars and supports which held the great wooden crucifix in place, as if she were viewing Golgotha from the wings and observing the technical expertise necessary for the performance. She was also behind the clock. The clock was a surreal, gigantic Gothic folly, carved in wood with a long gallery and intermittent turrets, topped by white saints, a great streaming sun upon its face, the eyes of which actually rotated in time to the ticking seconds. The thing proclaimed: *Unsere Zeit in Gottes Händen* — Our time in God's hands, puffed up behind its smug, fat cheeks, and glowered down upon the orchestra. Above the complacent sun stood Death, his skeleton face streaked, as if painted with cat's whiskers, clutching the raised hammer above his bell to count out the appointed hour. And next to him stood Judgement, her sword in

98

one hand and her own hammer raised in the other, ready to sound the quarter-hours. When the hour arrived, with an echoing groan, clatter and whirr from the creature's innards, Death turned his double hour glass upside down and banged out the time upon his bell, jerking his head from side to side, again and again and again. Another hour gone, another hour closer to Judgement Day. The mechanism inside the Lettneruhr, as it was called, had survived the RAF air attack in March 1942, but was considered too delicate to be stopped by anyone but an expert in seventeenth-century clocks. The expert had been summoned from Hamburg and was in fact busy with the saw-tooth wheels during the rehearsal. Unfortunately he managed to arrest only one of the inexorable wooden figures on the apex. The quarter-hours were already silenced. He had stopped not Death, but Judgement. Therefore, as six o' clock arrived in a trembling hiss of machinery, the hour glass turned over and into the eerie surge of unearthly music came that very human toll, calling us all to our final engagement, concerning whose approaching moment we possess neither power nor choice.

Dong, dong, dong. The hammer collided with the bell and Death's nodding head wobbled above the severed hands, which now divided the clock.

The Composer exploded, leaped from the podium with startling rapidity and blazed through the church like a comet, his white hair flying. He stormed straight towards the Judge, who shrank, rigid with surprise and alarm, back into the bishop's throne. She had heard the bell, but because she sat behind the clock she had no idea what had occurred. The Composer plunged up the steps and pounded upon the antique wooden door, which held the secrets of the clock.

'Um Gottes Willen, was machen Sie denn eigentlich?' he roared. 'What in God's name do you think you're doing?'

He was a mere ten feet away from Dominique Carpentier. She saw the liver spots on the back of his clenched hands as he dragged the door open, revealing a gnome-like figure in the entrails of the clock.

'Vorsicht! Mensch! Passen Sie doch auf!' yelled the expert. 'Watch it. Be careful! That door's fragile!'

A nerve throbbed in the Composer's throat. The two men screeched at one another. The Judge, certain that the Composer had never even seen her, picked her moment carefully and slipped away. As she pattered past the orchestra she noticed their amused relief that his rage had settled upon another, different victim.

★ ★ ★

'Where have you been? I looked everywhere. Reception said you'd gone out. Why don't you ever leave messages?' Gaëlle, surrounded by empty crisp packets and Coke cans, crouched indignantly amongst her scrunched duvet and cushions. 'I've watched two hours of cartoons on

TV5 and four lots of news on CNN. Are we ever going to eat? And don't you want to do some preparation for the interview? Where have you been?'

The Judge sat down on the edge of the bed and offered her Greffière a boiled sweet. Gaëlle, now aged twenty-eight, could still revert to torrents of childish demand when they were alone together. Now she bristled at the Judge, but accepted the sweet as a peace offering.

'I have been doing a little unexpected preparation for tomorrow. The Composer was rehearsing in the cathedral and I went to watch.'

'Really?' Gaëlle's eyes widened. 'What's he like? Schweigen says he's a monster.'

'A perfectionist. Short-tempered. Choleric. Lots of white hair. Physically very powerful for a man of sixty-four.'

'Ughhhh. You didn't tell me he was so old.' Gaëlle put out her tongue and revealed a large silver spike, solid enough to endanger the enamel on her teeth.

'Hmmm,' said the Judge, 'you'd better not smile tomorrow. And don't wear that T-shirt with the slogans.'

★ ★ ★

The Composer's house in the Effengrube stepped upwards into a Gothic red-brick gable, a little lopsided, but still elegant and luminous, pierced by a steeple pattern of tiny windows. The unshuttered squares on the lower floors were larger, double-glazed and utterly clear, so that

101

the sombre costumes of Gaëlle, now in a long, dark-purple coat, purchased that morning, and the Judge in flat shoes and Lincoln green, with tiny creases in her skirt, were reflected back, mirrored again in segments. They stood looking at themselves carved and divided up into oblongs of white wood. Two dark columns on either side of the double doors were decorated with modern wooden carvings of haunted faces and strange musical instruments, one of which resembled an elongated harp. An odd key lodged in the wood generated an electric chime. There was no name on the door. Large Italian pots, presumably frost-proofed and filled with rising bulbs, pushed outwards, colonising the pavement, and a torrent of winter jasmine, still heavy and golden with blossoms, nudged the doorway. The Judge calculated that the vegetation in Lübeck flowered at least two months after it had done in the Midi. The jasmine in her mother's garden expended all its force and beauty at the same time as the mimosa. Just to the left of the house a small dark tunnel led into the illuminated Gänge, the courtyards and passages with small gardens and tiny squares behind the houses on the street fronts. The Gänge contributed to the city's charm and were often full of tourists, ogling the tiny squares and pretty houses. The Judge peered down the dark shaft and saw, at the far end, framed by the red-brick archway, a different world of early flowers, sharp light, cobbles and tiny fences, sandpits, tricycles and climbing frames, a small domestic haven, well swept, exclusive, painted, polished. Gaëlle bent down to look; the curved brick vault brushed her spiked hair.

'Why don't the bicycles get nicked?' she demanded.

The Judge stood tense, expectant, her eyes screwed up against the sun that was licking long straight lines through the melting frost. She raised her hand to her tortoiseshell clip and checked that her black hair was firmly locked in place. I want to look neutral, plain; should I have changed my glasses?

'Do you think he's in there?' Gaëlle rang the bell again and stepped back; the Judge confronted the locked doors.

Both carved wings of the entrance suddenly opened and the Composer stood before her, slightly hunched in his own doorway, his rimless glasses catching the glare. They both drew back, startled, unprepared for the masked glimmer of each other's faces.

'Vous êtes Madame Carpentier? Entrez donc. Entrez.' He stood aside and waved them into his kingdom. He did not offer to shake hands with either of them.

They had expected the house, given the pierced Gothic front, to be filled with dark spaces, but once past the coats and boots in the vestibule they entered a great arc of light and green. A conservatory had been built at the back of the house, its roof rising to the second floor. The glass room extended into a walled garden, already flourishing with spring. The forsythia mutating from yellow into green; huge red geraniums standing proud of their earthen pots bolstered up the red-brick walls with even stronger colours. Then the Judge realised that the geraniums were actually inside the glass. They were standing in a greenhouse.

The high, lighted space oozed a strange mixture of wealth and austerity and promised neither comfort nor welcome. There were rows and rows of books, untidy, uneven, clearly often consulted, on either side of an open fireplace and a cold, unused grate. There were no ornaments and no personal photographs of any kind. A small pale painting of a sandy landscape appeared to be the only framed object on the walls. There were no curtains, no fabrics, no shutters; all around them arose solid surfaces of wood, brick, glass. The great double walls of glass climbed upwards, without fleck or smudge, so that they appeared to be waiting outside in the hard, bright light. The Judge let out her breath, resolved to be quite silent, and then realised, discomfited, that she could hear herself breathing. They could hear no sounds at all, other than their own. The space was sealed away from the outside world. The silence contained something uncompromising, habitual, terrible; as if they had stepped into a pocket of cold air. A giant piano, covered in sheets of music, crouched in a domed alcove, out of the light. All the chairs promised to be uncomfortable, but the Composer indicated that they should install themselves at the long table. He took his place at the head, his back to the illuminated garden. Gaëlle faced him out, frowning across the pale scrubbed wood.

'May we speak in English? My French is not particularly sophisticated. I understand from my secretary that you wish to record this interview and I trust that you will send her a copy of the transcription. As you know I am very busy with the Festival here in Lübeck. I can offer you an hour, perhaps an hour and a half of my time, but no more. Now, what did you wish to ask me?'

The house smelt of fresh coffee and cinnamon, but the Composer was clearly not intending to offer them anything to drink. The table was swept clear apart from one large candle in a blue dish at the centre beneath the lowered white dome of the lamp. The Judge relaxed and allowed the utter silence to grow around her. I have not travelled nearly two thousand kilometres to be intimidated by a probable madman who may, or may not, be a murderer. Gaëlle's insolent fearlessness also proved useful. She slapped her pad down upon the polished table with a resounding smack, produced her pen with the death's head spiked on the tip, and began to tap two fingers gently on the empty paper. The sound boomed like a drum.

Dominique Carpentier manoeuvred her chair gently on the flagstones so that she was facing the Composer and arranged her ring-binder file with all her notes upon her lap so that her attitude was more informal, and she could look at him directly. For a long moment they stared at one another, and she watched the curiosity mounting in his eyes. For the first time she acknowledged not only his power, but also his beauty. Behind the rimless glasses his eyes were a

105

terrible cold blue. The eyebrows still shone golden, a pale reddish brown, and the white hair, thick and rummaged, fell across them. His lined strong face gathered itself up into a grimace of concentration. He is recording me, weighing me up, in the same way that I am assessing him. The Judge instantly sensed an equality of strength in her antagonist and coiled every muscle, ready to spring.

'Well?' prompted the Composer. And so the Judge began.

'We know that you are an intimate friend of the Laval family. Both Anton and Marie-Cécile Laval. Were you aware of their involvement with the Faith?'

'Yes, of course. I am godfather to Marie-Cécile's two children. Ever since their father's death I have been a father — or perhaps a grandfather — to them. Marie-Cécile always had a religious bent. She was very 'catholique pratiquante' as she used to say, when she was a girl. I think Anton must have first introduced her to his beliefs. She remained true to her church. But she loved her brother. She studied his faith. She wanted to understand him.'

'Did they ever talk to you about the Faith and try to involve you?'

'There is something you must understand, Madame Carpentier, the Faith is not a proselytising religion. It is not some sect invented for financial gain, like the charlatans you spend your time investigating. It is not a religion at all in the ordinary sense. It is a chemin, a pathway towards knowledge. You

106

cannot discover the Faith on every street corner. You must be selected, initiated, chosen.'

'Many sects present themselves in that way,' said the Judge slowly, considering her words with great care. 'It's an effective selling point.'

'Comme vous dites,' said the Composer, refusing to rise to her jibe.

'So the Lavals never tried to involve you in the Faith in any way?'

'We spoke about it. It wasn't a secret. I knew how they felt, and I respected their views. But, Madame Carpentier, if you are as thorough as your reputation suggests that you are, you probably know as much about the Faith as any ordinary person who is not an initiate. Members of the Faith do not, as a rule, ever discuss the details of their beliefs with outsiders.'

He's not answering my questions, thought the Judge. Change tack.

'Where were you on the night of New Year's Eve, 2000?'

'I've already told your brutal Commissaire all this. I was in Berlin, preparing a New Year's Day concert to celebrate the millennium.'

'Did you make any attempt to contact Marie-Cécile Laval or her children on New Year's night?'

'Yes. I rang to wish her une bonne année.'

'And did you speak to her?'

Here came the first hesitation. The Judge looked down at the times and texts of the messages on her lap and counted the five missed calls: two before midnight, two well afterwards and one at four in the morning. He must have suspected something. Or known for sure.

'No. The lines were all occupied. I couldn't get through.'

'Did you try more than once?'

'Yes. I can't remember how many times.'

'Did you have any reason to believe that she would commit suicide that night?'

Was it suicide? Does he think it was suicide? Has he any idea what happened that night in the snow? Does he know she was shot? Does he know about the gun?

'None whatever.'

The Judge listened to his cool, measured replies and conjured the anxious urgency on the tape. *Cécile. Ring me today. I beg you. Ring me as soon as you can.* The apprehension in that voice confessed a thousand things, but one fear above all else. Don't go. Be there. Stay with me. Don't go. Don't leave me here alone. Don't go.

'What are your views on suicide, Monsieur Grosz?'

'My views? In what way is that relevant?'

'I merely ask. Were you angry that your friends — your closest friends by your account — were so ready to kill themselves and to leave this world behind?'

'Angry? Why should I be angry? I miss them. I was — I am deeply grieved at their departure.'

He paused and the Judge registered his use of the word 'departure' rather than 'death'. She suspected that only members of the Faith would describe their collective massacre as a departure. Yet even this slip sounded inconclusive. If she pounced on that one word he could simply claim

108

to respect their religious convictions and demonstrate his affection by using their terminology. The Composer looked up; he fixed her with his blue glare and she heard the truth in his voice.

'Sometimes I can accept their decision. Sometimes I cannot. I take my responsibilities towards Cécile's children very seriously. I am their legal guardian now.'

'Ah, yes.' The Judge appeared to remember. A copy of Marie-Cécile Laval's last will and testament rested in the briefcase beside her. 'Paul and Marie-Thérèse. But surely they are adults?'

'Were you capable of taking adult decisions at the age of seventeen, Madame Carpentier? Of managing a vineyard with dozens of employees? Or running a complex business?'

The Judge nodded.

'Tell me about your relationship with these children.'

'I will take care of them, educate them and provide for their well-being. That's clear enough, isn't it?'

'And you are fond of them?'

'Of course. They have grown up before my eyes.'

'I believe, sir, that you have no children of your own.'

The Composer stiffened slightly. The Judge, however, was not entirely sure what point of weakness she had touched. So she persisted.

'Can you comprehend, Monsieur, how a mother and father could murder their own unknowing, unconscious children for the sake of a belief that cannot, in the normal course of things, ever be verified?'

The strange, beautiful face before her darkened and closed.

'Murder, you say. I do not judge.'

'Yes, I do say murder. Tiny children cannot and do not commit suicide, which is an act that requires an adult awareness of what is at stake. The adult members of the Faith who took their own lives in the early hours of New Year's Day murdered their children first.'

The Composer glittered, roused.

'And do you have any children, Madame Carpentier? Children of your own? You do not, or you would answer me at once. I have told you that I respect my friends and their strange faith. I tell you that I do not judge them, and I do not because I understand what it means to dedicate my life to a vocation, a calling — as they have done.'

His voice rose.

'I did not choose to live alone, like a hermit, cut off from all the social ties, which other men value. I did not choose to circle the earth like the Wandering Jew, without love or comfort, to live on in uncertainty and unknowing. I am a man who creates beautiful things. I too am chosen. I hear a language more beautiful than anything in the world and it is my task, the task for which I was born, to transcribe that language and to donate this music, along with my life of service, to the kingdom of this world. That is my sacrifice, Madame, and I make it willingly, gladly. It is my offering of joy. I am a Composer who honours his calling and accepts his burden, just as Christ once willingly lifted up the Cross.'

'No one else can create my life's work. I have accepted a sacred trust and I will obey its laws. Yes, there are laws other than the ones you serve, Madame. I acknowledge my allotted task and I will carry this cross to my life's end.'

The Judge's face sharpened during this extraordinary speech and Gaëlle's fingers whirled silent across her pad. Get it down, Gaëlle, get it down, but don't call attention to yourself. Don't look up. The Composer took a deep breath.

'And now, Madame, if you have no further questions I wish to be left in peace.' He stood up.

'I have one more question,' said the Judge quietly, 'and something to show you.'

She reached into her briefcase and drew forth the Book. The cool authentic leather binding and strange folding clasp were placed in the man's hands before he had a chance to recoil, and his fingers settled carefully on the inlaid golden rim.

'Do you know what this is?' The Judge watched his every gesture. She remained seated, unmoved, intensely aware of Gaëlle's death's head pen frozen in mid-air. This moment, planned, anticipated, calculated and yet fraught with risk, had been forced upon her sooner than anticipated.

His eyes darkened, the black core swallowing the blue, and a faint red stain blossomed on his chin and neck beside the collarbone.

'This book belongs to Marie-Cécile Laval,' he said softly. The pressure in the room changed, as if they were descending rapidly inside a diving bell.

I have you, thought the Judge, I have you now. His hands closed around the book. A long stillness surrounded them all, and faintly, as if from another country, they could hear the birds calling to each other in the gardens and the distant tussle of horns and bells warning each passage of the boats through the locks on the river.

'You gave that book to Madame Laval.' The Judge risked this statement, but lowered her voice, making each deadly word distinct. 'I believe that you can also read the coded language written in that book.'

Two white lines appeared down either side of his face, which was now wrenched, cadaverous, into a terrible mask of pain. The Judge froze. She had expected bluster, denials, recriminations, rage — not the agony of a man crucified. She sat very still and cold, and waited for developments.

'I must now ask you to leave my house.' His violent grasp upon the book tightened and clenched. He rose up over them like a ghoul, his great shoulders and white hair shaking. 'Please leave.'

The Judge never flinched.

'Monsieur Grosz, that book is now a piece of evidence in an ongoing investigation conducted by officers of the French Republic. And I am afraid that I must ask for it back.'

'Get out of my house!' He towered above her, as dangerous as the hideous phantasm created by Frankenstein. The Judge stood up carefully and held out her hand.

'Give back the book and we will leave your house.'

Gaëlle, who was struggling into her coat, turned instantly to stone and attempted to vanish. The Judge barely reached the middle of his chest. One blow from his hand would have crumpled her into the flagstones. The Judge took one step closer, so that she was almost touching him, and looked up. This was the moment when the confrontation tipped in her favour. She stood too close to him. You cannot strike someone who is standing in your arms. She had stepped inside his defences, her nose and the dark frames of her glasses pressed fast against the window of his anger, and this uncanny lack of distance gave her the upper hand. She ushered the violence out of his countenance with her defiant, unwavering glare and reached for the book. He let her take it, like a man stunned.

'Gaëlle?' The tiny engine of her discipline growled back into action. She collected her briefcase and tucked the book under her arm. 'I believe that we have outstayed our welcome. Thank you for your time, sir.'

And with that she swept out of the house, Gaëlle scuttling behind her. As the door thudded shut the city erupted into a great peal of bells; the seven towers pounded out a crescendo of triumph and celebration. This was the first thing they heard as they returned to the world. It was midday.

5

The Printer of Lubeck

'Well? Is that it? Can we go home now? I don't ever want to see him again. Schweigen was right. He's a monster.'

They kicked off their shoes and lounged on the Judge's bed, flattening the sculptured duvets, which had all been restored into spiked points, like bishops' mitres.

'Our plane's not till midday tomorrow, ma petite chérie. And we have work to do. You're going to do a tour of the antiquarian booksellers with two photocopied pages, one all in code and one with code and German. And take this photograph, don't crease it, or bend the plastic. I had it laminated. I think you can see the book's binding quite clearly. Ask them if they have ever seen this book, have any copies ever been offered for sale and do they recognise the code.'

'I thought you had dozens of experts cracking the bloody code?'

'Well, two of them. They've already told me what it's not, which is helpful, I suppose. I thought that it might be unaccented Hebrew, without the vowels, like holy scrolls of the Torah. But it isn't.'

'And what are you going to do?'

The Judge fluttered through *gewusstwo*, the local register of businesses and service providers for Hansestadt Lübeck.

'Lübeck is famous for its printing industry. There are some very old publishers here. The binding on this book is at least fifty years old, if not older. One of our experts thought that the pages were taken from an older document because the paper is handmade but not watermarked, and the whole thing has been rebound. It's been typeset, even the title page, the ink actually hit the paper. We now know that Friedrich Grosz is F.G. — unless he has a double — and that the book once belonged to him. I'm certain that, in some irrevocable way, he is bound to the Faith. Lübeck is his home town. He was born here. If he had anything to do with the making of this book then I'm prepared to bet that it was restored, if not printed, here. I'm going to traipse round the printers.'

Gaëlle stretched out, groaning.

'I'm a recorder and an office clerk, not a policewoman. Isn't this Schweigen's work?'

'Yes, it is. But he's not here and we are.'

'Did he leave a message for us last night? I forgot to ask.'

'Several. I've asked Reception to intercept all his calls. And I've switched off the mobile.'

'You didn't! What if he has important information?'

The Judge peered at Gaëlle over the top of her glasses. She spread the map of Lübeck across her knees and began matching printers' addresses to the geography of the town.

'Don't worry about Schweigen, Gaëlle. At the

115

moment we know more than he does. And that's driving him mad.'

★ ★ ★

The morning betrayed them; it was raining in the streets. The sky sank, torpid and veiled in milky cloud, but the wind's breath stole down the river in warmer currents. The earth opened its pores, unclenched against the vanishing cold and basked in fine, fresh spring rain. The Judge slithered across the slick cobbles, treasuring the book, swathed in plastic sheets, stowed inside her black rucksack. She balanced her umbrella at a lower angle, against the advancing crowds. Everyone else appeared to be several sizes larger than she was. The scale of the Altstadt varied from street to street. Sometimes grand baroque buildings with grey window frames and white cladding reared up beside her, ending in dramatic stone statues, a naked Mercury and Pomona, one breast exposed, clutching her basket of white marble apples, ready to dart between the stately, garlanded urns. Sometimes the red-brick Gothic gables, neatly repointed and reinforced, pushed their steepled façades upwards like stage sets, the last gable standing proud of the red-tiled roofs with their long sharp slopes and high chimneys. The gables were often supported by metal rods as the buildings settled, over centuries, into the damp earth of the medieval island city. The town, beautiful, comfortable, at ease with itself in the spring rain, embodied its official policy, proclaimed upon the

116

Holstentor, *CONCORDIA DOMI, FORIS PAX*, Unity within the walls, peace before the gates. Pausing before the frilly windows of a patisserie, the Judge confronted an identical scaled model of the Holstentor, decorated in marzipan, bearing the same pompous declaration.

She turned up the Mengstrasse, away from the river, and wrinkled her nose: the lower reaches of the street stank of old, rotting, dead fish. A portly yet agile rat flickered down a crumpled entrance to a drain beneath the stone steps. She checked her map. The printers that once stood at No. 42 were no longer there. She stalked onwards through the rain, patient, thorough, unhesitating, learning the city as she negotiated the old streets, practising whispered German sentences, ready with her explanations.

The Judge travelled a good deal in the course of her work. She was used to the Anglo-Saxon countries, especially Canada and America. There she settled into suitable clothes, at ease with the tacky culture of the streets, the plastic hotels, unintelligible accents and appalling food. But she did not know Northern Europe and was troubled by this sharp green cold settling on the late afternoon, and the alien politeness of these people. She could not understand the casual talk around her and disliked the sensation of being silenced, shut out. The men and women she approached all fingered the book in its plastic covers, fascinated, entranced by its secret language. But it could not have been made here, not here, no, not here. Those methods of production, that stitched binding, old-fashioned, uneconomic, long fallen into disuse. But look, Madame, this stitching is immaculate, this book was made by hand. No one understood or even recognised the code.

A pile of brown boxes cluttered the doorway of the last house in the Engelsgrube, before the Siebente Querstrasse. Each one had the brochure's cover stuck to the carton, indicating the contents. A small brass plaque mounted the plastered wall.

> **BARDEWIG GmbH**
> **LÜBECKS ÄLTESTES VERLAGS-UND**
> **DRUCKHAUS**
> **Seit 1579**

She looked at the firm's logo stuck to the glass door; the slogan was a strange mixture of German and English.

> **Lassen Sie sich beeindrucken!**
> **Moderner Druckereibetrieb mit**
> **Full Service**

Something about the firm's claim to longevity and its sheltered position in the Altstadt filled the Judge with confidence. She shook out her umbrella and strode in without ringing the bell.

'Darf Ich Ihnen helfen?'

She stood surrounded by courtesies in a busy office filled with computers and bright light. This

118

was clearly the section that dealt with the publicity brochures. A few scrunched programmes for the Music Festival lay on the floor. The new schedules and timetables for the leisure boat-trip companies, based on the Trave and the Wakenitz, were stacked in piles beside her. She produced the book and her questions. A small flurry of curiosity greeted the strange code and the worn but beautiful, anonymous binding.

'I'll ask the Director.' The elderly woman in charge was the first person of the afternoon whose enthusiasm did not falter into a mass of categorical and discouraging denials. 'He may know. There is something familiar about the pattern around the rim.'

She set off into the darker passages of the building. The Judge gazed after her, realising that the narrow street façade concealed an obscure receding labyrinth of busy spaces; for, when the padded door thudded shut, far away, a small ghost of damp air flitted back through the house. For it was once a house, a great house for a rich family. The Judge read the small signs and details: a dumb waiter with sliding doors for transporting hot food to a first-floor dining room, an archway, now blocked off, which framed the great entrance, a curving stairwell with fine carved banisters ending in a fluted baroque column, and a handsome globe, all the countries of the world still visible through the dust. The stucco roses, entwined with vines and flowers, lingered on the ceilings although no trace remained of the lost chandeliers, dismantled, sold off.

The Director was Herr Hartmut Bardewig, the owner of the firm, a vigorous, red-faced man of fifty with thinning blond hair on his freckled scalp and a warm excited handshake. He clutched the book.

'Guten Tag, Madame. Frau Handl tells me that your mystery book looks like one of my father's productions. Let me see, let me see — '

He fished his half-moon glasses out of his breast pocket and fingered the binding. Then he opened the book. The Judge noticed that he paid no attention to the strange language, the marginalia or even the German commentary; instead he examined the stitching and the folded groups of pages. Then he closed the book entirely and peered at the tiny repeating pattern stamped in gold along the spine, faint but luminous like the edge of a Roman mosaic, lost beneath centuries of dust.

'Yes, yes, yes. That's his work. Indeed it is. This book is my father's work. And he bound it himself. Where did you buy it? It must be a very unusual specimen.'

He now appeared reluctant to relinquish the prize and turned the Book of the Faith over and over in his hands.

'May I remove these plastic covers? It's wonderful to see something so distinctive. He rebound many rare books in his time. Collectors' items. Some were sold at auction for amazing sums. This one is rebound. The paper is handmade. Very rare, very old. I think the paper may be French, but there's no obvious watermark. I could take a look with my lens and

120

see. But it's in good condition, worn but not damaged. Um Gottes Willen, what sort of a language is this?'

'Then you don't recognise the language?' The Judge hesitated between two verbs: 'erkennen' and 'wieder erkennen'. But Herr Bardewig was already reading the commentaries.

'Most odd. Is it poetry? Or biblical? Or that sort of seventeenth-century mysticism where the author pours out all her theological passions? Schöne Seelenliteratur. My father had dozens of volumes of that sort in his personal library. Very beautiful books, but none that looked like this.'

'Madame, please forgive me. We can't go on standing here in the dispatch room. Come through to my office. Frau Handl, bringen Sie uns bitte ein Kaffee. Please, please, do come through. Come this way.'

The Judge settled peacefully into an old leather armchair with a scarlet cushion and allowed Herr Bardewig to fuss over her comfort, wet shoes and long journey from the South of France all for the sake of an obscure book that she couldn't read. She understood that she was being welcomed and honoured in his father's name, and that her host's loquacious enthusiasm was utterly artless and unfeigned.

'I still have all his bookbinding machines. Even the hand press on which he used to print small runs of poetry. He was the founder of the Lübeck Poetry Society. Religious things mostly. Schwärmerei, I used to think, but he was minded that way, it meant a lot to him.'

He poured the Judge a large cup of hot coffee,

and faltered when she refused to accept any Kaffeesahne. 'No cream? None at all? Will you have a biscuit? That's my father's portrait up there, above the water cooler. Yes, that's my father.' He gazed beatifically out into the hall of the old baroque house.

The Judge rose up, cradling her cup, and stood looking into the dim space. The arched doorway was squared off beneath a fan light and decorated with dark, swirling woodwork. Framed certificates, licences and awards littered the walls beyond the august patriarch, who met her gaze. A stiff white collar and a dark suit, but yes, the same face as the son that stood beside her, rubicund, benevolent, courteous. The offices were located on one side of the doorway, the business on the other, and the old master printer himself surveyed all their goings out and their comings in, radiating familial solidity and magnificence.

'Oh yes, he was a great man in his time. He was always a printer rather than a publisher. He left that side of things to his partner. But he had a deep love of books.'

'And you are sure that this is his work?' The Judge put down her coffee cup and concentrated on her darker purpose.

'Yes, quite certain. Look, this is another of his books, one that he bound himself. This unusual repeating pattern is his mark, his signature. But I don't need even to see that crest, Madame. Look — ' He pointed to the tiny Gothic script squashed into the margins. 'That's my father's handwriting.' He ran his forefinger tenderly over

122

the words, not attempting to read them, but caressing each capital, as if reaching out towards the lost hand. 'This is wonderful — to see his writing again. But it's odd. I never knew him write in any of his books. He had a separate book for notes and ideas.'

The Judge decided to forestall any further speculation or questions.

'Have you any records? Any way of knowing when he might have rebound it? Or from whom he might have bought the book?'

'Oh, of course, we have all the old ledgers here. With all his orders and commissions, and all the work he did for himself. The project is always dated, described. He must have done this after the war. I can tell from the Stempel, this stamp, here. We still have that machine. He bought it in 1948. It's not in use any more. But I can't bring myself to destroy or discard anything that was precious to him.'

The Judge rose up from her leather perch, glittering.

'And may I see these ledgers?'

'Of course. I should be delighted. But I may have to get a duster. Wait a moment.'

Herr Bardewig disappeared into his nether vaults. By the time he returned the Judge had quietly photographed the frozen face of his dead father and noted the name of the painter and the date on the corner of the portrait. *1946*. The ledgers were impeccable: records of orders, the dates on which they were confirmed, executed and delivered, with a note of all payments received, whole or in part. Entire transactions were handwritten in the same flawless Gothic script, until they reached the 1950s, after which fragile, typed descriptions of the orders, completed on carbon paper, were stuck into the ledgers alongside the dates and figures. Something about the very accuracy and fullness of the ledgers, which exuded the sweet smell of past wealth and private business, disturbed the Judge. The records were also handbound in leather, massive, avaricious and replete; the firm intended to survive, apparently for ever. They leaned over the great books searching for an entry that might describe the secret Book of the Faith. Herr Bardewig inspected the code.

'What a very strange text! You thought it was Hebrew, didn't you? My father could read Greek. He read the New Testament in Greek. But he couldn't read Hebrew. And he couldn't have typeset this. You'd have to know something about the language. And no matter how carefully you follow the original you always make mistakes. You should see our brochure for the Buddenbrooks House. We all think we know a bit of English, but we had to do it three times in proof and the errors still got through. Are the characters Hebrew? Someone must have possessed a set of characters. The moulds would have been very expensive to make if there was just one copy. Economic madness! Have you found any other copies?'

'Not yet. We're still looking. You've never seen this language before?'

'No. Never. The paper is old though. Look, there is in fact a watermark. This paper is

French. I was right. Probably seventeenth century.'

The Judge saw the faint crown and circle, at last evident under the strong lamp. She had great difficulty reading the handwriting in the ledgers. Herr Bardewig translated the abbreviations.

'That means it was for his own use. So no invoice would have been issued. Let's look for that symbol. I wonder if the order was simply for this single copy. But we don't know that there is only one. And if he bought it in an auction he always bought more than one book at a time. So he may have rebound it with several other books.'

'Let's look for one single book first,' said the Judge. 'That will narrow the search.'

'Ah, that makes it much easier,' cried the printer, his finger now speeding down the margins of the years, 'he always notes the quantities in this column.'

They found one family Bible, one book on animal husbandry, an entire collection of medical textbooks on the science of anaesthetics, each one individually rebound, and nevertheless noted as one, the livre d'honneur, the memorial volume for the glorious dead in the Petruskirche, rebound without charge as a personal gift to the Parish, all the yearbooks for the Lübeck Musical Society, and a special presentation copy of *The History of Lübeck*, destined for the retiring Bürgermeister, for which the remuneration was exceedingly handsome, even allowing for an inevitable shift in the value of the Deutschmark. They had been searching for nearly two hours, and were beginning to lose heart, when a small entry in March 1957, crushed at the bottom of a page, an entry that they had already passed over, stopped Herr Bardewig's sliding finger.

'Look. What about this?'

Frau Handl knocked upon the door.

'I'm going home, sir. Will you lock up?' She looked suspiciously at the Judge. Who was this tiny visitor from France, this pretty woman with wet shoes, and black-rimmed glasses, who had absorbed the Herr Director's entire afternoon with a wild goose chase?

'Thank you, thank you, Frau Handl, schön freier Abend. Yes, I'll do it all. Put the catch up but leave the lights. Now what do you think, Madame Carpentier? Could it be this?'

5. Single copy for rebinding and repair 23rd March 1957. Das Buch des Glaubens, 280 Seiten. The Book of the Faith, 280 pages, Replace damaged cover, No titles, Rebind as stands. Two pages slightly torn, Repair as necessary, No. 480.

'Who placed the order? Or was it his book?' snapped the Judge.

'Privat Kunde. A private customer. The book was rebound for someone else. That's all that's noted. But if it was someone else's book why on earth did he write in the margins? I can't imagine him defacing any book, let alone one that belonged to someone else.'

'Was there an invoice?' The Judge gazed at the next page, hungry as the wolf spotting the child's blood-red hood coming through the trees.

'No. No invoice was ever issued. He rebound this book for free. But where's the delivery note?'

'May I photograph this entry?'

'But of course. Ah, you have one of those modern digital cameras. My daughter is clamouring for one. But they're still rather expensive. Most useful for documents. Here, I'll hold the light.'

They stood side by side in the warm office. The Judge noted the numbers and dates beside the record in the great ledger. The book had been returned to a person, or persons unknown, three weeks later.

'The missing delivery note? Does this number correspond to some other record that he kept?' The Judge had begun to have great faith in the dead patriarch's meticulous exactitude.

'Well, he kept everything in good order, as you see. But I don't have access to every aspect of his system now. We computerised the accounts not long ago.'

'But do you still have his private records of his book purchases? The ones he bought at auction and rebound?'

Herr Bardewig looked up at the rows and rows of dark and golden books above him.

'The books are all here,' he said. 'Wait a minute. I'll look in the household accounts. He managed those too. Mother never worried herself with the household bills because we always lived upstairs.'

Herr Bardewig accepted her challenge and vanished again into the company's archive. The

Judge looked at her watch. Seven o'clock already passed. She was the ferret, shaking a rat, and could not let go until she was certain that the thing was dead. The printer finally reemerged with two large cardboard boxes and an embarrassed confession.

'These aren't so well filed as I imagined they would be — loose sheets and only roughly in order. But here are all the existing delivery notes and household invoices from 1956 to 1960.'

They sat down at separate tables and began to hunt for anything relevant or the number 480. An hour later the Judge struck gold.

'Excuse me, Herr Bardewig, but I think I have it.' She held up a delivery note. 'There is no name on the ticket, which if I understand you correctly, was not your father's usual practice. But here is the number. 480. Would you be good enough to confirm the address for me? Is this a double S or a double F?'

'It's an F. Effengrube 19. That's in Lübeck, near the cathedral. Do you recognise the address?'

'Yes,' said the Judge, glowing, 'I do.'

But she gave nothing else away.

Herr Bardewig photocopied the delivery note for her and insisted on a small schnapps in celebration. They sat at ease, like old friends, and the printer talked on about the firm and his father's time; how he had learned the profession from his father and uncle, how as a small child he had been allowed to sit up and listen to the music and poetry in the great salon above them, which had now been divided into two rooms. He

128

asked very few curious questions concerning the provenance of the book and her unstinting search for its source. She rose to leave. And then it became clear that he had knowingly held his tongue.

'Is this book part of an investigation, Madame?'

'It is.'

'Not anything horrible? Or criminal, I hope?'

The Judge hesitated. It was always better to say very little about her work. Outsiders became intrigued, then spellbound. The sects touched an unconscious current of fantasy; a Kraken, which unfortunately needed very few underwater currents in order to awaken. As the years passed the Judge remained unimpressed by the mental strength of most ordinary people, for, with the lightest of prods, they became irrational and unhinged. The actual content of most people's faith beggared belief. Long used to floods of hysterical insanity poured forth upon the walls and ceilings of her office, the Judge scarcely flinched at the narratives of past lives, alien abductions, revelations from floating tablets, voices emerging from space, birds or bushes, and conclusive evidence of maternal reincarnation in the form of a sheep. She avoided precise explanations of her role as 'la chasseuse de sectes' whenever possible. Yet she owed this man a slice of honesty.

'It is a little disturbing perhaps, but I am a juge d'instruction. I gather evidence. I don't prosecute anyone. I present my reports to the Public Prosecutor, Le Procureur de la République. He decides if there is a case to answer.'

129

Herr Bardewig turned a little white.

'Ah, I see. That sounds very grand. My father was always somewhat mistrustful of the law. I can't think why. He wrote his last will and testament himself. Impeccable, unambiguous, like the ledgers. But he was a very private man. He had a secretive side.'

A tiny fragment of the puzzling labyrinth of connections before her suddenly settled in the Judge's mind and she turned her darkrimmed, magnified eyes upon the printer.

'Forgive me, Herr Bardewig, if I appear intrusive. But may I ask when and how your father died?'

The generous, open-hearted face before her closed like a trap. Regret, pain and a flood of unlocked memories swept past his mouth and cheeks like a rising tide. She had given him back a man he had honoured and adored. For one half-day his father had returned to the firm in his old shape, upright, exacting and just; his love for Das Buch des Glaubens manifested itself in the careful beauty of his work, made to last for ever. Now this chilly Judge had snatched away the beloved presence and his goodness stood eclipsed.

'It is not easy for me to speak about these things, Madame Carpentier. My father died in 1984, by his own hand.'

6

Endless Night

The first letter, and she always thought of this message as the first one, the first one addressed to her, outside the investigation, for it came bearing nothing but her name on the envelope, was delivered by hand to their hotel.

> *Effengrube 19,*
> *Lübeck*
>
> *Chère Madame,*
> *Please forgive my appalling rudeness to you and your assistant this morning. To hold, in my own hands, that book which belonged to someone I dearly loved was to bring him once more before me. It is a loss that I cannot accept and I allowed my feelings to govern my behaviour. But it is inexcusable bad manners on my part and I beg your pardon.*
> *I enclose two tickets for tomorrow's performance of <u>Tristan and Isolde</u> at the main theatre in the Bechergrube. I would be honoured and delighted if you were able to be my guests at this performance. Please accept my humblest apologies.*
> *Mit vielen freundlichen Grüssen,*
> *Friedrich Grosz*

'Well, there's no way I'm going to sit through

any opera, let alone Wagner,' roared Gaëlle, flinging down the letter on the Judge's bed, 'and anyway our plane's at midday.'

The Judge pursed her lips.

'Go and take off those wet clothes, Gaëlle, you've been sitting around in them quite long enough. I'm sorry that you had a fruitless search through the bookshops. But I'm afraid that I've already postponed our flight back until Friday.'

'You didn't! Without asking me?'

'Remember that you're on a mission for the French Republic, which may not require your services on the weekend, but certainly does so throughout the week.'

'How can you do this to me? I hate the food.'

'We will eat at a splendid, expensive restaurant tonight, I promise. And if you absolutely can't stand Wagner I won't make you go.'

Gaëlle collapsed flat across the duvets and let out a mighty cry of relief. She kicked off her soaking boots. The Judge rescued the Composer's letter and slipped it into a plastic envelope reserved for evidence. The phone rang, and there at the other end, baying like an abandoned hound, was André Schweigen.

'Alors? Dis-moi où tu es,' he yelled. Gaëlle snatched up her boots and fled, banging the door shut behind her.

DEM WARHREN, GUTEN, SCHÖNEN

The Judge arrived at the Lübeck Stadttheater forty minutes before the performance was due to begin, and stood on the pavement opposite, looking up. The theatre was dedicated to truth, goodness and beauty or rather, given the grammar of its declaration and the declension of the abstract nouns, to that which is true, good and beautiful. Not only are those three things not the same, thought the Judge, they are also rarely united in the same object or person at the same time. Musical performances were probably no different. And, so far as the Judge was concerned, only truth shone unambiguous, and non-negotiable. Beauty and goodness were up for grabs.

The Beckergrube was, or had once been, one of the more grandiose streets in Lübeck, with large and pompous houses, lumbering upwards from the Trave on either side. Most were now down-at-heel business premises, a tobacconist, an artistic flower shop with improbable dead pods arranged in the window, a mobile phone company which had placed a gigantic plastic 'Handy' on the pavement to entice passing customers, and several evil-looking cafés. In the midst of this stood the temple to dramatic art. Comedy and Tragedy flanked Apollo and the Nine Muses, a great frieze of figures beneath the pediment bearing the dedication to truth, goodness and beauty, in their individual or collective manifestations. The entire bombastic monument, a mountainous construction in art nouveau, dated 1908, with a solid brown stone face, and two handsome wings with tall windows, squatted before her, vast, bulbous and murky, with the odd glittering tile, in silvery diamond green. The Judge braced herself for battle, settled the tortoiseshell clamp in her black coil, steadied her glasses with her right forefinger, pulled her cashmere shawl more firmly around her, against the crisp spring dusk, and then marched across the road and into the theatre.

She gave up one of the two tickets at the box office, now besieged by a lurking queue for returns, where it was promptly sold to the first of the waiting Wagner fanatics. The opening performance, duly greeted with rapturous notices from all the local papers, sucked in the public from distant provinces. Roars of eulogy, now stuck up on giant boards all around the foyer, dwarfed the Judge. Vast black-and-white photographs showed desperate figures with their mouths open and their arms outstretched. *An Isolde for our times: Fräulein Maria Bayer in the title role, ravishing, passionate, seductive, nobly supported by Gerhard Klingmann as the knight torn between his love for Isolde and his loyalty to the King.* The Judge yawned and gave up trying to translate the superlatives. She decided to find her seat and read the programme.

Her knowledge of the plot was somewhat hazy, for while she knew the general outlines of the legend she entertained the common delusion that all operas were the same: ludicrous incidents, irrational behaviour, uncontrollable passions, overblown orchestration, and four fat folk bellowing at the footlights. The point of the evening was to spy upon the Composer, openly and at his own invitation, to exploit his repentance if at all possible, by gaining his confidence, then squeezing whatever information, or better still, confessions, could be extracted from this powerful, but slippery source. This man was a living connection to the Faith. Of that she was certain. But she knew now that she was dealing with something far more ancient and sinister than the usual run of sects, which, if they survived at all, became bourgeois, visible and liable to fiscal inspection. The Faith now assumed an ancestry that smelt of Masonic ritual and a hidden, deeper past than she had first suspected. The Faith remained uppermost in her mind. The opera was neither here nor there.

Dominique Carpentier disliked all manifestations of excess: older women who wore far too many trinkets, happy people, drunk and singing, love letters that made free with words like 'for ever' and 'all eternity', men who thought sport was significant. This deep and innate hostility to all those trivial joys which keep the advancing shadows at bay, tinged with a sharp, ironic tongue, led many of her colleagues to think of her as heartless and a little cruel. This was unjust. The Judge cherished a deeper passion, one that was as surprising as it was laudable: the desire to defend and protect the vulnerable, the feeble-minded and the mad from every predator, and, if necessary, from themselves. Through her office trailed a sad procession of victims, frail beings whose desperate need for security and belonging trapped them in narratives of faith, largely of their own imagining. The Judge pared away the delusions, leaving the people on whose

135

behalf she felt compelled to act naked, defenceless and ashamed. Reason is neither gentle nor kind, and the Judge believed in Reason with as intemperate a commitment to her own credo as any of the secret initiates who had given their hearts to the suicide Faith. She sought the Truth, and nothing but the Truth. Yet the Truth is not, and cannot be, the instrument of freedom for every one of us; and to know the Truth may well imprison gentle souls in wretchedness for ever.

The inner spaces of the theatre were solid, plain and unpretentious. Despite the early start — the performance began at six-thirty — many of the audience were wearing full evening dress, black ties and silken gowns, brandishing small, jewelled evening bags and trailing overblown chains of shining gems, entwined with leaves of gold. The Judge felt slightly underdressed. She never wore bulky costume jewellery. Inside the stalls the theatre felt suddenly smaller and more intimate. The great red curtains plummeted in folds like a waterfall. Yet the illusion of their proximity was so compelling she imagined that she could reach out and touch them. The distances around her shivered and shortened, treacherous, unstable. She identified her seat: six rows back from the stage at the very centre of the house. A quiet escape for a breath of air and to collect her thoughts proved therefore impossible. As she stood at the rim of the great sea of red seats, dismayed by the prospect of imprison-ment, she sensed someone surging towards her. The Composer appeared in the still largely empty theatre, magnificent and gigantic in full evening dress, every aspect of his presentation formal and meticulous. The iron discipline of the man, a façade she had so casually shattered, stood remade before her. He bowed, now reconstituted as a handsome, cultivated gentleman, inexorable in his determination to charm. He held out his hand.

'Madame Carpentier, will you humour a cantankerous, bad-tempered old man and shake hands with me?'

She accepted the gesture and the self-deprecating, shamefaced smile at face value. And she was not wrong to do so. The Composer's manner gave away his uncertainty at his possible reception.

'Please forgive me, Madame, for my unpardonable bad manners.'

The Judge bowed and smiled slightly. She had no clear advance plan as to how she should deal with sincerity; there was no doubt that the cordial welcome and diffident apology were both absolutely genuine. He wrapped her small hand in his and drew her down towards the orchestra.

'Was your assistant unable to come?'

'Gaëlle? I'm afraid that Wagner's not exactly to her taste.'

The Composer laughed, and inside the warm embrace of his laughter the Judge felt suddenly included and at ease. He continued, 'She had the most wonderful spike through her tongue and an array of pierced ear studs that are surely quite uncommon amongst lawyers. She must be a very unusual person.'

Had Gaëlle put her tongue out at the Composer? The Judge felt compelled to present excuses and explanations.

'She's discovered a Rockkneipe in the Marlsgrube and is spending the evening with some new friends.'

'Ah yes,' he grinned, 'I know that place. It hasn't changed in years. The crowd always looks exactly the same — Motorhead T-Shirts with the sleeves rolled up to their armpits, terrific tattoos — smoky air, thrice-breathed, and the music so loud you can't think. But the clients are all greybeards now. Like myself. I hope she finds someone her own age to play with.'

He took the Judge's arm, gentle, solicitous, a gesture that suggested old-fashioned manners rather than impudent familiarity, and led her to the middle of the low barrier above the orchestra. The space was cramped and dark, almost beneath the stage, only the lights on the music stands glowed like rafts on a sea of shadows. The brass section was arriving, carrying their huge instrument cases. They looked up at the Composer and his guest, startled and a little anxious. One of them ostentatiously turned off his mobile phone. The Composer's stand was illuminated from beneath as well as above, like an exhibition case, or the hotplate on a stove. She saw the full score of the opera; there lay the music, a language she could not decipher and had never valued, open at page one.

'Are you fond of the opera, Madame Carpentier?'

He was still holding her beside him as they

looked down into the pit, and this gentle reassurance encouraged her honest response.

'I've never been to one before.'

'Oh good heavens! *Tristan and Isolde?* Then you are climbing Everest, never before having set foot upon a mountain?'

He chuckled slightly.

'Madame Carpentier, you are a very courageous woman. I have conducted this opera many, many times in the course of my professional life. Yet each time I find something new, fresh and miraculous in the score. So, even for an old hand like myself, the familiar remains strange, uncharted, even obscure. Let me advise you how to listen. Do not rationalise. I know that you are a very rational person. A Judge must be so, to sift the evidence. But put that part of yourself aside. Do not assess things or calculate. Or really even try to listen. Let go of everything. Like loosening a rope. Is that the right metaphor? Yes, let go. And give the music time to speak to you.'

'I know nothing about music.' The Judge tried to disentangle her arm. But he held her more firmly and turned her towards him so that he could see her face. The house lights were up and the theatre murmured with the rustle of arrival, but they stood so close to the orchestra that his features, lit from beneath, took on an eerie magnificence.

'This opera is dear to me for many reasons. These are young singers; they are utterly dedicated. And I have worked them so hard. The soprano is singing Isolde for the first time. Wagner demands such stamina, I have asked

139

myself again and again whether she is ready to do this. Be indulgent and generous to them, Madame Carpentier. If you are not an aficionado you will be harder to persuade. To win you round will take a great effort. We will give you our best. Our very best.'

The Judge looked up at his fine lean face and registered his terrible intensity. She realised that he was proposing to offer the performance, as a special gift to her, as if she were the only member of the audience. But I know nothing of Wagner, nothing about opera, I cannot even read music; she retreated backwards in her mind, searching for cover. The Composer's next words disconcerted her utterly, for despite the hesitation in his voice he had grasped the most effective metaphor to silence her. He delivered his masterstroke.

'You are my Judge. Let this music be my advocate. May the music plead my cause.' His lips touched her hand. They were in full view of everyone in the house. Then he stepped back, setting her free at last, bowed formally, as if they stood before the Court and the King, then vanished away into darkness. The Judge found herself standing alone before the open score; apparently she had seized power in his absence and taken command of the orchestra. She fluttered hurriedly to her seat, and plunged her nose into the programme, turning each page slowly, understanding nothing.

She had not reckoned with the audience. Nobody else was there for the first time. These were the opera lovers for whom music-theatre in general, and Wagner in particular, was not just a passion, but a drug. The excitement in the stalls smothered her like a fragrant cocoon. Despite craning her neck till the veins stood out and ached, she could catch only the faintest glimpse of the Composer when he greeted the audience and the assembled musicians in the pit. The level of the orchestra sank until all that remained was an expectant rustle and the gleaming lights above the unreadable music, the sounds locked up in hieroglyphs.

Opera remains a miracle; partly because the cost of producing a performance is so prohibitive it can never be met by the price of the tickets. The art requires princely subsidies; its origins are aristocratic, and so is the grandeur of its spectacle. The plots may be improbable and the emotional content may well defy all sense and reason, but the form, infinitely mutable, remains extraordinary, subversive, insidious. Canny producers know that naturalism is the enemy of opera. We demand the big symbols and the gestures of excess. This particular production of *Tristan and Isolde*, set on a derelict Cunard liner manned by a chorus of mutinous, lecherous sailors, confronted the Judge with a vision so unlikely and bizarre that, for the first forty minutes, she stared, transfixed, in affronted amazement. Had she unwittingly attended a mass gathering of the sects she so effectively liquidated, she could not have been more disconcerted or perplexed. The singers wore formal modern dress with a 1920s atmosphere; yet the costumes achieved a shimmer that was both timeless and imprecise. The Judge crouched in her seat, baffled by the action and the incoherence of the music. Yet everything unrolled according to her prejudiced expectations: forbidden love, desperate conflicts of loyalty and trust, she loves this one but has to marry that one, who is this one's lord and master. So far, so predictable. But the music unsettled her nerves; a monolith of sound, oddly broken and discordant. Each theme she picked out modulated, mutated, dissolved and escaped, so that she could never keep hold of the threads. The Judge confronted a structure, which resembled the barrage in the mountains above Montpellier, a giant man-made dam behind which the waters mounted, pressed. She could hear the danger rising, rising. And so two conflicting emotions bubbled within her: anger and irritation at being forced to listen to something that she neither liked nor understood, and hypnotised fascination. Her gaze flickered across the rapt and concentrated audience: another sect, another sect. The Judge refused to silence her canny, analytic intelligence, as the Composer had advised her to do, for this gift operated not only through judgement, evidence and selection, but also out of an unacknowledged feral cunning. I am here for a purpose. This man is showing me something that I need to see, and presenting me with an argument that I need to hear. This is the fulfilment of that interrogation that was broken off, and the subject before me, a great secret love and a suicide pact, is both pertinent and sinister. She nestled into her red velvet perch, an animal on the watch, her muscles tensed, intent.

The effort did her no good at all. She could make no sense of that huge, impenetrable wall of strange, discordant, contorted patterns. She could hear the structures of logic building great towers of sound, but grew impatient; the action proved too static to engage her attention. Every one of the singers flung themselves into the enterprise with a passionate desperation that suggested the Composer would flay them alive if they didn't. Yet still they failed to reach her. Why am I sitting here? To what end? She decided to slip away at the interval. But no sooner had the house lights risen and the mountainous clamour of applause sunk away, than she found herself looking up at a young woman, elegant as an elf in black, with a short slick haircut, murmuring her name.

'Madame Carpentier?'

The Composer's assistant whisked her away to a small table in the restaurant attached to the theatre, where she was awaited by a light salmon salad and a bottle of champagne.

'Are you enjoying the performance?' The Judge decided to take pleasure in the bribe. She had suffered quite enough. And so, mellowed by supper and the expensive champagne, which had the decency and intelligence to be French, the Judge sauntered back through the well-dressed crowds and reclaimed her central position, to await the final denouement. These desperate lovers are surely doomed.

Wagner always comes home to roost. There is

a method that underwrites his power: complicate, prevaricate, withhold. Let the water's seepage through the dam become palpable, visible, viscous to the touch. Then unleash all that has been promised and desired in a mighty flood. Deliver the goods. The Judge had already sat through a lot of noisy, worthless posturing. She expected more of the same and nothing unforeseen. Yet she paid attention, much against her better judgement.

> Das Schiff? Das Schiff?
> Isoldes Schiff?
> Du mußt es sehen!
> Mußt es sehen!
> Das Schiff? Sähst du's noch nicht?
> Can you not see Isolde's ship?

The last act of *Tristan and Isolde* is about waiting, waiting in impatience and frustration, waiting, waiting for life to ebb, waiting for the dawn, waiting to see the one you love for the last time, waiting for death. And the music makes you wait. Was it simply the effect of the champagne? The Judge felt the tension easing from her jaw and shoulders. She let the cashmere shawl slip down across her back. Let go. *Let go of everything. Like loosening a rope. Is that the right metaphor? Yes, let go.* And this was her undoing. The action of the piece remained static and improbable, but the music began to tell another story. We will not always be condemned to wait, forgotten at the gates. This forbidden love, which we have sacrificed, will be returned

144

to us tenfold. We see the one we love, the one who has gone on before us, striding ahead, stepping away into darkness, but we know in our flesh, in the kingdom of this world, that we have but to take one step, one single step across that threshold, to seize the glory that awaits us in that eternal, endless night.

The young soprano had a voice not yet sufficiently confident or powerful to sing the Liebestod upon her knees beside the body of her dead beloved, as it is usually performed. And so the ending of the opera took the audience by surprise. A soft screen descended between the singer and the spectacle of the assembled court, mourning the hero's death, their heads bowed in grief. The soprano stepped forward and the house lights glowed. She stood, no longer an actress in an opera, but a real, breathing human being, a woman whose beloved had died in her arms, less than two metres away from the Judge.

Mild und leise
wie er lächelt . . .

O Death where is thy sting? O Grave, thy victory?

Seht ihr's, Freunde? Seht ihr's nicht?
Immer lichter
wie er leuchtet,
stern-umstrahlet
hoch sich hebt?

Now she was speaking directly to the

audience, her arms outstretched, her face radiant with joy. For the Night beckoned, that Endless Night of pleasure, the lavish promise of eternity and the enraptured dream. The girl reached out towards the audience, begging for their blessing and consent. For what awaits us on the other side of death? Glory, glory, glory: I have seen it with my own eyes and I give you my word. The darkness behind the young singer opened out into a windy dawn, so that the figures, silent as statues, stood dark against the transfigured light, and the Judge, no longer able to see or breathe, found her face awash with tears.

She imagined that the endless curtain calls would give her time to recover her equanimity, but the soft tired face of the young soprano, overflowing with exhaustion and delight, her blonde hair slicked against her cheeks, moved the Judge still more deeply. When the audience rose to acclaim her, the Judge rose too, her rushing tears in free fall. She saw the Composer, applauding his own cast and orchestra, the same exhausted satisfaction on his features, through an uncontrollable blur of tears.

Then it was all over.

★   ★   ★

The audience in her row separated like the Red Sea before Aaron's rod and set out home, half in one direction, half in the other. The Judge was left, hesitating and worn out, gathering up her bag and shawl, flattened, as if she had been prodded through an emotional mangle. Then the

146

Composer reappeared at the end of the row of red seats. Several people spoke to him, one man shook his hand; he brushed them aside and stormed towards her like a crusading knight who has at last spotted a maiden in distress and need of rescue. She felt his hands upon her face, wiping away her tears. He said nothing for a moment, but pressed a large, folded white handkerchief upon her, then spoke, almost in a whisper.

'Thank you, Madame Carpentier. Your tears are the dearest compliment we could wish for. You have believed in us and heard us truly. We cannot honour you enough.'

The Judge wrestled with her feelings, which had been sliced to ribbons, and fought like a tiger to regain her distance and composure. She looked up at the Composer, but could not tell if his savage blue eyes had really softened into a shifting grey mist or if she was still mastered by unpardonable emotions. Something was missing.

'My glasses! I've lost my glasses.'

He turned all the neighbouring seats upside down and found the still undamaged spectacles beneath the preceding row. At what point had she lost them and ceased to see clearly? She had no idea.

'I'm sorry,' she murmured, 'I'm not usually so uncontrolled.' She felt his giant hands gentle upon her shoulders.

'We are now spending all our time apologising to one another, Madame Carpentier. But there is no need to be sorry. For these tears you must never apologise. Never.'

147

He uttered these last words with such vehemence and intensity that a precise thought crystallised in the Judge's mind. She had lost this night's battle. On enemy territory she had been vanquished. I must escape from this man. Now.

'Would you be so kind as to call me a taxi?'

He swept her out into the foyer and began to negotiate with one of his assistants. She realised that she had mislaid the russet cashmere shawl, excused herself and darted back inside the theatre. The shawl lay draped upon the carpet at the end of her row like a healing wound. The Judge snatched it up, unfolded the Composer's handkerchief and blew her nose, hard. As she settled her glasses and her vision cleared, she saw a thick folded book, the size of a college lecture folder or an artist's sketch pad, resting on the seat before her. It was the Composer's score, the full score of Wagner's *Tristan and Isolde*. She picked up the volume with the intention of giving it back to him, slowly turning the pages as she made her way past the vestiaire. The theatre was packing itself away for the night. She heard bangs, thumps and voices filtering out from behind the closed tabs: the set was either being dismantled or reconstructed in another form. The spare programmes, the spring *Spielplan*, listing all the forthcoming attractions, and the Music Festival brochures stood in neat stacks along the counter. The bar and snacks had already vanished. The adjoining doors leading to the restaurant stood darkened, locked. The Judge glanced down at the blue marks and odd comments written in German down the margins of the music; it seemed that the Composer was answering back, responding to the score.

Suddenly she stood still and stared. A bleak, lost fragment of her brain that had been muffled, dulled and silenced snapped aggressively back into life. For there, beside the Liebestod, that terrible hymn to extinction and eternity, scratched along the blank gaps at the edge, gleamed a sequence of blocked-out letters, which resembled unaccented Hebrew. There, in the Composer's own hand, shone the living, secret language of the Faith.

7

Servants of Isis

'What bothers me most,' said Gaëlle, chewing her upper lip, 'is that you haven't had him arrested yet.'

'On what charge?' replied the Judge. 'Planning to bump himself off at some future date? Knowing that his friends also intended to kill themselves? Hard to prove. And anyway, non-assistance à personne en danger is all I'd have. Being able to read and write an ancient secret language? Behaving like a maniac and then being excessively charming to make up for it? None of these things are crimes, Gaëlle. In his law or ours. And I haven't even got enough on the Faith yet to nail the whole thing as a sect. I have no official members, no legal or associative structure, no registration or documentation. And no trace of the money. We haven't even found the gun that was used to kill Madame Laval.'

Gaëlle rummaged in her dossiers, mutinous.

'Well, trump something up. Plant the gun on him. Like they do on TV.'

'Fine. I'll get Schweigen on to it at once. But in order to plant the gun on Friedrich Grosz we have to find it first.'

The Judge set aside three fat dossiers dealing with the Faith, which dominated the left-hand side of her desk, and drew down the bulging folders on Agape: Healing through Love, which presented a far simpler profile. All our illnesses result from a dearth of fraternal love and the care of healing hands. Be prepared to part with an initial subscription fee of three thousand francs, non-returnable, and after a sequence of six sessions with a self-help group of like-minded believers, led by a specialist, anything — even miracles — will be possible. The publicity contained testimonies of those who had signed up as doubting Thomases and still been cured of everything from psoriasis to cancer. One woman suffered from 'tingling in the knees', but the faith of her Agape group had lifted her mind to greater, higher things and the tingling miraculously disappeared. The guru, Thucydides Magistos, supposedly Greek, turned out to be one of her usual suspects. The Judge had encountered him once before as the leader of an Egyptian cult, the Servants of Isis — *We are the servants of Isis, sworn to obey Her commands* — which sought to restore the ancient religion in the Western world. The guru, then accompanied by an ample matriarch, proclaimed her holy, the true reincarnation of the Goddess Herself. The lady, at least, believed him. She turned out to be not fraudulent, but mad. Isis suffered from fantasies of immediate deification and demanded a human sacrifice, preferably a handsome Osiris, whom she would rip to pieces with her own mighty hands and teeth, and then reconstitute, using sacred tears as glue. The willing initiate was rescued, the Goddess Isis locked up in an asylum, and the guru fined prodigious sums. The Judge could produce no conclusive evidence to prove that he was party to the sacrifice plot, and he denied it before the tribunal with convincing passion, claiming that Isis held him in thrall.

Now Thucydides Magistos narrated, in thrilling detail, his own conversion experience, remarkably similar to St Paul's uncomfortable encounter with Our Saviour on the road to Damascus, as recounted in the Acts of the Apostles, a tale the Judge suspected of being the source. *I was proud, I would not believe, but God's humbling hand pointed out the Way. He told me to arise and enter the city, for I am His chosen vessel to bear His name before the gentiles and kings and the Children of Israel.* His whispered prayers in Greek proved extraordinarily efficacious and even arrested the progress of gangrene in one old lady's foot. The Judge sifted through the specialist reports from the doctors. Those members of Agape: Healing through Love who suffered from fatal diseases had died anyway, but in comfort and peace, accompanied by their purchased, loyal friends.

Gaëlle typed and filed their interrupted interview with the Composer and then closed the great grey shutters of their office windows against the midday sun, which had just cleared the Church of Our Lady of Compassion, and sent a long, solid shaft of light across the dark parquet. Cool air, trapped beneath the high ceilings, kept the office temperature at a comfortable 23° C. The Judge refused to install an air-conditioning unit on principle. The planet must be defended from the misnamed 'climatisation'. Their desks stood confronting one another, so that neither woman could see into her companion's computer or know exactly which documents turned between the other's fingers. Gaëlle could not distract herself from the Faith, but defended her private enquiries from the Judge's searchlight eyes. Why could she not simply file the case, under 'Awaiting Fresh Evidence', like all the others, inconclusive, pending? Her difficulty arose from a personal antipathy towards both Schweigen and the Composer. She guarded Dominique Carpentier with the ferocity of a jealous god, and these men absorbed too much of her Judge's precious attention. Gaëlle studied the ballistics reports, comparing the diagrams, graphs and figures. Finally, she risked resurrecting the debate.

'Hey, listen. If the same gun killed both Anton and Marie-Cécile Laval, and yet forensics seem pretty sure they shot themselves, personally, if you see what I mean, with no outside help, but the suicide gun has vanished, doesn't that mean that there is always one person present at these mass departures who doesn't go too? One person who stays on? And if there's one person unaccounted for, then one person is still available for prosecution,' Gaëlle persisted, bent on revelation by deduction.

'Indeed,' said the Judge, not looking up, 'but it needn't be the same person at both departures.'

'And it wasn't the Composer in either case,' sighed Gaëlle, openly disappointed. 'His alibi checks out. He was seen by at least two thousand people on both occasions.'

There was silence in the office. The city quietened at midday.

'But wouldn't that one person have nightmares for evermore? I mean — at seeing everyone they knew and loved lying there dead?'

The Judge looked up.

'Not necessarily, Gaëlle. It all depends on your relationship to death. On what you think it means.'

The Judge saw a young woman leaning towards an enchanted public, her arms outstretched, persuading each and every one of them that our longing for the everlasting night will never be in vain. Embrace the joy of endless, endless night and follow, follow me. The Judge shivered slightly, then fixed her Greffière with a determined stare.

'Put the Faith away, Gaëlle, and help me finish off these lunatic disease-healers. We'll come back to it soon enough.'

★ ★ ★

And so, the Faith, mired in several bulging dossiers, was confined to the cream cabinet in the Judge's office — unsolved cases, affaires non classées — pending further information and fresh developments. Two months passed. Gaëlle cut out all the articles in the local and national press describing Madame Laval's well-attended memorial service, held in the same parish church where the Judge had been baptised. There were discreet hints concerning the dreadful circumstances of her tragic demise, but no one used the

154

word 'suicide', although *Le Nouvel Observateur*, which was running another series on contemporary sects, dared to describe the New Year's Day departure as a massacre. The Judge rang them up and complained. That night, long after the offices had closed and the security guard had done his round, then settled down to watch the football on a secret little television that resembled a security screen, the Judge sat on before her desk, her astral charts spread out across the green leather. She could not justify any more official working hours brooding over the Faith, but she was convinced that something strange lay just beneath her fingertips, dark to her eyes, but livid with revelation to those capable of reading the haunting trails of stars.

The republic of reason seemed in full retreat, for the annual turnover generated by clairvoyants, mediums, commercial mystics and visionaries now amounted to well over four million euros in the new currency. She tried to calculate the sum in francs, but abandoned the attempt when she read that every other person living in Martinique was actually in touch with the beyond. Dominique Carpentier's enlightenment values of reason, justice and humane discipline were evidently out of step with the times. The little shops selling idols, crystals, fragrant candles, Buddhas, Krishnas, magic herbs in silken sachets, beads and bangles, which guaranteed health, longevity and sexual power on a scale unimaginable to ordinary mortals, flourished in every city, lurked in corners of bookshops, advertised in women's magazines, could now be contacted direct via our website;

one white witch, a pagan defender of Gaia, even gave astrological readings over the phone. All you need is a gullible soul and a credit card. The sects were led onwards to glory by rich men. The Greek guru enjoyed the use of a villa in Tuscany and a condo on the beach in Miami, handsome gifts from devoted followers, undeclared for tax purposes, for the guru owned nothing in his own right. He had risen above property. His spacious dojo in Paris was funded by an English aristocrat, who flew over on Wednesdays to attend the miraculous healing sessions, where, after an hour and a quarter of martial arts practice, they all got in touch with their lower abdomens. O Lord, I wander among the foolish and dawdle before the gates of Paradise, where the angel stands, bearing his drawn sword. The Judge bowed her head in unbelieving prayer and terrible exhaustion.

Her mobile lit up and shivered across the desk without ringing. She peered at the number. Withheld. She looked up at the clock. Fifteen minutes to midnight. Then she snatched up the phone.

'André? Where are you?'

'Outside. Looking up at your window. Security won't let me in.'

The Judge rose up, stiff and joyful. She flung open the shutters and leaned out. Two floors beneath her, in the narrow cobbled street, gazing upwards through the orange shadows, stood André Schweigen. She greeted the wide smile and square features of the man who had stifled fires with his bare hands for love of her.

'I've just driven down,' he called.

'In the middle of the night?'

'It's too hot in the afternoon. Come downstairs. I've got some news. And some fresh evidence.'

André Schweigen kept the Faith alive. The case mattered more to him than any other because it opened the doors to the Judge.

★ ★ ★

Her house lurked breathless and shut up on a little hill, north-east of the city, surrounded by a blank stone wall and a discreet curtain of pinède. She irrigated her garden via a computer-controlled system of pipes, which hissed and spat in the dark. They heard the spray and smelt the water as they climbed out of their cars. Schweigen hesitated before removing his small case from the boot. She had not invited him to stay with her. A warm wind stirred the stunted pines; Schweigen began to justify himself, standing there on the gravel in the perfumed dark.

'I did try to tell you I was coming. I left three messages on your answerphone here,' he announced. 'The switchboard had closed at your office and you usually turn off your mobile at work.'

'It's all right, André. You can stay the night. I was feeling a little dispirited. I'm glad you're here.'

She fiddled with her keys. The terrace lights all came on in a burst and immediately fizzled with insects. Her mother's clafoutis lay prostrate in the fridge, untouched. Had the fruit congealed into rubber? She prodded the flan in hope.

'She only made it for me on Sunday morning. It'll be delicious. Here, have a fork.'

They wolfed the poached apricots, then slopped down a carton of iced tea, sitting side by side at the kitchen table, like naughty children, staying up late without permission.

'Where does your wife think you are?' asked the Judge, pushing her plate away. Her house remained cool, even in summer, behind the blue shutters and the deep stone walls. Schweigen shrugged, irritated and a little desperate.

'I told her I was bringing the evidence to you. So she thinks I'm here. With you.' The Judge raised one eyebrow and delivered her ironic smile, then she took off her glasses and rubbed her forehead. He looked carefully at her tired eyes.

'I see. Well? What have you come all this way to show me, André? Where's the evidence?'

Schweigen retrieved a self-sealing plastic sack from his briefcase, which contained a small blue box and a folded square of Christmas paper.

'Look.'

He rewrapped the box in shining decorated foil. The Judge watched intent as the paper fitted perfectly, each crease tense and exact around the gift. She had no need to read the card, still swinging from a shining silver thread, for she knew the words by heart: *To my darling Marie-T, Je t'aime, ma petite chérie, Bisous, Maman* — in the elegant careful hand of Madame Marie-Cécile Laval.

'We bagged up all the waste-paper baskets and anything of interest in the dustbins. Remember? This box was concealed under the lower bunk in the children's bedrooms and only discovered when we released the chalet back to the owners. They're going to sell the house. Even though I told them nobody actually died there. The woman kept the box, just in case. You found the paper downstairs. It was the address on the box which made me put them together. Look.'

He held the cover up to the light suspended above her kitchen table; the engraved letters gleamed gold against the blue:

GOLDENBERG'S
Montpellier

'You know them?' He looked at her, smug and expectant.

'Of course. I bought my bracelet there.' Schweigen glowered at the bracelet, jealous of its constant presence upon her arm.

'I thought I'd find out what Cécile Laval gave to her daughter. She had already planned her own death. It was her last gift. It must be significant.'

The Judge stretched and yawned. It was half past one in the middle of the night. André had devised yet another implausible and extravagant excuse to spend taxpayers' money and come in search of her. His love rendered him unreliable and unprofessional.

'André! What if it's not significant at all? What if it's a harmless golden necklace or a charm bracelet? What if Monsieur Goldenberg doesn't even remember what he sold to whom in the Christmas rush? Anyway, I thought Marie-T wasn't even at the chalet when they all went up the mountain.'

'I must try.'

The Judge stood up and stacked their plates in her tiny dishwasher. Schweigen faced her out, dogged and obstinate. She watched him, inscrutable; but as she studied his grey eyes, measured each deepening line on either side of his mouth, she began, despite her irritation, to comprehend his sincerity. She realised that he loved her with a violence that she could neither control nor return; but that his hunt for the remaining members of the Faith was just as genuine, and as relentless. Both passions were entwined in the fibre of the man. His obsession with his work matched her own; but his search was not impersonal, detached; the blue box from Goldenberg's was not a slight excuse. His love was written across his face, his shoulders, his clenched hands, and so was his resolve.

'Come to bed,' said the Judge.

Schweigen breathed out, a long sigh of tiredness and release, and reached for her hand. She closed her fingers tight within his palm and he felt her short nails sharpen against the skin.

★　★　★

'Schweigen's here, isn't he?'

Gaëlle's mouth clenched, sullen with resentment. Here they were, June almost over, the beaches swollen with early tourists and holiday-makers, the Faith shelved, the Lübeck trip fading, all the interviews and reports analysed, typed up, filed and recorded on disc, hard copy in the dossiers and the information downloaded on to the office M-Drive. The trail had gone dead, and yet, behold the apparition of André Schweigen, confident, aggressive, spotted swaggering across the car park. The Judge got up, stretched and walked to the window. She looked down into the street, fixing the spot where he had stood. She emerged from the short night of five hours' sleep limber and subtle as a cat. Gaëlle glared at her loveliness, the sleek black wedge of hair, her olive legs and flat, black classic shoes.

'So? What's he doing here?'

This time the rebellion escaped from Gaëlle's carefully policed intonation, and the Judge swivelled round, ready to cuff her Greffière's multi-pierced ears.

'He has fresh evidence on the case, Gaëlle. I know you don't like him, but watch your tongue.'

The affair between Schweigen and the Judge was never mentioned or acknowledged, and this silence rebounded like an echo between the two of them, as if they were two stone cliffs with an abyss below.

'Oui, Madame le Juge. We are the servants of Isis, sworn to obey Her commands.'

The Judge laughed out loud at this demure, but calculated piece of insolence, and tapped the top of Gaëlle's vast and yellowing computer.

161

'To work, my girl. Anything on the pseudo-Greek guru's personal accounts?'

'Not yet. Interpol are sending me a complete printout.'

'Fine.'

'Shall I disinter the Faith?'

'Not yet. We'll wait for Schweigen's call.'

This came soon enough. Just before ten o'clock Schweigen rang direct from the counter at Goldenberg's.

'Dominique? Would you reassure Monsieur Goldenberg that he is not breaching any sort of confidentiality if he tells me exactly what he engraved on the golden locket the late Madame Laval presented to her daughter, before she arranged her departure to the stars? I don't want to bother with a warrant for a bon de commande.'

A voluble protest from the besieged jeweller could be heard in the background.

À ma fílle bien-aimée
(To my beloved daughter)
Maríe-Thérèse
Suís-moí
(Follow me)

The oval locket had contained a recent laughing photograph of Madame Laval, digitally enhanced and then cut down to size. The loving message whose meanings spread outwards in ripples of possibility had been carefully engraved on the secret cavity inside. The Judge smoothed out the bon de commande and gazed at the handwritten words. Then she looked up, scowling at Schweigen's triumphant defiance.

'André, this proves nothing whatever.'

He ignored her. 'Will you summon the girl for an interview or shall we go up to see her?'

These were his alternatives. The Judge hesitated for a moment.

'Gaëlle? Can you raise the Domaine Laval on the telephone. I'll arrange a brief meeting this morning if possible.' She rounded on Schweigen. 'I imagine that you are driving back to Strasbourg tonight? Yes? Good. Then we'll take both cars. The Domaine is on your way.'

'I'm coming too,' snapped Gaëlle, who had felt excluded long enough.

8

Persephone's Double

They skimmed the suburban villas spouting from
the red earth and rose up towards the vineyards
that pulled away from the city in precise and
everlasting green rows. Some fresh souches,
strung along wires, gleamed thin and green, their
roots clear of weeds, with a young rose planted at
the end of every row. The roses functioned as the
early-warning system against odium, mildew and
black rot. The Judge loved the rhythm of the year
in the vineyards; the pruning in January, spraying
the plants with sulphur in the early spring, when
the narrow roads became downright dangerous
as the great green machines, like elongated
moving croquet hoops, trundled along between
the flowering ditches. The early-summer landscape threw all its remaining moisture into a sea
of white flowers and clouds of red roses,
trumpeting the rich time of ripening green
before the coming of the great heat and sagging
leaves. The weather counted for everything. Pray
for rain in May and June, then a boiling summer
with the odd mild thunderstorm, no hail, please
God, no hail, and a warm September right up to
the vendanges, and the jubilant arrival of the
seasonal workers; they were Spanish when she
was a girl, now Poles and Romanians trudged
down the steep rows, gathering in the harvest.

164

Here they come, sometimes entire families, all ages, shouldering the great red plastic buckets and refusing to slacken their pace on the stony red earth of her father's land, and his father's before him. Her childhood had followed this rhythm, and she would never have left the family estate had she been born the eldest son.

They paused in the olive groves to make sure that Schweigen was still behind them.

'Your parents grow olives, don't they, Gaëlle?' The Greffière was sitting beside her, mute and truculent, rattling her jewellery like a gladiator's weapons.

'Yes. Et alors?'

'Did you help with the ramassage when you were little?'

'I had to. We all bloody well had to. They made me work in the olive groves and I hated it. I hated being stuck in that tiny village, where everybody knows everything about you. I shall never live in the country again. Ever.' Gaëlle gazed at the vines and groaned.

The Judge stifled her laughter and concentrated hard on Schweigen's blue Clio speeding behind them beside a line of swaying cypress trees; these looked rickety and overweight, bulged into one another and loomed over the road. She glanced at Gaëlle, and amusement transformed into affection; the Judge hoped that she had never worn her heart upon her sleeve with such obvious and unselfconscious charm. Gaëlle would be no good as a judge; when she was angry she glowered, when she hated people she told them so, and then proclaimed all her

165

reasons, while her death's head symbols glittered with aggression.

The Domaine Laval swept upwards across the glossy slopes, long shimmering rows of vines glistening in the windy sun. The house faced south-west; they caught sight of the façade for a moment as the Judge pulled up the narrow road towards the iron gates. The buildings gathered together, unpretentious, but massive, great walls of fortress stone and glowing red tiles, the windows often narrow, shuttered. The roofs, recently repaired using a mixture of old and new tiles, tricked the eye, so that it was difficult to guess which slope had been entirely resurfaced. Cypress trees nuzzled the walls, dark against the glowing stone. The wealth of the Lavals lay before her, in the long red slopes of their terroir, and the stony red earth that had been cultivated, tended and loved for thousands of years.

DOMAINE LAVAL
VIGNOBLES DU LANGUEDOC
VENTE DIRECTE
VIN EN VRAC

The symmetrical cross of Languedoc at the heart of the family crest completed the sign and appeared as the label on their bottles. The red wines won prizes, but connoisseurs bought the rarer sweet white wines from the higher slopes. The gates stood open and the roar of agricultural motors thumped towards them, then sputtered and receded. Two Dutch cars, the sun roofs half open and buzzing with trapped insects, occupied

166

the yard. The dogs, laid out on the concrete, raised their heads, then slumped back twitching beneath the soft ministering hum of fattened flies.

The arched stone entrance to the vast caveau rose up directly before Gaëlle and the Judge, and on the right stood the smoky glass doors to the offices; this was the yard, upon which the house turned its back. The immense walls of the cellars were two metres thick, the roof constructed of domed stone like a cathedral. The Domaine's working buildings crouched against the hill and a large part of the deep storage cellars tunnelled underground, so that the temperature within remained at 18°C, winter and summer. Every known form of credit card, spattered like bunting down the frame, decorated the main office doors and inside lurked the various millésimes, displayed in gift boxes upon a row of barrels. Someone was in the barn, hosing down a trailer, singing.

The Judge parked next to the Dutch, peered into the office and waved at the woman tempting her tourists with tiny gulps of wine in smart glasses, also available in gift boxes, engraved with the family crest.

'Myriam!' she mouthed.

'Excusez-moi!' The other woman bounded through the glass door and hugged Dominique.

'Madame le petit Juge! Are you here to see Marie-T?' She stared at Gaëlle, whose murderous expression intensified when Schweigen appeared in the yard. 'Mon Dieu, le Commissaire. That won't go down well. I ought to tell you, not after what happened in February. He hasn't been back since.'

Schweigen was climbing out of his car. The Judge raised her voice. She knew perfectly well what had happened in February, but decided to make use of the debacle.

'What went wrong before? No one's told me in any detail.'

'Tell you later,' hissed Myriam, looking anxiously first at Schweigen and then at the Dutch, who were helping themselves to another swig from a bottle worth over three hundred francs. 'But Marie-T was expecting to see you, only you. And she wants to talk. Only to you. But — ' Schweigen loitered on the edge of their conversation. Myriam shrugged, gave up and raised her voice. 'Go round to the front. You know the way. Give them a call when you get to the steps.'

The Judge nodded and marched off with her Greffière clamped to her heels like a blood-hound.

'Gaëlle? Do you know exactly what happened?'

'Oh yes. I'm sure I told you. Schweigen came here with his thugs. There was probably a punch-up. And they got thrown out. He made the Composer sound like the aggressor in his report. But I bet it was fifty/fifty.' Gaëlle managed an evil smirk. She got out her notebook, ready to record the next ugly scene. 'How do you know Myriam? Is she your spy in the house?'

'Not exactly. We went to school together.'

Schweigen joined them, took off his jacket and rolled up his sleeves. The Judge turned on him, fur bristling. 'André, keep this civil and courteous. Let me do the talking. Marie-T is only seventeen and we'll get more information out of her by being kind and listening.'

Myriam hovered, gesticulating, just inside the office door. The Judge smiled back as they turned the corner.

★　★　★

She had danced with Myriam at the New Year's Ball, here in the Great Hall at the Domaine Laval, twenty-five years ago. Those were the rich days when the old man, Bernard Laval, her father's friend and hunting companion, still ruled as master of the Domaine. Mademoiselle Marie-Cécile Laval blossomed, playing her part as the elegant older daughter, recently married, inheritor of the greater part of her father's wealth; her beauty ogled, envied, admired, the woman every young girl at that New Year's dance had wanted to become. She was the first to take the floor after dinner when the musicians struck up, nestled in her father's arms. But no one else stood up to dance, despite the voluble encouragement of everyone over fifty still installed at the tables or standing smoking in the bar. The boys, all wearing white ironed shirts, proved too shy to stand up with any of the younger girls, and so Dominique Carpentier bowed to her friend, serious as a chevalier come a-courting, and Myriam, resplendent in a flowered dress sewn up at home, for no money ever ran spare for impractical clothes, tucked her hair behind her ears, blushed, and then offered up her slender waist to her partner's nervous grasp. They whirled away across the old stone floors, intoxicated with champagne, woodsmoke, the smell of pine cones blazing in the grates, breathless, giddy, delighted. When the boys plucked up courage and sauntered towards them the girls were off, laughing, spinning, taunting, teasing, their skirts flared and their faces glamorous in the firelight. And the old men and women clustered on the benches clapped and shouted at their audacity — Dominique Carpentier, the boyish clever one in spectacles, and Myriam, just sixteen, whose full lips and breasts pleased the old ones. Here was a girl full of promise and sensual opulence, a foreshadowed future overflowing with love and children. The Carpentier girl will never marry. She has some other work to do in this world. And now the two gazed at one another through glass, one woman cheerfully wed these past ten years and mother of three, working for the Domaine where she once danced, and the other, solitary, inflexible, stalking her quarry through the vineyards of her childhood.

★   ★   ★

The little party of three rounded the corner of the house. The vines surged like a green wave almost to the bottom of the steps. A narrow grassy path, now burned back and browning in anticipation of the great heat, delivered them to the main entrance. Huge pottery vats overflowing with red geraniums topped the stone balustrades. The long terrace stood in shadow, sheltered by an orange-and-white-striped electric awning, which protruded from the medieval walls like a grotesque decorated tumour. At the far end where the terrace circled the house and two solid doors gave access to the kitchens, the table was already laid for lunch, three places, real white starched napkins laid across the plates, lovingly encircled with engraved silver rings.

'Est-ce qu'il y a quelqu' un?' called the Judge, leading the attack. 'Marie-T? C'est Dominique Carpentier.'

The salon remained dark with shadows, all the shutters blank against the sun. Is there anybody there? The Judge began to climb the steps.

The Composer loomed suddenly above them, a terrible apparition, his unsmiling face and white hair as arresting and eccentric as that of the disturbed Count, discovered lying in his native earth.

'Bonjour, Madame Carpentier. We are expecting you, but not your companions.' He stepped into the bright sun and blocked their advance. His face clenched against the glare; he nodded at Gaëlle, but scowled at Schweigen.

'This isn't a social call, Monsieur Grosz,' snapped the unwelcome Commissaire, 'and we haven't come to see you.'

'I am Mademoiselle Laval's godfather and legal guardian. I will not have her interrogated,

171

especially not by you, Monsieur le Commissaire. You may remain, Madame Carpentier. But I must ask your Greffière and Monsieur Schweigen to leave at once.'

Impasse. The Judge made a snap decision.

'Very well.' She turned around so that the Composer could not read her face and flung all her persuasive intelligence into a long hard stare at Gaëlle and Schweigen. If there hadn't actually been a punch-up in February a real fight seemed inevitable now. Back down, André, for God's sake, back down. This is my decision, and I will take the consequences.

'Gaëlle, guide Monsieur le Commissaire back to the village. You know the way. I'll ring you at your parents' later on and pick you up on my way back.'

Schweigen opened his mouth to object. The Judge raised both her eyebrows. Schweigen muzzled himself with a massive shudder, but held his ground. Va-t'en André! Mais vite! The sweat was running down both sides of his clamped jaws. He turned without a word and rampaged back down the steps and round the corner of the house. Gaëlle lingered; anger rising like a red tide from her collarbone stained the side of her throat in a glut of blood. Stand-off. The Greffière is the recorder. Her juge d'instruction should not conduct formal interviews without her recorder. The young woman would not be dismissed.

'Gaëlle?' prompted the Judge.

'We are the servants of Isis, sworn to obey Her commands,' snarled the Greffière and bolted.

The Composer intervened as she stormed off down the steps.

'Isis? What does she mean? What's she talking about?'

'Gaëlle is teasing me a little,' smiled the Judge.

This was so clearly not the case and the menace of Isis so obviously offered as an outraged insult that the Composer threatened to pursue the vanishing Greffière. He glared, hesitated and then set off after the girl. What on earth did he intend to do? Box her cheeky ears with all their pierced studs and cuffs? The Judge touched his arm gently and stopped him in mid-stride, and it was this gesture, unpremeditated, peculiarly intimate, which transformed the space between them. He turned to face her and looked straight into her eyes, past her glinting lenses, past her redundant diplomatic smile. Suddenly the Judge questioned her own judgement. Why had she decided to remain alone with this man? She remembered the weight of his hands on her shoulders, and a vivid, bitter taste rose in her mouth; she heard the stifling intensity of Wagner's strange music, sensed the tears pouring down her cheeks. The Composer's face unravelled into a mass of indecipherable lines, and she knew he was remembering the same things. Then she saw something else in his eyes; an electric attention, not to her role as the Judge, but to her, Dominique Carpentier, and to her alone. She caught her breath and sucked out the dry taste from under her tongue. The Composer relaxed and bowed to her, ushering her back up the steps, returning her smile at last.

173

His whole face changed when he smiled, as if the dictator's mask peeled back, revealing another man, one anxious to conciliate and to charm.

'Marie-T and I were speaking of you last night. I wanted to see you again. Very much. But how to approach you? I couldn't think of an excuse. And then — pouf! — it happens like magic. Three months go by and we are thousands of miles apart and then you ring up to say that you are coming. I am delighted. Marie-T thinks I have rubbed the lamp three times. Will you have lunch with us, Madame Carpentier? We were hoping you would stay to lunch.'

He guided her into the cool interior. She had passed over the threshold.

The walls of the Domaine were also two metres thick and the perceptible drop in temperature veiled her like a shroud of muslin. She was Judith stepping into Duke Bluebeard's castle. Had she ever entered this salon on her childhood visits? She remembered the steps and the timeless vats of red flowers, but not this shaded space. The old wooden floors, polished honey smooth, proved hard to negotiate. Her feet encountered a rug, and looking down she saw a dim red expanse of darkness. The shutters remained closed tight against the heat. All around her massive dark cupboards, two chests shining with polished darkness, uncushioned eighteenth-century chairs, their dark seats looming from the dim walls; the room breathed darkness, square blocks of dark rimmed with gold jostled on the walls, but so dark that no

174

subject could be discerned. She could make out a lamp and a writing desk. A telephone. A sofa draped in dark rugs. A low table with a white vase, and she could smell the lilies, rising pale in the darkness. And then she saw something that she remembered: a large stone egg, calcified and immovable, an egg abandoned by the dinosaurs. A small cache of these eggs had been discovered on the estate decades ago and now formed part of the distinctive marketing image. Madame Laval designed a new label for the white wines with the eggs just beneath their name and the children had named it their Vin Dinosaure. She reached out and fingered the stone egg.

'I remember this. It's always been here.'

'I wish I could remember you. Everybody else does. You came to the dances with your parents, didn't you? I can remember your father very well. You were famous for leading off the dancing. Myriam tells me you always chose the prettiest girl in the room. And her husband says that it was always Myriam. Marie-T remembers you with awe. You frightened them all rigid with your cleverness. Let me get you an apéritif. We have un peu de tout. Un petit muscat?'

His careful, hesitant French gave her the advantage and the illusion of security. As the subtle, darkened room took shape around her, the Judge settled into a high-backed leather chair and set down her briefcase, which now seemed charged and dangerous. The tiny box from Goldenberg's and the shining Christmas paper lurked like living creatures inside their plastic prison. I have to bring them out. I have to mention these terrible things. The oblivious Composer was cracking ice cubes and outlining his summer schedule.

' . . . so I will not be very far away from you. We are performing at the Festival in Aix and I am conducting three performances of *Aïda* at the theatre in Orange. We are to have real elephants. Yes, I can promise you hundreds of naked slaves, real elephants and for the execution scene — real sand. Imagine that! Now, would you like some ice?'

'How do you execute someone with sand?' The Judge stared at him, mystified.

'Ah, I forgot that you don't know the opera. Somehow I assume that you know everything I know. The lovers are buried alive at the end. We can use the Roman theatre to good effect. It is open-air, as you know — an odd booming acoustic. But the sand is very easy to recycle. We are building a cavern like a tomb at the front of the stage and we will bury the structure in real sand.'

'Buried alive?' The Judge shuddered.

'Verdi has some wonderful ideas.'

The Judge sensed that she had lost control of the conversation and cleaned her glasses carefully. When she looked up someone else had entered the room. A tall pale girl, fragile as a fresh shoot in a faint green dress, softly closed the door and came straight towards her. The Judge stood up. She had last seen Madame Laval's daughter cowed in black at her mother's side, a child, anxious not to bawl or sniff, clutching her white rose. The child still lingered in the young woman's shy glance, her bent head. She walked straight up to the Judge, who was startled to find herself the smaller of the two, then bent her face to be kissed, as if the Judge was an intimate friend of the family.

'Bonjour Madame Carpentier, merci d'être venue.'

The Judge faltered, speechless. Here was Persephone's double; a young girl, uncannily like Myriam at the age of seventeen, slender, cautious, re-emerging from Pluto's kingdom. The Judge's eyes widened as she stared into the past. Here was the girl she had once loved, restored to her at last, with the promise of eternal spring. She had planned a formal interview; her now discarded strategy had taken Marie-T's youth and disturbing bereavement into consideration, but had followed a more restrained and austere script. The girl began apologising.

'I'm really sorry that Friedrich asked Monsieur Schweigen to leave. It must have seemed very rude, and it wasn't his fault, it was mine. You see, last time, when he came in February, he kept asking me questions I couldn't answer. And he spoke so loudly. I started crying and couldn't stop. He must think I'm feeble-minded. And I'm not at all really. I miss Maman so much. I know she's happier where she is, but every day I want her here.'

The Composer stroked the girl's head gently.

'Don't take on so, ma petite, I'm sure Madame Carpentier understands.'

The girl slid her hand into the Composer's

177

giant paw and squeezed his finger. Then she stretched out the same hand to the Judge as if she was claiming her role as the link between them. The Judge accepted the girl's warm grasp and rapt seriousness. She imagined Schweigen yelling at this fragile, soft face and felt a ripple of indignation. As a silent rebuke to her brutal, absent colleague she lowered her voice.

'I'm sorry that Monsieur Schweigen alarmed you. I'm sure he thought that he was only doing his job.'

A bell chimed far away beyond the closed doors, across the shining wooden surfaces, through the darkened rooms.

'Bring your drink with you, Madame Carpentier. We always eat on the terrace.'

The vile striped sunshade had managed to spawn another on the dark side of the mas. The Judge noticed that they had been recently installed and were electrically powered; Marie-Thérèse registered the Judge's sceptical glance and apologised for these concessions to modernity.

'Maman would never have tolerated them. We always used to have a big white sunshade. I don't like them. I said so to Paul. Do you remember him? My elder brother? He had these put up a month ago when he was down from Paris. He's very cross about the continuing investigation. It means we can't sort out the inheritance. Monsieur Schweigen was very short with him. He just said, 'Le criminel tient le civil en état.' Basta! You have to wait.'

'Did you know that Friedrich is my godfather?

178

Yes, godfather to both of us. He held me in my little white shawl when I was baptised. Your uncle wasn't the curé then; it was his predecessor. Do you remember Père Michel? Your uncle has fourteen parishes to run now. And there are only two priests at the presbytery. I think the Church should ordain women, don't you? Maman thought so too. After all, we have women judges, why not women priests? Do sit here, then you can see the vines. They are wonderful in all seasons, don't you think?'

They sat down in wind and shadow. The red dust rose up in little clouds at the roots of the vines, that green sea, stretching away into the white glare of midday. The Composer waited until both women were seated before settling himself between them at the head of the table. The Judge noticed the silence. All the tractors and trucks in the yard on the far side of the house no longer trundled away across the slopes or down the drive. All sounds within stilled at midday, even the faint bangs from the kitchen ceased. The Domaine Laval fell under a hushed spell of quiet. Their napkins rustled in the tug of the wind; in the hard light reflected from the green vines and the red earth, the Judge studied both the lunch and her companions. Charcuterie, home-made, gherkins, thinly sliced, tiny onions soaked in vinegar, a green salad now being turned over in the Composer's hands, cold rosé, a dark, rich colour, no label, produce from the estate. Madame Laval's daughter returned the Judge's careful stare with an anxious, ardent confidence. Was everything all right? Would she try the olives? Did she like the pâté de campagne? Maman taught me how to make it. And I'm really no good in the kitchen. The Composer held back. He let his god-daughter talk. This steady flow, laced with polite civilities, appeared to be utterly unguarded, spontaneous, an unerring artlessness which held the Judge at bay.

Who was this calm girl, who had buried her mother not four months before, and now played at being hostess to the investigating judge? Her identity rang like a bell in Dominique Carpentier's imagination. She bore the unlined, haunted profile of Persephone, painted a thousand times, the lost daughter, reclaimed from the under-world, clad in delicate spring green. The Judge scrutinised her features, seeking a likeness to the enraptured dead face of Marie-Cécile Laval, but saw none. This strange fair skin and blonde hair, untouched by the sun, suggested another race altogether, a wandering child from a northern land where distances remained imprecise, the sun low, red and huge, a land where nights never came to pass in summer. The girl raised her eyes to the Judge, her uncanny face drenched with smothered grief. The Judge embraced this unspoken appeal without hesitation. This girl has been given to me, and I will defend her.

Dominique Carpentier felt the Composer's giant hands encircling her glass, pouring her wine, pressing her with simple delicacies. She knew he was watching her; every time she looked up, she met his eye. Although she could not grasp the meaning of his intent absorption in her every comment or gesture she felt neither uncomfortable nor ill at ease. She worried a little that she should have been. He did not appear hostile, but the very lucidity of his attention glittered with purpose. For the first time the Judge registered what manner of man stood before her. Were he asked a direct question, it would never occur to him to lie. Had she been too cautious, too oblique in her earlier interrogation? Most of the prophets and gurus she interviewed were quacks, charlatans and frauds, men on the make. Their motives were financial or venal — or both. Lying became as natural as breathing; often they had completely lost their grip upon the truth and raved on before her, convinced that they too saw aliens descending from heaven alongside their disciples. Very few, apart from the reincarnated Goddess Isis, proved to be certifiable, dangerous lunatics. The Composer did not fit into any of the categories under which she filed her usual suspects.

Marie-T stood up to clear the plates. No, no, you stay there and talk to Madame Carpentier, the Composer insisted. He disappeared into the house and returned with a giant platter of seafood, oysters, moules, bigorneaux, cushioned in ice and surrounded by glistening chunks of fresh lemon. Had they been preparing this feast all morning, in her honour? Not possible. Gaëlle had rung the Domaine shortly after ten. The Judge's astonishment must have risen to her face because the Composer leaned forward, his smile gloating and boyish.

'Once we heard that you were coming — you should have seen the activity. The kitchen revved into top gear. Panic in the household. *The Marriage of Figaro!* Act Two. Myriam drove down to town like a racing demon to hunt for the oysters. For you — nothing less than the fatted calf!'

Marie-T glowed with pleasure and rubbed her long hands together. The midday shadows rippled up and down her skirt as she rose to pour more wine. The Judge limited the girl's generosity to half a glass and surveyed them both in suspicious disbelief. What is this? What does this mean? Am I being courted and bribed? The Composer covered a thin slice of bread with a fine layer of butter and presented it to her as a gift.

Dominique Carpentier had presided, stony-faced, at a sufficient number of interviews with deluded maniacs, con men and criminals to recognise her antagonists. Her judgement remained shrewd, unclouded, cold. She saw two things in this man's strange lined face and extraordinary blue eyes: the desire to give her pleasure, and a passionate attention to something private and invisible, hidden in the depths of her. He sought her good opinion, yes, but he was also listening, listening carefully to the shifting depths of her feelings and reactions, as if he could hear the currents seething far below the polished surface of her sealed face. And yes, he was watching her, anticipating her needs, retrieving her napkin, worrying that the sun was creeping across the old tiles towards her, lowering the appalling sunshade, and laughing as it twitched and jerked, but he was always listening, listening to her with a disinterested intensity that took her breath away.

When they had finished their coffee Marie-Thérèse handed the Judge her vital opportunity to redeem the time and pursue her abandoned investigation.

'Have you seen the garden since Maman transformed it completely? It now looks quite different — after ten years of work and a new irrigation system. She began rebuilding the garden when I was a little girl. I remember the brambles smothering the cherry tree. Oh, it was a beautiful place even then. Like a secret jungle. I love sitting out there now; it's where I feel closest to her.'

The Judge couldn't remember any garden at all near the house of the Domaine Laval. Beyond the yard with the caveau were the wine cellars, cut back into the soft rocks. The dry riverbed lay below the pinède at the foot of a barren escarpment, and the little Gothic chapel built above the vault, which she had once fixed in her binoculars, stood further away, on the edge of the vines at the end of a rough track. On her left the vines swept down the great slopes, vanishing into bright sunlight and symmetrical purple distances. Marie-Thérèse registered her puzzled frown.

'Did you never go into the garden? Even when it was all overgrown? Oh, then you must come. Please do.'

They stood up.

'I will wait for you here, Madame Carpentier,' said the Composer, settling among the bleached cushions on one of the cane chairs and apparently proposing to survey the vines. 'The garden is Marie-T's treasure. She will be the best person to show it to you.'

9

Green Thought

They passed into the house and down a cool corridor with silent doors to the right and left. At the far end the Judge saw an oblong square of bright light. A cool rush of air, sucked out of the dark caverns in the house, swept stealthily towards this distant white space. Marie-T held out her hand, childish, confiding.

'Mind, there are always old boots and gardening tools in the corridor. Maman's things. I can't bear to clear them up.'

She clasped Dominique Carpentier with a simplicity and tenderness, which startled and moved the Judge; this girl too was an Israelite in whom there was no guile, and here was her naked demand, to be recognised and loved. Together they stepped carefully towards the light. Suddenly they traversed a vast cold space. By now the Judge was used to the cavernous emptiness of the Domaine, but here she paused and looked around. The giant fireplace yawned black and void, empty of grates, logs, fire irons. The bare walls soared upwards into darkness. There were windows facing south, tightly shuttered. She felt the smooth uneven cold of the flagstones oozing through her soft leather soles. This must be the Great Hall. Her companion paused and turned; Marie-T's face gleamed like a pale oval portrait in the gloom.

'Yes, this is where my grandfather always held the New Year's Ball. The orchestra sat up in that gallery at the other end. We still call it the hayloft. I think this used to be the barn when the mas consisted of nothing but farm buildings.'

They stood side by side in the hushed cold.

'I danced here. With Myriam.'

'Would you dance with me?' The jealous smallness of the voice emerged not from a woman, but a child. The Judge peered up at Marie-T, startled. Then she laughed.

'But of course.' The Judge bowed before the pale sad face and held out her arms.

'Can you waltz? Remember — your grandfather was a gentleman. We weren't allowed to rock and roll. We had to dance like ladies.'

The Judge watched Marie-T smother her surprise. The girl stood ready to be placed in position, like a stiff, musical doll about to dance on top of an antique wind-up box.

'I lead,' commanded the Judge.

And there in the cool and massive dark of the empty hall she swept the girl off in a huge silent arc beneath the bare musicians' gallery, past the dark stacks of chairs and the great dusty drapes which rose almost to the roof, and then fell in swathes of moth-ridden velvet to the stone floor. They crossed a solid blade of white light flung down from one unshuttered square just beneath the eaves, which sliced the flagstones like a spotlight. Dominique Carpentier suddenly identified the radiance on her partner's face. Marie-T had seen her dance before, and had longed to be chosen.

The moment passed. They slithered to a halt, laughing, embarrassed and a little out of breath.

'It's much easier to keep time with the orchestra.' The Judge smiled in the darkness. 'We'll have to practise. Now show me your garden.'

She found herself at the top of a long flight of stone steps with large pots on either side to protect anyone descending from falling over the mossy rim. They were now at the back of the house. She felt the heat on her head and shoulders, but below her nestled a damp green space, filled with colour, small spiky palms, and the scent of syringa in blossom. The garden lay between the great medieval foundations of the old mas and the cliff itself; a narrow space, sunny but sheltered, drenched in running water and vast damp leaves, oozing green. The summer colours of Languedoc, both the houses and the earth, are hard and red: umber, ochre, burnt sienna. The greens too stand solid, full vines shading the early grapes, the dark masses of pinède rattling with cicadas, and the whisper of fallen pine needles, which form a brown carpet beneath your feet. By midday you hear nothing but the clatter of cigales, but here in the garden against the soft green silence they made a different music, a gentle rustle, proclaiming their presence like a greeting.

She was standing on a stone path in the marbled light beneath a cherry tree spangled with ripe fruit. Marie-T reached up and plucked a handful of dark-red cherries. They stood side by side, sucking the fruit and spitting the stones into their palms; the Judge examined each façade in turn. There was apparently no way out other than the way they had just come. To her left she noticed an old stone wall, taller than a man, with several pear trees carefully tended and pruned on espalier, stretched out in full sun. Two smaller apricot trees, more recently planted, the golden fruit small, still unripe, pushed outwards away from the wall. Where did it end? A giant mass of wild acanthus masked the point where the wall encountered the cliff. The leaves spread out like dark green skirts, clinging to the red earth and the rising rocks. They walked forwards into the lush, damp world. The Judge heard water, and the sound of water falling into water; all the foliage appeared to breathe, as the garden reposed in the midday heat, animate, sleeping. The huge cherry tree dominated the core, but the Judge recognised olives, lemons, manda-riniers, shimmering in the sun. To her left was a small white summer house, governed by a mature wisteria, whose serpent trunk had reclaimed the fragile wrought-iron structure and engulfed its decorated trellis. The flowers were long over, and a drifting mat of dried petals shimmered on the floor. Whoever had planted the garden loved white blooms and strong scents. They sauntered through an archway of opulent jasmine and white roses. The jasmine blotted out every other fragrance for a moment, but once they were clear of the pergola another scent dominated the air, sweet, stifling, odd.

'What's that scent?' asked the Judge, curious.

'Datura. Don't you have these in your garden? They do so well in the Midi.'

The long flowers drooped in massed bunches, extended tubular blossoms, like an orchestra of trumpets at rest. Many were ivory white, but others were painted in strong colours, yellow, orange, gold. Marie-Thérèse gently lifted one of the flowers and the scent flooded upwards into their faces.

'The other name is Trompette du jugement. Isn't it strange to think of Judgement Day as colourful and beautiful? But Maman said it would be so. The painted sculptures in the church are all bubbling vats of damned naked people. I used to find them horrible and frightening.'

So this was her mother's garden: a quiet, overflowing paradise of drenched white scents. They approached the cliff and a small pool into which the stream dropped. Tiny ripples undulated outwards against the green rocks. The bamboo planted round the pool on the shady side had begun to proliferate out of control. The Judge noticed new shoots pushing up into the rough grass. A giant bank of arum lilies, odourless but intense, clustered on the sunny side of the pool; their leaves formed a massive green darkness against the white. The women sat down on a stone bench amidst the shadowy bamboo. The Judge removed her glasses for a moment; all that she could see was hunched masses of green and white. Marie-Thérèse leaned forwards and stirred the pool, the angel churning the waters. As she did so the Judge

189

noticed a small golden oval on a fine chain that escaped from her dress collar. This was the moment to speak, exploding in sunlight before her. She reached out and caught the shining necklace in mid-air.

'Marie-T, is that the gift your mother left for you last Christmas?'

She had no idea what reaction to expect, but the girl smiled, undid the chain and handed the trinket to the Judge with the same ardent candour that characterised her every gesture.

'Yes, it is. It opens like this. Look, here's the catch. And that's the last photograph I have of Maman. It was taken in November, on my seventeenth birthday. She looks so happy, don't you think?' The girl leaned over the open locket in the Judge's hand and peered at the lost, laughing face. The Judge dared not decipher the tiny inscription. 'At first I couldn't wear it. It was as if the thing burned my throat. I was too angry and unreasonable. But gradually I understood that I couldn't own her. I couldn't decide for her. Friedrich is a great help. I talk to him all the time, every day. I try to see things as he does, but I don't always succeed. He loved her so much, as much as I do.'

The Judge sat very still, cold all over, in the unimaginable space that had opened up before her. She had no need to win this girl's confidence or manipulate her trust. Marie-Thérèse simply opened her heart, artless, confiding. The Judge tensed on her cold seat, shifty and culpable; for the first time in her life she doubted her own ethics of interrogation. Her

190

interpretation of justice required her to occupy the moral high ground with irreproachable integrity at all times. This meant that there was never any room for doubt; she was the white knight with the drawn sword who galloped among the heathen dispensing light, justice and righteousness. Now she had joined the fantastical duke of dark corners, who spent his time conning gullible maidens into intimate confessions. She went on, never raising her voice.

'Did you know what was going to happen?'

'No, or I would have begged her not to leave us. But the people who died with her were her closest friends. Her inner circle. I knew them all well. So did Friedrich. They were always here. Visiting. We went on holidays together.'

'And did you know that they were all members of the Faith?'

The girl shuddered a little, then, twisting the golden chain in her hands, she caught the Judge's arm and drew closer.

'No, no, not exactly. Or at least I did know that they were part of — or maybe shared — something important and enormous. That's what hurt most.'

The tears were overflowing now.

'She shut me out. I was excluded.'

The Judge put her arm around Marie-T's shoulders and squeezed her gently. The girl fished out a tissue from a hidden pocket in her dress and blew hard.

'I'm sorry. It really is better now. I don't mind talking about her.'

'When did she give you this gift?'

'Christmas Eve. At the chalet. We always have the presents with champagne before dinner on Christmas Eve.'

She can't drive. She doesn't have her permis de conduire. How did she leave the chalet? And when? Why isn't this in the dossier? How could we have overlooked this detail? According to Schweigen's record Marie-Thérèse was never at the chalet. She was with the Composer in Berlin. And she couldn't explain her mother's card, abandoned in the waste-paper basket. So either Schweigen's initial report is inaccurate; and this girl was lying then — or is she lying now? But, knowing André Schweigen as well as she did, Dominique Carpentier suddenly saw him, four months earlier, dogmatic and overbearing, bullying this frail feather of a girl, insisting that she talk about her mother's suicidal lunacy, when the child was gazing up at him through the deep waters of a well, fathomless and cold, knowing that her mother's corpse still lay frozen in a walled slot, labelled and suspended between death and burial. No wonder she had simply capitulated to grief. And he got nothing out of her but tears. How do I pursue her now? Don't react. Prompt. But push gently.

No caution was necessary; Marie-Thérèse overflowed with information. 'We went off on Christmas Day. Maman looked radiant then. We had soup and jambon and she sat beside me. Bad weather was forecast. She insisted that we set out early.'

'We?' The Judge hardly dared to breathe.

'Friedrich, of course. He took me with him. I

192

adored his New Year concerts. I went to as many as I could. We caught the afternoon plane from Strasbourg to Berlin.'

The Judge forced herself to relax and finger the fresh segments of bamboo. A belligerent hostility towards Schweigen spilled into her mouth. She felt her neck redden. *Am I to do all my own judicial investigations from now on? Every single procès-verbal? As well as the paperwork?*

'So Friedrich — Monsieur Grosz — was with you for Christmas?'

'Oh yes. He's always there. Every year. He has no family of his own. We are his family.'

Cécile. Ring me today. I beg you. Ring me as soon as you can.

'We kept ringing when we saw the storm on television. They were directly in its path. That's why we were so worried when we didn't hear. They rang on Boxing Day to say that they were fine. Many trees down, but they still had electricity when many other people didn't. But then — then we didn't hear. Maman sent me a text. *Bonne Année.* And the lines are always saturated at New Year. But Friedrich seemed to have a presentiment that something was amiss. He kept trying. Up to the last minute he kept trying.'

There was a long humming silence. If the Composer had known about the planned departure surely he would not have kept ringing and ringing? But if he was as close to the Faith as she believed him to be how could he not have known? The Judge could no longer construct the

193

emotional jigsaw before her eyes. The snowy mountains of the Jura seemed far away in the past; they leered at her like apparitions from another world, already extinguished, only faintly remembered.

'Marie-T, look at me. What did your mother mean when she gave you that gift? *Suis-moi?* Why did she say *follow me?*'

The green girl seemed to rise up stronger in her mother's garden when she turned to face her Judge. She drew a huge tight breath.

'Maman? What did she mean? Ah — that I couldn't say.'

Her eyes were red and shining. The Judge registered at once the ambiguity of this reply. For the first time Marie-Thérèse was not being entirely frank; something was being withheld rather than concealed. And now her manner seemed prim and restrained, the good little Catholic girl, entertaining an important guest.

'I'm so pleased that you saw my mother's garden. Shall we go back to Friedrich?'

10

Consequences

There were consequences, of course. The Judge was not the only person bristling with indignation and reproaches. Gaëlle sulked all the way back to the office in breathtaking heat with a ferocity at once disconcerting, unprofessional and just. A dim cloud hung around her heavy metal ears and the Judge was forced to ask every question twice. She rang Schweigen's mobile from the office. He pulled off the motorway, ignored her attempt to describe her private interview with Marie-Thérèse Laval, and began screaming.

'I don't understand you. You sleep with me the night before and then dismiss me as if I meant nothing to you and you don't need me. You go on and conduct your own damned investigation. You aren't kind, Dominique, you aren't fair, you aren't even rational.'

She froze him out.

'When you have remembered your manners, André, send me an e-mail. But don't, I repeat, don't try ringing me back.' And she slammed down the phone. Gaëlle, who had listened in to every word, strolled off to the photocopier, whistling.

The high cool of the office enfolded the Judge as if she were an exhibit in a cabinet, mummified and arranged in orderly calm. She sat very still. This must be Schweigen's first and only affair with another woman; he was possessive as a husband, and as potentially unhinged. He now rang her at least twice a day; his voice clanging down the lines like a distant chorus of howls. The Judge flicked the phone into silence and began to write out a chilly factual account of her encounter with the Composer and his god-daughter, a report so bald and disengaged that the business might as well have been conducted in her office. The judicial narrative was therefore not entirely accurate. Like an old-fashioned anthropologist, lost somewhere on the Dark Continent, she wrote herself out of her research, and ceased to be a presence, influencing her own findings. The occupants of the Domaine Laval emerged as foreigners in their own land, a race observed. But in the days following this encounter, just as the holidays immersed them like a great wave, the supposed foreigners were also on the case.

Marie-Thérèse sent her a brief, warm note, longing to see her again soon. The plea was formal, ardent, heartfelt, as if two currents struggled in the young girl's heart. The Judge read them correctly: the need for secrecy and the longing to tell.

The Composer sent her flowers.

A purple twisted installation of orchids, with copious instructions on their needs and welfare, arrived at her home, arranged on twigs, with their roots sunk in a solution that kept them alive for all eternity. She inspected the strange, exotic shapes with curiosity and suspicion. How had he discovered her private address? Yet, after all, she had seen where he lived in Northern Germany, and perhaps the source was innocent enough — her uncle, Myriam, even her parents could have provided the information. But living flowers? Orchids, whose very shapes appeared obscene? The gesture seemed too intimate. Here she was, trying to inculpate this man, for, at the very least, non-assistance à personne en danger, or at the worst, moral corruption, fraudulent diversion of funds and being an accessory to murder. Yet he courted her with orchids. Their colour, livid and suggestive, took up residence on the kitchen table. She tried not to look at them.

Then the second letter arrived; the second letter addressed exclusively to her.

Dear Madame Carpentier, he wrote
formally in English,
Please forgive me for not writing to you in your language. My French, as you know, is very stiff and limited to arguing with singers and musicians. I will return to the Midi for the Avignon Festival within a week and hope very much to see you again. I realise that our initial meetings have taken place within the strange, sad context of the loss of my friends. But I do not wish this relationship to remain constrained by the legal boundaries of your investigation. I have not ceased to think of you since I saw you standing in my theatre with the tears flooding your face. I could not bear it if our connection were to cease now.

197

I must see you again. Chère Madame, please allow me to visit you, speak to you, face to face.

I remain, your devoted and obedient servant,
Friedrich Grosz

Devoted servant? The significance of this archaic formula was beyond the Judge's English; she was forced to look it up in her dictionary and emerged no wiser or enlightened. Connection? Relationship? They didn't have one. But he was the principal subject of her investigation. She strode round her living room, picking up stray newspapers. Now she crackled with guilt and irritation at her colossal error — I let myself be taken by surprise, indeed almost incapacitated — by an emotional evening at the opera. And this man pounced upon her weakness. Her tears remained a shameful secret. Neither Schweigen nor Gaëlle must ever know. A faint prickle of unease tingled in her fingers as she examined the letter and its envelope. The German stamp, his address in the Effengrube, the Lübeck postmark, his firm, clear hand and the careful, precise folds. She was sought out, cornered. Yet the register of the letter was conciliatory, beseeching. He addressed her as a supplicant, not a master. The power to withhold and deny remained hers, and hers alone. But did it? The letter lay there, flaccid and inert, like a failed magic trick.

Standing alone, drinking a bowl of black coffee in her tidy, silent kitchen, before leaving for work in the brief cool of early day, the Judge's unease erupted and overflowed. She took up the letter and read it once more. In her hands she held a declaration of love from a perfect stranger. She possessed only the power he allowed her to have; he was tracking her down. How could this be sincere? She stood seething with anxiety and uncertainty, both unwelcome sensations, and alien to the Judge. This untoward assault upon her privacy and self-containment unsettled and disturbed her equilibrium, as much as Wagner's music had done, many months before. Yet the Composer's directness disarmed her utterly. She could find no words to reply.

⋆　⋆　⋆

She spent the early evenings of the following week fending off Schweigen's calls and studying the coded guide. Her linguistic experts had produced no key to the blocked signs; the text remained secret and opaque. She concentrated on tiny fragments of the Book that were written in German and Greek; then she recognised the symbol for the sun — Helios. Many sects sought out myths as supporting structures for their invented faiths, and the Judge possessed an extensive research library of gods and legends. Sometimes, buried in the advertising, she found entire chunks of bogus science copied directly from the sources in her office. She contemplated prosecutions for plagiarism rather than mendacious publicity, but confined herself to a few dry comments alongside the parallel passages in her report to the Parquet. Lord, what fools these mortals be. The Judge reached for her illustrated list of sun gods, whose cults were frequently revitalised.

The sun usually figured as the principal and most reliable source of divinity in resurrection mythologies. The Judge took a detached view of the phenomenon; that great disc of exploding hydrogen and helium meant no more to her than any other star; our sun, a single dying star, the force that powers all things and draws all life towards its flaming core. The most popular version of the sun god, who reappeared in her files, year after year, was Ra, also known as Re-Horakhty. The Egyptian deity crossed the sky by day in a boat rather than a chariot, only to be swallowed up by the goddess Nut, and emerge reborn as a scarab beetle on the following morning. His symbol, prominent on the cover of her dictionary of sun gods, represented a winged disc, but he reappeared on the frontispiece in the shape of a man with a falcon's head. Ra. The sun god Ra. She tapped the curved beak of the god with her forefinger. Good evening, Great God Ra, explain your evident connection to the Faith. The ancient Egyptians appeared crucial in some respects. She had marked a carefully drawn tablet covered in hieroglyphs with the actual dimensions noted beneath, which was apparently reproduced in its entirety. The blocked code below must be some kind of commentary, because the hieroglyphs reappeared at intervals throughout the text. Here was a sequence of figures close to the symbol of the sun; this is a saros, the measurement that describes the repeating cycles of the solar eclipse. Eighteen years, eleven days and eight hours, thus each part of the globe has a chance to see a total eclipse, maybe every thousand years or so. Ra's golden eye remained, fixed and staring; his black pupil dilated, vast. And here is a fragment of poetry:

Ja! Ich weiß woher Ich stamme!
Ungesättigt gleich der Flamme
Yes! I know where I began!
Insatiable as flame

The phrase sounded eerily familiar. This is part of something else, something longer. I read this when I was studying philosophy. But who wrote these words? She could not identify the source. She copied out the lines and the two linked coordinates immediately following, then looked up the figures, which were clearly measurements.

Altarf (Mag 3.5) RA 8h 16m 38s Dec 09° 10′ 43″
Sirius (Mag 1.47)RA 6h 45m 15s Dec 16° 43′ 07″

Cancer and Canis Major — the faintest of the constellations and the one containing the brightest star visible in the sky. In what ways are these opposing things significant? How are they linked? The stars in the constellation of Cancer were actually dimmer than one of the deep-sky star clusters, known as the beehive cluster or as

M44, an open cluster of seventy-five stars at the centre of the constellation. We use the stars to calculate distance and time. The stars we see, or think we see, may no longer exist, for the light that brings them to us travels across billions of years. Therefore we are looking directly into the past.

The Judge spread out her astral charts and stood up, the better to gaze at the heavens, now flattened beneath her fingertips. We have only begun to map this endless void, this image of eternity itself, uncharted matter that spans hundreds and billions of light years. It is beyond all our imagining. The Judge inspected the little pool of swirling bugs circulating in the beam of her desk lamp. Her mind balked before infinity, even as she contemplated the Great Wall of Galaxies, some five hundred million light years long, two hundred million light years wide, fifteen million light years deep. She floated outwards between these unimaginable masses of helium, hydrogen gas, and dust spinning out into the massy void; if matter accounts for a mere ten per cent of space then for the most part the universe is simply empty, great chasms of non-being, where nothing is. And the earth was without form and void, and darkness upon the face of the deep. Nothing will come of nothing. Speak. She issued her command out loud, her voice hollow in the warm air.

How is Cancer linked to Canis Major within the philosophy of the Faith? The Romans called the time when Sirius rose before the sun the 'Dog Days', because it was the hottest time of year. She looked up Sirius in the Egyptian calendar. Sirius was Sothus, the god who caused the Nile to flood. Sirius is one of the stars closest to the sun. The sun is supposedly located in Cancer during the summer solstice. The Judge scrabbled through Schweigen's report on the first departure, the mass suicide from the mountaintop in Switzerland. Yes, the 21st of June 1994, Midsummer's Night. All right, but the solstice is sacred to dozens of sects, including the Druids, who are now immensely respectable. She looked up the latest charts. The sun in fact reaches the summer solstice in Gemini. And if all these numbers are just lists of stars, why are they there? It doesn't get me any further if I can't crack the code.

But the Judge had noticed something strange and interesting, which she stored away for future reflection. The Guide had been compiled at different times, before being beautifully rebound by Herr Bardewig's father. Some of the oldest designations for the constellations appeared to be based on Ptolemy's Almagest and the star magnitude system devised by Hipparchus in the second century. But there were more recent twentieth-century designations. And even one or two handwritten annotations containing information that could only have come from the Cassini mission, still under way, and due to reach Saturn's system in 2004. And here was some data clearly credited to the Hubble Space Telescope. Followers of the Faith were still studying the stars and noting all the latest information. But why? Suddenly she found a passage in English, the familiar letters blossomed amidst the code. *Who art thou? That we may give an answer to them that sent us. What sayest thou of thyself? He said, I am the voice of one crying in the wilderness.* 'St John.' The Judge breathed his name softly again and again, 'St John.'

And so the Judge gave up on heavenly bodies, and turned her attention to earthly things: bank accounts. For at last Schweigen had procured copies of the Composer's most recent bank statements and the most recent set of audited accounts in the name of his orchestra. This material, not all of it legally acquired, and therefore inadmissible in court, had just arrived in two huge folders. She skimmed Friedrich Grosz's bank statements, curious, surprised. He was a very rich man. No doubt he had filed those orchids under general expenses. She calculated huge regular payments to the orchestra, which was run as a non-profit-making artistic enter-prise and performed regularly at benefits for excellent causes: typhoons in Bengal, the Iranian earthquake, the widows of a mining disaster in China. She paused over the orchestra's name — *An die Freude*, that means joy — the orchestra of joy. There was no management company, but a benevolent association, chaired by Grosz himself. *An die Freude Freunde* — the friends of joy. The committee met twice a year to receive the forthcoming programmes, travel plans, lists of guest artists and to check the budget. The same names appeared, again and again. The association Secretary played in the orchestra — the first violin. The Treasurer performed as one of their regular bass-baritones, a handsome black man with distinguished features who also made popular commercial CDs, featuring gospel songs (*Swing Low Sweet Chariot*), calypsos (*Jamaica Farewell*), and cover versions of Frank Sinatra's greatest hits (*I Did It My Way*). The profits from all these productions sank straight back into the orchestra's accounts.

If in doubt follow the trail left by hard cash. Follow the money moving silently across frontiers and through unknown cities, seek out the dark accounts headed by acronyms and no human names. The Judge steadied her spectacles, poured herself another glass of still, cold water and set about her long slow task of charting the transfer of money. And it was all there: there before her on the green screen and in the long printouts with serrated edges provided by Interpol. Here are the large sums marked as private donations, bequests exempt from all tax obligations or upon which the orchestra's administration recuperated the tax. These accounts have been approved and cleared. She set out the list of names in both departures and studied Gaëlle's careful double columns: donations made in sterling, dollars, Deutschmarks, Swiss francs. Gaëlle had left each amount in the original currency but translated the sums into French francs and euros so that the Judge could distinguish between contributions that were regular payments and others that appeared as special gifts.

A small flurry of capital sums, often

substantial, leaped out at her; like faint but visible galaxies of stars — 1992, 1993, 1994, 1997, 1998, 1999. She began cross-referencing the amounts passed through the orchestra's audited accounts with the donations and bequests left behind by the suicide dead — the only known members of the Faith. And the truth shone brightly back from the scroll of figures. The anonymous cash donations, like stolen antiques, began to acquire identities, histories and a specific provenance. This was where some at least of the vanished sums of money had come to rest. The orchestra was the hidden host, the financial façade for the Faith; this was their siège social, their legal entity. And at the core of this structure stood the Composer, solid and fixed as the sun in the Ptolemaic universe.

So this is how the whole thing is financed. Look where the money goes. And here a strange surprise awaited her. This is a secret charity; these acts of benevolence and goodness take place in silence and darkness. The money is passed onwards through music to heal the wounds of this world. The Judge had never encountered a sect that was financially above reproach. Someone, somewhere, must be lining his pockets. And so she continued, into the cooler small hours of the early morning, her computer illuminated, checking websites, charities, hospitals, desert clinics, schools, scholarships, foundations dedicated to scientific research, a lifeboat in Norway, helicopter-rescue services, housing, farming, rural development projects. She found a network of names, logical as a labyrinth, to which she now clasped the key. By three in the morning she had garnered one hundred and twenty names, the quick and the dead, a harvest of the educated, privileged elite, powerful, well-placed women and men, all of whom were linked to a curious array of good causes. But the colossal sums that had vanished in the aftermath of the New Year's Eve suicides did not appear and could not be found. She stood up cautiously, closed her eyes and stretched her back; her acumen and energy had drained away, as if the Faith, intent on drawing her into the net, had leeched all her strength. It would soon be day.

She drove home through the glimmering streets, watching the dawn people heading for work. The biblical quotations spattered throughout the Guide now crystallised into a strange maze of significance, a latticework of goodness, accessible to rational intelligence. Take heed that you do not your alms before men, to be seen of them: otherwise ye have no reward of your Father, which is in heaven. Members of the Faith operated like the Masons, their creed a secret temple, dedicated to righteousness and salvation. The Judge stamped on her accelerator and all her plastic water bottles, stowed in the pockets of her car doors, shivered and rattled. I don't believe this, it doesn't add up: a secret society of suicides dedicated to Justice, Truth and Mercy? Something else is here before me, something I can't see. And I can't see it because I am too tired to think. If they want to save this world why are they so anxious to abandon us? What other course are they plotting in the stars? But when thou doest alms, let not thy left hand know what thy right hand doeth. I am God's eye. I wish to see both the left hand and the right.

11

Flamme Bin Ich Sicherlich

She arrived back in the office at eleven-thirty on the following day wearing a straight shift of cream silk, dark glasses with prescription lenses and a broad-brimmed black straw hat. The effect was aggressive, glamorous and eccentric. Her battered briefcase landed amidst the abandoned chaos of the orchestra's accounts with a violent smack.

'Gaëlle,' she snapped in the tone that indicated she had no time for moods or sulks, 'get André Schweigen on the phone for me. I need his linguistic expertise in German to make certain that I understand the tax forms and the audited accounts. We need to speak to someone high up in the Berlin tax office. And we must summon up the Composer once again.'

Gaëlle, on her way to the water cooler in the corridor, bearing a large jug of clinking ice cubes, flung open the door. Her voice, suave and ironic, never missed a beat.

'Summon the Composer? You don't need to. He's already here. I'll leave you to it, shall I?'

And she marched out, rattling her chains, past Friedrich Grosz, who stood framed in the doorway, gigantic, sunburnt, startled to find himself at once expected and announced, when he had clearly been uncertain of his welcome. He bowed and addressed her in French, opening with a sequence of carefully rehearsed sentences.

'Madame Carpentier? I trust I am not disturbing you? I wondered if you would do me the honour of having lunch with me?'

For once the Judge was grateful that she had not yet settled into her working day and was still wearing dark glasses indoors. There was a terrible pause, and both parties hesitated, baffled, embarrassed. The whirling fan above them hummed and clicked. The Judge found herself desperate to escape from the incriminating accounts spattered across her desk and Gaëlle's malicious satisfaction at her discomfiture. She removed her hat and laid it over his name, printed and signed with his own hand, the name that leaped from a dozen documents visible before her.

'Thank you for the orchids, Monsieur Grosz, and yes, I should be delighted to have lunch with you.'

She began to advance upon him so that he was forced to retreat from her office. At the last minute she snatched up her briefcase again. She felt the Book of the Faith glowing inside, like a radioactive brick.

'Did you have anywhere particular in mind?' she asked sweetly.

It turned out that he did.

★   ★   ★

The Composer stowed the briefcase carefully away in the boot of his Mercedes and held the

210

door open: sink down, sink down inside. Two low black leather seats resembled rocket-powered devices for ejecting astronauts if blast-off went wrong, and the folding sunroof had apparently vanished into the carcass of the beast. His white hair swirled about the dark glasses as he drove. She noticed that his cream shirt matched her dress, but that someone had ironed the sleeves into crisper, more elegant folds. She sensed the wind plucking at her tortoiseshell comb and leaned back, clutching her loosening black hair. She had not been driven about in a sports car for well over twenty years. The entire expedition dissolved into an irresponsible and adolescent prank, as if they were skiving off school. The Composer leaned over when they paused at the lights.

'Is the wind too strong? Does it disturb you? Shall I shut the sunroof?'

She heard the gentle inflection in his voice; she could not be mistaken. For one small moment her stomach shrank in bewildered alarm. Lead us not into temptation, but she pushed the sensation aside. This man, with his temper and his fame, his name that means nothing to me, remains my subject, the focal point of my investigation, the creature around whom I extend my web. He must never perceive my intentions. I can withdraw, masked and cloaked, at any time. And yet still she reached, surreptitious, furtive, into her shoulder bag and switched off her mobile phone, thus closing off the safety of the abandoned office behind her. Why had she changed her mind? How did she justify the risk? The thought was precise: this man deserved, at the very least, her full attention.

Dominique Carpentier took her charisma for granted. She turned heads in church when she was seven, adorable in her first communion dress, clutching the great white candle that proved too big for her. Teachers waited for her upstretched hand in class, loving the bright frown of the cleverest child. And the entire assembly in the Great Hall, amidst the winter's dark of the New Year, had paused to watch her dance. She was accustomed to admiration and expected to command. She anticipated winning this intellectual tournament with the Composer; just as she always won everything else.

The land beside the route nationale slipped into great coastal lakes, the shallow masses beyond the airport, spattered with flamingos, and the pegged rows of oyster beds, dark blots against the ruffled blue. The Composer shouted the odd comment across to her, but otherwise watched the road and drove fast. Great convoys of lorries, nose to tail, holiday cars with billowing roof racks, a posse of bikers bound for Spain, all turned up on to the motorway. She saw the green shimmering hill of Sète materialise out of the heat, a murky outline, vague, incorporeal. The Composer knew exactly where he was going. They avoided the port and streets engorged with traffic either side of the canal, nipped past the semi-derelict railways yards and climbed up into the bushy pines amidst the comfortable villas and tiny walled roads above the Église Saint-Louis and the Quartier Haut. The Composer was telling her that the town council planned to extend the esplanade into a huge walkway as far as the beach. She lifted her glasses, rubbed her eyes and tried to remember his most recent bank statements; the Mercedes wasn't new. Did he own several cars? They arrived in front of a peaceful pale-yellow villa in much-watered gardens, bulging with sweet scents and the rhythmic chatter of the cicadas.

'Where are we?'

'The Hôtel Belvédère. It's small, quiet. Full of elderly people who've been coming south on holiday for years. Like myself.' He grinned, a wonderful boyish smile beneath the dark glasses. 'You'll be the youngest person here. You like fish, I hope? The food is fabulous. *Poisson du jour, selon arrivage.* I won't let you eat anything else.'

'Then it's just as well that I like fish.'

The Judge, as a matter of course, noted the number of the car, registered in Montpellier.

'Do you need your briefcase?' He caught her staring at the boot. She shook herself slightly.

'No, I don't think so.'

He took off his dark glasses and fixed her, aggressive and intent.

'Do you want to continue your investigation over lunch, Madame Carpentier? Or may I have the pleasure of your company?' The frightening blue eyes swept over her. She snatched off her own dark glasses and installed her usual black rims; the effect was of a knight's visor snapping shut before the battle, and they faced each other, there on the gravel in the singing shadows, swords drawn.

'Perhaps we had better get one thing clear now, Monsieur. I am here as your guest, but I am still a juge d'instruction and one of the open dossiers on my desk concerns you. You, your friends — dead and alive — your orchestra, whatever connections you may have to the Laval family and this mysterious sect you call the Faith. If you think that I'm going to shelve all that and just enjoy eating fish with you then you're very much mistaken.'

He changed colour and appeared to grow in size, like the Incredible Hulk.

'Sect? You think we're a sect? Like the Christian Scientists? Or the Moonies?'

Dominique Carpentier noted his use of the plural, but her pedantic streak got the better of her.

'The Christian Scientists are not a sect in France and their teachings are mostly very sensible. I suggest that you read Mary Baker Eddy's *Science and Health*. You are confusing them with the Church of Scientology, which has long been subjected to state repression and anti-cult opposition, particularly in the USA. And as for the Reverend Sun Myung Moon's Unification Church, or the Moonies as you call them, they are one of the religious movements who delimit the elements used to define a cult, and in France they are indeed usually described as a sect.'

She delivered this speech with absolute composure, as if she expected him to take notes.

For a moment the Composer glowered at her, rebuffed and enraged. Suddenly he bellowed and shook with a great explosion of laughter.

'I adore you, Madame Carpentier. You are the most extraordinary woman I have ever met.' His face underwent a weather change, and contorted into a snarl. 'But you know that I adore you. Why didn't you answer my letter?'

And now he wasn't laughing. This radical shift of subject, violent as a fist in the chest, disconcerted her completely. The letter! In her passion for his bank statements, she had forgotten the letter. But still, she was quick off the mark.

'You have answered it yourself, Monsieur. You have what you wanted. You are speaking to me now, as you demanded, face to face.'

He began shouting. A row of fascinated faces appeared on the terrace above them, peering through the geraniums.

'I've made it quite clear that I'm in love with you, Madame Carpentier, and I am perfectly happy to say it out loud. And to say it directly to you. You cannot have misunderstood me.' He glared at her, then his features sharpened into a feral scowl, shrewd, knowing. 'You did not. You are far too intelligent. Well then, why are you here?'

The Judge, taken aback by his ferocity, recoiled two steps into the shade of a pin parasol that was being attacked by caterpillars. The tell-tale silk webs smothered many of the branches. Given time, this tree will die. The Composer stood before her, controlling the gravelled space, hands on his hips, his jacket pushed back, his eyes narrowed against the sun.

'Well?' he snapped, 'answer me.'

She recovered herself at once.

'I am conducting an investigation, Monsieur Grosz. And your personal feelings are your problem. Not mine.'

He stood frozen, savage, for a moment; then shook himself and walked round an imagined circle in the gravel. The watchers in the geraniums retreated slightly, but she could still see the audience, awaiting the denouement. The Composer looked at her ruefully, smiled, and bowed.

'Touché, Madame. That is quite true, it is my problem and mine alone. And now I am being very rude. I have started arguing with you before lunch rather than afterwards. Will you ever forgive me?'

He held out his hand. At this point a white-suited waiter, poised at the top of the hotel steps with his mouth open, dared to chip in, seeing that the argument had not actually come to blows.

'Bonjour, Monsieur Grosz,' he squeaked, 'Your table is ready.'

'Ah, thank you, thank you. Madame?'

His hand was still outstretched towards her; the moment sizzled in the heat. The audience in the geraniums leaned forwards — what will she do? And this tiny answered gesture, apparently without any great significance, determined the strange chain of events that followed. For Dominique Carpentier really did consider recuperating her briefcase, calling a taxi on her mobile, and, after a suitable absence, long enough to have eaten lunch with the enemy, pedalling back to her office, and never, ever again allowing herself to speak to this man alone. But what piqued, angered and aroused her, almost in equal measure, were his audacity, his directness and his charm. He still stood before her, his open hand naked as a promise without conditions, another Israelite in whom there was no guile, a man incapable of deceit. She knew, and her sixth sense told her truly, that not only would he never lie to her, but that he was incapable of doing so. And not only to her, but to anyone. In some strange and horrifying way his music, his passions and the Faith were bound to one another with holy cords, 'too intrinse t'unloose'. She was the rodent in the storehouse, niggling at the hidden bonds, overturning the vats, meddling in those rich mounds of grain. And yet, and yet, she would not retreat, could not let go. She held out her hand to him. He drew her across the little distance that remained between them and kissed her fingertips. They stood arranged in sunlight amidst the roar of the cicadas, like a formal composition or a couple about to dance. The faces in the geraniums withdrew, smiling in relief.

'Say you forgive me for fighting with you,' he insisted.

In her haste to contradict him she had changed her glasses; now she was blinded in the glare she felt, once more, at a disadvantage. He still grasped her hand with an intimate intensity that alarmed her. This man conducts his business in public exactly as he would do behind closed doors; he doesn't care who sees us, and anyone may hear. She squinted upwards.

'I do forgive you. But you are on trial, Monsieur Grosz. You have been warned.'

He chuckled and encircled her with one giant arm. She began to wonder how he had fitted into his own car as he rushed her up the steps. The unfortunate waiter was still standing in the doorway, confused and twittering.

'The terrace, Monsieur? With the view? You did say that you wanted the sea view?'

'What if I'd said no to lunch?' muttered the Judge as they were whisked towards champagne and pointed starched napkins.

'Then I'd have eaten my daurade on my own, looked very miserable and got drunk on champagne.'

The elderly couples in the dining room all looked up at the tall, white-haired ogre of a man with the beautiful tiny princess scampering, captured, beside him, for they made an extraordinary entrance into the upper world, like the lost bride and her groom. They sat facing the huge and distant curve of endless blue. The Judge put her dark glasses back on to look at the menu. The entire restaurant kept a close eye upon the strange pair in case they fell to yelling at each other once again. She spotted the Composer peering at her over the top of the wine list. The waiter offered to open the champagne.

'Thank you. We'll open it ourselves in a

218

moment.' He hissed across the table,' Let me order for you.'

'I am used to ordering my own food, Monsieur Grosz,' she bristled back. The neighbouring tables laid down their forks.

'Faites-moi plaisir!' he begged. Then he leaned towards her and whispered, 'Your hair's coming down.'

And indeed it was. Dominique Carpentier shivered like a ruffled bird, dishevelled and in disarray. She started to get up with every intention of withdrawing to the Ladies, but immediately his great hand shot out and closed hot about her wrist.

'Please don't go. Do it here. No one cares. I can't bear to let you out of my sight. I'm afraid you'll vanish.' His voice overflowed with alarm.

The ridiculousness of her situation struck her in the face as she thumped back down into her seat, pulled out her comb and wound her long hair back into its usual black coil. The audience cautiously resumed eating moules, bream, lotte, terrine de poisson, tarte au citron, tarte tatin, and every shade of sorbet. He stared at her, transfixed. She glowered back. He reached for the champagne. The Composer's refusal to conform to any kind of expected behaviour undermined all her plans of attack. Why am I here if I am unable to control the discussion? Who's calling the shots? Is this an acceptable state of affairs? Suddenly she smiled. She could no longer pretend they were strangers.

* * *

'I must tell you what happened in rehearsal last night. We're performing Beethoven's Ninth. A local choir — they're very good — their choirmaster has drilled them to perfection — and my usual soloists. The performance always goes well if it's a local choir: everybody's entire family seated in the audience, willing us to succeed, and the music carries you off in transports of joy. Well, the bass is American, a great big black man with a barrel chest, he's quite wonderful, and as he began — '

Here the Composer forgot himself and began to sing. '*O Freunde, nicht diese Töne* — and all the buttons on his waistcoat flew off and hit the first violins like machine-gun bullets — ping, ping, ping — chaos in the orchestra and the sopranos folded up screeching, laughing like rag dolls!'

'How does he survive in a waistcoat? In this heat?'

'Precisely. Quite impossible. Marie-T has found a solution. We're performing outdoors in the palace courtyard. I've made a fuss about the choir. They have a huge canvas sail above them to stop the sound going up, up, up and vanishing. So it's not at all formal. We don't have to wear evening dress. Marie-T ran up a shirt for him on her mother's sewing machine. Eight hours work, all told. The shirt is all Hamlet sleeves and folds, and the tenor is also wearing a white open-necked shirt. We're not in Berlin or Vienna now. Down here I think we can be more informal.'

He stretched out his arms; the cream sleeves

were turned back and the hair on his forearms shone ash blond.

'Look,' he said, 'this was one of Marie-T's prototypes for the concert shirt.'

Then they talked about Marie-T. The Composer clearly took his role as guardian to heart.

'She finishes her Bac next year. And do you know what she wants to study? Law! And all because of you.'

'Me? I never suggested that to her.'

'You didn't need to do so. It's your example that is so compelling. Marie-T has always wanted to be like you. She saw you dancing when she was a child.'

The Judge merely raised one eyebrow. So Marie-T had said nothing about the strange moment in her grandfather's Great Hall.

'Tell me what you wanted when you were her age. I feel so old when I talk to her. I can't imagine what she feels or how she sees this world. I was born in 1936. Before the war. Can you believe that? I am not even of her parents' generation.'

'But you don't seem old,' reflected the Judge, aloud; she looked up quickly, afraid that she might sound rude.

'I'm delighted to hear you say that, Madame Carpentier. I lie awake, panic-stricken that you might view me as a dinosaur. I am over twenty years older than you. Time doesn't matter to me. But even I am locked in this world.'

He used the verb 'enfermer', which puzzled the Judge. Locked up, shut in, like chickens awaiting the fox. He asked her about her childhood and the Judge recalled the long boredom of her adolescence.

'Well, soixante-huit and the sexual revolution certainly didn't disturb our village.' She smiled. 'I wanted to be a philosopher, like Sartre or Michel Foucault. I certainly didn't think of law. Not at first. And in order to be anything at all I had to leave my parents and my childhood behind.'

She found herself talking about who she had once been, and that small, ferociously ambitious slender girl who loved dancing seemed as remote and lost as the days of embroidered flared jeans, agitprop street theatre, the MLF and *Le Torchon brûle*, glam-rock, the songs of Jacques Brel and revolutionary socialist politics. At first his concentration upon every word disconcerted her, made her hesitate, slow down, but gradually, the quality of his attention, the fact that he was so clearly committing every frown and gesture to memory, and the deep quiet that she sensed, listening within him, calmed her unease. The Composer was a man at peace with himself, for all his explosions and irrational outbursts. It was this that anchored his presence at the table before her. The dining room emptied out behind them and the afternoon breeze tugged at the tablecloth. By the time they rose, full of fish and champagne, her senses were no longer sharpened against his danger. She felt cradled, safe.

'Shall we have coffee in the gardens?'

He held out his arm to her, gallant as a

nineteenth-century prince, and she accepted him without hesitation.

★   ★   ★

The belvédère from which the hotel took its name turned out to be a summer house perched on the last terrace above the main building. A steep flight of damp steps led upwards to the frivolous little cupola, painted with tiny white flowers, surrounded by a verandah. The cane furniture, laden with cushions, suggested a peaceful afternoon snooze in well-fed somnolent heat. A sea breeze ruffled the wisteria strangling the balcony, but before them lay nothing but a giant white haze. Even the sea unfolded into a white glaze of light, as if a veil had descended, cutting them off from the working world. The Judge, clutching her coffee, stretched herself out upon a floral sofa, clearly designed for the frail and elderly. Without warning the Composer leaned over and removed both her shoes. This gesture, which amused rather than annoyed her, gave them the exact measure of the distance they had travelled in two hours. She curled and extended her naked toes in a patch of faded, blustering sun; the wind brushed the soles of her feet. Despite the roar of the invisible cicadas, she became intensely aware of every approaching sound and the distant rhythm of the sea.

He sat beside her, gazing into the light.

'You're unlike most Frenchwomen. You don't wear any paint.'

'I was wearing lipstick this morning,' she

corrected him. 'And as you haven't allowed me out of your sight I haven't had time to touch up my paint, as you call it.'

'Good. Don't. If I'm on trial, you're under arrest. You must understand how greedy I am as far as you are concerned. I have you near me now, for a few precious hours. But you will never have much time for me.'

The sudden sadness in his voice made her look round at him.

'On the contrary, I spend nearly all the time we are apart thinking about you and trying to dig up information on your background, personality, history and career. And the last two hours have amply demonstrated the limits of my methods. I have dossiers full of facts, none of which match the man.'

His delighted roar of laughter shook his huge frame and the chair beneath him shuddered. The white hair fell across his eyes; he flung back his head to shake it free.

'Really? How wonderful! So I've succeeded in disguising my bad temper, autocratic manners and impossible character.'

'Oh, completely.'

They settled into a companionable silence that is the usual hallmark of friends who have known each other for years.

'Don't you have any more rehearsals to attend?'

'Yes. This evening. I've been flung out by my lighting engineer for brazen interference. We've been working together for decades, so he can say what he likes. You must meet him. He thinks that light is an abstract language, like music.'

She reflected on this for a moment.

'But it is, isn't it? Light doesn't use words, but has the power to rouse the emotions.'

'And that, Dominique, is the root of your mistrust of music.'

For the first time, he used her Christian name. She decided to take no notice of this collapsing barrier. Instead she merely nodded her agreement, sacrificed the pawn, and made her much meditated move across the board.

'If I ask you something about the Faith, will you tell me the truth?'

Oddly enough the question now seemed neither risky nor impertinent. She was at last sure of her ground, and they were sitting side by side, close together, facing the sea far below them. She could see his hands, his knees, his worn jeans and leather moccasins; she watched his jacket trailing on the tiles, but she could not see his face. He answered without hesitation or disquiet.

'Yes, of course. You can ask me anything. And you know quite well that I will always tell you the truth as I understand it — and as far as I know where truth lies.'

'Where does the poem come from —

Ja! Ich weiß woher Ich stamme!
Ungesättigt gleich der Flamme — ?'

He corrected her German pronunciation.

'Stamme. That means 'originate from', it's a 'sch' sound, not like 'stammer' in English. Don't you know it? *Ecce Homo*. It's from Nietzsche.'

He recited the poem, just as it was written in the Guide.

> *Ja! Ich weiß woher Ich stamme!*
> *Ungesättigt gleich der Flamme*
> *Glühe und verzehr' Ich mich.*
> *Licht wird alles, was Ich fasse,*
> *Kohle alles, was Ich lasse.*
> *Flamme bin Ich sicherlich!*
>
> Yes, I know where I began!
> Insatiable as flame
> I glow and consume myself.
> What I grasp turns to light,
> What I leave becomes cinders.
> I am surely flame!

'I see you have been studying the Guide! I'd write it all down for you, but I don't think I could translate it properly into French.'

'Yes, I have been reading the mysterious book. But we haven't yet cracked your code.'

She stared at her own toes; he laughed softly.

'The language is only for initiates to know. But nothing would give me more joy than to teach you how to read that book.'

The day's heat flowed over them both, like an incoming wave, yet as he spoke, her skin rose up against an inner gust of cold, peculiar, unforeseen, and a quick thread of fear passed through her. The instinct of self-preservation swirled in her stomach, bounded through her heart. I must never, never know these secrets. I

226

must never understand his code. She sat up straight and looked at him. One of the cushions fell to her feet. But the Composer seemed unaware of her alarm. He leaned back, tranquil, languid, giving no sign that he had said anything disturbing or out of the ordinary.

'Tell me,' for now she risked everything, and the question was unpremeditated and therefore unprofessional, but her fear screamed within her: save yourself, save yourself, and the only safety that remained lay in knowing the scale of the monster before her, 'what is the Faith?'

He took hold of both her hands and swung round to face her, the chair scrabbling the tiles; he looked straight into her eyes. She saw tiny flecks of hazel amidst the dangerous blue. She had never been so close to him. He did not raise his voice; there was neither urgency nor hesitation in his words, simply the desire to be as clear as possible.

'The Faith is a way to live in this world and a doorway into the life to come. It is a very ancient pathway towards wisdom and has always existed in the margin of other faiths. This is not to say that the Faith, as you call it — for bien sûr it has another name, a secret name — is in any way derivative. Our teachings and the hidden knowledge we transmit are borne through the millennia by members of our people, who may well apparently be highly placed representatives of other monotheist religions: Judaism, Christianity or Islam. Sometimes we have been burned as heretics or traitors. We are engaged in a long search, like the Grail Knights, but we are

227

also watchers, the people who remain awake while all else sleeps.'

'We are also known as the people of the dark, because in our mythology, which has been studied for hundreds of years, we follow the Dark Host, the charioteer, Auriga. You may have noticed the maps and charts of the night sky buried in the Guide. Auriga is easy to see in the northern sky because of Capella, the most northerly star of the first magnitude and the sixth brightest star in the night sky. You know that astronomers have always mapped the night skies; mariners have always used them to steer across the world. Those are our traditions, our inheritance. But Auriga possesses one intriguing characteristic. Within this cluster of stars are two eclipsing binaries. Do you understand this?'

The Judge held her breath and said nothing.

'Well, one is Zeta Aurigae, the scientists now call this an orange giant — I rather like the term — which holds a smaller blue star in its orbit. The giant eclipses the blue star every 2.7 years. This causes the star to fade for a period of six weeks. But in the same constellation we see Epsilon Aurigae; the ancient Arabic name for this star, which we continue to use, is Almaaz. And this is what modern astronomers describe as an eclipsing binary star, for Almaaz has a mysterious dark partner, which we cannot see, but which eclipses the star every twenty-seven years. And the eclipse lasts for two years. This means that this giant star — it's about two thousand light years away from the sun — is being eclipsed by something far greater than itself. But exactly what this dark companion is, we cannot know. My people call it the Dark Host. Astronomers think it may be another star veiled in dust. Perhaps one day we will know. The next eclipse will begin at the end of 2009.'

He paused; and all around him the bright day began, imperceptibly, to ebb, despite the throbbing cicadas and the windy heat. The Judge sensed the change at once, as if the Dark Presence he invoked seeped out of his words and infected the blaze of southern summer, muting the heat, softening the sounds, darkening the world. The wind stilled, dropped.

'We only know of the existence of the Dark Host because of what it conceals. But we can hear this Dark Presence at the heart of the charioteer, whose horses' heads are pointed towards eternity. We can record its voice.'

'The thing speaks?' The Judge had heard enough; her scorn gave her away. She pulled back from him, incredulous, and thrust her feet into her shoes. He shrugged, and smiled slightly, as if he had anticipated her reaction.

'I am a musician, not an astronomer. You can ask Professor Linford at the Jodrell Bank Observatory in England. He is the world expert on Epsilon Aurigae. He seldom calls it Almaaz. He has been listening to the radio signals for decades and will tell you whether what I have said is true or not.'

'So we're being addressed by something in the stars?' Her self-possession, now utterly restored, wrapped her away from him, and her voice rang out, taut, ironic, cold. The Composer never flinched, but faced her down.

'Show me a little more respect, Dominique, and hear me out. We are part of everything that is. This is the voice of our own souls speaking to us, across infinite distances. Do you expect me to tell you about little green men and flying saucers? They don't exist and never will do. We are all that there is, and the Great Mind speaks in us, through us.'

'We find the love of God in one another. Earth and heaven are locked together in the perpetual explosion of creation and eternity. All time is collapsed into the drama of a splintered second. We seem to follow our small lives like a thread, across the few years we possess, when we inhabit the kingdom of this world, but inside every second here, within every moment that I stand before you — loving you more than you will ever be able to grasp — I touch the colossal space of endless night, *die ewige Nacht* of all eternity, where there is no loss, no grief, no churning time, only the endless night of union and joy, the moment that endures for ever, this moment that we can grasp now, with our bare hands. We are such lonely creatures: the poor, bare, fork'd animal, longing to be accompanied, to be comforted. That loneliness is an illusion; for we are surrounded, secured. You know — for it is written — that the very hairs of your head are all numbered. 'Now therefore with angels and archangels and the whole company of heaven we laud and magnify your glorious name, evermore praising thee and saying Holy, Holy, Holy.' How many times have you spoken those words and neither understood nor believed them?'

'The people of the Faith belong among that company of heaven. We stand on both sides of the doorway; we are the guardians of the gateways and the crossroads.'

He spread out his great hands and bore down upon her like an accusing deity.

'Look at me. Speak to me,' he demanded.

'I'm here. I'm listening,' she snapped back.

'I love you, Dominique Carpentier, and not just now, in this moment, and this life. But for all time and throughout all eternity.'

★　★　★

Gaëlle was pacified with two cream cakes when the Judge finally pattered back into the office at almost five o'clock. She kissed her Greffière on both cheeks and handed over the freshly baked bribes. Gaëlle grinned and kissed her back, and so peace reigned between them.

'Any calls?'

'Schweigen. Felt like every half-hour. He's got info on the accounts.'

'I'd better clear all this up.'

The accounts were still there, buried beneath the black straw hat. They sat down together.

The afternoon began to darken around them, that first shadow that the Judge had sensed beneath the white cupola lengthened and extended its grip upon the city and the surrounding land. They printed off all the material on the floppy discs and opened a new filing system for the financial records of the

Faith. By seven they were almost finished, when a sudden power cut stopped them short. The Judge watched the green screen tremble and fade, then gave thanks for her mass of hard copies.

'There's something I don't understand,' said Gaëlle as they stood side by side at the window, looking out at the clammy black streets, pregnant with thunder and the coming storm. 'Why are we so bothered with this mad sect? They don't hurt anybody but themselves with their crazy suicide ceremonies. So far as we know they don't embezzle funds or seduce children. And they only seem to murder their close friends. You say that they support all sorts of charities we've never heard of — to whom they'll presumably leave all the cash. So why don't we just let them kill themselves off?'

The Judge stood still, thinking hard. Then she said, 'Écoute-moi bien, Gaëlle, I didn't want to alarm you. You're a young woman with your whole life ahead of you. The reason why I am so concerned with the people of the Faith is because I do not believe that we are dealing with just a suicide sect; they believe in the approaching Apocalypse. They are leaving the earth and taking their children with them. They think that the Apocalypse is imminent. No, I know what I've always said — plenty of people think that the Apocalypse is coming up tomorrow. Human beings are much given to signs and wonders. But the members of the Faith, or at least the ones I know about, are all highly placed in society. They aren't misfits, dropouts, or women whose husbands don't love them. The chief government adviser on the environment and global warming was in the Swiss departure. So were two scientists from the nuclear research station at Grenoble and the Director of Research in Astrophysics. How many of them are there? Who is still here? *And what are they doing?*'

Gaëlle clapped her hands over her mouth and gasped at her own stupidity.

'You think they're actually working towards that Apocalypse? You think they'll try to make it happen?'

The Judge watched the first distant bolt of forked lightning dividing the sky and entering the earth. She wiped the sweat from her forehead and began to count.

'I have no hard evidence, Gaëlle. I cannot be certain. But there is a pattern in the dates of their mass departures, and a trail of significance too exact and rational to be coincidence moving in the stars.'

She had calculated that the storm was still at least fifty kilometres distant, but her count proved too short. The cataclysm exploded over the mountains of Haut-Languedoc in a theatrical spectacle of white fire and black rain, far closer than she had allowed in her original calculations.

12

Agape: Healing Through Love

Within two days the third letter came. Postmark Avignon; presumably he was still occupied with the Festival. She stalked straight out of her kitchen and into the tiny office, the unread letter in her hand. The music programme slowly fluttered into focus on her screen: Beethoven's Ninth, all tickets sold, returns only — scheduled for Saturday night. He was conducting a concert of his own music, also sold out, on Friday in the theatre. Was there any danger that he would liberate himself from rehearsals and appear upon her doorstep? Not unless he abandoned the orchestra. No, she was safe from arrivals and apparitions. She took a deep breath and opened the letter. Once more he had written in English.

My Dearest Dominique,
I must risk your anger at my impudence in addressing you thus, but I cannot wait. I am an impatient man. Yet in one thing I am like a woman — when my heart is full I must speak. And my heart is full of you. Please don't think that I do not listen to you or understand you. I do. Your fame as 'la chasseuse de sectes' made it inevitable that you should be burdened with this terrible investigation. Yet I cannot wish the fault

undone, because it has brought you to me. And I know, without your words, why you despise all religions and mistrust anyone in thrall to a great idea, or even a wild hope. You are someone who is utterly alone and your solitude is that of the truly independent spirit. You are the child sitting reading in the corner of the playground. You hold in absolute contempt the need of weaker people to belong to something greater than themselves. And you dislike anyone who longs to be told what to do and how to live. I have grasped this aspect of your ferocious character. But I am not only a composer; I am the conductor of an orchestra. An orchestra is one single, breathing, living thing, like a body that awaits its commands from the brain. Sometimes you must join together with others to create something greater than yourself. You must see that, Dominique. My music cannot exist without my musicians and my singers.

Please do not wilfully misunderstand me. For if you do you will misjudge me.

I must see you again. And very soon. I beg you to allow me to visit you. I will come wherever you suggest and agree to whatever conditions you wish to make. My commitments here end on Sunday and my assistant will take care of the orchestra. They have five days' repose before we begin our rehearsals for Salzburg. Kilometres of Mozart, naturally. Please answer me. I beg you to answer me. So far as you are

concerned I have no pride and no shame. I
love you with all my heart and it is my
greatest joy to tell you that this will always
be so.
  F.G.

The Judge misread 'impudence' for 'impru-
dence', looked up both words in her dictionary,
and found herself unable to decide which
defence would be the most suitable. Repose
resembled 'repos', but seemed oddly archaic.
She had never seen the word used in a letter,
only in advertisements for sun loungers. She
imagined the orchestra, lifeless and frozen like a
vast modern sculpture, magnificent in repose,
only to be summoned back into vitality by
Mozart's crescendos, limpid and demanding, a
great bell, ringing across two hundred years. The
Judge experienced no unease listening to
Mozart. Mozart's structures exuded logic and
security. They represented no emotional threat;
the mathematics of beauty did not disturb her.
She had neither knowingly heard nor ever seen
any of the operas.

He expects me to answer this letter, yet he has
given me no address, phone number or e-mail.
Or maybe he thinks that it's all in his file on my
desk. She rang Gaëlle, announced her late arrival
at the office and then looked up the Domaine
Laval in her personal address book. The
commercial arm of the enterprise could be
reached under Myriam's work number.

'Myriam? C'est Dominique à l'appareil.'

'Salut, ma belle. You've caused quite a stir

here. Marie-T never stops talking about you. Congratulations! She's utterly bewitched. I thought she'd never smile again when her Maman went off so disgracefully. I know we shouldn't speak ill of the dead, but let me tell you, now that the first wave of shock is past, there are some very angry people here, who don't think too well of Madame Laval. I mean, how could she do it? Her son's a monster and he might well inherit the estate. Did you see how he's ruined the façade of the mas with his orange awnings? I've a mind to ring the Beaux-Arts. It's a listed medieval building. What was it that you wanted, ma bibiche? When are you coming to see us again? Marie-T says you'll be here next week.'

'Next week?'

'Mais oui, aren't you here for the fête en l'honneur de l'orchestre on Sunday? Or were you coming on your own later in the week?'

The Judge invented a banal reason to rush, sent her best to Marie-T and rang off. She poured herself a powerful slug of bitter coffee and then sat quite still, looking at the phone. She was everywhere anticipated, expected, cornered, coerced. What course of action should she choose? As she drove into work, anxious and puzzled, she decided to do nothing. The best course of action, when surrounded by uncertainty, is always to do nothing. Watch, listen, wait. Let them declare their hand first, give themselves away, let them come to me. Gaëlle also sat looking at the phone, but she had her huge black watch, the strap covered in spikes, laid flat upon the desk, and a mysterious tally of figures and letters on a large white sheet before her.

'Bravo! You made it. Look, I'm keeping score. Schweigen and the Composer are vying with one another to catch you first. They ring alternately, at precise intervals, like a pavane.'

'For God's sake Gaëlle, alert the switchboard. Put it on automatic response and suppress the sound. Or we'll never get any work done.'

*　*　*

They sent out for pizza at twelve-thirty. Gaëlle chattered away in buoyant good humour.

'Here, have my pepperoni. They're too hot for me. Isn't it a bit of a dangerous game you're playing? Schweigen's out of his mind with worry.'

'What game?'

'With the Composer.'

'What game?' The Judge fixed Gaëlle with a deadly stare, but the young woman waltzed on regardless, utterly certain of her ground.

'It's clear to me, but I don't think Schweigen's grasped your tactics. You're infiltrating the group, aren't you? The Composer almost certainly thinks that he can eventually recruit you to the collective suicidal madness. And if I were you I'd go as far as you dare. Get to meet the inner circle. You'll probably bump into Monsieur le Procureur. I've always thought he was ripe for the funny farm. Then you can get his job and take me with you. We'll have a much bigger office and two secretaries.'

238

Gaëlle chomped the crusts, shook the mini-bottle of vinaigrette with unnecessary violence and then tipped it over the salad.

'You'd like this mixed? I mean anybody can see that the Composer is crazy about you. And that's perfectly understandable. Bit odd, though — you could have him arrested for fraud and murder any day now. But the fact that he worships you could be useful. You'll be able to reel him in like Ahab's whale.'

'I didn't know you read Melville.'

The Judge tapped salt on to her hard-boiled egg and nibbled at the thing.

'The film was on telly last night. Version originale. Entire crew of the *Pequod* looked like members of the Faith. Or any one of our sects for that matter — obsessed, deranged!'

'So you think he'll try to recruit me?'

'Not a doubt. It's like you said. They want people with positions in society, good jobs, influence. All that stuff.'

Gaëlle sucked a tomato; the juice overflowed down her pale chin and stained the white skin, carefully guarded against the sun; she usually looked like a vampire. There was a long thoughtful pause, a beat in the air between them.

'It's all very murky and ambiguous. I wish I was dealing with your TV scenario,' said the Judge, her voice suddenly anxious and sad.

'But it's always murky, isn't it? Like being a double agent. I'd ring Schweigen if I were you. He's still cut up about that day at the Domaine and he hasn't seen you since.'

'He's a married man, Gaëlle.'

The Greffière raised both pierced eyebrows, which disappeared into her stiff, lacquered fringe.

'Oh, is he now? Well, what a surprise! I'd never have guessed!' She grinned at the Judge, but her voice, drenched with irony, suggested a different outlook on the facts. Gaëlle suspected that Schweigen's wife and son mattered more to the Judge than could ever officially be admitted, in any court.

At two o'clock the Judge had a meeting with the local médecin légiste to discuss the case of one of the Agape victims. The unfortunate woman, suffering from terminal liver cancer, had, upon falling into the arms of the sect, refused all noxious chemical cancer treatments and plumped for the holistic, organic option of raw fruit and vegetables, fresh air and deep-breathing exercises, encircled by her loving group. The collective gathered round her bedside as she died, singing and praying, radiating a tsunami of supportive love. The family promptly prosecuted the sect for manslaughter and sued the association for compensation.

'The question is: for how long would she have lived if she had continued with the conventional cancer treatment? That's very hard to say, Dominique. Here's the report, which gives four comparative cases, all of which concern the same kind of cancer. Her disease was terminal. She had weeks to live, not months, and if you want my candid opinion, the sect was the best thing that could have happened to her. She was accompanied in her last days by loving friends, not her hysterical, demanding relations. Believe me, I know, I had to deal with the family. They couldn't believe she was dying, and made her do the shopping and the housework, when she could barely walk. At the end she was tranquil, serene, at peace with herself. She accepted her death. Elle est partie comme une plume. She floated away. I was there.'

The Judge flicked through his report.

'But the facts, Michel? Would she have lived any longer?'

'One week? Maybe two? And so dosed up on diamorphine she'd have been a virtual vegetable. She had secondaries everywhere. She was better off with those men and women who never reproached her for leaving them.'

'All right.' The Judge sighed and signed in his report. The dossier bulged over the edge of her desk.

'How's it going with the suicide sect? Any more of them surfaced? I read the report from Strasbourg. I gather they've released all the bodies to the families now.'

'It's gone quiet,' said the Judge.

'Quiet?' Gaëlle blurted out, incredulous, all her earrings rattling. 'It erupts often enough in this office. We had their guru in here not three days ago.'

The Judge swivelled in her chair and delivered the tiger's glare.

'Sorry!' Gaëlle clapped both hands over her mouth. The médecin légiste got up, palms raised in surrender.

'OK, OK.' He delivered a wide smile. 'Top

Secret,' he added in English and strolled out.

At four the Judge checked her e-mail. They had a new Outlook system, which involved a long, flickering delay between reading the list of new messages and accessing the chosen text. The most recent message, sent at 15.57, was from Schweigen. For a long moment her fingers hovered over the keys. Schweigen continued to clamour at her door, like an angry child, menaced with desertion. The mistress is usually thought to be powerless in that tacky little theatre where the predictable drama of the betrayed wife, the married man and the other woman unfolds in continuous performance. And, usually, she is powerless. But in this case the mistress held the winning cards and knew it. Were I to demand that he should abandon his wife, his child and his career for love of me, he would not hesitate. This situation therefore represents an unacceptable risk. The consequences are unforeseeable because Monsieur le Commissaire is an unpredictable, impulsive man. He is neither prudent nor discreet; he is unnerving, dangerous. I cannot command his emotions; and I am quite unable to contain his behaviour. The married man is supposed to be the spider at the centre; cold, self-seeking, manipulative, duplicitous. André explodes like a lunatic, lets his colleagues hear everything. Suddenly she smiled. I have never made love to a man who lost himself so utterly, that complete boyish abandonment of all restraint — he doesn't care who sees what he feels, has never cared who knows. This love comes first for him, and he will not, cannot change.

The tiny electronic arrow settled on Schweigen's name and the screen sprang to life.

> Dominique, I can't get through on the phone and your mobile is switched off. They tell me you have meetings all day. Gaëlle informs me that you interviewed Friedrich Grosz again three days ago and that you will need some help from the Brigade Financière. When can I expect your report? I respect your methods and I won't interfere. But please don't shut me out. André

This reasonable and moderate plea surprised and moved the Judge. She touched the box marked Reply and paused before the blank, shimmering screen.

The internal phone vibrated on her desk.

'Madame Carpentier? You have a visitor in Reception. She says you are expecting her.'

'Gaëlle? Do I have another meeting?'

'No, I'd have told you.'

'Who is it?' the Judge snapped at Reception.

'Marie-Thérèse Laval.'

There was a strange pause as the Judge hesitated, repeated the name, her eyes blank, staring at her Greffière. They do not flee from me, they seek me out.

'Shall I go down and get her?' volunteered Gaëlle.

'No, I'll go.'

And so the Judge pressed Send and closed

down her e-mail. André Schweigen, wedded to his dull screen, hundreds of miles away, received his own careful words, meticulous, edited down from the torrent of rage and loss he had first written, yes, his own words thumping back towards him, an empty electronic pulse, with a white gap of silence lodged above them, where the Judge had written nothing. He accepted this peculiar gesture like a slap across the face, and strode out to the lavatory, where one of his colleagues saw him, plunging his curiously naked head into a basin of cold water.

Then he stormed back into his office, hammered out a very different e-mail and pressed Send without even bothering to reread the screen.

How dare you refuse to reply to me? Expect no further cooperation from my office.

It was ten minutes past four when the Judge negotiated the last bend on the stone staircase and stepped down into the marble corridor with the great white globes suspended above her on iron rails. The shutters stood at half-mast, so that huge white blades of afternoon sun whitened the floor at intervals. Light, dark, light. She traversed the long cool space with even strides; her gaze fixed upon the figure stretched out on a leather armchair by the columned entrance. Marie-Thérèse Laval sat with her arms folded across her stomach and her head thrown back, her bare legs extended across the white slabs. She wore

244

soft green slippers like a Bacchic dancer, and she gazed straight upwards at the frieze of mythic figures that cantered round the ceiling. Something about the uncoiled glamorous length of her, the casual possession of all available space, the unguarded manner, and the ease with which she had settled herself in a public room suggested the aristocrat, the woman used to owning bright things, whose grace and reserve derived not from timidity, but from the languor of great houses, where all the necessary work is done by servants. Every angle of her body suggested calm and wealth. The Judge stood still in shadow, concentrated upon the image before her.

Was it the young woman's slenderness and elegance? Was it the way she raised one long arm above her head to steady her shoulders against the curve of her chair? Was it the way her long hair fell down over her back? Or the fact of her colours, gold, ash blonde? The resemblance was now so powerful that the Judge wondered at her own obtuse stupidity — the facts of the case now rolled towards her across the cold tiles, suggestive, ambiguous, undeniable.

Of course. She's his daughter. This girl is the Composer's daughter. And although her confidence in her own intuition remained absolute, she needed to draw a hard circle around her morsel of gleaned knowledge. The second thought, barbed, suspicious, mounted in a whisper to her lips.

'Who else knows?'

⋆ ⋆ ⋆

'Madame le Juge!'

The formality of the girl's greeting was quite at odds with her quick bound towards Dominique Carpentier and the ardour of her embrace. She steadied herself against the Judge, excited as a greyhound that has at last reclaimed its master.

'We're having a petite fête for the orchestra on Sunday at the Domaine. It goes on all day, lunch in the courtyard and supper later with Friedrich's colleagues and cronies. The singers have promised a little concert. Just for us. For our pleasure. You will come, won't you? Friedrich has begged me to intercede with you. He's put all his trust in me as his ambassador.'

The Judge looked up at her; she was guileless, radiant, importunate. Now Dominique could see only his face, faint as a ghost, in the young woman's smile. Her inheritance, tenuous, yet visible, glowed like a map, lightly traced across her cheekbones, present in the lines of her mouth and the fine down beneath her ears. This is how he looked as a young man.

'He could not have sent a more persuasive messenger,' smiled the Judge. 'Thank you. Of course, I should be delighted to come.'

Marie-T beat out a delighted little dance of pleasure with her feet. 'Are you free now? Can you come and have a cup of coffee with me? Oh please, just ten minutes.'

The Judge sent a message back to Gaëlle via Reception and sallied forth into the fiery summer streets, where the leaves hung limp in the airless swirl of traffic, and spillage from the fountains evaporated at once upon the burning stones. Marie-T attached herself to the Judge's arm, bending to hear her and to look into her face. The intimacy of this unconscious gesture and its concentrated intensity recalled the Composer's manners even more forcibly than the likeness that shimmered before her. The Judge measured out her replies, vigilant at every word. Does she know? She calls him Friedrich, but she names him as her godfather, her guardian, the children's legal representative. But does she know him as her father? How can she not know when it must be clear to everyone who ever sees the two of them together? She must know. In the depths of her, somewhere, she must know. And yet — the Judge was used to negotiating that abyss between knowing something and being told the truth. Now she found herself listening to a torrent of merry chatter; her secret trespass into other lives could easily remain disguised.

'It's the first time that we've held a big fête for lots of people without Maman, and I'm in charge. At first I was really scared, but Myriam's backing me up with the catering and we'll serve our own wines — starting with the apéritif de châtaignes — have you tried that? No, I'm paying for your coffee; I've lured you away from your work — lots of people are probably being sent to jail because you're here with me. Would you like an Amandine? I'm going to have one. So the wine is no problem, but it's things like the flowers. Maman set out these huge vats of flowers, all from her garden, and I don't know when she did those, they were always dripping with fresh water. And then the benches; we hire those from the salle des fêtes, but somebody's got to go and get them. We couldn't find the oilcloth we use to cover the tables, and then when we did it was mouldy and smelt horrible, covered in huge spots of black fungus. So Friedrich burned the lot yesterday — clouds of stinking smoke, and we had to buy it all new. Now we've got lovely bright colours: yellow and blue with olives and cigales, the Germans and the Swiss love those patterns. The tables will look splendid. But I've got to count out all the glasses, cups, cutlery, all the plates, and make sure we've got enough. Maman never used paper trash or picnic plastic. It's all good porcelain belonging to her family, and something always gets smashed. Every year. Oh, and we open the great doors into the hall. Getting the things to open is a real performance and last year we disturbed nests of giant spiders and everybody began screaming. Friedrich did too. He says he didn't and that he doesn't mind spiders, but he was just as full of fear and trembling as Maman and all the rest of us.'

She paused, took in the Judge's owl-like poise, and vast, magnified dark eyes; then burst out, gleaming with golden, satisfied joy.

'I'm so pleased you're coming. Friedrich will be overjoyed. He speaks of no one but you.'

13

The Fête

A hot wind scorched the mountains on the day of the fête and plucked at the shining oiled table-cloths, which flapped like sails, buckled into ridges and then flew away in the dust. Someone was sent down to the village café to borrow two-dozen plastic clips and secure them to the tables. When the Judge arrived, cautious, early, intending to stake out her ground, so that she could assess the incoming opposition, she found chaos in the courtyard, the Composer desperately wedging napkins beneath plates and Myriam standing, helpless and frantic, in a whirlpool of red earth. Two of the staff were moving the tables laden with the apéritif: glasses, olives, bowls of crisps, rolls of smoked salmon on tiny slices of toast, roasted peppers in vinaigrette, back into the Great Hall, beyond the hot fingers of the ceaseless wind.

Myriam and the Composer saw her descending from her car at the same moment and hurtled across the courtyard in a flurry of greetings. Myriam got there first, kissed her three times, and wailed like a child.

'Ma petite chérie! Help! We need you. Nous avons besoin de toi!'

The Composer almost slithered into them both, still clutching a festive packet of decorated yellow napkins.

'Madame le Juge!' He met her steady, unsmiling gaze, caught her hand and gently kissed her fingertips. 'You find us one hour late in the Garden of Gethsemane. The wind is a disaster.'

Myriam jabbered on, noticing nothing, not even the suggestive stillness between the Composer and his Judge.

'Where is Marie-T?' The Judge decided to greet her hostess first.

'She's in the kitchen. C'est la Bérézina! Did you ever see such a wind? But what shall we do? It's so strong one of the tables is sure to blow over. And there'll be dust in the food.'

The Judge took command.

'We'll move the tables round to the back of the house. Further under the trees. It's blowing from the north-west. There'll still be a bit of wind but the tables won't be caught by the big gusts, and when the sun comes round we'll be in the shade. Is there a hose in the barn? We can easily lay this dust with a bit of artificial rain.'

'Thank God you've come.' Myriam yelled in at one of the windows. 'Marie-T! Madame Carpentier is here and she needs someone to set up the sprinklers.'

And so the Judge and the Composer, side by side, dressed for a wedding in their smart summer clothes, hauled tables and chairs across the courtyard, rearranging them in the shade of the great plane trees, beneath the speckled white trunks and the broad leaves, already yellowing, hardening in the heavy air of August. When Marie-T and her helpers appeared in the doorway, laden with more plates and knives, they found the guest of honour, hot and a little dusty, watering the parched earth.

'Spread it around. We don't want rivers of mud.'

The Composer adjusted the sprinkler, grinned up at her, then suddenly altered the angle so that the Judge was covered from head to foot in a damp soft spray. The down on her arms rose, spattered with cool drops.

'Mais qu'est-ce que tu fais?' she yelled, leaping backwards, completely unaware that she had abandoned the formal term of address. She had always referred to him as 'vous'.

'Come inside,' he said, catching her arm and leading her away. 'You look hot. We both need a glass of cold water.'

He marched her through the Great Hall. Anyone could overhear them, indeed the entire staff of the Domaine might have witnessed the Composer's presumption and his insistence. The Judge paused at the entrance to the kitchen, a scene of frantic action and boiling smells; the scullery, four doors down, hung over the secret garden against the cliff. Through the barred window she saw bright light spattering the dusty leaves of the fruit trees. The Composer flung open the fridge, the inner light flickered in the shadows.

'Ah, Evian. Here are all the bottles.'

There were no glasses. He wrenched off the top and handed her the cool ribbed plastic. The Judge gulped down a third of the bottle of cold water, then smoothed her burgundy sheath, which had creased into two lines, one beneath her breasts and the other at the top of her thighs. The dress had almost dried out, and the effect of being watered like a flower surprised her; the sensation of renewal, readiness, energy suddenly returned. The Composer took hold of the bottle and drank the rest, his eyes half closed, his burning hand still clamped to her arm.

'Stay with me. Sit here for a moment.'

She looked down the long cool shaft of the scullery; there were no chairs. He lifted her gently on to the great freezer, which hummed and bubbled beneath her, then slumped against the wall, gazing out at the garden through the iron bars. She bristled a little at being placed like a doll on a shelf so that her feet no longer touched the floor. His palpable need to touch her, to be physically close to her, proved both disconcerting and conspicuous. She felt compromised in the eyes of others.

'Did you like the garden?' His unexpected question startled her a little.

'Yes, it's beautiful.'

'Her mother planted everything, you see. It was her gift to us.'

The Judge cooled; her mind snapped open. The habitual poise of the one used to asking all the questions, despite being perched on a freezer, flooded back. She dared to ask the dangerous things, quiet, casual, offhand.

'You must miss her too, as much as Marie-T. Were you together for many years?'

The Composer continued to lean against the wall, looking away from her, the plastic bottle crackling in his grasp.

'Yes, I do miss her. Especially in this house. We were lovers once. I was a young man. It became impossible to see her after Marie-T was born. Her husband was an angry, jealous man and that was one of his conditions. But the estate was hers; so was the money. Then she was widowed and the door was open. But by then the world had changed so much. My life was elsewhere; we saw each other as often as possible but we were never involved again. Yet the tenderness remained.'

The Judge sat very still, every nerve clenched, calculating the pitch of her voice. *If I ask him now he will tell me everything. I have set the trap.* But she had no chance to scissor him with her questions; he was too quick for her, and his emotions were too raw. Suddenly ricocheting off the wall, he caught her up in his giant grasp.

'Don't ask me about the past. It still hurts. And it shouldn't do. I don't see things clearly. I see you. And I see you as if you were illuminated. You haven't answered my letter. You never answer me. You just think up more questions. I've brought you here to make you talk to me. Answer me now.'

He held her fast. The Judge was unable to climb off the freezer.

'Put me down.'

For one awful second they glared at one another; their faces inches apart, he smelt of warm sweat and cinnamon. She resisted his incendiary grasp and wriggled violently. He swept her down on to the tiles; she saw the barred windows and the garden beyond, then her glasses, slightly dislodged in the scuffle, misted up.

'Monsieur Grosz, control yourself.'

He let her go at once.

'At last you said my name. One part of it at least. Why won't you call me by my name?'

The Judge adjusted her dress and her temper; then set about polishing her glasses with the lining of her skirt.

'Please don't do this again. I shall have you prosecuted for assault if you insist on treating me like a toy.'

'A toy? But I have laid myself at your feet, Madame.' He grinned and swept his white hair back.

'Am I too old for you? Is that it?' Suddenly he clouded up, visibly distressed.

The Judge melted. 'Gaëlle thinks so.'

'I knew it. She's been preaching sermons against me.'

He bulged into the entire space between the freezer and the door, like the gigantic symbol of the Macrocosm. She found herself smiling back at his candour and impertinence. The Judge knew, she always knew, when a man was lying; she had a nose for perjury, and this man was made of truth. The puzzle to be solved did not therefore rest in the Composer himself but in his entourage, and in the labyrinth of relationships, friendships, connections and memories surrounding him. She did not doubt this much-declared passion; his persistence had become not only peculiar, but flattering, and she realised that she could pinpoint the moment of his disintegration more precisely than he would ever be able to do. For before her she recognised the same

254

absorbed and passionate stare that had engulfed her in the theatre at Lübeck, months ago, despite her lost glasses and blurred vision. He had seen her then for the first time.

'Am I interrupting something?' A figure darkened the passage.

The language was German; the voice urbane, familiar, self-possessed. The Composer let out a great whoop of joy.

'Johann Weiß — meet Dominique Carpentier. This is the leader of my orchestra, my first violin and my right hand. He speaks all my languages, and, I imagine, all yours.'

'Enchanté, Madame.' The violinist, already brandishing a glass of the famous apéritif de châtaignes, bowed low. 'Let the festivities begin! Et que la fête commence.'

To her relief the Composer was called away to welcome his orchestra, now being rapidly disgorged from a flotilla of cars and several minibuses. Johann escorted the Judge back through the Great Hall and out under the trees. He spoke fluent French, with a deliberately comic accent, and bubbled incessantly, like a man on the brink of raucous laughter. The Judge realised that she was the only stranger; everyone there knew everyone else. Marie-T spun past, giving her a jubilant squeeze, and admonishing Johann to take care of their most precious guest. The babel of languages overflowed into the dark spaces of the house and gusted through the tiny whirlpools of dust still floating in the yard. The wind dropped and the women's bright dresses settled against their thighs. The Judge fished out her prescription dark glasses and, undercover, sifted the festive crowd, her eyes steady as needles seeking north. She assumed the secure, professional role in which she was most at home: the woman who watches, absorbs information and refuses to arrive at hasty conclusions, the woman who waits. But her concentration was perpetually uprooted, distracted. Almost every single member of the orchestra sought her out, shook her hand, claimed her acquaintance. She was more than welcome; she was anticipated, awaited, honoured. This was as disturbing as it was gratifying; she too was being observed, with an absorbed and rapt attention that undercut her confidence. *What has he told them? Who do they think I am?* The Judge nodded and smiled, like a distant cousin arriving at the wedding, who suddenly discovers she is the mother of the bride.

The Composer sat her down between Marie-T and the first violin. She made no objection to this careful pincer movement, for they dominated the head of the tables and she had an excellent vantage point from which to gather faces, voices, gestures. The orchestra unfurled carefully down either side with much snickering, grating of chairs and unstable benches. She felt surrounded by arguments and laughter. Were they arranged by instruments or languages? She had no idea. The Composer wolfed down charcuterie, cornichons, tiny sour onions and several glasses of muscat, while he conducted a violent argument about Mozart with a woman on his left to whom she had not yet been introduced. Their exchange in German was too rapid and technical for her to follow. The Judge sat isolated, disconcerted by a ripple of unbidden irritation. I could be at home, working, reading. What is the point of being here if I can't spy on them and follow their discussions? He pounced upon her like a giant cat.

'What do you think, Dominique? You must have a view on the Mozart symphonies.'

'I don't. I am not a musician and I very rarely go to concerts.'

The first violin chuckled. 'Then we must set to work and convert you at once.'

He nodded at the Composer, but Friedrich Grosz had fixed her once more with his savage gaze, hunting out the muscles on her face, the tension across her shoulders. She felt him searching for the memory of her uncontrollable tears as the young soprano poured out her ardour and her longing for the endless night of all eternity, within which there is no loss, no separation, no division. Look, we have reached the place where the stars shine still and time no longer rushes on, the place where hours, days, weeks stand motionless and frozen, caught in the bright ring of unchanging perpetuity.

She spoke again, hypnotised by the energy of his glare.

'You know perfectly well that music disturbs me.'

'Exactly!' exploded the Composer, as if she had given him all the evidence he needed to carry off victory in the dispute, and he began to gabble once more at his companion.

Suddenly he stopped, turned to face her and Johann Weiß, paused, and then declared in English,

'Music alone opened the gates of the under-world. It was the song of Orpheus that broke Pluto's heart and released his Eurydice. The appeal is irresistible. But does music make promises that it cannot fulfil? For it is the most Romantic of all the arts' — he abandoned his thought to his native tongue — '*denn nur das Unendliche ist ihr Vonvurf*. But the eternity of love was never granted to Orpheus. He looked back.'

The Judge frowned, baffled.

'Bullshit,' cried Johann, including the Judge in his revolt, 'you know perfectly well that the Promise — *das Versprechen* — is there and that it will be kept for all time. Music opens the doors of the unknown kingdom, that world which has nothing to do with the external world of the senses. And the kingdom is both the source of all our longing and our destiny, our final goal. We have the right to be insatiable in this world, and everything, everything shall be given to us. But we must keep our part of the bargain. And so far, we have been faithful in every respect.'

The Judge, rigid with attention, nibbled her warm toast and goat's cheese. She could not follow the intricacy of the argument, but she remained convinced, without any doubt, that she was hearing, at this table, spoken freely and without inhibition, the exalted language of the Faith.

★   ★   ★

Johann Weiß began to play at dusk. Insects thronged round the lights high on the walls of the Great Hall, which lit up the vast rafters and

258

the dusty plaster. Myriam eased off her shoes and tucked her arm around the Judge as they leaned against one another, settled in white plastic chairs by the great medieval doors, their backs pressed against the studded patterns of round nails. The single sad thread of sound rose up into the old building, nourishing the gentle chink of dishes from the kitchens and the soughing of the plane trees, brushed by the fading wind. Everyone else stretched out, red-faced, exhausted and replete, ready to be quiet, breathing the sound of a single violin and its melancholy retelling of the old songs. The Judge forced herself to suspend her seething brain. She had drunk two glasses of alcohol in eight hours; she was probably the only sober person left amidst the cheerful hundred, all of whom were happier, at rest. Yet these were the places of her childhood; here she had played among the great vats, home from school, hiding from her father and Myriam. And here she had danced, on these very tiles, enjoying all eyes upon her. Had the family been initiates even then, followers of the sacrifice sect that swallowed fortunes, futures, every prospect of independent happiness? Who had known? Was it here, on her doorstep, even then? She looked at Myriam's dark head, and the little gold hoops in her ears. What had her best friend known, but not told? No, as far as Myriam was concerned her mistress had been duped and murdered, deceived into a grim pact of slaughter. The events of New Year's Eve had revealed the fabulous Madame Laval to be both cowardly and

259

gullible, a lesser woman than we had all believed, not the great lady, who had managed a profitable business for decades. The Judge fiddled with the black Japanese comb, not her usual tortoiseshell grip, and therefore less comfortable, that held her hair high as a geisha's, primed for an evening's stint in the Tokyo bar. The violin dipped and soared as the sad songs ceased, banished from the night of joy, and the dance began.

Where had they hidden their instruments? For now there were three other fiddles and a double bass, informal, improvising, smiling at each other with no score placed before them. She felt the Composer's oppressive concentration upon her, his eyes never leaving her face. He loitered in the shadows, leaning against the stacked tables, Marie-T perched above him, pounding his shoulders in time to the quickening stamp. Two men had begun to dance. Was it the *sevillanas* from Bizet's *Carmen*? Or simply a melody everybody knows? She watched their arched backs and rigid hips; the dance unfolded in a drama of pounding feet, fierce gestures and fixed scowls, the sinister glare of the possessed. Someone was singing, an angry blazing shout, and Johann Weiß hammered his heels against the ground as he played. Everyone clapped, angrily against the beat. And then, as suddenly as it had begun, the dance was over, and the two men, back to back like victorious gladiators, raised their arms in victory.

'Tu te souviens?' Myriam squeezed her shoulders. 'Do you remember, ma bibiche? How we used to dance?'

'Mais oui. Of course I do.'

And there was Myriam, smooth and slender, a young girl of sixteen, swirling like an unleashed djinn, in the balance of her arms. I grew up here. This is my childhood friend. But what else could she remember that might have passed for the natural oddness of adult life, but in fact marked the presence of something dangerous and strange? The Judge ransacked her own past for signs and wonders, for anything that could tell her how long the Faith had been rooted in her native earth, and emerged with empty hands.

★　★　★

She could not leave without thanking her young hostess. Marie-T, effusive in her gratitude, nevertheless managed to dissolve into the singing night when the Composer appeared, impatient at her elbow.

'Where is your car?'

They marched to the far side of the buildings where the vines began. The pruned vines now shuddered in the first cool of night, the great leaves peeled back to expose the grapes. The muscat will be first. Sometimes, on these slopes where the sea heat gushed inland with the burning wind, they would begin the harvest as early as the last week in August. The Judge prodded a fat cluster with her keys, assessing the water content.

'When can I see you again? I have five days before I must leave for Austria. I will agree to anything, Dominique. Only don't withdraw from me. That's all I ask.'

'It's not all you ask.' She shook herself with discomfort and impatience. 'Can't you understand that so long as the investigation continues I cannot see you without being hopelessly compromised? I actually have to write reports on you. I shall have to write a report about this day.'

There was a silent space between them; she could see his white hair ruffled above his eyes and heard the distant laughter in the night. He stretched out his arms in a gesture of frustrated irritation, his sleeves rolled back, ready to fight; now he loomed above her like a wrestler.

'Well? What does that matter? I'm not a trivial person. And I have nothing to hide from you. You can write all the reports you like.'

No one could hear them now, or witness this conversation. The Judge felt safe from all observers, indeed safe from everything except her own temper. She drew a deep breath, ready to extract herself from his demands. But as she searched for the curt reply ending in goodnight, the Composer sensed her hesitation and pounced.

'You came with me to the Belvédère, you may not have answered my letters, but you have not returned them either, and I am certain that you have not merely added them to the mounting pile of papers in your legal files. You came here today. You give me great hope, Dominique, hope that one day you might consent to love me, or at least return one tiny glassful of the love I have for you.'

She reached the tipping point. No man had

ever dared to assess her behaviour; even the Procureur gave her a free hand. No man ever assumed that he understood her feelings or her motives, and no man, not even Schweigen, had dared to comment on her inner intentions or decisions. This man interfered with her freedom of motive and movement. Incensed, provoked, and now blazing with anger, the Judge actually raised a clenched fist against him and snarled back.

'Don't hope. Never hope. Don't count on me.' She found herself shouting. He pinned her arms to her sides and her back against the car, then yelled straight into her face.

'You can't stop me loving you. And nothing you can do will ever change that!'

He stepped back. She sprang into her car and dropped the keys on the floor, her hands trembling. She saw his giant white shape, magnificent as a colossus, striding away down the vine rows to open the gates of the Domaine. For a second she caught him, grim-faced, in the blaze of her lights, then sped past in a white blast of dust. She refused to slow down, or look up.

★　★　★

The Judge awoke in the grey, cool dawn and stood before her lighted fridge in the half-dark, gulping fruit juice straight from the packet. Something was becoming clearer to her. The clues gleamed in tiny corners of her mind, like beads on a necklace, fallen from the broken string, scattered and lost, splayed across the stone tiles. She heard Johann Weiß, his voice raised, jubilant — *you know perfectly well that the Promise is there and that it will be kept for all time* — and then she heard his music; the sombre mourning cry of sadness, absence, loss, his homage to the travellers who had passed onwards, treading the path we all must take, into the glowing dark. They swayed with the sad songs, and accepted their collective sorrow; no one asked him to play anything different. Then she heard the key shift into the major and the dance of joy began. For sorrow may endure for a night, but joy cometh in the morning. Something in the pattern of the performance and the shape of the fête itself flashed a warning to the Judge: the feast and then the dance. She stood still, sober, thirsty and exhausted, looking out into the whitening grey. The familiar shapes of shrubs, palms and fruit trees flickered darker as the light gathered about them, steady and intense. The shutters were still open. She had not bothered to lock them when she returned home, simply flinging her bag and keys down upon the kitchen table. The familiar hum of the automatic arrosage ceased. Soon, it will be day.

Had Friedrich Grosz paid for the fête? She began to cost it out — over eighty, maybe a hundred people had sat down at those long tables. The pleasant shimmer of wealth accompanied the orchestra; the musicians were opulent, casual, well dressed and at ease with one another. True, the mixture of languages had confused her, but when you cannot understand exactly what is being said you watch and listen for other things, an unguarded tension between the speakers, the way in which they hold themselves apart, unspoken assumptions, a connection that is scarcely visible, embedded in a dismissive gesture, an intimate glance, a bending of the head. These people knew and loved one another as clearly as members of a united family. They had opened out to enclose her as one of their number. Why? And why had they seemed so much closer than colleagues, friends? She could account for some of this. They worked together, lived together, travelled together, they must spend more time in one another's company than they ever did with their families. Many string quartets contained a core of blood relations. The closeness she had observed between members of this orchestra suggested bonds that were equally powerful. Yes, they were there, the remaining members of the Faith, or some of them at least, and she had seen them, at the table, talking, eating, dancing in the night.

But what could she do with this information? As long as she remained close to the Composer she was touching the sect at its core. Of that she was certain. But the Composer had not expected the departure of Marie-Cécile Laval and her Christmas guests; of that too she had no doubt. His grief rose up, monstrous, unfeigned, and as powerful as his love for his unacknowledged daughter.

Well, what was André Schweigen actually doing? Beyond sending her savage or importunate e-mails?

Suddenly the Judge saw two connected glittering beads from the broken string rolling towards one another as if they had been magnetised. André Schweigen was still following up the startling sums of money that had vanished along with the wealthy dead left behind in the New Year's snow among the broken trees. He had discovered nothing but a sequence of dead ends. Even modest donations to unspecified charities proved impossible to trace. One super savings bonus account, lodged in Zürich, that had contained two hundred thousand Swiss francs, emptied out in the run-up to Christmas. No one spends that much money decorating the tree or buying oysters.

Everything shall be given to us, but we must keep our part of the bargain.

The Judge picked up her glasses, pulled her cotton kimono tight about her waist and strode into her office. The computer was on stand-by. She opened her e-mail and ignored all the waiting messages. One was from Schweigen. She opened the box. And there lay the brisk contradiction of his last two messages. *How dare you refuse to reply to me? Expect no further cooperation from my office.* The Judge sat baffled before her computer's mysterious bulk. Why have I missed this? Surely I replied? Another message suggesting that she should visit a website entitled *Doctors and Nurses* gave her a moment's pause, but she disregarded the contents of the screen and tapped out her new message with ferocious rapidity.

Date: Mon 14 Aug 2000 04 :57 :23
From: Dominique Carpentier
To: André Schweigen
Subject: Financing the Faith
Priority: High!
Headers: Show All Headers

André, I am still investigating the finances of the orchestra and I need some more urgent information. Find out where their siège social is located. Try Berlin or Lübeck. The Brigade Financière should be able to help you. The company has just finished a tour at the Avignon Festival and is engaged to perform at the Salzburg Festival next week. Friedrich Grosz is not only the Artistic Director, he is also Chairman of the Board. Or their association, whatever the legal definition in Germany. Insist on seeing all the accounts associated with the orchestra. Go back to 1990 (at least, earlier if you find anything odd) and make sure that you get hold of any accounts not used for immediate running costs. I don't yet have any evidence of substantial donations in the last financial year that would match the money which disappeared in the wake of the New Year's suicides. Check every account held under the names of the main signatories on the orchestra's management committee. Keep me informed. Dominique.
PS.I will always reply to you, but perhaps not in the manner you expect. We are far more than colleagues now, Andrè. I expect your cooperation. I can ask you for anything and I will not be refused.

267

This e-mail, sent at 4.57 a.m. on Monday morning from the Judge's home address, confronted André Schweigen with the red exclamation of alarm as soon as he arrived in his office. Immediately, he rang her mobile, only to be short-circuited by her usual message. Nevertheless, he flung himself into the fray with tingling zeal. She was back. She needed him. And here were her commands. Like a hunter, who hears one branch snap in the forest, and exaggerates the scale of the prey, Schweigen mounted an expedition of some magnitude, and readied himself for the chase.

14

Prayer for the Dead

Many people are still on holiday at the end of August; so, although the stealthy evenings now crept across the city, cooler and more sudden, the pavements still burned at midday and the tables in the Allées bubbled with noisy foreigners in shorts. Work in the office remained slow, as they waited for the promised reports that never came. Gaëlle spent her time poking through the dossiers and then scouring the Internet. They filed all the dead cases. The Judge read an entire manuscript on faith healing with an eye to mendacious claims. No word came from either Schweigen or the Composer. She held herself clenched and ready for another eruption in the office, but the silence extended over five long days, and she faced the next week disappointed and relieved.

Then Gaëlle discovered something strange, which startled them both.

'Hey, you know that celestial phenomenon the Composer told you about? The eclipsing star?'

'Yes?' The Judge had included a carefully edited report of the conversation at the Belvédère in her dossier on the Faith. The Composer's peculiar claims proved to be the safest territory; she had therefore recorded every word he said.

'Well, I've found something here about the star. It's a prayer included in the Egyptian Book of the Dead. Must date from around 3,000 BC.'

The Judge rose up and leaned over Gaëlle's computer. There, in the British Museum's catalogue of curiosities, given pride of place upon the website, was an oval stone, roughly carved like a small hand, scratched with ancient Egyptian hieroglyphs. The Judge gazed at the open palm. She had seen the thing before, carefully drawn, with the actual dimensions noted beneath, apparently reproduced in its entirety. There is a whole page of coded annotations surrounding this object in the Book of the Faith.

'Look. It says here that it's a prayer to the charioteer, Auriga. And the reason that it's on display is because the star is especially bright this month. The eclipse isn't due to begin until 2009. Nine years to go. Here's the translation in English.'

The Judge scrolled down quickly, saying nothing. Patterns of nine. The thing eclipses every twenty-seven years. Nine years to go.

Pray, pray for my soul — that the Dark Host may embrace me and restore me. Let no evil approach my dwelling. Anoint my servants with the holy oil of sanctuary that we may pass safely across these dread waters and that at our rising the Dark Presence shall grant us joy perpetual.

The Judge pressed Print without speaking.

270

Across the years she heard a foreign voice, shaking in the air. I have overlooked this. This is my fault. How can I have overlooked this prayer for the dead? Why did I neglect the translation? Gaëlle was still reading.

'What does 'anoint' mean?'

'To pour over something, or I suppose to smear on if it's oil. It's a sort of holy consecration. Like extreme unction when you're dying.'

'Ughhhh. Horrible.'

'It's supposed to be comforting.' The pages ground slowly out, emerging into the printer's tray. The Judge fingered the stone upon the screen, tracing its outline, wondering at its scale.

'Where is this thing on display?'

'London. In the British Museum.'

'When?'

'Now.'

A still pause opened up between them.

'Can I come with you?'

'No,' smiled the Judge, 'not this time. I can't claim the journey on expenses unless it proves to be directly related to the investigation. And you must keep things going here. I'll be gone one day, two at the most.'

Gaëlle tore at her spiky hair in mock despair.

'You are abandoning me to my fate, O cruel one!'

The Judge laughed. 'Careful. You're beginning to sound like the Composer.'

'Really? Is that how he talks?'

The Judge decided that she had already said too much.

She negotiated the holiday queues at the airport and was standing, thoughtful, in departures, bound for Gatwick on the daily shuttle, when André Schweigen rang the office, seething with victory. He burbled at Gaëlle, who forced him to repeat himself, slowly.

'I've got a trace, a firm trace. There were six huge anonymous donations to the orchestra all made on the same day in December 1999 and all with the same stipulation, that the money could not be transferred until January the 3rd of this year. All the donors insisted on anonymity — some from France, some from Switzerland — but I bet I can already put names to the dead. The Brigade Financière is tracking down the French donors and Interpol are investigating the Swiss sources; that will take longer, maybe much longer. And it's all gone to a subsidiary called the Foundation, run by the orchestra's Company Secretary, the first violin, Johann Weiß. He's using the orchestra like a private bank. Where is Dominique? How did she know? I've rung her mobile and it's switched off. Where is she?'

'In the air by now, en route for London. She's hunting down a hieroglyphic stone.'

★ ★ ★

The Judge found a small hotel in Bloomsbury from which she could walk to the British Museum. Her journey seemed frivolous, escapist, almost festive. She settled in an art nouveau Pizza Express, chewed upon a rubbery cheese-and-mushroom pizza, drank two glasses of bad

272

red wine and read the English newspapers from cover to cover, even deciphering the advertisements. She rang her parents to explain her absence and listened to Schweigen's excited sequence of messages, satisfaction spreading through her like floodwater finding its designated channels. She didn't ring him back, but stretched out her feet beneath the table, coiled her ankles around one another and stared out at the muggy drizzle and the London night. Now what precisely am I doing here? Am I an ordinary visitor staring at an arcane system of belief? Or am I still a juge d'instruction conducting an important investigation? Perhaps I am simply Dominique Carpentier puzzling out a man who tells me that he loves me? Indeed, a man given to incessant declarations. And what am I to think of this?

She took the Composer's three letters out of her leather case, the first innocent invitation to the opera, and the two subsequent culpable diatribes, seeking her out and drawing her in, and flattened them beside the printout from the British Museum website. The Dark Host is the name given to whatever it is that eclipses Epsilon Aurigae. The Ancient Egyptians were celebrated astronomers, they had seen it and named this Dark Presence. And to them it was sacred, potent, holy. They too believed in life beyond the grave. The Dark Host is associated with Anubis, the Jackal, also a charioteer, which is a traditional image for the God of the Dead. The Dark Host is the coachman, one of the Four Horsemen of the Apocalypse. Swing low sweet chariot, coming for to carry me home. Because I would not stop for Death — He Kindly stopped for Me — The carriage held but just Ourselves — And Immortality. She read his last words to her. *I love you with all of my heart and it is my greatest joy to tell you that this will always be so.* Well, he certainly doesn't stint on hyperbole. She took off her glasses, cleaned them carefully, then read his words again. The tightness across her lips gave way as she gazed at his cautious handwriting. Despite her cynical wariness she was touched to the core by the unhesitating, robust energy of his excess. She sensed the urgency in his demand. Am I part of his greater purpose? How can he love me? He barely knows who I am. What can he offer me that I do not already have? He is all desire and demand, like a child — I want, I want, I want — and what I want is you. Nothing will ever be enough for this man.

She decided to reinspect his entourage, now that she had observed them all at close quarters. She pulled Johann Weiß to the front of her mind. My first violin, my right hand. *We have the right to be insatiable in this world. Everything shall be given to us.* The Judge saw a massive hoard of starving people, naked or in rags, mutinous at the gates, ferocious with justified claims. Do we have the right to be insatiable? I think not. So distribution should undo excess and each man have enough. In this corner of Europe we have enough and more than enough. But I'm being too literal. These people think in symbols and metaphors. Are they beyond the reach of my

274

analytical imagination? Her eyes clouded and she removed her glasses, staring straight ahead.

Wealth, comfort, possessions — that isn't what he means. So what does he mean?

She saw the Composer, earnest, unleashed, lost in the tempest of his own convictions, appealing to her across the laden tables. And then, despite her rage at his presumption — how dare you impose your feelings upon me? — she felt the fabulous beauty of his candour. He had chosen her. And having made his choice he would not change or bend. He was in thrall to his perception of a woman he could neither abandon nor possess. She was indeed his Judge.

And I? What do I feel for you? Answering his letters was professionally unthinkable. But she saw him again before her at the theatre in Lübeck, demanding her opinion and acknowledging the tribute of her tears. And now he was courting her with his uncontrollable sincerity. She had been right to warn him. Don't hope. Never hope. Don't count on me.

★ ★ ★

The Judge presented herself, her identity cards and her passport at the museum offices as soon as they opened on the following day. She explained her mission, a straightforward and brief prepared speech, including the minimum of gruesome detail, to a fascinated administrator, agog with curiosity to learn that a modern suicide sect was actually inspired by one of their current exhibits.

'You'll be wanting the Keeper of the Stones, Professor Hamid. He received the fax from your office and he's in today. I'll call him.'

And so she found herself shaking hands with a tiny, serious, dark-skinned man whose white beard and crinkled, grizzled hair were on a level with her glasses.

'I'm really an expert on the Assyrian antiquities,' he began to apologise, 'and my colleagues in Egyptology are on holiday, but I'll help you as much as I can with the Auriga Stone. That's what it's called.'

He led her past giant black statues of winged and sculptured creatures with lion's claws and huge slabs of ruffled rock for beards, through the great hushed gallery of the Elgin Marbles, already filling with visitors, towards the Egyptian sarcophagi and glass cabinets of mummified cats. Spotlit in a case on its own, lay a tiny black stone, smaller than her own hand, the thumb and fingers roughly sketched. A large sloping board beside it explained the hieroglyphs and the object's provenance in several languages; an astrological chart illustrated the impending eclipse. The stone hand, cradled in velvet, with its gouged signs, glinting, unintelligible, disturbed the Judge. Her work did not usually encompass crime scenes, exposed cadavers and precious objects as evidence. She worked with printed sources: documents, photographs, tax affidavits, accounts, medical reports, duplicitous publicity, leaflets. The Faith had drawn her on to a lurid terrain where unbalanced emotions fluttered naked against her face, and inexplicable

276

delusions had a history stretching back into antiquity.

The Professor allowed her many minutes to gaze upon the stone, rapt and concentrated, then drew her away to a little distance from the exhibit, so that they were standing in front of the golden mask on the lid of an Egyptian coffin. The frozen stylised features looked strangely androgynous, as if the dead pharaoh, recently the recipient of a successful face lift, was truly contemplating a life among the angels in heaven, where there is no marriage, or giving in marriage. The achievement of serenity seemed to be the gift of death itself, which no philosophy could, with certainty, procure, and no faith guarantee. She peered at the peeling gold, the barred stripes and the strange cartoon images of stick men and elongated birds. The god Anubis, his wolfish face vivid and alert, braced himself for the last passage in the black boat. Death is a river, the Stygian waters into which we step, only to be drowned for ever.

A small crowd of visitors, following an official guide, surrounded the Auriga Stone. Professor Hamid lowered his voice and bent towards her, so that his comments did not suddenly gather up a group of interested tourists. She could still see the illuminated stone.

'The shape suggests that it was a votive offering or a talisman, actually placed in the coffin with the deceased, possibly in their right hand. It was found among the grave goods inside a coffin that had been ransacked. We are still finding untouched tombs in the Valley of the

Kings, so there is a chance we may discover another of these stones. But at the moment it is unique. The text is known, indeed clearly copied, almost verbatim, from the Egyptian Book of the Dead.'

The Judge leaned towards him; they appeared to be concocting a conspiracy across the sarcophagus.

'My assistant tells me that this prayer dates from a period over three thousand years ago. Is that correct?'

'Maybe. It could be even older. Prayers are curious things. They often have an oral history that predates their written sources. You see, prayers are repeated like ballads. They belong to a priesthood, and a people. This prayer for the dead may well have been common property, belonging both to peasants and to kings. It may be very ancient. What is most interesting is that the eclipsing star appears to be a known phenomenon, even in these very early days of astronomy and navigation, and to have a mythic, religious significance. Almaaz is uncommonly bright; ancient mariners must have noticed that one of their guiding lights simply vanished for more than two years. The eclipsing presence is traditionally known as the Dark Host, or the Dark Presence — and we still call it that today.'

The Judge tried to identify the earnest little Professor; he called the star Almaaz, but he was clearly of Arab origin, which might account for his use of the name. Did his casual use of the plural indicate the community of scholars? She

278

was quite certain that she had never seen him before but his voice, quiet, calm, foreign, seemed eerily familiar. I have heard this man's voice before. She gazed at him, uneasy and intent. He spoke with such sinister, uncanny authority. She decided to draw him out.

'Did the Egyptians attach great significance to this eclipsing star?'

'Well, we can't be sure. The Dark Host is clearly a metaphor for death itself. And it was found in what was once a wealthy tomb. The stone itself is humble, yet the writing suggests a priestly scribe. We are at a disadvantage because the tomb was raided, probably at the end of the nineteenth century, so that we shall never know what else was buried with this king. All the precious treasures were stolen. This modest stone, embedded with the embalmed corpse, remains our most significant find.'

The Judge watched the museum visitors gazing at the cryptic stone. Some barely glanced at the learned explanations, and then passed on. Some consulted their exhibition catalogues, others studied the chart of the stars, clearly puzzled and amazed. Do we all long for signs and wonders, the map that guides us towards salvation and eternity? Here, surrounded by the swaddled dead, the Dark Host gathered significance and power. The Judge shivered; for when the Composer had first described Epsilon Aurigae to her on the sunlit tip of Sète, poised on the edge of the sea, she had assumed that he was recounting a myth, or even making it up. But here lay a prayer to the Dark Host and the pupa

279

of the pharaoh, who had believed in His eclipsing Presence.

'Would you like to come into my office?' The Professor bowed, a model of courtesy, gently pointing out a locked corridor behind the coffins of the defunct kings. 'I can show you a little more about the stone and suggest some useful books.'

The Judge entered a long dusty room that looked more like a laboratory with a massive library of reference books hugging the walls and stacked boxes around several cluttered desks. She noticed dozens of sturdy wooden crates bearing white labels and a sprawl of shattered ceramic bricks being reconstructed like a jigsaw. A flaking lion's head shimmered in fractured segments.

'This is a wall from a temple in Babylon,' explained the Professor, indicating the ruined fragments of lost empires with great pride. 'We're making good progress. My German colleagues in Berlin are proving most helpful.'

The tall windows were masked and dulled, so that no direct sunlight entered the room. She heard a faint tapping through an open door beyond the dusty tables, but no one else appeared.

'Cup of tea?' The Professor unveiled an elderly kettle and a tray of mugs. The battered white cabinet beneath was in fact a fridge. The Judge settled into her grimy surroundings; the long space felt like a shabby version of her own office with its high ceilings, cream walls and successful spiders wedged between the upper beading and the strip lights. Professor Hamid produced two small honey-and-coconut cakes in a little white box and presented them to her with a flourish. He spread out a tea cloth, aged and stained, but with the ironed creases still fresh, on the table before her and arranged the sugar and milk.

'Are you returning to France today? Yes? A pity, for there will be some guest lectures on belief systems in the ancient world offered at my college by a Classics scholar from Cambridge. I'm based at UCL, just around the corner, but I only teach postgraduates now and precious few of them if they aren't involved in the big research projects.' The next statement slid easily between the cakes and mugs. 'I gather that you are investigating that mysterious death cult known only as the Faith?'

He paused and looked at her for confirmation. The Judge gave nothing away, so the Professor continued.

'I must say, I'm very intrigued. So few people know that it has a modern incarnation.'

The kettle boiled, and the Professor pottered about the sink, warming the tin pot, which had apparently survived many archaeological expeditions.

'Is the Faith very ancient then?' demanded the Judge, mightily annoyed. At last he had touched her defences. 'I've been researching the matter on and off for six years, and apart from some German texts and eighteenth-century symbols which could have been filched from the Freemasons, I couldn't find any historical trace of the sect, or indeed of any suspicious mass suicides.'

281

'Ah, that's because they aren't a suicide sect as such. They believe in the dark world, a life beyond this life. And the only person who would know who they all were at any time would be the Guide.'

The Judge sensed a rush of cold in her legs and spine. 'I thought that the Guide was a book.'

'It is. A very sacred, holy book. We have lots of quotations from that text in other sources. It is a kind of encyclopaedia, a glossary with which we can decipher other texts. But it is mostly written in a code that no one has yet been able to fathom. It is intelligible only to initiates.'

'But you said that the Guide was a person.'

'Both a person and a book, according to my information. The Guide is the Keeper of the Book, just as I am the Keeper of the Stones.'

He waggled the teapot at her and delivered a jovial chuckle. The Judge gazed at him, horrified that all this knowledge lurked in a department of classical antiquities just two hours' flight away from her office, and had never been discovered. She began to justify herself, as if the little Professor had just accused her of professional incompetence.

'But I couldn't find out anything about the Faith when the first suicides occurred in Switzerland. We knew nothing of this history. Or this stone.'

Then she fixed him, accusing. 'Is all this common knowledge among scholars of the ancient world? I found no references to the Faith. None. Anywhere. How do you know?'

But Professor Hamid was pouring tea and

offering her a steaming chipped mug.

'I have no lemon. Do you mind milk? Please forgive me.'

'I'll take milk. Thank you.' She waited for him to begin again.

'Well, the Faith certainly is a very ancient creed. And no, very little has ever been written about the Faith itself, its theology and significance. It is like a shadow; it exists in the margins of other faiths. Akhenaton, the famous pharaoh who attempted, unsuccessfully, to introduce an abstract monotheism to his people, is suspected of being one of them, if not the Guide himself. All we have are their prayers. And most beautiful they are too. That prayer on the stone outside is quite specific and mentions the Dark Host, a key figure in their cosmology. The pharaoh who was buried with that prayer in his hand must have been a member of the Faith. So yes, it is over five thousand years old.'

The Judge avoided his eye and frowned at her fingernails. 'Professor Hamid, I believe that I have a copy of the Guide locked up in the safe at my office.'

'Ah. You have it. Are you sure?' He whistled. 'I would give anything to hold the Book of the Faith in my hands.'

There was a terrible pause, and the two stared at each other, hesitant with revelation. Then he said, 'Madame Carpentier, I do not believe that you are aware how precious that treasure in your possession actually is. Take care of it, Madame, for it is almost certainly the only copy that now exists. Only one ever exists at any one time

283

throughout the long serpent of creation. And it is passed on, along with the knowledge of the Faith, to the next Guide.'

The Judge sat before him, transfixed, balancing her mug of tea. The Professor continued, his voice even, each word careful, measured. But there was no mistaking the menace, or the command.

'You must return the Guide to its Keeper. For that is where it belongs. The guardian of the Guide bears a sacred trust. The law has no business harbouring this holy text, for it is a book of secrets. And some cruel harm will come to you if you do not give it back.'

'How do you know that?'

'Ah! The Guide is like a Grimoire. You do not have the key. The person who knows most about the Faith, and who has helped me with the Auriga Stone, is Friedrich Grosz, the Composer. And I believe you already know him, do you not?'

The Judge froze, as if facing a cobra, with raised head and outstretched hood, but the Professor pattered softly on, never raising his voice, a civilised intellectual negotiating an ordinary moment in an ordinary world.

'He came to London last week to set up our little exhibition. He told me you would soon be here.' The Professor beamed and raised the teapot, in gentle impatience, as if he was explaining the obvious. 'And here you are!'

15

The Château in Switzerland

The Auriga Stone claimed pride of place among the new postcards at the British Museum. The Judge bought two, one for the file and one for herself. Then she strode out of the museum into damp sunlight and traffic fumes, reached the midpoint of the courtyard and stopped dead. She stood, caught between the great fluted columns and the spiked black gates, puzzled, angry and confused. Am I a puppet to be pushed to and fro by these mysterious people? And could I arrest the lot if I knew who they were? On what charge? There were no small children among the first departure and the murderers among the second mass of suicides are all dead. All except one. There is at least one killer still out there and we are still looking for the gun. But that's not my business. I must leave Schweigen something to do.

She began to walk in a large circle. Every citizen is free to believe what he or she likes, we're all free to believe any madness we choose, as long as we don't break the law. And if the donations to the orchestra are declared, and within the tax limits, then no law has been broken. Am I wasting my time chasing ghosts? The Faith is a chimera, an ancient cistern, now emptying out. It poses no danger to us, any more

285

than Isis and Osiris. And I'd lay money on the proposition that every single obsolete god that ever possessed a temple, grove or holy well still has a band of faithful disciples, holed up somewhere in the mountains, sacrificing goats.

She paced the forecourt of the British Museum in a tightening circle, then stepped out into the street and flagged down a black taxi.

★   ★   ★

But the curious events of the summer, now dying slowly and peacefully, cooling into the vendanges and la rentrée, the eternal rhythm of the school year and the grape harvest, would not settle in her mind. She added another report to her file on the Faith, giving in full every single detail of her discussion with the Professor, and continued with her usual round of work, in which the ubiquitous sects played only one small part. Schweigen's piecemeal research into the finances of the orchestra had so far revealed only one thing. Many wealthy lovers of music supported the enterprise magnificently, anonymously, and in line with the tax laws. The list of names remained incomplete; the work continued. Schweigen's double frustration thundered down the lines from Strasbourg; the file was on its way and his wonderful excuse to see the Judge had evaporated. She sent back two sentences. Thanks very much. At least we know. Once more the investigation came to a dead halt within the maze. The only solid element in the inquiry, which flickered like a beacon, persistent, unseen,

286

was the Composer himself. And he too was silent. No more letters, no more calls. Had he ceased to pursue her? She did not believe this. She kept his three letters in her briefcase and read them all, one after another, whenever she was alone, biting her lip.

Gaëlle departed on holiday with her family at the end of August, leaving the Judge buried in a fat dossier on a chain of health clinics that were clearly being used for laundering drugs money.

'There. Hunt the evidence. That should keep you out of mischief.' The Greffière kissed her Judge on both cheeks. 'Take care of yourself. Try to eat every lunchtime. And properly. Not just slices of pizza.'

'Where are you going?'

'Egypt. Sharm el-Sheikh. And I'm not going to bother with Luxor or the pyramids. In fact I'm not going to move from my air-conditioned hotel room or my sunbed on the beach. You ought to come with us. You never go away on holiday.'

'Send me a postcard.'

'Promise.'

And so the Judge brooded in her office, discontented and alone, at first answering the phone herself, then finally switching it over to Reception.

The fourth letter lay waiting in her green post box at home on the night of Gaëlle's departure; the postmark smudged and the date missing, but his handwriting remained firm and clear.

My Dearest Dominique,
Forgive me for shouting at you. I meant

what I said. So please understand that the volume indicated nothing but the strength of my feelings. You say don't hope, don't count on me. But I do and I must. I cannot believe in chance or accidents. And I am not wrong. Don't mistake my certainty for arrogance. This love is too strong and too vast to be contained. I will count on you and I will wait. I am waiting for you now and I will wait for ever.
   Friedrich Grosz

The offices were almost empty; an unexpected heatwave accompanied la rentrée on September the 3rd. In the weeks that followed she covered for her other colleagues and worked overtime. She spent hours studying the Guide, staring at the strange solid script and the quotations in other languages. You must return the Guide to its Keeper. For that is where it belongs. The eccentric little Professor, wielding his teapot, may well be one of them, trying to frighten me. Well, I don't scare. The Guide is the Keeper of the Book. Das Buch des Glaubens. And was it passed from Friedrich Grosz to Marie-Cécile Laval? So which one of them is the Guide? And what does that mean? She gazed at the initials. This is his handwriting, not hers. The notes and commentaries are all his. But the Book was in her possession. Did she pass on the Book and then set out with her friends towards the snowy mountain? The Composer did not expect Madame Laval to take her own life. Of that the Judge was certain. Was she then the Guide? Or

288

had he chosen her? And had she reneged on the commitment? In which case who was left to pass on the knowledge of the Faith? She tapped her pencil against the desk and gazed upwards at the fan churning the air above; the blades shovelled heat into high corners of the room. She drew the shutters across her windows and watched one hard shaft of light waver against her desk. The Professor declared that the Faith was not a suicide sect, but a death cult. And in its own way Christianity is also exactly that — a mystery religion with death and resurrection at the core.

She fingered the Guide. This is the only copy that exists. And it is passed on, along with the knowledge of the Faith, to the next Guide. The Book itself had no mystical significance for her. The Professor described it as a Grimoire — a book of spells. Occult knowledge was synonymous with nonsense in the Judge's mind. But she was intrigued by the idea that somewhere, in someone's memory, all members of the Faith were added up on a list, accounted for, like subscribers to a golf club, generations of them, following one another across the centuries, then the millennia, marching to glory, the triumphant saints. *Suis-moi.* And then, suddenly, at ten o'clock in the morning, sitting at her desk in the office, one more piece of the puzzle slotted into place before her. Marie-Cécile Laval had given her daughter an expensive, beautiful present, which contained a command, a command that I have misunderstood. *Suis-moi.* I assumed this woman meant go on, kill yourself, follow me into the ecstatic, shared, eternal dark. But no mother,

289

not even this one, on fire with the madness of the Faith, ever orders her daughter to die. Marie-Cécile Laval didn't mean that. She meant: *Follow me — come after me — take my place.* That's why Marie-T was unsure of her meaning. She had no idea what role they had prepared for her.

The Judge snatched up the phone and rang Myriam at the Domaine, her discarded papers slewed across the desk. Then she replaced the receiver before anyone had answered and drank a large glass of water in one long breathless gulp. She stood utterly still for a moment, interrogating her deduction. Then she redialled the number.

'Domaine Laval — service commercial — j'écoute.'

'Myriam?'

'Ma belle, quel plaisir! Où es-tu?'

'In the office. Is Marie-T at the Domaine?' She took a huge, steadying breath. 'And do you know how I can contact the Composer? Monsieur Friedrich Grosz?'

'Monsieur Grosz? Alors, neither of them is here at the moment. There's some sort of reunion in Switzerland. I'm not quite sure where, but I can find out. Is it urgent?'

'I don't know. But yes, it might be. Do you know where Monsieur Grosz is next performing with his orchestra?'

'Alors ça, non. Aucune idée. But that's easy enough to find out. They've got the future programme tacked up on the kitchen door. I'll look up the dates and ring you back.'

The Judge prowled around her desk, angry at her own indecisiveness, her feelings troubled and confused. I should stand back, let a little time elapse, consider this summer's events in a colder mood, from a rational distance. But why did she sense there was no time left? A reunion in Switzerland? In 1994 a gathering of the Faith around Anton Laval had led to a mass of abandoned bodies clasped in one another's arms. I must save that girl from her own longing for her mother and from them, whoever they are. She saw Marie-T coming towards her across the tiles in the Domaine, a slender messenger in a green dress, hesitant and insecure, anxious to please and to be loved. And then she saw the girl again, her long bare legs stretched out, her arms folded across her belly and her head thrown back, looking up, up, up at the assembled gods and the frozen stars. She grabbed the Guide and hugged its bulk against her stomach; the leather felt warm through her shirt and the lock left a square red mark upon her hand. Dominique Carpentier had reached a crossroads, her experience and intelligence counselled caution, patience, the long careful assessment of motive and risk. But now she stood on the brink of a dark pool, and beyond her, on the far side of the still water, two people waited, two people who had inexplicably reached out towards her, the Composer and his teenage daughter.

She jumped back against the water cooler as the phone went off like a bomb.

'Dominique? C'est Myriam. His next engagement is Saturday September the 23rd in London;

guest conductor with the London Philharmonic. It's a concert performance of *Fidelio*, the Beethoven Festival, which comes at the end of the Proms. He's working with his usual singers, all the same ones that performed at Avignon, but not the whole orchestra. And the reunion took place last night at the Château de Séverin. It's about an hour, no, maybe half an hour, beyond Lausanne on the Swiss side of the lake. Do you want the address? I can't find a phone number, but I've got the address. And I can give you Marie-T's mobile.'

The very ordinariness of Myriam's helpful voice forced the Judge to acknowledge how far she had travelled towards an outburst of obsessive hysterics. She began to see fan shapes spread before her, which resolved into bodies, their eyes open, their mouths fixed and smiling.

'Thanks, Myriam. You're marvellous.' She wrote down all the information and watched her damp, shaking hand leaving a smeared trail across the pad. When did I last eat a proper meal without Gaëlle? I work all the hours God made, and neglect to eat. No wonder I'm light-headed.

She rang Marie-T's mobile, *Laissez-moi un petit message*, but she could find no words. Her sense of impending threat remained obscure and therefore, to her conscious mind, both unlikely and ridiculous. She drank half a litre of water and sat staring at the Guide; the stealthy unease crept through her bones. That fête at the Domaine was important to them both. I was their chosen guest. And I have let them down. Don't hope. Never hope. Don't count on me.

For the first time the Judge realised the appalling scale of her rejection. I think that the subjects of my investigations must be mentally deficient and somehow less than human. These two people opened their hearts to me and I sent them packing. Why? Because my professional convictions prevent me from seeing the justice in any other narrative of reality that differs from my own. Their Faith is ludicrous and insane. I therefore dismissed them along with their monstrous delusions. But no one becomes worthless simply because they believe something different from yourself. Does my knowledge and education always give me the right to condemn? My role remains clear: to save and to protect.

The astronomical charts of the middle heavens still covered one wall of her office. She wheeled around and stared at the deep-blue map spattered with white points and the fine black lines between them. She saw the same patterns again, fluorescent on the ceiling of the children's room in the freezing chalet. Their Faith follows the rhythm of the universe, as do all faiths, the patterns of the seasons and the phases of the moon. I never really listened to them. I did not care to understand. In my mind, they were already judged.

She rang the office administrator and told her she was going home. As she surveyed her tidy office before turning out the lights and the photocopier, her eye caught the gold clasp on the Guide, which lay closed and silent upon her desk. I must lock that up. She was halfway to the safe when she paused and stood still. The Judge was never again able to account for her reasoning, or for her actions, in the moments that followed. She swept up the Guide, for this is indeed the only copy in the entire world, placed it carefully in her documents case, where it consumed all the space, and marched out of her office into the first cool wind of the day.

Her locked house simmered, airless, stifling. The shutters onto her verandah had not been opened for a week. Her green plants had all wilted and died in the dark. She flung open her shutters and saw her shrubs and the wonderful Datura, les trompettes du jugement hanging their heads, shameful and parched. There had been no rain for almost a month, just dry thunder passing over the mountains. The computerised watering system had turned itself off during the power cuts and never been reset. She tested the system; then set the sprinklers to work throughout the garden all night long. She ran cold water over her wrists and flung open the fridge.

Four plastic bottles of water lay on the bottom shelf; a dried segment of St Nectaire, shrivelled in its wrapping, settled, stinking faintly, inside the door. She finished off a bottle of sour-sweet gherkins in vinegar and abandoned the cheese to its fate. No fruit, no wine, no bread. I've been eating once a week — dimanche midi — with my parents, and that's it. How did I come to this? She opened a small tin of tuna, and, still standing at the sink, drained the brine and fished out each mouthful with a cake fork. The salt taste skimmed her throat.

She loosened the tortoiseshell clasp and ran her hands through her thick black hair; her scalp felt unpleasant, greasy and damp. She caught the smell of her own sweat. The Judge strode into her bathroom, threw everything she was wearing into the washing machine and turned the shower's force to maximum. She scrubbed her body and her head until her skin was singing. Then she dressed for battle in black. By the time she had locked her rucksack into the boot and climbed back into her car her mind was clear; strait was the gate and narrow was the way that lay before her.

She set out for the motorway.

★   ★   ★

By mid-September the A9 is clear in the evenings, and once the Spanish lorries bound for Italy lurched on to the A54 beyond Nîmes, the Judge found herself left looking at empty lanes, white cliffs, windy skies, and the shadows lengthening out from the feet of the cypress trees, those long rows of dark green guarding the frontiers of the garrigue and the rim of the vineyards. She had no plan, only an inner conviction. The Composer and his daughter were asking me for help in however strange and obscure a way, and I would not listen to their appeal. My manner was too rigid, guarded, cold; they were creatures to be observed, from the far side of the glass. I played the witch at the feast, plotting against my hosts. She stopped at the motorway services and deliberately chomped her way through the solitary, remaining plat du jour, rôti de porc et ses petits légumes, drank a bottle of water and a double espresso, and drove onwards, north, always north, with the blazing orange sunset draining the light behind her.

The night was almost upon her by the time she circled Valence and turned east, towards Chambéry, Annecy. She saw the dark edge of the mountains of the Vercors, folded white rock, and the falling shadows, darkening across the farms and orchards just below the wooded edge. She increased her speed, pounding down the column of her lights through the tunnels, all her windows snapped shut against the stale air lingering around the dim green discs marking the escape zones. She emerged into white moonlight, the Alps hulked above her, a jagged dark line, free of mist, against the still deepening blue.

At the Swiss frontier, just south of Geneva, she was stopped by the douanes and the motorway police. They stood round her car, curious and bored.

'You must buy a vignette if you are driving on the motorways.'

'I'm only here for one day. Why is it so expensive?'

'It's valid for a whole year. That is, until the end of January.'

The Judge shrugged, changed two thousand French francs into Swiss francs, paid for the exorbitant vignette and drove onwards into the dark.

Once past Lausanne she slowed down and watched the lights bobbing on the black water.

The great lake shimmered to her right; the traffic ebbed. It was gone eleven at night. For the first time she doubted the wisdom of this impetuous journey. Should she search for a hotel in Vevey and approach the Château in the morning? She looked at her map. The Château de Séverin was not marked, but the village was there, perched on the narrow precipice above her. By the time she had climbed all the way up the mountain it would be well after midnight. Visitors at midnight! Only the messengers of death — doctors, priests, police — came to the door after dark. And yet something almost tangible, like a fine silk thread, drew her onwards, upwards. The vines flashed autumnal in her lights, the walnut trees stretched out above her. On either side of the uncoiling road a sequence of red poles marked her way, appearing and vanishing as she looped and turned. These must mark the path for the snow ploughs, so that even in the worst weather the roads stand clear. A green municipal scoop of salted grit loomed before her, then disappeared into the ascending dark. Séverin. Here was the village, silent, unlit. No street lights, cobbles underfoot and a strong smell of crushed grapes on the roadway. Was the vendange already over? She slowed right down and crawled past tiled barns, painted gates, tidy houses, their gardens filled with golden rod and the purple flowers of Michaelmas. Far below her she saw lights moving on the surface of the lake. Suddenly the flickering dark landscape sank from view and a great stone wall appeared directly before her in the car's headlights, blotting out all else. Follow the wall to the gates. Two hundred yards later the black gates rose up, as if conjured out of the darkness. *Private Property. Keep Out.* But the gates stood open. She turned on to the sandy gravel, dipped her beam and followed the trail towards a tiny square of light far ahead, suspended in space. The gatehouse. There was another, inner court. She stopped the car, cut the engine, and sat still in the cooling velvet night. Crickets, frogs, damp grass recently cut, smelling green, fresh, cool. She climbed out, stiff, exhausted, and stretched her arms high above her head. Then she set out towards the warm blotch of light, her rucksack over one shoulder.

The window proved too high in the wall above her to see what lay inside, but she tapped anyway on the warm glass and waited. No answer. She felt her way along the rough façade. Where was the door? Here, beneath my fingers, and it will be open. The Judge felt a pattern of iron bolts, a rusty decorated swirl, and then the lock. She heard the latch rise beneath her hand. Yes, this is the lock and the doors are open. She slithered on the damp cobbles in the courtyard, but the steps leading up to the main entrance were lit by two yellow globes balanced on the stone curls, which ended the staircase with a flourish. The Judge stood looking into a handsome tiled hall through clear glazed doors. Where was the bell? Should she creep away now? Or waken the sleeping house?

The bell, a real one, hung just above her, and a leather strap, glistening and slippery from the light rain, that once encircled the neck of some Alpine beast, unfurled beside the clapper. The Judge pulled gently upon the strap. To her surprise another bell sounded inside the house to the right. She waited. Then she saw an old woman wearing a headscarf and slippers coming towards her. They peered at one another through the glass. The Judge braced herself for another language, but the woman, neither unfriendly nor surprised, simply asked in French, 'Yes? Who is it? Can I help you?'

'My name is Dominique Carpentier.'

The door opened at once.

'Enfin, c'est vous! Bonsoir, Madame, bonsoir. Mais vous êtes très en retard! Entrez, entrez.'

The Judge hesitated on the threshold. Once again she was expected and announced. They are waiting for me, even in the long watches of the night, they are waiting. She was disconcerted, but no longer surprised. The old woman, even smaller than she, resembled an ancient wizened root and for a moment the Judge harboured a vision of the giant Composer, lurking in his Swiss castle, transformed into an ogre sur-rounded by dwarves. Then she entered the Château.

High decorated ceilings and another great yellow globe descending from the moulded plaster rose — the tiled corridor clearly stretched the length of the building. The silence around her deepened. Were they all asleep? Was no one there? The old woman answered her unspoken questions.

'They've gone to Geneva. Monsieur Grosz

took Marie-Thérèse to the airport tonight. He will be back. But very late. Shall I show you to your room? Or do you want to wait?'

The eerie sensation of walking into a prepared future, about which she possessed no knowledge and over which she therefore had no control, assaulted the Judge. She stood absolutely still for a moment, confronting two vast carved doors leading into the reception rooms.

'I'll wait.'

'Would you like a hot drink? Tea? Chocolate? Coffee?'

'I don't want to give you any more work.'

'Oh, it's no trouble. I usually wait up for Monsieur Grosz and then I lock all the doors. But now that you're safely here I'll go to bed. Let me get you a drink. You must be very tired after such a long journey.'

'Tea, then. Thank you.'

One wall of the long drawing room was divided into high glass doors, overlooking the lake. Far away she saw the distant lights, skirting the rim, jewels in the dark, then the great expanse of black, and on the far side, the continuing necklace of diamond lights. The great shapes of the Alps bulged upwards, vast, distant, black. The dark sky opened up from time to time as the wind shovelled the clouds slowly across the dome, revealing a deeper darkness in the gulf. The moon had set. And so the Judge took up her position by the French windows and stared out into the rolling night. The land before her stretched away into darkness and distance. Immediately outside the windows she saw a dim terrace, and as her eyes steadied against the shadows, the outline of a Chinese summer house, glimmering white in the long tunnels of light from the glass doors. She viewed the world in monochrome, like an old film.

The drawing room extended, luxurious and opulent as a dark-red serpent, long and comfortable, all the way from a baroque marble fireplace at one end to a huge grand piano at the other. A stack of folding chairs leaned against one wall, deep sofas and armchairs still bore the dents, lumps and disarray of recent occupation. She gathered up two fallen cushions. A crumpled newspaper lay scattered on the floor, open at the detailed European weather maps. The television eye glowed red, waiting. The Judge switched it off, then stood back to assess the objects before her. What can I read from this space and these colours: reds, orange, gold? The room smelled of woodsmoke, alcohol and wealth: lamps, books, a wine glass abandoned on a small table, the wood inlaid, gleaming, with solid shafts of mother-of-pearl. Whoever lived here, and she found it hard to believe it was the Composer, lived well, in rural security, comfortable in the world, the host at the banquet, one of the masters.

The Judge unshouldered her rucksack, took off her black jacket and sank into the embrace of an opulent sofa facing the lake. She felt her eyes closing. I have been driving, almost without interruption, for nine hours.

'Voilà! Your tea and some lemon cakes. I wasn't sure what you would like.'

When the old woman had gone, pattering

301

away down the long halls, the Judge inspected the tray. Eat me, drink me. The cakes tasted rich and delicious. I'm hungry as the Wolf was when he met Red Riding Hood. She brushed the crumbs from her black jeans and eased off her shoes, clutching her china bowl of tea. Don't fall asleep. Stay awake. Lie in wait for him. But the room was warm and the dying logs in the fireplace shuddered, settled, glowed, went out. The Judge set her empty bowl down by the plate on the soft red rug and was asleep before her dark head even touched the cushions.

★　★　★

She never heard him enter the long drawing room. The Composer padded like a cat towards her and stood looking down at the Judge, whose glasses, twisted sideways, had left a red mark on her cheek. He gazed at the dark rings under her exhausted eyes and then knelt beside her, lifting her into his arms.

'Dominique?' He carefully removed her glasses and put them in his jacket pocket. It was gone two in the morning. She shivered and raised one hand to rub her eyes.

'Oh — you.'

The heat from his throat warmed her cheek. She tried to sit up, suddenly alarmed that she might still be driving and had fallen asleep at the wheel.

'It's all right. I'm here.'

'Why are you so late?'

She dropped all pretence of anger, formality or

302

distance. She simply closed her eyes again and snuggled into his arms. He massaged the red patch on her temple where the glasses had cut into her.

'I'm sorry,' he whispered, 'Marie-Thérèse wanted to get home. She has school on Monday. The plane was late. I wouldn't leave her alone at the airport.'

'Is she safe back?'

'Oh yes. She's already landed. She'll ring tomorrow.'

The Judge began to surface from the borders of sleep.

'Why aren't you surprised to see me?'

'You rang Marie-T on her mobile. But you didn't leave a message. She knew it was you and she believed you would come. That's why she waited as long as she could and then took the late plane. We both waited for you.'

'Where are my glasses?'

He squeezed her and laughed.

'You want to begin your investigation again? Now?' He cleaned her glasses on his handker-chief, then opened them up and handed them back. She sat up and looked at him. The thick white hair needed a trim. The lines on either side of his mouth had lengthened and deepened. He looked older, very tired and a little sad.

'I've come to do something so unprofessional that I can hardly believe it of myself.' She reached for her rucksack. 'I've brought this back. Because I believe it belongs to you.'

The Guide is the Keeper of the Book. As she put the Book of the Faith into the Composer's

303

hands she needed no further confirmation of the justice of her instincts and the ethics of what she had done. The joy in his face spread like an electric surge throughout his body, his habitual heat, almost becoming visible.

'I love you, Madame le Juge, with all my heart.'

'So you keep saying. I'm flattered, Friedrich, but now I've done what I came to do.' She straightened her back. The night gaped in the windows.

'I won't let you go.' He clutched the Guide to his chest as if she and the Book had become one. He was so close she could feel the heat in his breath.

'I'm hungry,' wailed the Judge.

* * *

The kitchen curved over her like a huge tunnel until he turned on the lights, and then the roof lifted away into a high dark where a washing rack swayed on a pulley, the drying dishcloths white and crisp like elderly ghosts. She saw an old range flanked by a modern gas stove and dishwasher. This stood open and a mass of soiled dishes lay upended in a row, waiting to be scoured. Out of sheer investigative habit the Judge counted the plates: twelve, there were twelve of them. One clean plate stood aside on the dresser. She guessed this had been her plate, which still lay waiting, ready and expectant. As if reading her thoughts the Composer reached for the white plate and set it before her. She noted the huge cupboards and the door into the larder, which had a small yellow grille at eye-level, like a prison slot. The kitchen was stocked with provisions adequate for a visiting army.

'Is anyone else still in the house?'

'No. They've all gone. We're all there is.'

They sat at the kitchen table in the middle of the night eating bread, ham, salami, smoked salmon, fruit and cheese. For a while they gnawed hungrily at the food in companionable silence, anticipating each other's wishes. He cut thick chunks off the loaf for her; the butter formed an oval with a stamp at the centre in the shape of a cow. She sliced off the cow's head. He poured out two glasses of dark wine.

'I can feel your ribs when I hold you. Why have you stopped eating?'

'I don't know. I find all this very unsettling. I was alarmed by Professor Hamid.'

'Did he frighten you?'

'No. Well, yes. Maybe a little. I blame those fearful Egyptian mummies. They were lying all about me, with their eyes fixed and black. And in some obscure way he menaced me.'

The Composer stared at her, clearly disturbed. 'Explain.'

'He said that some great harm would come to me if I did not return the Book to its Keeper.'

A deep sadness seemed to settle over the Composer, and a tired anger rang in his voice. 'We are not here to be feared, Dominique, but to build goodness and hope in this world.'

'Now you explain,' she snapped. 'Explain everything to me.'

He pushed his plate aside.

'There is a schism in the Faith. Hamid will have told you that we are not a suicide sect, like Heaven's Gate or the jungle cult of the Reverend Jones, although that may be how we are represented. We are the hidden people of light and darkness, but the impending millennium and the Apocalypse texts in the Guide caused uncertainty, delusion and many fears. And, in my view, have resulted in catastrophe.'

'What texts?'

He rose, cleared the food away, cleaned and dried the table carefully, then laid down a clean napkin on which he spread out the Book of the Faith, so that she could see the strange block script. He began to read, one finger encased in his own serviette, like an anatomist opening a corpse, moving slowly from each letter to the next.

It will begin with the fall of the towers in the new world. We must read this as the first sign. This is the beginning of the change, the transformation which marks the conclusion of all time. There will be wars and rumours of wars, for evil will be unloosed from his prison and shall go out to deceive the nations which are in the four quarters of the earth to gather them together to battle: the number of whom is as the sand of the sea. The people of the mountains and the plains shall wither and die, for their crops will shrivel and their cattle

shall be scattered. The sea will rise up and sweep over the land, for the earth will be opened and commanded to yield up the dead, and before the great wave the cities of the East will be swept away into the ocean. And yet the West shall not be spared. His hand shall stir up the boiling waters of the gulf into storms of such terrible magnitude that the force of their destruction can never be predicted or foreseen. And in the South the rains will cease and locusts will consume the grain and fruits they have tended. These are the signs that will appear without warning. But again this is only the beginning. Do not fear the signs marked in this world, for the deeper pattern is moving in the stars. The people of this world will sense the impending Apocalypse. The fish in the seas will choke upon blood and the sky will be empty of birds. Their prophets will predict the destruction of their green continents. But they cannot know what is being prepared for them. Starvation and slaughter will follow the people of the desert lands and the Four Horsemen of the Apocalypse shall be unleashed. It will be as it has been written and recorded for thousands of years: war, famine, pestilence and death. They are coming. We must continue, as we are, steadfast in silence and darkness, serving the ancient cause

of reason, liberty and enlightenment. But when these signs are upon us we shall know that the time of waiting and watching is now past and the shaping of Apocalypse has begun.

He fell silent.

'But all this sounds exactly like Revelation. The last book in the Bible,' objected the Judge, now crackling with renewed scepticism.

'Precisely,' said the Composer and closed the Book, 'for it was written over two thousand years ago. And the rhetoric of Apocalypse is common to many religions. But some of our number were bewitched away from the path of truth. They were unable to hold their souls in patience. You know perfectly well that it is written: that one day is with the Lord as a thousand years, and a thousand years as one day.'

The Judge knew the Bible well, not from childhood study, but professional research.

'So you don't believe in the Apocalypse?'

He poured her another glass of wine and handed her a bunch of sweet grapes.

'It's not my business to speculate on the date of the approaching end to all things. Our tasks are set in this world. And we are forbidden to leave before we are called to die. The only person who is permitted to step forth through fire into darkness is the Guide himself. We know that our real lives begin beyond the grave, but suicide is forbidden, just as it is in Christianity and Islam. We must live out our appointed days. I tried hard to calm this insidious, spreading enthusiasm, but

308

as you know I failed, even with those closest to me.'

'So you knew nothing about the planned departures? You suspected nothing?'

He did not reply, simply pushed back his chair and slumped against the dresser. The cups rattled. He looked utterly defeated. So he hadn't known. The Judge gloated over the justice of her own deductions. The house creaked and shifted in its sleep around them.

'How many of you are left?' she asked softly.

'They were all here tonight, but I cannot present them to you. Not yet. Not yet.' He took her hand and drew her up from the table. 'Come. Follow me.'

★   ★   ★

Sometimes she imagined the entire conversation as a hallucination, brought on by exhaustion, hunger and an irrational desire to know everything, no matter what the consequences. They sat in the long drawing room, drinking tea before the renewed flutter of sparks licking the damp logs. He held her closely in his arms, defending her against the liquid dark outside the windows.

'I acted as the Guide for forty years, and yes, now I am exhausted and defeated. I could not hold the group steady and united. Their motives and desires were too diverse. Too many powerful individuals disputed the terrain with me. The Guide remains as the interpreter of the Faith, the guardian of our people, their arbiter in

309

disagreements. I had the final word. If you like, I was their judge. Why has it been so hard for me to protect my people from themselves?'

The Judge recognised her public role here, and her own countless defeats, but said nothing.

'The Guide is not a function that is inherited. The person must be chosen, trained. Not everyone could do it; she or he must have real authority.'

'So women have acted as the Guide?'

'All the first Guides were women. Mostly they were priests. Or at least that's what we read in the old stories.'

He spoke of the distant past, then fell silent for a moment.

'Who was the Guide before you?'

'He was a very wise old man who lived in Lübeck. A great musician, but not a professional. He befriended me when I was a child. He taught me all I know.'

'And after you? Who comes after you?' whispered the Judge, knowing the answer before she spoke. She felt the slight shudder of horror that ran through him.

'You know, Dominique, you know. I chose Cécile.'

Suddenly the Judge felt all her energy returning. She shook herself free of the Composer and stood up, her back to the fire and her face in darkness.

'Marie-T! She wanted to pass the task on to Marie-T.'

The Composer looked past her into the fire.

'Yes. She did. And I cannot allow that. I will

not sacrifice my daughter.'

'What do you mean?'

'The Faith is a great joy to us, but it is also a burden, a sacred task. Your life is not your own. You cannot choose your own paths. It is like a monastic calling. You must have firm shoulders and great strength of mind to survive. Marie-Thérèse is fragile, une enfant sensible. She cannot negotiate quarrels, bickering, arguments. This happens within any community, but within the Faith — ' He broke off, shrugged, then continued, his voice low and fierce.

'I have not allowed Cécile to draw Marie-Thérèse into the Faith. I have kept her out. Cécile sank into terrible depressions, then dangerous enthusiasms. She and Anton turned themselves into missionaries of apocalyptic madness against my will. And I will not let my daughter die before she has lived. I want her to live out her days in happiness and safety. We are not slaves to masochistic suffering as some Christians are. We believe in joy, the same revolutionary joy that is the legacy of the Enlightenment. If the Faith is to degenerate into an insane, unbalanced, suicide sect then I want her to have no part in it. I wish for her only the blessings of the Faith — joy, life, freedom.'

'And what is my role in all this? Why have you sought me out?'

'I want you to become the Guide.'

The Judge froze, then strode to the windows and looked out. The lake was still there, flat and dark, with the lights tracing the edge. She took a deep breath, to stop herself shouting.

311

'Are you out of your mind, Friedrich? You want me to take over from you as the leader of your sect? I cannot think of anyone less suitable.' The Judge faced the dark, unflinching. 'I believe in nothing.'

'But you do.' His voice seemed to come from a long way off. 'You believe in all the Enlightenment values of the Republic. You believe in justice, liberty, solidarity, and the right of all your citizens to live in peace, free from poverty and fear. And you believe in the law.'

'But I don't believe in God or destiny. Or anything up there, out there.'

The Composer stood up, stretched, and his giant shape unfurled upon the long wall of the drawing room, across the bookcases and above the piano. He smiled at her, shaking his head, as if she were an apparition, a wondrous and unexpected miracle.

'The Kingdom of Light is a citadel, built in the hearts of men. You shine like a warning flame, Dominique. You are radiant with that very light.'

She almost stamped her heels in rage. She felt belittled, patronised.

'How do you know what goes on in my head? You know nothing about me. And if I take your place and learn how to mouth all this nonsense, are you then condemned to die? To die at once? You said that only the Guide could choose to die.'

The horror of all this seemed utterly grotesque. But the Composer remained unruffled.

'I would have to teach you many things first. I

could not leave you to struggle in darkness and unknowing. You do not yet understand the Faith. We would be together night and day. For many years, I hope. I would give you all the rest of my life.'

'But then you'd leave me? You would choose to die?'

'Sterben um zu leben. I die in order to live, more fully and for ever. Death is not a state. Or even an event. Listen to me, Dominique. It is a door, a door through which we stride into eternity, into the eternal glowing darkness of vision, glory, freedom, joy. You cannot imagine, in this small world, imprisoned by the limits of your senses, constrained by these four walls of flesh, what boundless glory awaits you. I will wait for you there, beyond that door. The first thing you will know is that my arms are tight around you, and once we are there I will never, never let you go.'

'Then hold me now.'

He made no move towards her, but opened his arms. She crossed the dangerous space between them. As he folded her against him she touched his simmering heat. Flamme bin Ich sicherlich. He was already flame. Her cool lizard skin brushed his bare arms, her ice cheek came to rest against the throbbing pulse in his jugular vein. Their roles were already reversed. She was the one dedicated to that cold night of death lodged in the far stars, and he was doomed to serve in this vital, boiling world of hunger and blood, for all eternity. The urgent words of denial and rebellion bubbled within her.

'But I want you now. In this life. Now. I don't believe in for ever. I don't. There is only now. Only this moment.'

She felt his gentle laughter, a hot wind stirring in her hair.

'And yet I have chosen you. Not just for this life, but for all time. How can you be so bound to the kingdom of this world? Surely your own Catholic faith taught you to look further, deeper? To look up? I will teach you so many things, Dominique. And it will be my joy to do so. You are so precious to me. You are my jewel, buried in sand, uncovered by the very music you resist. You stand revealed to me.'

'Buried in sand? Like Verdi's lovers? You believe that this life amounts to nothing more than a tiresome prelude to the grave?' Now she was actually shouting.

'No, no.' He kissed her forehead gently, but continued to speak. 'There is no grave. And for me there will be no grave. I will vanish into light, air, darkness. And all through your long life I will stand beside you, waiting for you to accomplish your work, this immense work that is entrusted to both of us. And once your time here in this strange green world is completed, then you will step into eternity, the great ring of pure and endless night, the night of boundless love.'

She sounded like a disappointed, bawling child, even to herself.

'But I want you now. Now! In this world. There is nothing else but this world. And I think you're insane!'

The heat of his body engulfed her, as if he was

314

already consumed by fire aboard the Viking ship. And for one terrible moment she felt herself sinking, vanishing. She pulled herself away from him, flung open the nearest French window and lurched out into the wet grass. The freezing night washed over her; she gulped down the shock of the mountain cold, and felt herself shivering. Wrapping her arms about herself she picked her way through the soaking earth, unable to see anything at all on the black mass before her. A man's passion held no terrors for Dominique Carpentier; this was just one more field in which she excelled, like mathematics and jurisprudence. And to the outcome she was largely indifferent. He loves me, he loves me not, he loves me. The deepest currents within her never surfaced and were never touched. But now, in this man's arms, she had sensed her cold intelligence obliterated, and she was shaken to the core. The combed vines and the glassy blackness of the lake with the Alps beyond, ghostly in the night mist, refused to remain a backdrop to this moment of temptation, like a painted scene before which the Composer seduced her with his outrageous propositions, for the very landscape heard his voice, and shivered, animate, listening, intent. She was surrounded, trapped.

'Dominique?' She never heard his approach. He caught her and she felt his giant hand cradling her head. She lost her footing in the slithering grass.

'Look up,' he commanded softly, 'look up.'

And there above her reeled the Great Bear and

Pleiades, the vast dense mass of stars, suffocating, close, the long veiled trail of the Milky Way, exploding with light, a dance of such glamorous enormity that her breath stopped in her throat. As if for the first time, she saw the huge immensity of light and distance, stretching away into nothingness, a soft glimmer on the outer edge of the universe, and then the endless galaxies beyond. She heard his voice coming towards her from the passionate brink of all created worlds, seen and unseen.

'Everything already is. Everything exists. It is both before us and within us. All we have ever done is discover the names. We spend our short lives finding the words to say it. You and I have always been here, now and for all eternity. Did you never listen to your uncle when he was teaching you your catechism? He was teaching you the first fragments of the Faith.'

16

Follow me into the Kingdom

She stumbled out past the gatehouse in the first grey-blue light of coming day, dishevelled and unsteady, like someone drugged. Where had she left the car? Could she still find her keys? With each step she struggled to regain her chilly equilibrium. Her mind shuddered and gaped, as if she had stepped into a distorting fairground mirror and retained its grotesque shape. There was another car parked, just behind her own. As she reached for the lock a huddled form crouched behind the wheel of the intruding vehicle sprang into life and leaped out before her — André Schweigen.

He must have spent the night collapsed in the front seat. He looked like a homeless tramp, unshaven, battered, trembling with cold.

'How did you find me?' The Judge, suddenly lucid and terrifying, almost roared into the dawn. 'And what are you doing here?'

'Gaëlle. She's on holiday in Egypt and she's desperately worried about you. Both the phone in the office and your mobile have been clamped on to the answering service for over a week. You haven't answered any of your e-mails. You don't respond to messages. She rang me and I traced you here via Myriam at the Domaine.'

'André — I am not a child and I don't need a

317

minder. Now get back into that car and follow me down the mountain. We're going to find an expensive hotel in Vevey and sleep till midday.'

But by the time they reached the dozing desk clerk at the Grand Hôtel Continental neither of them could speak; the Judge was exhausted and Schweigen had been transformed into a living block of ice. The only rooms available formed the honeymoon suite. Schweigen booked the suite with fabulous views down the length of the lake and the Judge paid on her credit card. She ate all the chocolates laid upon the pillows, both hers and his, then pushed him into the bathroom and told him, without ceremony, to thaw out and eliminate the lingering stench of sleeping rough before coming to bed. He could barely see her, brandishing the hotel toothbrushes and picking out shampoos, through a cloud of steam. They muttered to one another, grateful for the familiarity of each other's movements and gestures, unable to initiate any explanations. She was almost asleep before he joined her in the vast four-poster, tasselled with satin and gold.

'Don't talk, André,' she whispered, as if she were ill or drugged. 'I can't stand it. And in answer to the questions that are written all over your face — yes, I spent what was left of the night with the Composer. No — I didn't have sex with him, but yes, I am in love with him. And don't throw one of your jealous fits. I'm not up the mountain in his bed. I'm down here with you in the honeymoon suite. Goodnight.'

And she pulled the duvet over her head to shut out the light.

The sun illuminated the honeymoon terrace and
the long rows of vines directly below the Grand
Hôtel Continental from nine o'clock onwards.
André Schweigen, sleepless in luxury, watched
the light growing from behind the Alps, and saw
the lake changing colour, from black to leaden
blue. The Judge, he reflected with some
irritation, slept as if there was no original sin in
this world, and no impending consequences
following her terrible declarations. Had she
changed sides? Gaëlle thought not, but the
outspoken Greffière possessed a boundlessly
loyal spirit; she would never betray her Judge, in
thought, word or deed. And in any case André
Schweigen now discovered himself capable of
understanding only one thing. She loved another
man. She had told him so. The fact that she had
never returned his devotion in any shape or form
was neither here nor there. If he went on loving
her, and he had no choice but to do so, then that
was enough. But now there was someone else.
She loves someone else. He paced the borders of
his mind and found the dangerous edge, perilous
as the Wall of Death. Here he lay, poised on the
brink. What should he do now? Morning blazed
in the windows. His wife had sent three
desperate text messages. He no longer possessed
the words with which to lie, and so he merely
read the messages again and again. At last, André
Schweigen blacked out his mobile, settled down
beside the sleeping Judge and closed his eyes.

When he finally awoke it was well after midday

and the Judge was standing on the terrace, wrapped in a white fluffy bathrobe with the hotel's sinister logo stitched in gold glowing across her back, her face raised to the sun. Someone was tapping at the door.

'Entrez,' cried the Judge, and a uniformed flunky oozed into the suite bearing a vast silver tray, overflowing with breakfast, two flutes, and a bottle of champagne.

'Félicitations! Madame, Monsieur,' murmured the apparition. 'The management would like to wish you a very happy stay at the Grand Hôtel Continental.'

'Thank you.' The Judge helped herself to a glass of champagne and escorted him out of the suite. She stalked back to the four-poster.

'Cheers, André!' She handed him the fizzing golden cone. 'This is the honeymoon suite and we appear to have done the decent thing and regularised our situation at last.'

Schweigen sat up and gulped down half the glass. The room flickered to the beat of her smile. For one moment their complicity was complete and Schweigen grinned broadly. They had escaped together and were now on the run.

'Didn't they notice that we haven't any luggage?'

'Perhaps they think we've eloped?'

Then Schweigen remembered her confession. He flung away the moment of intimate peace between them and roared, 'You're with the wrong man,' as he clambered out of bed. He tried to pull on his trousers, but rage triumphed over dignity and his right foot got stuck. She knelt down and pulled his foot through the hole.

'Don't start up, André. Please. It will stop you thinking straight and we need to stay calm.'

She carried the tray out on to the terrace. Her use of the plural immediately sent a message of reassurance to his muddled, exhausted brain, and he followed her out into the gorgeous day. The air smelled of September, the first fires, damp leaves, and a chill rising from the dark lake. In the shadow of the mountains the water remained black, with a faint mist clinging to the surface, as if the thing was living, breathing. The Judge set out breakfast on the glass table, her brisk, assured gestures shimmering with confidence and certainty. Cheese, pâté, wurst, eggs. Where are the croissants and the pains au chocolat? She rummaged through the sweet treasures.

'Here. Orange juice. Drink it up or you'll pass out.'

'Did he ask you to marry him?' André exploded, nevertheless obediently guzzling orange juice at her command.

'Well, he did make me a proposition and yes, I think you could call it a proposal. So in a manner of speaking, yes.'

André gazed at her in horror. Her glasses had darkened in brightness, and so she sat, her bare legs and toes stretched out to greet the sun, munching pains au chocolat. She was eating his share as well as her own.

'And what did you say to him?' He held his breath.

'What every cautious woman says. I played for

time. I said I'd give him my answer in a week.'

'A week!' Seven days vanished in the flicker of her black hair falling across her face. Seven days and she would be lost to him for ever.

'Don't look so tragic. I haven't said yes.'

'But you will.'

'Why do you assume that?'

André nearly crunched the champagne glass to splinters in his hands.

'You told me last night that you were in love with him.' He found himself shouting. The Judge swivelled in her seat, her darkened eyes invisible behind the black frames.

'And I will never lie to you. That man has paid me the compliment of loving me with his whole heart and offering me the things that matter most to him. He has asked me to watch over his daughter. And I love him for his confidence and his trust in me. But I am not a madwoman, André. Friedrich Grosz and I stand on either side of an immense divide, like an abyss beneath the ocean. He cannot see it. He has a faith that knows no limits. For him nothing is impossible.'

She paused. André let out his breath with a long seething hiss.

'And for you it is impossible?'

'I didn't say that.'

Then something else hit Schweigen like a slap; she had concealed information from him.

'Marie-Cécile Laval's younger child. The girl. That's his daughter?'

'Yes.'

'How long have you known?'

'About a month and a half.'

Schweigen stood up and clutched the wrought-iron balcony, his knuckles white.

'I can't stand this, Dominique.'

'André, sit down. Listen to me. And keep your nerve.' He collapsed into the honeymoon cushions.

But for a moment she didn't say anything at all, merely handed him a slice of dark bread spread with garlic cheese and poured out the coffee. They ate in silence, gazing down the lake, which stretched away into a glaze of mist. The landscape draped before them, like a curtain of endless beauty, softened into golden light. The lake, shadowed, unclear, now appeared as difficult to comprehend as the nature of the decision the Judge had sworn to make within the week. Would she abandon her past? Unthinkable. Marry an old man, albeit a disturbingly energetic vieux Picasso? She hated music, never listened to it and didn't even own a hi-fi system. Had she suddenly become domesticated and begun dreaming of a family? Schweigen could not imagine the Judge managing kitchens or clutching children. He suddenly realised that he had no idea how old she was. The smooth, timeless olive face gave little away.

'How old are you?' he demanded, all caution gone.

'Forty-two. The same age as you.' She smiled at him. 'Do you think we might order some more champagne?'

'Are you mad?'

'No. This is the honeymoon suite, remember. I think it's included in the price. Anyway, I gave them my personal credit card number. We're not on the fiddle and it's Saturday. Order another bottle, André. But remember, they think that you are now Monsieur Carpentier.' She flung back her head and laughed.

He gave up, staggered forth into the bridal drapes and fumbled about for the telephone.

★　★　★

She remained both affectionate and preoccupied throughout that long afternoon. Towards the end of the day they walked down through the vines to the woods by the lake's edge. The dry earth crumbled under their shoes and they disturbed a hare on the brink of a tall mass of uncut maize. The creature shot away from them, its huge arched legs forming a jagged pattern as it vanished up the bank and into the golden woods. The light shivered and slid across the surface of the water and tiny waves lapped against the pebbles on the artificial beach. The hotel owned a brace of small boats, padlocked to the jetty. Schweigen and the Judge sat side by side on the warm planks, their feet hanging just above the water.

Only now did Schweigen remember what he had intended to tell her. And, mirabile dictu, they began to take up the investigation again. Whatever she thought about the impassable abyss between herself and the Composer, she still stood beside him, on the same side. The Faith, and the dismantling of its power, still bound them together.

'Dominique, I found something in the documentation for the Foundation set up by whoever is now running the Faith. Weiß is the director of the fund, but there is a legal Deed of Trust, properly drawn up and witnessed, which names two other trustees in the event of Weiß's demise: Professor Hassan Hamid and Friedrich Grosz.'

The Judge caught both knees with her arms and rested her chin between them. She thought for a while, but made no reply.

'Do you think they're creaming it off?' André desired this with all his soul. He wanted to believe every possible ill of the Composer.

'Did either of them sign this Deed of Trust?'

'No. They're just named.'

'Then they probably know nothing about it. What is the purpose of this Foundation?'

'I don't know. Not yet.'

'Then keep digging.'

'You want me to go on?'

'But of course.'

Schweigen shuddered, incredulous. He imagined the Judge, now coiled like a spring beside him, as the crusading saint, bearing the white banner of righteousness, the sword of justice unsheathed in her bare hands, sea-green incorruptible, and possessed of no human feelings whatsoever. She says she loves this man; yet she would put the handcuffs on him herself. He imagined her as the Grand Inquisitor — cold, ruthless, obsessed. Her next question was therefore unexpected.

'And what, may I ask, have you told your wife this time?'

325

There was no animosity or judgement in her voice. She simply sounded curious. He looked at her, puzzled, and then suddenly certain that the fact he was married had mattered to her, all along.

'The truth. That I had spoken to your Greffière who feared that you were in some sort of danger, and so I was going to find you.'

'And what did she say to that?'

André Schweigen hesitated, sheepish, rueful.

'She asked me if I cared about you in a way that I shouldn't.'

'And you replied — ?'

'That I was in love with you. That I had been in love with you for years, and that I always would love you more than anything or anyone else. I felt better saying it. That's the truth.'

The Judge whistled and took his hand in her own. He crushed her lizard cool in his warmth. They sat side by side for many minutes without speaking. The times they had spent together rose before her. She could no longer see the shadow of parting which had haunted every encounter. The Judge heard the echoes in the simplicity of his declaration and recognised the resemblance between André Schweigen and the Composer; they were both given to extremity, generous men swept by the giant winds of irrational, powerful emotions and tempted to take mad risks. And they both trusted in truth. The truth cannot be spoken, clearly and with conviction, and remain unheard. When my love swears that he is made of truth — she stopped the thought before it formed, and wisely kept her insight to herself. They watched the mist thickening on the lake.

'Well, André, I'm amazed. And very flattered. I have heard exactly what you said. But I will need to think about that too. And you'd better drive straight home and face the music.'

★ ★ ★

Gaëlle sliced open the post in the office, sitting bolt upright. She had been transformed, by a mere three weeks on an Egyptian beach, into a bronzed god. Her Cleopatra haircut blocked into an exact geometry of lines and layers was held steady by the same transparent gel that had maintained the original black spikes. Her eyes, rimmed with kohl, re-created the looming gaze of Isis, and a large beaded collar, brilliant with white threaded shells, yellow ceramics, jade, onyx, and cobalt blue stones of lapis lazuli replaced the death's heads, silver rings and chains.

'It cost a month's salary. Do you like it?'

'Yes, I do. It looks unbelievably vulgar, but wonderful. You can carry it off.' The Judge thumped her briefcase on the desk and kissed her Greffière.

'Are you livid with me for putting Schweigen on your tail?'

The Judge paused; it had never occurred to her to be angry with someone whose only motives were loyalty and love.

'No, of course I'm not cross. It was actually very useful to have him there in the end.'

'There are two e-mails from him already — both marked urgent and personal and tagged with receipts. Do you want me to open them? And are you going to tell me what you were doing in Switzerland?'

'No, I'll read what Schweigen has to say. And yes, of course I'll tell you, but all in good time.' The Judge settled her glasses and peered into her screen.

> Dominique — my belle-mère has moved in and I have moved out. I'm living with my brother. Please use his home e-mail. Or ring me. André.

'Oh no. Schweigen has finally lost his mind,' groaned the Judge.

'What's he done?' Gaëlle practically leaped over the desk. The Judge closed the screen.

'He's left his wife.'

'Oh no!' Gaëlle clamped her hand across her mouth, smudging her Death-Ray Red lipstick. 'What will you do?'

'For the moment, nothing whatever. I've made no promises.'

'Do you think it will blow over?'

'No.'

'Did she find out?'

'No. He told her.'

'He must be mad.'

'As I said.'

And so the two women settled back to work and the rhythm of each other. The Judge hunched down over her desk to read her incoming reports and prepare the week's interviews. An incendiary incident involving an adolescent gang on the outskirts of Béziers had led to the destruction of an entire Renault showroom. The gang, all aged under eighteen, and of encouragingly mixed ethnic origins, confessed their intention of peacefully setting fire to one or two cars on the forecourt. The spectacular blaze and accompanying fireworks were entirely unexpected, although delightful, and therefore not their fault.

'Help me process the little shits,' snapped her colleague. 'You and Gaëlle can deal with the girls. I know two of them. Their social workers are already here and the police are trying to track down the parents.'

The affair made the national news. Every single member of the gang had numerous warnings and previous convictions: handbag snatching, car theft, selling drugs in class, burglary and vandalism. They had all been excluded from the local schools and were now being educated through a special scheme in a boot camp run by ex-army officers. And so the Judge had little time to reflect on her strange situation or the Composer's proposal. But she was not easy in her mind, or even entirely certain that she knew exactly what she had agreed to consider. What alarmed her more than anything else was the sinister sensation that she had overstepped a professional line and was now standing on the brink of something unthinkable. Was she simply the chosen dupe of a powerful, charismatic lunatic? She took off her glasses. The text before her became a blur and the Composer took shape as she had last seen him, exhausted, urgent, passionate. Why had he excluded his daughter from any knowledge of the Faith? Did he in fact doubt the credo he preached with such intensity? *If anything should ever happen to me, take care of my daughter. She admires you so much. She wants to study law and to learn how to dance. She wants to be like you. I am afraid for her, Dominique. I would be easy in my mind if I knew that you would watch over her.* And that promise she had made, without reflection or hesitation, because the care of one slender, fragile girl seemed a little thing compared to the enormity of a secret faith, thousands of years old, whose nature was beyond reason or understanding. For if I studied the Faith with an open mind surely all I would see would be a fraudulent pack of cards, like a Tarot reading, specially adapted to seduce the gullible and the frail. Surely I would see what I always see — mendacity and delusion? Study the Faith? As a serious task? I cannot, I cannot. The only proofs that exist are those provided by my own senses, and they tell me that there is no other world but this, no supernatural patterns, and no destiny charted in the stars. I would have to see first, before I could believe. Except I shall see in his hands the print of the nails and thrust my hand into his side, I will not believe. Blessed are they that have not seen, and yet have believed. But even then, could I ever bring myself to believe in anything irrational, mystical, uncanny?

Or make myself sufficiently fanatical to convince anyone else? This is ridiculous. My job is hard enough as it is.

Dominique Carpentier no longer had any clear plan of attack against the Composer; he was obviously a madman if he thought that he could persuade 'la chasseuse de sectes' to become the titular head of the very sect that had given her the most trouble. Yet the Faith had proved to be the one sect that had piqued her interest and commanded her attention, precisely because it was not fraudulent or corrupt. The eerie familiarity of the Composer's certainties confirmed one thing: the Faith existed as a wild river running parallel to the disciplined canals of orthodox monotheism, Christianity, Judaism and Islam. The Faith was the night side of conventional belief, the Dark Host itself. How could she argue the Composer into disbelief? He had already given most of his life to the Faith. This was the peculiar problem which agitated the Judge through the days and nights that followed her wild drive to Switzerland. But she had promised to give him her answer within seven days and she intended to keep her promise.

'What are you thinking about?' demanded Gaëlle.

'I was arguing with the Composer in my head,' said the Judge, replacing her glasses. Gaëlle began to say something, thought better of it, and bit her tongue.

★ ★ ★

331

One of the delinquent adolescents became suddenly violent on Wednesday afternoon and destroyed a chair and the water cooler in her colleague's office. He was overpowered by two gendarmes and removed in handcuffs with a cagoule over his head to stop him biting his captors.

'It's the drugs,' said Gaëlle, calmly trying to salvage the flood of paper cups floating on the carpet. 'The poor lad's probably in the withdrawal stage. And they aren't being held in prison, so his supply's been cut off.'

The Judge frowned upon this worldly knowledge. Wherever she looked, inadequate human beings, driven desperate by demand and desire, lashed out in perpetual protest. The Judge drew a line across the pad upon her desk.

'I'm going home, Gaëlle, to watch something exceedingly silly on the television.'

But the world would not back away from her door. She lay down, her bare feet unfurled upon the sofa and a tall glass of apple juice in her hand, when her mobile, which she had set to Vibrate, wobbled across the glass on her cane table and threatened to explode upon her cold white tiles. If it's Schweigen I'll turn the damned thing off. But here is the voice of Marie — Thérèse.

'I'm sorry I missed you at the Château last week. I'd set my heart on seeing you there. I've left two messages and sent an e-mail. Did you get them? Are you fearfully busy? I expect you always are. You're mentioned in the paper as one of the judges dealing with the Renault showroom

332

fire. Is it awful? Must be. One of the boys is only thirteen. Can I come and see you tomorrow? We're going to London on the afternoon flight this Friday to be all ready for the concert. You are coming to London, aren't you? Friedrich thinks you are coming. He won't be discouraged. He keeps saying you must come and that he's sent you the tickets. You will come, won't you? It's the weekend. May I take you out to lunch tomorrow? Please say yes.'

The Judge found herself smiling, unresentful of this interruption, and amused by the girl's importunate enthusiasm. She possessed the power of granting happiness, and the generous, open-handed gesture of granting a wish charmed her, pleased her. She had begun to love the sensation of being courted, admired, and mattering to someone else. Suddenly this child's admiration magnified before her, into a pearl of great price, and she closed her hands about the gift.

'Of course, come at twelve.' Then the Judge took the risk. 'Is Friedrich with you?'

'No. He's already joined the orchestra in London. It's the London Philharmonic, not his usual team, so he's got masses of rehearsals. It's just me.' A sliver of alarm entered her voice. 'Were you expecting him? You don't mind that it's just me?'

The Judge relaxed.

'Don't be silly. I'll look forward to seeing you.'

★ ★ ★

Gaëlle was in the high-roofed front hall, with all the gods and stars above her, when Marie-Thérèse bounded up the steps. The Judge watched the two young women shaking hands. They appeared to originate from quite different cosmological systems: Gaëlle had cloned herself as Isis in a miniskirt with powerful shoulders and a benign fixed glare, Marie-T impersonated Persephone, on lease from Pluto's gloom, shining in her embroidered green spring. But the world beneath their feet has tasted the first gust of autumn. The Marin darkened the sky above the Allées and the medieval streets; then a nasty salt wind had them all reaching for their jackets. As the revolving doors swung round, a faint wash of white sand slithered across the stones, and the first leaves from the plane trees, still green but poised for the change, fluttered against the steps. A moist fog covered the mountains of Languedoc; eating outside was unthinkable.

As she listened to Marie-T's cheerful optimism for the vendanges — the harvesting of the muscat was already well over on the Domaine — the Judge found herself formulating enquiries that, coming from a concerned parent, would have seemed ordinary and suitable. When do you complete your Bac? This year or next year? Well, you really should be thinking in terms of a university qualification. Unless you've already decided to run the Domaine Laval, in which case a course in management and accounting is, I think, essential. What is your brother's opinion?

They debated the various merits of the law, languages, philosophy, which the Judge had first studied in Paris; psychoanalysis, which fascinated the Composer, and about which he possessed dozens of books, including the *The Complete Psychological Works of Sigmund Freud* — or perhaps a more practical degree from the business school.

'I've got no ear for music. But Friedrich doesn't seem to mind. Maman didn't either. We love his music. But we're amateurs. Friedrich says it's just a gift. Either you can hear it or you can't.'

The Judge nodded. And as she did she realised that the Faith, mysterious, secret, unseen, was written in a higher register than the one to which she habitually listened. And yet, and yet, the Judge never mourned the liars who were fraudulent, duplicitous, predatory; the people who caused her genuine grief were the passionate faithful, bristling with conviction, entirely persuaded of their own reckless creeds. I can deal with crooks, but not genuine fanatics. And I have no patience with romantic obsessions, the products of wilful wish-fulfilment. And is that how I have judged Friedrich Grosz? Have I imagined him as a character in one of his own unintelligible operas? A man whose motives are dark to me?

Marie-T gabbled on cheerfully about a young man who had asked her out. Should she say yes? What did Madame Carpentier think?

'I think you should call me Dominique. And I'm not sure. Do you like him?'

The two women sat before their empty plates, gazing at one another and following quite different trails through the forest. Do you like

335

him? Yes, I do. Immensely. He has given me his full attention. Does anything else matter so much? Do I want him to hold me in his arms and go on talking to me? Suddenly the Composer's presence filled the empty space within her, his white hair and the heat blazing in his giant frame. She saw his lined face, enraged, then smiling, heard his voice, cheerful, amused, telling her that her hair was falling down, threatening to follow her into the lavatory, teasing her in a shower of drops, keeping her warm against the frozen dark. She turned her long stare upon his daughter, who was fiddling with her necklace, hesitating over her emotions, plucking at her sleeves.

'Oh, I don't quite know what I feel or what I want.'

She lifted her eyes to the Judge's face, and Dominique Carpentier gazed straight into the Composer's eerie, intense blue presence. Well, you may not know what you want, ma petite chérie, but I do. I desire your father with my whole heart and if that means taking on some mad cult that should have been obliterated thousands of years ago, then I will.

She took his daughter's hands in her own.

'You must listen carefully to what you feel. What you really feel, not what you ought to think or want. And don't let other people influence you. What do you truly desire? Right at the core?'

Marie-Thérèse flushed, startled. The Judge grinned, reading her face.

'Then do that,' she said.

On the night of Friday the 22nd of September, the night before she flew to London, the Judge sensed something strange and loose, flapping in the bushes behind her. She was walking in her garden in the cool of the day, checking the sprinklers before resetting the computer to water her shrubs and trees. A few days' chilly drizzle had hardly penetrated the dry red earth. She stood still, listening. A wild cat, perhaps? The light wind dropped. She heard it again, a faint crackle, then a muffled rush, as if a fire was just beginning. Bonfires were still forbidden and very strict regulations governed outdoor barbecues built on the brink of the garrigue. The heat had briefly returned towards the end of the afternoon and the white haze over the sea generated an odd yellow glare as the light dimmed, ebbed. The Judge looked out over the hills from the garden of her little villa, searching for a dark trail of smoke, the first sign of fire. Surely it's too late in the year to worry about the garrigue bursting into flames? She could see nothing.

But as night fell a peculiar unease settled over her. She packed her rucksack ready for the journey and chose her clothes with care. Even in high summer London had been autumnal, cold. The bulging dossiers on the Faith lay out-stretched upon her dining-room table. She flicked through the pages of notes, reports, autopsies, pausing over Schweigen's signature and his rough translations of the earliest Swiss reports dating back to 1994. She knew most of

337

the material by heart. Now she looked more carefully at the astronomical reports from a British professor based at the University of Manchester, who was responsible for a network of radio telescopes known as the Merlin Array. Schweigen had left no stone unturned. The original reports had been updated, along with the main Lovell telescope itself, towering above the Cheshire plain. The dish had been realigned and was being recoated with galvanised steel plates. In reply to her enquiry about the Auriga Stone the Professor had kindly written back. Yes, the stone was well known to modern astronomers, who had the greatest respect for the ancients. And she was perhaps aware that the Crab Nebula in Taurus, a supernova created by the explosion of a giant star, had been observed and recorded by Chinese astronomers in 1054. I expect that you know our work on gravitational microlensing, which enables us to detect objects such as neutron stars and black holes which emit no light. We have no idea what the Dark Presence accompanying Almaaz actually is, but our studies of mass distribution within the galaxies we record and observe will eventually give us enough data to risk a hypothesis.

She laid down the letter. Astronomy enacts the drama of measurement. And we are intent on measuring infinity. One day we shall be able to weigh each single ounce of gas, light, dust. She bit her lip and set aside the documents. But we cannot measure the effect of that micro-distance between rising fifths, or a burning palm against my cheek. Then she heard again the Composer's voice, patient in the face of her incredulity. We are part of everything that is. This is the voice of our own souls speaking to us across infinite distances. The Faith is a way to live in this world, and a doorway into the life to come. She slammed the file shut and sat listening to the dark outside.

And then she heard it again: a faint rustle and snap of something close, even present in the room. The Judge stood up and turned on all the outside lights. She could see nothing. Suddenly she plunged into the second file, looking for a report, an address, a particular number. What is the code for Germany? 0049. That's it.

'Herr Bardewig? Guten Abend. Verzeihen Sie . . . habe Ich Sie gestört? This is Dominique Carpentier, the French Judge who enquired about your father's book, back in March. Do you remember me?'

'Of course. Das Buch des Glaubens. With the wonderful binding. How is your investigation progressing?'

The Judge heard her own voice, unsteady with urgency.

'I'm sorry to ask you this and I know how painful it must be — but you told me that your father took his own life, but not how. *How did your father die?*'

There was a deep silence on the other end of the phone. The Judge held her breath. Then the printer's voice returned to her.

'He died in the fire. We believe that he deliberately set fire to his old warehouse on the other side of the river and that he flung himself into the flames. He used some kind of industrial phosphorus that was traced by the police. That's how we think he died. He gave no hint, no sign that he was intending to leave us. His body was utterly consumed. We had nothing to mourn. There was nothing left, nothing but ash and dust. So we buried a small urn with ashes scraped from the remains of the blaze.'

There was an even longer silence on the line.

Then the printer spoke again. 'Are you still there, Madame?'

'Yes,' whispered the Judge,' thank you.'

★ ★ ★

Evening shadowed the slick streets. She strode down the wet pavements, shouldering her black rucksack and counting the number of people before her in the taxi queue. The coffee on the Gatwick Express proved undrinkable, but she calculated that she had no time to eat a proper meal before the concert. The city rushed towards its various destinations, theatres, restaurants, cinemas, clubs, home. She made no arrangements for the night, booked no hotel, and left her mobile switched off. Let it come. Whatever is to come, let it come. The taxi driver wanted to chat. She could barely understand him. What are you going to see at the Albert Hall? The Proms have finished. An opera? They don't do opera at the Albert Hall. It's an opera presented as a concert performance. Well, wouldn't be my thing at all. Nor mine, thought the Judge, looking out at the grey chill settling over the white squares

340

and the towers glazed with light, shining in the damp. It is as if I have stepped forwards in time, into the autumn, into the dark.

The Albert Hall looked like a gigantic brick cake with several decorated tiers. She saw the Composer's name on every poster, his face on the programmes for sale just inside the door. She had arrived too early to enter the auditorium and from inside she heard the soaring squawks of the orchestra, rustling, settling, like a giant black bird. She abandoned her rucksack in the Cloakroom and then set off round the building, looking for the stage door. Two members of the Composer's entourage were standing outside, smoking. The Judge recognised them from the fête at the Domaine, but did not know their names. They knew her at once.

'Ah! Voilà! Madame Carpentier!'

'You're coming to the concert? The tenor's first-rate.'

And she could hear the singers rushing up and down their scales, then two long notes held for a moment before dying away.

'Is Friedrich here?'

'Yes. He's locked in the office. He had an urgent call from Switzerland.'

She stepped inside the stage door anyway; the corridors were crowded, not only with members of the orchestra but the choir, some of whom, brimful of energy, and all wearing black shirts, like a Fascist youth movement, scampered down the corridors, pushing past her. Where was the office? She hooked one of the technical staff and murmured in English.

'The conductor? Monsieur Friedrich Grosz? Where is the office?'

A porthole in the door contained slightly distorted glass, but she could see him, hunched like a vulture over the table. His shoulders were rigid, and his great hand, spread out flat upon the wood, remained still, like an outstretched claw. She tried the door; it was locked. She tapped upon the glass. He did not hear her. She stared for a moment at his unkempt white hair and then noticed that he had removed his white tie. The thing lay scrunched and abandoned on the thick dog-eared score. I am less than three metres away from him, and he does not know that I am here.

Again she began to rationalise the circumstances. He is a busy man, about to conduct an important performance. The phone call may have been urgent. Perhaps one of the singers is ill. Marie-T will have told him that I intended to come. He knows where I am sitting. He will interpret my presence as the answer, the answer he desires and that I promised to give. And so she turned away from the door and settled herself in the vast red-and-gold cavern of the Albert Hall.

The concert had sold out. An impatient queue waiting for returns stretched away from the box office and curled round the building. Some people wore evening dress, others turned up in jeans, grimy jackets, wet raincoats, and pushed past her to their seats. A hollow echo in the corridors regurgitated the muffled noise of talk, food being wolfed down quickly, programmes, scrunched newspapers. The informality amused the Judge; the whole thing was vast as a football stadium and the public presented themselves groomed for an outdoor performance. Yet something festive and intent washed over all; everyone had already decided that they were going to love the music and enjoy themselves. She looked round for Marie-T. Where is she? She knows where I am. She noted the seat number when she looked at my ticket.

And suddenly she saw the girl, the green dress shining among the dark suits, the tall fair head craned above the crowd. She watched the Composer's daughter searching for her. But just as she was about to wave she recognised the small grey man beside her: Professor Hamid, in full evening dress with white tie and silk scarf, elegant and dapper, two programmes tucked under his arm. He scanned the stalls, also searching for her face. The Judge looked down and away, startled. Hamid, the Keeper of the Stones. And of course it was obvious; he isn't just an expert on Egyptian astronomy, he too must be a member of the Faith. The Judge found her own sudden shiver of repulsion unaccountable and strange. It's the not-knowing. I am so used to holding all the cards, always knowing more than the helpless people before me. I suspected him, but was not sure. And even now I cannot be utterly certain. I do not know what I know.

The choir filed in, taking their places on the raised rows of seats above the orchestra. The great dome rustled and hushed. The Judge

343

noticed the absence of Johann Weiß at once. A young woman with short hair took his place as the first violin to a warm outburst of applause. Where is he? But of course, it's not the Composer's usual orchestra. Yet still — something was wrong. She risked a glance to the far end of the rows behind her. Marie-T was buried in the programme and Hamid was gazing at the gilt decorations on the boxes above. No one else seemed concerned. Then she felt the spreading expectation throughout the auditorium and saw the Composer's great white mass of hair and broad shoulders following the singers: two women in bright silk gowns, the men in evening dress. The audience erupted with a great boom of applause.

Is it possible to be impatient with Beethoven? The Judge fiddled with her programme, seething in irritation. How long will this take? She fixed her eyes on the Composer's hands, his fingers on the baton, she calculated the tension in his back, his white hair shaking as he lunged down to kiss the hand of the first violin. She braced herself in surprise as she saw the long lines of pain and stress that marked his cheek when he turned, his glare drawing in the brass and the woodwind. She could not see his entire face. Suddenly he wheeled around and bowed to the audience; amidst the thunder of welcome she caught the caged glance of a creature gathering all its remaining force, crouched and ready to spring.

The entire first act tortured her powerful calm, her habitual self-control. She wanted to see his face again. Beethoven set out his stall, his only opera, the only one of the many he tried to write, whose success was uneven and late in coming. But the Judge could barely listen to Beethoven. The thing was sung in German. She locked her understanding against a language she knew perfectly well and fought the impulse to fidget. She had absorbed the synopsis in the programme, but now found it impossible, given that the singers were standing still and bellowing over the footlights and the music stands, to follow the plot.

A prison, a dungeon, a tyrant, his jailer, the daughter Marzelline, who is in love with a woman disguised as a boy, the eponymous Fidelio, who is in fact looking for her husband, incarcerated somewhere in the prison by the evil villain. All the elements of opera condensed into a static tableau of pure music. The Judge, bored and cross, contained herself with difficulty. This was all an unnecessary prelude to the real action of the evening: her confrontation with the Composer. The odd moments where the singers appeared to drop out of character and actually spoke rather than sang disconcerted her completely. So too did the rapt and reverent attention of thousands of people all around and above her. It was like being part of a congregation whose beliefs she did not share. She clenched her fists and fixed her concentration solely on the man she loved; she had no idea what he was actually doing in front of this disparate engine of noise and movement; he seemed to be hauling on invisible ropes, as if struggling to control a ship in full sail and high winds. She noticed that he actually mouthed the text back to the singers; he knew the opera by heart. Neither the principals nor any member of the choir took their eyes off him for an instant. He was the centre of the great wheel churning round him. She longed for the concert to end, and sat biting her lip.

Marie-T found her in the interval.

'Isn't it wonderful? I'm so happy you are here. Have you met Professor Hamid from the British Museum? He's one of Friedrich's friends.'

Professor Hamid gravely raised her fingers to his lips. His face, set and serious, further disturbed her equilibrium; his entire presence appeared heavy with undisclosed knowledge.

'Mes hommages, Madame.'

'Yes, we have met.' Her cold eyes scanned him, wary, suspicious. The moment passed. The Judge settled back for the second act, now radically ill at ease. There was no reason for Hamid not to be there, but his presence caused an upheaval within her. Why? She could not make sense of her own discomfort.

The second act of *Fidelio*, even presented as a static concert performance, is irresistibly dramatic. And the singers rose to the task. Florestan, waiting for death in the darkest corner of the prison, imagines that he sees his wife as an angel come to release him, and, in one of the most extraordinary shifts from the minor to the major key, oppression gives way to liberation and despair is transformed into hope. Even the Judge, her spirit muffled and overwrought, heard the moment, and the promise: *Ein Engel — der führt mich zur Freiheit ins himmlische Reich*. An angel leads me to freedom in the heavenly kingdom. The production eschewed all costumes, scenery and props, all except one. As Pizarro the tyrant rose up to stab his victim the soprano reached into her small jewelled evening bag and pulled out a gun, clearly visible to all the audience, which she pointed straight at his chest. A gasp rippled through the Albert Hall. The drama of the incident was compounded by the sudden call of the trumpets, the trumpets of judgement and salvation. Leonora cast away her pistol, seized the tenor's velvet lapel, and announced the moment of universal salvation with a mighty roar:

> Es schlägt der Rache Stunde!
> Du sollst gerettet sein!
> The hour of vengeance is at hand!
> You shall be saved!

And the choir, unleashed at last, belted out their hymn to joy, justice and love, for just slightly more than ten minutes. The climax struck the Judge as unlikely as it was compelling. But she too was swept away in an explosion of rejoicing.

The Composer commanded the orchestra to its feet and as he stood, facing the bright hall and rapt thunder of the public, his still face swept round the stalls, searching for her. Along with everyone else the Judge had risen to her feet. But he had already seen her and his face, tense, lined, obscure, illuminated with excitement and relief. She saw him clearly at last, beyond her reach, his arms raised in triumph, his face transfigured with certainty and joy.

17

Jodrell Bank

'We're staying at the Dorchester. Professor Hamid's gone on ahead. Friedrich booked you a room. It's terribly expensive. You mustn't think of paying. He says the orchestra will foot this one. Quick! Taxi!'

And so she was swept away on Marie-T's arm, into the rainy night, hearing the hiss of traffic through the wet, seeing the drooping trees turning downwards, inwards towards the dark. The uniformed porter at the hotel wanted to carry her luggage and seemed disconcerted that she didn't have any.

'Here's the key to the suite. Slip it in the slot and the lights come on. You know that system? The Professor might be up there already. 502. I'm just going to sort out supper and champagne. We've stayed here before. I know everybody in the bar.'

The Judge took the lift. As she stepped out on to the hushed dark carpet she became instantly aware of someone waiting. The long grey coat and scarf were familiar, so was the obstinate stubbled jaw and the shaved down on his naked head. Schweigen.

'André! Qu'est-ce que tu fais ici?' She clamped her hand upon his arm in horror. But her stalker refused to give way.

'Just listen, Dominique. And don't say anything. There's been another mass suicide. Again in Switzerland. At that château where I found you last week.'

'When?'

'Last night.'

'How?'

'We don't know. Probably poison. But the last one out must have torched the building. There's very little left and most of the bodies are burned beyond recognition. They'll have to be identified by DNA and dental records.'

'How many?'

But she already knew the answer. Nine. There had been twelve plates in the dishwasher. The Composer, Marie-T and the Professor were still here. The thirteenth plate had been hers. Nine. There were nine bodies consumed by fire.

'How did you know?'

'It's my investigation. I know.'

'Well, the Swiss will fuck it up now. So far as I can gather there were no French nationals in this departure. They were either Swiss or German.'

'Why are you here, André?'

He took hold of her shoulders and shook her until her glasses were dislodged and her tortoiseshell clamp came loose.

'To make sure you weren't one of the dead,' he yelled.

She wrestled out of his grasp.

'You're mad.'

'So are you!'

'Am I interrupting anything?' Professor Hamid, suave, self-possessed, still wearing his camel coat, appeared in the doorway; the dim rooms, comfortable and luxurious, unfolded behind him in a sequence of crystal and mirrors. He stood aside. Schweigen, unaccountably aware of the geography of the suite, strode in, pushing the Judge in front of him.

'Monsieur Schweigen?' The Professor held out his hand. André ignored him and prowled round the sitting room, turning off the television, which welcomed Mr Friedrich Grosz and family to the Dorchester in flickering yellow letters. Hamid sat down on a deep golden sofa, which settled around him, like a throne.

'Well, I gather that you both know about the recent Swiss departure. A tragic business, which we have tried — and failed — to prevent. At least no one else was hurt in this terrible catastrophe. And no children were involved. I have something to give to each one of you, which I must do quickly, before Marie-Thérèse arrives with her bottles of champagne.'

He unearthed the Guide, Das Buch des Glaubens, from beneath the cushions and presented it to Dominique Carpentier, who dropped her black rucksack to the floor and accepted the gift with both hands.

'This is from Friedrich Grosz, Madame. He has given it to you for safe keeping. And I am sure, that if you come to visit me, which I hope you will do, I can teach you how to read every word.'

He glanced at Schweigen, who was studying each object in the room in turn, as if committing everything to memory, before trying his hand at naming them all in a quiz show.

'Monsieur Schweigen? This is for you.' And he produced a small-calibre pistol from the inside pocket of his coat. The Judge and Schweigen froze. She pressed the great book against her chest.

'Please don't be alarmed. It's not loaded. And it is the gun that was used to shoot Professor Anton Laval and his sister, Marie-Cécile. I am very happy to make a detailed statement to the British police concerning both their deaths in front of you, Monsieur Schweigen, at your earliest convenience. Your presence as the investigating officer in the last case and your familiarity with the events of 1994 will be a great help, both to the authorities here, and indeed, to me. Needless to say, our friend Monsieur Grosz knows nothing about any of this, and should you see him again I would be grateful if you would say nothing. Or at least not yet. We all have our methods of persuasion and I know that I could never bring him to approve of mine.'

The Professor paused, wrapped the gun carefully in a white handkerchief, and handed it to Schweigen. Then he leaned forward slightly and weighed every word.

'As you have no doubt gathered, I too am a member of the Faith, but I cannot believe in a God who demands the deaths of all who serve Him. And despite the vows of secrecy and obedience I have taken I will not honour that trust. Friedrich Grosz is a man of great faith, he will remain faithful to the last, *but the Guide cannot outlive his people*. He must follow them, even as they have followed him. He has gone to the foot of that great telescope on the Cheshire plain, the place where we first witnessed the tangible presence of the Dark Host. You must find him, and save him if you can. He gave me this. It is for you.'

The Judge tore open the envelope bearing the hotel's crest. The Composer's handwriting rose unsteadily towards the edge, each word slithering into the next. *Follow me, Dominique — follow me into the Kingdom.* The Judge stood rooted, frozen, her eyes filled with darkness. Schweigen took the paper from her, read the single inscrutable sentence and then stood still, baffled. The Professor settled back into the golden sofa, as if his part in the business was now over, and looked at them both, an unworried host whose guests seemed unable to relax amidst the opulent furniture.

'I'm going with you,' snapped Schweigen and dragged her away from the Professor, who had begun nodding sympathetically, as if everyone had agreed with his recent momentous revelations concerning the nature of God. The door flew open and Marie-Thérèse, clutching four tall glasses and a sweating bottle of champagne, wrapped in a starched white cloth, careered into the room.

'Here I am. We've got a whole chariot of food and more drink coming up behind me. Oh! What's the matter?' She took in Schweigen and flinched in shock, her voice rising. 'What's happened? Tell me what's happened. Where's Friedrich?'

The street lights glowed orange across the map spread out upon the Judge's knees. It was nearing four in the morning, but the dark had not begun to lift. They had left the M6 and were lost in a small town called Holmes Chapel. Two roundabouts had returned them to the main street. Jodrell Bank was everywhere signposted and nowhere to be found. At least they had outrun the rain, and beyond the sleeping houses a clear half-moon glimmered over the gently swaying trees. The great oaks and chestnuts, now embracing one another across the roadway, loomed like tents, untethered, dripping, inse-cure. Schweigen had reached his limit. He could no longer think clearly. He had never driven a left-hand-drive car on the left before, was unable to see anything before overtaking, and remained convinced that his beloved Judge was fatally deranged.

'You can't know he'd come here. It's the middle of nowhere. What if Hamid's lying? He's probably gone back to Lübeck. Or Berlin. Or what do I know?'

'Gone home. Without his daughter? Never.' Her voice was no longer steady and her face already streaked with tears. 'André, please listen to me. I know what I'm saying. The people of the Faith have departed. There is no one left. And he has given the Guide to me. He will choose the place that is closest to Almaaz. Hamid is right.'

'Almaaz is a star, Dominique. It's billions of light years away.'

353

The Judge gave up.

'Try left here.'

They hurtled out into the countryside. The flat plain gave way to a gentle undulation and they passed under a nineteenth-century viaduct. The Judge peered out through the windows. Keep going, don't leave this road. Another brown sign bearing the image of the radio telescope flashed past.

'Left, left, left,' screamed the Judge.

And then they saw the dish, fabulous in the ebbing night, a giant white circle, gently indented, hundreds of feet high, vertical on its moorings, a long proboscis pointing straight outwards into the night sky. Neither Schweigen nor the Judge was able to speak. The huge uncanny structure towered above the trees. No houses or lights disturbed the white presence that lifted its perfect face toward the heavens. As they drove closer they saw that the dish was supported by two massive watch towers, tall as pylons, and a network of iron girders, forming another curved mass beneath the solid, parabolic circle. Far beneath the dish a small herd of black-and-white cows grazed on the dark grass. The gigantic shape loomed over the quiet fields, blanched white as a unicorn in the moonlight, its great horn interrogating the stars.

'Something's going on,' snapped Schweigen, and flung the car through the open gates. Why was there no security? What are those lights? The Judge gripped the dashboard. A policeman wearing a bright-yellow reflecting jacket flagged them down.

'I'm sorry, sir. You can't go any further. There's been an incident.'

Through the green-mesh fence they could still see the flames beneath the trees, as if a bonfire of some magnitude was slowly dying away. As the car's engine fell silent the Judge heard the same loose flapping rush and crack that she had heard in her garden, and a strange steady hum from the giant circle poised above them. She sat, open-mouthed in horror, beside Schweigen, who was still trying to understand his English colleague.

The Judge staggered out of the car, the tears now streaming down her face. Above her the giant dish slowly moved, a gentle roaring from the engines driving the rails on which it turned, to follow the colossal, ceaseless flood of dancing stars, far, far back in time and moving endlessly away from the green world.

'I'm afraid someone has set fire to themselves at the foot of the dish. Very strange business. God knows what he used. They saw it from the control room. The body went up like an exploding torch.'

'Ash and dust,' howled the Judge. 'There'll be nothing left, nothing but ash and dust.'

And then she collapsed, hammering her fists against Schweigen's chest. He had no idea how to comfort her, and gazed at her wet face, lurid and twisted in uncontrolled wretchedness, awash with tears. The blue flashing glare of the police cars and the fire brigade in the last gusts of night air never disturbed the cows, who continued chewing steadily, their long tails drawn out behind them in the wet grass.

'She's not the widow, is she, sir?' murmured the policeman.

'Pas vraiment.' Schweigen hesitated. His English failed him. 'No, she's not his wife. She's his Judge.'

'Righto, sir. I'll send someone over to talk to you.'

The officer then stood beside the car, utterly confused.

Schweigen rocked her in his arms. He was an honest man. A piece of truth smouldered in his pocket.

'Dominique, listen. I don't understand this any more than you do. But he wasn't planning to die tonight. He can't have known that the last of the Faith were bent on organising another departure. You heard what Hamid said — *the Guide cannot outlive his people*. The Composer didn't choose to die as they did. But he had to follow them. That's what he believed he had to do. Look. I found these in the hotel. Two tickets for Lübeck on the morning plane. One of them's in your name. He was going home and he counted on taking you with him.'

The Judge sat up straight, her face garish and macabre in the swivelling blaze from the squad cars.

'Taking me? I can't go. What do you mean? I won't go.' She raged into his face. She gave no sign that she had understood him.

Schweigen abandoned explanations. The lights contradicted the eerie silence of the great white dish; he heard the birds stirring uneasily in the long, bulbous line of trees. Even the voices surrounding the barrier tapes came to them muffled and hushed. Schweigen tried again and spoke for the Composer, who had left them, discarded and stranded, beneath the great white dish, amidst the gathering dew and the flat English fields.

'He loved you. He wanted you. He loved you as much as I do.'

★ ★ ★

On the 12th of June 2001 the Assemblée Générale ratified the draft legislation that defined a sect in precise philosophical and legal terms. The sects could no longer operate on any French territory, neither within the hexagone, nor overseas. Dominique Carpentier watched over the passage of this law into the architecture of the French state with quiet satisfaction. Under the terms of the Composer's will she became Marie-T's legal guardian and spent a good deal of her time at the Domaine Laval, revising philosophy and literature. The final exams loomed over them both. The Judge rediscovered her passion for Racine. They read *Andromaque* together, startled at the emotional excess which emerged from satin corsets and rhyming couplets. The Judge occupied Marie-Cécile Laval's bedroom whenever she stayed at the Domaine, but she changed nothing in the room. She displaced no objects, altered no wallpaper, bedspreads, ornaments or photographs.

Every two months the Judge flew to London

to visit Professor Hamid, who had been released on bail, pending his hearing. The British courts decided that he presented no danger to the general public; the Judge harassed his defence team with documents and suggestions. No one could decide where the preliminary hearings should be held. His extremely detailed declaration described two murders, prior to the mass suicides, one in France and one in Switzerland. But nobody initiated any extradition proceedings. The Judge decided to delay the paperwork, thus giving him time to finish his monograph on the recent discoveries uncovered at the ancient astrological monuments in Nineveh. The Book of the Faith remained under lock and key in the bowels of her office. She never allowed the Book to leave the reinforced steel safe, and in that sense she became its Keeper, and its Guardian.

Afterword

Explanations and acknowledgements are not usually added to a work of fiction, but a few words are necessary here. My French-speaking readers will have noticed that I have anglicised the shortened spelling of Marie-Thérèse. Her name would usually be written in French as Marité, or Marithé. To an English eye, unused to French, this would appear to be an entirely different character in the fiction. I have therefore spelt her name Marie-T throughout, in the interests of clarity.

Thank you to the team that produced this book: my agent Andrew Gordon at David Higham, my editor and publisher, Alexandra Pringle, and her colleagues at Bloomsbury, especially Erica Jarnes and Alexa von Hirschberg. I would like to thank Mary Tomlinson in particular, for her astute attention to the detail of the text.

Novelists need help with their inventions. Thank you to the following friends and colleagues: Monsieur and Madame Agneau, Myriam Buades, Lucie Barthès, Ghyslène Chantre, Simone Chiffre, David Evans, Richard Holmes, Anne Jacobs, Peter Lambert, Jenny Newman, Michèle Roberts, Sandrine Sire, Rose Tremain, and all my neighbours, past and present, in the village of St Martial. Jacqueline Martel created the garden at the Domaine Laval. Françoise Brutzkus-Gélinet, Avocat à la Cour d'Appel de Paris, advised me on French law and I am very grateful to her and her colleagues. Dr Tim O'Brien at Jodrell Bank has been very generous with his time and astronomical expertise, and for sharing his knowledge of Hebrew, I am grateful to Professor Philip Alexander from the department of Religions and Theology at the University of Manchester. My first readers are Janet Thomas and Sheila Duncker, and I thank them for all their critical help, suggestions and encouragement. Janet Thomas is one of the other writers who keep me going when the going gets tough. Claude Chatelard painstakingly corrected my French, and Lisbeth Lambert checked the German, for which I am exceedingly grateful. Needless to say, all the remaining errors are mine alone.

I have taken the usual geographical liberties every writer takes with physical space, so that it will be impossible for anyone to find the Judge's offices in Montpellier, the Domaine Laval, the house in Lübeck, or the Hôtel Belvédère on the slopes of Sète. So far as I am concerned all the characters and sects I have described are entirely fictitious, but the Dark Host is real, and, by the time you are reading this book, the eclipse will already have begun.

Patricia Duncker
Aberystwyth, 2009

We do hope that you have enjoyed reading
this large print book.

Did you know that all of our titles
are available for purchase?

We publish a wide range of high quality
large print books including:
**Romances, Mysteries, Classics
General Fiction
Non Fiction and Westerns**

Special interest titles available in
large print are:
**The Little Oxford Dictionary
Music Book
Song Book
Hymn Book
Service Book**

Also available from us courtesy of
Oxford University Press:
**Young Readers' Dictionary
(large print edition)
Young Readers' Thesaurus
(large print edition)**

For further information or a free
brochure, please contact us at:
**Ulverscroft Large Print Books Ltd.,
The Green, Bradgate Road, Anstey,
Leicester, LE7 7FU, England.
Tel:** (00 44) 0116 236 4325
Fax: (00 44) 0116 234 0205

Other titles published by
The House of Ulverscroft:

MISS WEBSTER AND CHÉRIF

Patricia Duncker

Elizabeth Webster is a cantankerous spinster pushing seventy. Forced out of her school-teaching job, she unleashes her sharp tongue on everyone in the English village of Little Blessington. Then, after suffering a near-fatal illness, her doctor sends her on a journey to a North African country to recover. There she ventures into the desert and has a brush with terrorism. Miss Webster, however, no longer cares overmuch about anything, least of all Islamic politics and suicide bombers . . . Just weeks after her return there is a ring on her doorbell. Standing there in the darkness is a young Arab man of astonishing beauty. Worryingly, he is carrying a large suitcase. But who is Chérif? Why is he there and what does he want?

TOOTH AND CLAW

Nigel McCrery

Carl Whittley must stay at home and care for his crippled father. But he has distractions. He's just tortured a TV presenter to death and he's planning to blow an anonymous commuter to pieces. Also remaining at home is DCI Mark Lapslie, his rare neurological condition has forced him to leave his family and to avoid the police station. His superiors regard him as a nuisance to be avoided. As the spate of brutal deaths catches the media's attention, the Chief Superintendent brings in Lapslie. He knows this case could break him, then the press will be placated and he will be free of the troublesome DCI. But the deadly game Carl wants to play might be just what Lapslie needs to come out of hiding.

DARK TIMES IN THE CITY

Gene Kerrigan

Danny Callaghan is having a quiet drink in a Dublin pub when two men walk in with guns. On impulse, Callaghan intervenes to help the intended victim, petty criminal Walter Bennett. Who sent the assassins? With a troubled past and an uncertain future, Danny Callaghan finds himself drawn into a vicious scheme of revenge. The police grope for answers, and a gang war moves towards a bloody showdown. In a city on edge, affluence and cocaine fuel a ruthless gang culture, and a man's fleeting impulse may cost the lives of those who matter most to him . . .

THE STONE GALLOWS

C. David Ingram

After three months in intensive care, DC Cameron Stone could recall his high-speed pursuit of a vice baron through Glasgow that took the life of a teenage mother and her child. And Audrey had left him, taking their son, Mark, with her . . . Unable to return to his old job he works for a private detective, trying to track down a teenage runaway. It's been a bad week. Access to Mark gets difficult. He's roughed up when he finds his runaway, and there's the daubing on his door: 'Burn in Hell Baby Killer.' The only brightness on his horizon is his growing friendship with Liz . . . But things get worse for Stone — somebody is out to destroy him and everything he loves — unless he gets to them first.

STILL BLEEDING

Steve Mosby

After his wife's death, Alex Connor just wanted oblivion. Only his friend Sarah kept him going, but she's been murdered. And whilst the police have the killer, they don't have her body. The gruesome search for her drags Alex back into the land of the living — and the dead. Policeman Paul Kearney is tracking a killer who's abducting women and draining them of blood. He's drawn into a world of dark desires that people will go to great lengths to hide. Wound together by their search, if they're to save themselves and the people they love, Alex and Kearney must go to a place where normal rules don't apply — where people trade murder memorabilia, and a place where life is only the first thing you lose.